PRAISE FOR *BRAVE FACE*

A 2019 ALA RAINBOW BOOK LIST TOP TEN TITLE
A 2019 *BOOKLIST* EDITOR'S CHOICE BOOK FOR YOUTH

★ "Razor-sharp, deeply revealing, and brutally honest."
—*Booklist*, starred review

★ "Raw and moving."
—*SLJ*, starred review

"Beautiful and forceful . . . A bold, banner announcement that there is a future for everyone."
—*Shelf Awareness*

PRAISE FOR *THE PAST AND OTHER THINGS THAT SHOULD STAY BURIED*

"Only Shaun David Hutchinson could take on love, family, friendship, life, and death so deftly, hilariously, poignantly, and thoughtfully. . . . This is a book you can't put down even if you wanted to."
—Jeff Zentner, William C. Morris Award–winning author of *The Serpent King*

"A fearless and brutal look at friendships and the emotional autopsies we all do when they die. . . . You will laugh, rage, and mourn its loss when it's over. If you haven't been reading Hutchinson, this is a brilliant place to start."
—Justina Ireland, *New York Times* bestselling author of *Dread Nation*

"Biting, hopeful, and laugh-out-loud funny. Dino and July's story is a heartfelt exploration of how our friendships shape us, even after they're dead and gone."
—Francesca Zappia, award-winning author of *Eliza and Her Monsters* and *Made You Up*

★ "Hutchinson is going to knock your socks off. . . . His intelligent writing will seduce readers with its complex and spunky characters, lively dialogue, offbeat humor, and emotional depth."
—*Booklist*, starred review

★ "A grotesque, mordantly funny, and tender look at friendship, for fans of . . . Adam Silvera's *They Both Die at the End.*"
—*SLJ*, starred review

PRAISE FOR *THE APOCALYPSE OF ELENA MENDOZA*

★ "Provocative and moving . . . A thoughtful story about choice and destiny."
—*Publishers Weekly*, starred review

★ "Hutchinson artfully blends the realistic and the surreal. . . . An entirely original take on apocalyptic fiction."
—*SLJ*, starred review

PRAISE FOR *AT THE EDGE OF THE UNIVERSE*

★ "An earthy, existential coming-of-age gem."
—*Kirkus Reviews*, starred review

PRAISE FOR *WE ARE THE ANTS*

★ "Bitterly funny, with a ray of hope amid bleakness."
—*Kirkus Reviews*, starred review

"A beautiful, masterfully told story by someone
who is at the top of his craft."
—*Lambda Literary*

★ "Shaun David Hutchinson's bracingly smart and unusual YA novel
blends existential despair with exploding planets."
—*Shelf Awareness*, starred review

ALSO BY SHAUN DAVID HUTCHINSON

Brave Face: A Memoir
The Past and Other Things That Should Stay Buried
The Apocalypse of Elena Mendoza
Feral Youth
At the Edge of the Universe
We Are the Ants
Violent Ends
The Five Stages of Andrew Brawley
fml
The Deathday Letter

SIMON & SCHUSTER BFYR
NEW YORK LONDON TORONTO SYDNEY NEW DELHI

SIMON & SCHUSTER BFYR
An imprint of Simon & Schuster Children's Publishing Division
1230 Avenue of the Americas, New York, New York 10020

Jacket designed by Sarah Creech
Interior designed by Mike Rosamilia
The text of this book was set in Chaparral Pro.
Manufactured in the United States of America
First Edition
2 4 6 8 10 9 7 5 3 1
Library of Congress Cataloging-in-Publication Data
Names: Hutchinson, Shaun David, author.
Title: A complicated love story set in space / by Shaun David Hutchinson.
Description: First Simon & Schuster BFYR hardcover edition. |
New York : Simon & Schuster BFYR, 2021. |
Summary: Sixteen-year-olds Noa, DJ, and Jenny awake on a spaceship, unaware of how they got there or what is coming, but soon Noa and DJ are falling in love.
Identifiers: LCCN 2020014569 (print) | LCCN 2020014570 (ebook) |
ISBN 9781534448537 (hardcover) | ISBN 9781534448551 (ebook)
Subjects: CYAC: Space ships—Fiction. | Love—Fiction. | Gays—Fiction. | Science fiction.
Classification: LCC PZ7.H96183 Com 2021 (print) | LCC PZ7.H96183 (ebook) | DDC [Fic]—dc23
LC record available at https://lccn.loc.gov/2020014569
LC eBook record available at https://lccn.loc.gov/2020014570

FOR LIESA,
WHO HELPED ME NAVIGATE THIS SHIP
AND NEVER COMPLAINED WHEN I GOT US LOST

This book contains a scene describing a sexual assault in chapter fifty-four of the section titled "The End of a Very Long Day," as well as references to the assault in the chapters that follow.

STRANGERS IN SPACE

ONE

I WOKE UP ON A SPACESHIP.

I'd crawled into bed, my hair still damp from the rain, and shut my eyes, expecting to wake up in the same place I fell asleep. As one tends to do. But, no. When I opened my eyes, I was most definitely *not* in my room any longer. Nor was I in my apartment in Seattle or even still on Earth.

I didn't actually wake up *on* the spaceship. Rather, I woke up outside it, wearing a spacesuit. Drifting in the vacuum where there's no oxygen or gravity, and basically everything wants to kill you.

You might be thinking that I knew I was in space because I saw stars. It's a good guess, but wrong. The first thing I saw was a note on the heads-up display inside my helmet.

You are wearing a Beekman-Hauser X-300 Vacuum-Rated Spacesuit.

You are in space, floating outside a ship called Qriosity.

There is no reason to panic.

My name is Noa North, and I am not ashamed to admit that I panicked.

"Help!" I screamed so loudly that my voice cracked. Not that it mattered—there was nowhere for the sound to go. It's a common misconception that sound doesn't travel in space. It does; it just doesn't travel well. That didn't stop me from screaming, though. And flailing my arms and legs as if doing either was going to help. Cut me some slack. It was my first time in space.

Also, hopefully my last.

Warning! Your heart rate is exceeding the maximum recommended beats per minute. Please attempt thirty seconds of relaxed breathing.

"Are you kidding me?"

Your health and well-being are no laughing matter. This alert has been a courtesy of Vedette Biometrics, a subsidiary of Gleeson Foods.

"I'm sorry, what?"

The notification disappeared, replaced by a series of readouts that were no doubt intended to be helpful but which meant nothing to me. I wasn't totally useless. I could build any piece of furniture from IKEA without committing murder in the process, I played a mean game of *Mario Kart*, and I could whip up a salted caramel buttercream that would blow your mind, but I had no business being in a spacesuit.

And, yet, there I was.

I did manage to locate the suit's oxygen levels in the mess of information overload. I supposedly had seventy-four minutes remaining. I hoped that was enough time to get somewhere safe, though I wasn't sure what "safe" even meant anymore.

"This is fine. I'm not going to die. I am not going to die." My helmet was transparent on three sides and let me get a good look at my suit, which was pea-soup green with eggplant accents. "I am *not* going to die in this outfit."

Being in space seemed unlikely. People didn't just wake up in space. But I had two choices: one, accept that this was real and that I wasn't dreaming or on drugs or in hell being punished for the time in sixth grade that I tied tampons I'd stolen from Mrs. Russo's desk to Luke Smith's shoes; or two, do nothing, wait to run out of oxygen, and pray that I hadn't made a horrible mistake.

I was tempted to do nothing, don't think I wasn't. It was the path of least resistance, which my mom and all of my teachers from first grade on would agree was my favorite. But I wanted to live, which meant I needed to stop freaking out and start trying to save myself.

I patted the suit down and discovered a tether attached to my belt around the back. The ship my hud had named "*Qriosity*" was immediately in front of me within reach, so I fumbled about, using the hull to slowly turn myself around.

That's when the harsh, unrelenting reality of my situation hit me. I wasn't *looking* at the stars, I was surrounded by them. Space was empty and filled with shards of light. It was terrifying and brilliant, and I was just a minuscule part of creation. I choked on the beauty of it, and I was strangled by fear.

Immediately, my brain short-circuited. It couldn't process that I was floating when it thought I should obviously be falling. Wave after wave of nausea flowed through me, threatening to overwhelm my senses.

"Don't puke in the suit. Don't puke in the suit. Don't puke, don't puke, don't puke." I squeezed my eyes shut even though that was the worst thing I could do, but I didn't care. All I knew for certain was that vomiting inside the suit was probably an awful idea that I should avoid at any cost.

I quietly repeated Mrs. Blum's macaron recipe until the sick, dizzy sensation subsided enough that I could open my eyes. Nothing had changed. The stars were still there; I was still outside the ship. It was time to remedy that. I grabbed hold of the tether and pulled myself along it hand over hand.

Despite the stars, most of the useful light was coming from lamps on my suit, and those did little more than create a weak bubble of illumination that extended about a meter around me. I could see the hull of the ship as I passed it, but I couldn't see the entire ship. I didn't even know what the other end of the tether was connected to.

"This is ridiculous. Who the hell wakes up in space?" I'd heard of waking up in Vegas, and once, the year my mom sent me to summer camp, Danny Forge woke up in the middle of Stonecana Reservoir in a canoe, but no one ever woke up in space. Except that I had. My brain kept trying to point out that it was impossible that I'd gone to bed in Seattle and woken up in space, but I couldn't deny what I was seeing with my own eyes.

"This is how people lose their minds, isn't it?" I said aloud. Talking helped keep my stomach calm. "You have to consider the possibility that you're actually sitting on the forty-four bus in your jammies, mumbling to yourself, and that a bunch of strangers are filming you so they can post it online for the likes."

That scenario seemed more likely than me being in space, but I had to assume that this was real until I had proof that it wasn't, or I'd spend all my time questioning everything.

Ahead of me, pale orange lights bloomed around an open hatch that I prayed was an airlock. The tether was connected to the hull on the side of the opening. I pulled as quickly as I could in the suit. It wasn't as bulky as movies had led me to believe it should be, but it was still awkward to move in.

Gentle blue lights filled the airlock as I floated inside. The moment my boots touched the floor, a notification appeared on my hud. **Lithos Inc. Mag Boots have engaged.** I shifted from leg to leg, grateful to no longer feel that I was going to spin off into the dark nothing. I detached my tether and watched as it was slurped up by a mechanism outside and disappeared.

The airlock was about the size of a small elevator, but I'd take its cramped confines over the endless expanse of space any day. I just needed to figure out how to shut the door and fill the room with oxygen so that I could get out of the suit, which was growing more claustrophobic by the second. I spied a palm-size touchscreen built into the wall that looked promising. I tapped it with my finger to wake it.

Cycle airlock?

I had never wanted anything more in my life. I was going to get out of the suit and breathe air that didn't smell and taste faintly of tin and sweat. I was going to get on my hands and knees and kiss the floor. I didn't know if there was gravity in the ship, but if there was, I was going to jump up just so that I could fall back down. Sure, zero-G sounds fun in theory, but the reality sucked and I wanted off the ride.

I reached out to tap the button that would affirm my deeply held desire to cycle the airlock when a voice spoke to me in a soothing Southern accent. "Uh, hello? Is anyone out there?"

I turned my head, trying to pinpoint the voice's source.

"Anyway, my name's DJ. I don't know how I got on this ship—at least, I think it's a ship—but I'm pretty sure it's going to blow up."

TWO

IT WASN'T ENOUGH THAT I'D WOKEN UP ON A SHIP. I'D woken up on a ship that was going to explode.

"Hello?" I said. "Can you hear me? Where are you?"

"I can hear you!"

This time when DJ's voice came through, I realized it was inside my helmet. Because, of course it was. Where else would it have been coming from? Any embarrassment I felt over not realizing it sooner was overwhelmed by the visceral sense of relief that flooded through me. I didn't know who DJ was, nor did I care. I wasn't alone anymore.

"What the hell is going on? Where am I? Did you do this to me? I swear to God when I find you, I'm going to make you wish—"

"I didn't do this." DJ's voice cut through my rage. "I'm somewhere called Reactor Control. That's what's stenciled on the door, anyway. There's a huge chamber with a bunch of pipes running out of it that I think *might* be the reactor, but I'm just guessing here. I was kind of hoping *you* knew what was going on." He sounded a bit winded.

"Oh." I felt like a jerk for losing my temper, especially since DJ and I seemed to be in the same screwed-up situation. "Sorry to disappoint you, but I'm clueless. I mean, I'm smart, except when it comes to math. I'm awful at math, but I'm decent at everything else. Anyway, you said something about blowing up, and I'd really like to *not* do that, so how do we keep it from happening?"

DJ was quiet for a moment, and I worried that he'd decided to abandon me. I found myself desperate to hear his deep, soothing voice again. There was something familiar about it. The tenor and tone wrapped around me like a hug, and I was incredibly grateful that DJ hadn't actually bailed. "The note on the computer says there are a couple things we need to do to keep *Qriosity* from exploding." He paused. "*Qriosity*'s the ship, I guess."

"Yep," I said. "Got it. We're on a spaceship. What do we have to do to prevent the ship from blowing up?" I wanted out of the vacuum suit so badly that I was willing to do just about anything to make it happen.

"Uh, so the instructions say we have to patch a leak in coolant conduit F-dash-519 and then shut down the reactor."

"Sure, sounds easy."

DJ hesitated before saying, "I know my way around computers

some. Mostly taking them apart and putting them back together, and I know a handful of programming languages too. I also spent a summer rebuilding the engine of a '62 Mustang, but I don't know how useful that'll be in this situation."

A buzz like an electric current began pulsing through my brain.

Warning! Your heart rate is exceeding the maximum recommended beats per minute. Please attempt thirty seconds of relaxed breathing.

I had to get out of the suit or I was going to die. The idea began small but swelled in size until it had shoved my other thoughts aside. I couldn't think about anything other than getting out of the damned suit. I reached for my helmet, my clumsy fingers searching for the latch that would release me from this smelly, canned-air prison.

"Hey? You still there?" DJ's voice squeezed in. It was a gentle tap on the shoulder that pushed through the nonsense and noise and stalled my hand.

I stopped, suddenly aware that I had nearly removed my helmet in an unpressurized airlock. If it hadn't been for DJ, I would have done it and died.

"I'm here," I said.

"You okay?"

A manic, frantic laugh escaped my lips. "Of course I'm not okay! I'm supposed to be at home in my bed, but I'm in space. I'm in space, DJ! Nothing about this is okay!"

"There are worse places to wake up."

"I doubt it."

"Stuck in a slimy cocoon spun by an evil alien that tortured you with bad jokes until it was time to eat you?" DJ said. "Snuggled up in the guts of a tauntaun? In the hallway at school, late for first period, wearing nothing but your socks?"

"Fine!" I said. "You win. There are worse places to wake up." I shook my head and smiled in spite of myself. "You've put way too much thought into this." Talking to DJ like we were friends hanging out helped me regain some sense of calm. He had a comfortable ease about him. Talking to him made me feel like it was possible we were going to survive this. Whatever *this* was.

"You got a name?" DJ asked.

"Noa."

"Cool," he said. "Hey, so, I know this is a lot to ask, but there's a countdown in here saying we've got about seventeen minutes before the reactor overloads—"

I shut my eyes, ignoring the rest of what DJ said, and breathed until I was completely calm. Okay, fine. Mostly calm. The low-level panic and feeling of impending doom were going to stick around no matter how many breaths I took.

"We can do this," I said, mostly to myself. "Where's conduit F-519?"

At the same time as DJ said, "I don't know," a path to the conduit appeared as an overlay on my hud. And, of course, it led back out the airlock.

"That figures," I muttered.

"What?"

"The conduit is outside the ship."

DJ fell quiet again, and I wished he'd stop doing that. I wanted him to fill every second of silence while I was stuck in the suit. He could have recited the periodic table of elements or read *Moby Dick* aloud and I wouldn't have complained. Much. All right, I *would* have complained, but I wouldn't have made him stop.

"I bet *Qriosity*'s got spacesuits," DJ said. "If I can find one, I can get out there and fix the leak, but that means you're going to have to come to the reactor room and—"

"I'm already in a suit," I said. "I woke up outside the ship. I'm in an airlock right now. I was about to come inside when you called. I haven't even pressurized it yet."

"Good," DJ said. "That's good. You can fix the conduit and I can stay here and take care of the reactor."

"Lucky me." I didn't know anything about shutting down reactors, but I was jealous of DJ because at least he got to be *in* the ship. I would have traded places with him in a second, but apparently, time was one thing we lacked.

"You think you can handle it?" DJ was asking.

"No?" I said. "I don't know. This is my first spaceship. I don't even know what fixing a coolant conduit entails. But I'm out here and you're in there, so I guess I'm going to have to try."

I felt like if I concentrated hard enough, I could picture DJ's face, which was ludicrous, of course. Just wishful thinking in the dark.

"Don't take this the wrong way," DJ said. "But we've got

about fifteen minutes before *Qriosity* blows up, so if you want to keep living, I'm going to need you to do a heck of a lot more than try."

The touch panel asking if I wanted to cycle the airlock was still taunting me. All I had to do was press it. I even considered doing it and saying it was an accident. Except, then I would've been responsible for destroying the ship and killing DJ, and I really hated having to apologize.

"Right," I said. "I can definitely maybe do this."

"That's the spirit!"

"And if I can't, then we both die in a fiery explosion and it won't matter anyway."

THREE

I DIDN'T WANT TO DIE, EVEN THOUGH I MIGHT HAVE SAID I did.

Look, I was dealing with some stuff, okay? I was walking home in the rain with a milkshake in one hand and a bag of Dick's burgers in the other, and some oblivious ass in an SUV, who was too busy texting to be bothered with paying attention to the road, rolled through the crosswalk and nearly hit me. Yes, I lost my temper. Yes, I threw my milkshake at him as he shrugged and drove off. Yes, I yelled, "Why don't you just kill me next time?!" at the sky and started to cry, while strangers on the other side of 45th pretended not to stare. It's not like I actually meant it.

After that, I gave the burgers to the homeless guy who was always hanging around the bus stop, went home, and crawled into bed. But, honestly, I hadn't been serious about wanting to die, and I hoped that whoever was out there making those decisions understood that I'd just been having a really bad day.

Not that this day was turning out much better. Though, I supposed if I managed to make it back into the ship without suffocating, I'd count it as a win.

I trudged along *Qriosity*'s hull, following the path on my hud, taking careful, measured steps like I was crossing a tightrope over a pit of vipers. It was eerie not hearing anything outside of my own breathing inside the suit. I could feel the impact of my boots attaching to the metal hull, and my brain expected to hear the sound of each step and didn't know what to do when it didn't. It left me feeling unsettled and anxious.

Adding to my disquietude was that I couldn't see much of the ship beyond the globe of light radiating from my suit. The path on my hud disappeared into the darkness, and it could have led me right over the edge and I wouldn't have known until it was too late.

"How's it going with the reactor?" I asked when the silence began to get to me. It had probably only been thirty seconds since I'd last heard DJ's voice, but it felt like forever.

"I'm not real sure yet."

"That's not reassuring."

DJ's sigh carried through the speakers inside the helmet, bringing his weariness along with it. "I don't know this computer, so I'm going through everything hoping I find something that says 'shut down reactor.'"

"Sounds fun. Trade you?"

"Does it make me weird if I would?" he asked.

"A little," I said. "I don't know why you would want to be out here, though. Every step might be the one that sends me hurtling off the hull into space, where I'd slowly suffocate and die in the icy embrace of the frigid void."

DJ hesitated a moment before saying, "I'd still do it. I always wanted to be an astronaut when I got older."

"How old *are* you?"

"Sixteen," he said.

I stumbled. I threw my arms out to steady myself, but that was pointless in a zero-G environment. Thankfully, my mag boots held their grip. It still took me a second to regain my balance.

"Noa?"

"You're sixteen?"

"Yeah, but—"

"So am I." I should have been moving, following the path to the coolant conduit, but finding out DJ was my age had shaken me. "Don't you think that's messed up? Who the hell kidnaps a couple of sixteen-year-olds and sticks them on a spaceship?" My voice rose an octave and cracked.

"Everything about this is unusual," DJ said. "I don't think us being sixteen is more or less weird than the rest of it."

Maybe DJ was right, but that didn't stop my brain from spinning. "Why us?" I asked. "And why here? What do they want from us, and how come I can't remember how I got into this damned suit?"

DJ's voice was like a soothing hand between my shoulders.

"Whoa there, Noa. Slow down." His words cut through the anger and fear. "I want answers too, but we'll never get any if we blow up."

It was terrifying logic, but it made sense. I needed to move. I focused on putting one foot in front of the other, marching toward my destination. "Hey, DJ?" I asked. "Where are you from?"

"Small town in Florida called Calypso. You've probably never heard of it."

I hadn't. "Is everything people say about Floridians true? Do you ride alligators to rob banks and whatever?"

"Heck yeah," DJ said, though he sounded a little distracted. "You're not a true Floridian until you've committed at least one stupid crime from the back of a gator."

Anyone who could crack jokes while the specter of death hung over them was okay by me. "So what do you really do?" The path on my hud finally reached an endpoint a couple of meters ahead. "Wait, don't tell me. You're a surfer. You've got a perfect tan, a sunburned nose, and blond hair because you spend as much time as possible catching waves in the ocean."

Up close, this section of the hull looked similar to everything else I'd passed. I saw nothing to distinguish it from the rest. But my hud had me kneel in front of an access panel and then offered up a helpful set of instructions. **Step one: Open the panel.**

"You got the blond hair right," DJ said, "but I'm about as white as Wonder Bread, and I definitely don't surf."

"How do you live in Florida but you don't surf? Isn't that against the law?"

"Don't know how to swim." DJ sounded a bit sheepish. I kept trying to picture what he looked like, but he remained a pale, blond blob in my mind.

I opened the panel and immediately spotted the problem. "Damn."

"What?" DJ asked.

"You should see this pipe," I said. "The thing's as big around as my thigh, and thick, too, but it's got a raggedy hole in one side. Looks like it was burned with acid or something."

"Can you fix it?"

My hud had outlined a pouch attached to my belt, and the instructions told me that the next step was to smooth the surface of the conduit before applying the sealant patch. In the pouch, I found a sponge-shaped object with a side that was rough like sandpaper. "Yeah," I said. "I think I can."

"You sound like you believe it."

"I guess I do." I started grinding down the rough edges around the hole in the conduit. I didn't know anything about DJ, other than that he didn't know how to swim, but I was grateful that he was on the other end of the line to talk to. I tried to picture Becca in the reactor room, and no. She would've demanded to speak to the manager and then probably set the place on fire. And Billy?

Nope. Billy was the last person I wanted to think about.

"What about you?" DJ asked. "Where're you from?"

"Seattle."

"Guess that means we weren't abducted from the same city."

"We weren't even on the same side of the country," I muttered. "Wait. When you say 'abducted,' do you mean by aliens?"

I heard the pause in DJ's breathing, and I wasn't sure whether he was considering his answer or was busy with whatever he was doing to keep us from exploding. After a couple of seconds, he said, "Why not aliens?"

I hadn't thought about it much until he asked, but the more I did, the more the idea seemed unlikely. "Does this feel like an alien ship to you?" I asked. "Granted, I've only seen the inside of this suit and the airlock, but all the text on my hud is in English."

"You're probably right," he said. "Besides, there are lots of other things that could've abducted us."

"Such as?"

"Sentient computer programs run amok?"

I snorted. "You watch way too much TV."

"My dad says the same thing all the time," he said. "Doesn't mean it can't be true."

DJ had me there, and I didn't know what else to say. There was an ease talking to him that I rarely found with others. I was frequently awkward and shy around strangers, but DJ drew words from me, seemingly, without even trying. I suspected it was because we weren't actually in the same room together. He was little more than a voice in my helmet.

Once I'd finished smoothing the conduit, the instructions told me to use one of the mesh patches in my pouch to seal the hole. The patch was made of thin, flexible metal strands woven together as tightly as silk. I peeled the backing off to expose the adhesive and pressed it carefully against the surface of the pipe.

"Question for you," DJ asked. "I've located the controls for shutting down the reactor, but doing so requires turning off a bunch of other systems, and I'm not real certain what any of them do."

"Okay?" I was finishing the last step, which involved smearing a thick, pasty goo around the edges of the patch.

"I think I can work out what 'oxygen reclamation' does and that I shouldn't mess with it, but I've got no idea what 'stasis regulation' or 'photonic interface' might be for. Any guesses?"

I shook my head, forgetting DJ couldn't see me. "I can bake a cake no problem, but I can barely update my phone without breaking it. I don't think this is the kind of situation where you want *me* taking guesses."

"You bake cakes?"

"Yeah," I said. "I bake lots of things, but I don't think that's what's important at the moment."

"I know. It's just that I love eating cakes."

It was weird to be laughing when my life was in danger, but it also felt good to bleed off some of the pressure that had been building inside my skull. And hearing DJ's lighthearted laugh on the other end of the comms made me feel, just for a moment, like I was safe and nothing could harm me.

"If we survive, and there's a kitchen on this ship, I'll bake you as many cakes as you want."

"Deal," DJ said. His laughter faded into silence and then the silence turned uncomfortable. "So what do you think? Should I turn off these systems even though I don't know what they do?" I began to repeat what I'd said before, but DJ cut me off. "We're in the same boat, Noa."

"Technically, it's a ship," I said. "And I'm not actually in it."

"You know what I mean." DJ sounded tense. He wasn't joking anymore. "I don't know what these systems do either, and I'll make the decision if I have to, but I don't want to be responsible for killing us if I can help it."

I understood where DJ was coming from. It was a lot of pressure. I still didn't think I was the best person to advise him, but I was the best DJ had, and I couldn't let him down. "Is there any other way to kill the reactor?"

"Not as far as I can tell."

"We'll definitely die if you don't shut those systems off, and we'll only possibly die if you do. The choice seems pretty clear to me."

DJ let out a relieved sigh. "Okay. Good. That's what I was thinking too."

"You got this, DJ," I said. "And I'll try not to be too pissed off if you accidentally kill us both."

DJ's rich, deep laugh filled the emptiness. It was bigger than the ship and brighter than the stars. "Thanks for that. I guess."

"You're welcome." I closed the panel and stood. "Now hurry up. I've finished patching the conduit and I'm coming in. I can't wait to get out of this stupid suit."

"All right," DJ said. "Say goodbye to water filtration."

"Bye, water filtration!" I reached around my back to grab the tether, but it wasn't there. I froze, seized by panic. The tether wasn't there because I'd taken it off at the airlock and hadn't reattached it. The tether wasn't there because I was a moron. My heart fluttered. It stopped. "Damn it."

"What?"

"Nothing," I said. This was fine. I was going to be fine. I had my mag boots, and there was no point worrying DJ about something he couldn't fix. I'd walked from the airlock to the conduit without the tether; I could make the return trip, no problem.

"You've gotta stop doing that," DJ said. "Unless you're *trying* to give me a heart attack."

"Sorry." One slow, careful step at a time, I made my way back to the airlock. The halo of lights surrounding the entrance grew brighter as I neared it, and this time I wasn't going to let anything prevent me from cycling through and shedding my suit.

Even thinking about the suit made me anxious. I needed to talk to keep from panicking. "What do you do for fun, DJ?" I asked. "Obviously nothing water related."

DJ didn't answer. I hoped he was only preoccupied with shutting down the reactor, and I didn't want to bug him and cause him to make a mistake, but I was also kind of on the verge of freaking out.

"DJ?"

"Sorry," he said. "I don't do much, I guess. Just normal teenage stuff."

"Normal teenage stuff? That sounds like the kind of answer

a fifty-year-old dude who's never been a normal teenager would give."

I had only been playing, but DJ sounded annoyed. "I don't know. Does it matter?"

"Just making conversation. Do you play any sports?"

"I like running," he said.

"Because of all the cake you like to eat?"

The silence before DJ answered was loud. "No. I just like to run." More quiet. Thankfully, I was nearly at the airlock. Just a few more meters. Ten, max.

"I'm a jerk," I said. "I make jokes when I'm nervous. I also talk a lot and I can't stand silence. My mom says it's because I was born premature and spent the first month of my life in an incubator." Five meters. "I had heart problems too. My mom teases me that I was born with a broken heart."

The heavy exhale of DJ's sigh rushed through the speakers in my helmet, and even that sound was a relief. "Sorry. I'm concentrating on not messing this up."

"What's the verdict? Are we going to live?" Four meters.

"I can shut down the reactor as soon as you're in the airlock."

Three meters. "I'm nearly there. Don't wait on me."

DJ paused. "You sure?"

"Positive," I said. "Kill it."

Two meters.

One meter. There was the end of the tether right where I'd left it.

"Here goes," DJ said.

A shudder rolled through *Qriosity*, and I immediately wondered if I'd made the right call telling DJ to shut down the reactor before I was inside.

"DJ? Maybe—"

The lights around the airlock flashed red. The inner airlock door irised open, releasing the air that was trapped in the antechamber as a fist that tore through the opening and smashed into me at the speed of sound. I felt a moment of resistance as my boots gripped the hull, but the attractive force wasn't strong enough to save me.

I pinwheeled my arms. I reached for the tether, a handle, anything I could grab onto, but it was already too late.

I could only watch as I flew backward, away from the airlock. Away from the ship and from DJ.

"We did it!" DJ yelled through the comms. "*Qriosity*'s not going to blow up!"

Warning! Your heart rate is exceeding the maximum recommended beats per minute. Please attempt thirty seconds of relaxed breathing.

"Noa? Are you there? Noa?"

When I was finally able to speak without fear of puking, I said, "We have another *minor* problem."

FOUR

SPACE SUCKS.

Space is scary. It's filled with stars that expand and explode and sometimes collapse into solar system–devouring black holes; there are meteors capable of destroying planets and, potentially, aliens that movies had convinced me were violent and had a taste for human meat. I know that every Earth-bound kid dreams of going into space and sailing among the stars, about boarding a rocketship to a planet no human has ever walked on, but I had never been one of them. Human beings had no business going into space. I was proof of that.

I'd been in space less than an hour and I was already dead. My frozen corpse was going to drift through the void between stars forever, and no one but DJ, who probably wouldn't outlive me by long, would know what had happened to me.

So I'll say it again: space sucks.

"How much oxygen have you got left, Noa?" DJ was doing his best to sound like this really was nothing more than a minor problem, but I could hear the alarm in his voice in the wobble of his words.

"Forty-three minutes," I said. "You know? From out here, *Qriosity* looks like a bus with wings and a hump on top." I couldn't see any detail on the ship, but I could see it outlined by the stars. "It figures that my first spaceship is a flying dump truck." A sour laugh bubbled out of me.

"Stop talking like that." DJ's voice was a whipcrack. "I'm not letting you die out there, so you can just put that out of your mind."

"Sure. Whatever." I appreciated DJ's attempt to reassure me, but my situation was hopeless and I saw no use in pretending otherwise. The only way DJ could save me was if he learned to pilot the ship he *just* shut down and came to fetch me, which I didn't see much chance of happening unless DJ was a spaceship savant.

"Keep talking to me, all right?" DJ said. "What's the last thing you remember before waking up out there?"

The irony of my talking to keep DJ calm was not lost on me, but it's not like I had anything better to do. "I was in bed, trying to sleep. It'd been a bad day."

"Why? What happened?"

"Well, there was the car that nearly hit me, and I threw my milkshake, which was stupid, *and* it was raining. But I guess it really started with Billy."

"Billy?"

"My ex," I said. "I wouldn't have even gone to Dick's for the milkshake and burgers if I hadn't run into Billy at Target. I should've gone to the one at Northgate, but all I needed was face wash and I didn't want to have to take the bus. It was my fault, really."

DJ said something, but I wasn't listening. I was thinking about seeing Billy standing in front of the notebooks, examining each one like it was the most important decision he would ever make—and for him, it probably felt like it was. How I froze when I saw him, and the moment before he saw me, when I could have taken off but didn't. The hurt that morphed into anger in Billy's eyes when he finally looked up and realized it was me standing at the end of the aisle.

"Noa?"

I tried to shake Billy out of my head. "Have you ever been in love, DJ?"

"Once."

"Sorry."

"Why?" he asked.

"Because love is a lie. It's not some deep and meaningful connection between two people built over stolen moments and awkward glances and hot chocolates. It's not a holy expression of the profound understanding you have for another person or a sign from the universe that you've found the one human being in the world that you're fated to spend the rest of your life with.

"Love is chemical warfare. It's your body responding to their pheromones by juicing you with feel-good hormones and then spraying your own cocktail of pheromones into the air. It's serotonin and dopamine and oxytocin. You can get the same high from eating a bag of chocolates, did you know that?"

DJ cleared his throat. "Uh, I didn't."

"Well, you can," I said. "And the longer you spend with someone, the more addicted to them you become. Your body craves the chemicals their body churns out." I laughed bitterly. "Love turns us into junkies."

I suppose if I didn't have a one-way ticket to a long, drawn-out death in outer space, I might have been embarrassed by my rant, but I had run out of energy to care what DJ or anyone else thought of me.

"That Billy guy really hurt you, huh?"

"I don't want to talk about it anymore," I snapped, even though I was the one who'd dumped my trash out there for DJ to pick through.

"Sorry." And he sounded like he really, truly meant it, which made everything worse.

"It's fine," I said. "I just . . . let's talk about something else. What about you? What's the last thing you remember?"

There was a three-second delay before DJ answered, and I worried in that short time that he'd shut off the comms so he didn't have to stay with me until I died. I was scared of dying, sure, but I was *terrified* of dying alone.

"I was in the shower," he said. "I think."

"You were kidnapped from the shower?"

"I think." He definitely sounded distracted. A small part of me wanted to believe that DJ was going to find a way to rescue me, but I couldn't afford to let hope in. Hope was even more dangerous than space. "I'd gotten home from running, and I was sweaty and covered in gnats."

"Gross."

"Yeah," he said. "You learn pretty quick not to breathe through your mouth."

I didn't want to think about all the bugs DJ had swallowed to reach that realization, and quickly changed the subject. "Who's missing you at home? Parents? Friends? Siblings?"

"I don't think—"

"Look, these are probably the last minutes of my life. I know you didn't ask to spend them with me, and I sure as hell didn't think I'd be spending them with you, but this is where we are, so can you please just humor me?"

The weird thing was that while I would have liked for my mom or Becca to have been on the other end of the comms, I wasn't upset that it was DJ instead. I barely knew anything about him—I didn't even know what he looked like—but, so far, he was the only thing about space I didn't hate.

"It's just me, my dad, and my older brothers," DJ said. "My mom died when I was born."

"I'm sorry."

"Thanks, but it's tough for me to miss someone I never met, you know?"

"Kind of," I said. "It's just me and my mom at home. My dad

took off when I was three. Drugs, though my mom said he had some mental problems and that I shouldn't hold it against him."

"Couldn't he have gotten help?"

I shrugged even though DJ couldn't see it over the comms. "There was a homeless guy I used to see everywhere in my neighborhood. He was always sitting at one of the bus stops I had to pass on my way to and from school. For a while when I was in sixth grade, I got it into my head that he was my dad, which was silly, seeing as we didn't look anything alike. It was just . . . it made me feel better to think he was there, even if he wasn't."

I didn't give a lot of brain space to my dad. Most of the time he was little more than a ghost who haunted me and my mom around the holidays. There was a small part of me that thought I'd find him one day. I never expected us to have some big reunion where he apologized for leaving, but I thought, at least, I might get the chance to know him.

Now I never would.

"Hey, DJ?"

"Yeah, Noa?"

"Do me a favor," I said. "Figure out who did this to us, find them, and kill them for me."

"Can't do it," DJ said. "I'm a pacifist."

I balled my hands into fists. "You're a pacifist? Like, you won't even fight to defend yourself?"

"To defend myself, yeah, but I'm not just going to walk up to a person and murder them, no matter how much I think they deserve it."

This was a ridiculous conversation, and it was even more ludicrous that it was pissing me off. "I'm dying here, DJ. Are you seriously going to deny me my dying wish? Can't you at least lie to me?"

"I could," DJ said, "but what would be the point? You're not going to die."

I was sure that I'd misheard DJ. That he'd said something entirely different from what my brain thought he had. "Say that again."

DJ's laugh was as bright as a supernova. "You're not dying today, Noa. Now hold on tight. I'm bringing you in."

Before I could process what was happening, the back of my suit began to vibrate. Soon, my entire body was shaking, and I seemed to be slowing down. I didn't know how far I'd traveled, but *Qriosity* was little more than a tiny dark blob in the starfield.

"What the hell is going on?" I asked, equal parts terrified and exhilarated.

I came to a complete stop, and the vibration in my back ceased for a moment before starting up again, only this time it was pushing me forward. I felt a gentle nudge against the inside of my suit as I sped toward *Qriosity*. "How . . . ? DJ? Did you . . . ?" I was having difficulty forming words and organizing them into coherent sentences.

"When I was digging through the computer's operating system, I remembered seeing controls for the spacesuits. Turns out those controls allowed me to remotely activate your thrusters. Once I figured that out, all I had to do was program in a firing pattern that would stop your flight away from *Qriosity* and put you on a trajectory back to the ship. Nothing to it." DJ really did make it sound simple. Like my life had never actually been in danger.

I barked out a laugh. "Oh yeah, sounds super easy."

"I'm good with math," he said. "Math and computers."

"I'm good at using a calculator." I had convinced myself that I was going to die in space, and now that I wasn't, I could hardly believe it. I didn't know what to do or say. "How am I ever going to thank you?"

"There was some mention of cake?" DJ said.

"As many cakes as you can eat," I said. "I'll stuff cakes in you until you beg me to stop."

DJ's gentle laugh filled my helmet. "Suddenly this is sounding less and less like a reward."

Now that I was returning to the ship, a small ember of hope flared within me, and I nursed it into a flame. "How long will it take to reach the ship?" I asked. "I can't wait to get out of this suit and to meet you, and I have to pee so bad I can taste it."

"Let me see," DJ said. "You're moving at a speed of . . ." His voice faded in and out as he talked himself through the problem, and I wasn't paying attention because . . . math. "Twenty-three minutes and forty-seven seconds."

I hesitated, glancing at my hud. "Can you fire my thrusters again and speed the trip up a little?"

"If you really have to go, I bet you can go in the suit."

The flame flickered. "That's not it. I mean, yes, I am almost definitely going to pee in this suit, but DJ, I only have sixteen minutes of oxygen left." I checked the readout on my hud twice to make sure.

Nothing from the comms.

"DJ?"

"I . . . Noa, I used the last of your propellant to set your course back. There's nothing left."

The flame died.

I began to laugh. A full-throated belly laugh that filled the suit. I laughed so hard that I absolutely peed a little. I hoped DJ was right about the suit being equipped to handle it. I didn't want to die drowning in my own urine.

"Noa, don't. I'll work something out. Breathe shallowly, okay? We've still got time."

I laughed because, if I didn't, I was going to cry, and I had no idea what would happen to tears in zero-G. "This is perfect," I said. "I'm going to make it back to the ship; I'll just be dead before it happens."

"Stop talking," DJ said. "Talking uses oxygen."

"This figures, you know?" I said, ignoring DJ. "My entire life has been one disaster after another."

A bang echoed through the comms, followed by DJ's choked voice. "You're not going to die, Noa. I won't let you!"

"It's fine," I told him. "It's not your fault. You don't even know me, okay? For all you know, this is exactly what I deserve. Don't waste any more energy trying to save me. Save yourself, okay?"

"Noa—"

"Just . . ."

"What?" DJ said.

"Don't leave me alone out here?"

I could hear DJ breathing, so I knew he was still there, but he didn't speak for what felt like forever. A second is a second no matter what, right? It's a measurement, and those are kind of absolute even if they're made up. But time is also relative to the person experiencing it. That's why the last minute hugging your best friend before they leave for LA to spend the summer with their grandparents feels shorter than a heartbeat, and why the last minute before the last bell rings on the last day of school feels like an hour.

Those seconds between my begging DJ to stay on the line and him answering were the longest of my life. They stretched out like they'd been sucked into a black hole and spaghettified. A second is a second, except when it's forever.

"I promise I won't ever leave you," DJ finally said.

I had nearly suffocated in the waiting, and now I could breathe again. "Still wish we could trade places?"

DJ's laugh was wet, like he was crying, which I tried not to think about so that I didn't start crying too. "I would, you know?"

Strangely, even though I'd never met DJ in person, I got the impression that he was sincere. He wasn't just saying he would take my place to make me feel better. He would actually do it if given the opportunity. That's the kind of person he was. And I was the kind of person who would have let him.

"If you make it back home," I said. "Do me a favor and tell my mom what happened. Her name's Emma North—"

"Please don't do this, Noa."

"And tell her it was me and not the cat that knocked down her little Christmas tree with the crystal ornaments on it that Gamma had given her. She's hated Jinx ever since, and the poor cat doesn't deserve it."

Maybe it wasn't fair of me to unload this crap onto DJ, but someone had to make sure my mom didn't spend the rest of her life wondering where I'd gone the way I knew she wondered about my dad. She needed to know that both of us hadn't abandoned her.

I'm sure it was my imagination, but the air in my suit felt thinner. DJ didn't say much as I babbled on about nothing. I told him to find Becca and make sure to tell her that she did *not* look good with a perm and I should've been honest with her, but I'd had a crush on Sanjay too and I'd hoped her hideous perm would make him lose interest in her.

I told him about Mrs. Blum and her bakery where I'd learned to bake. How she'd watched me after school, when I was younger, on the days when my mom had worked late at the hospital where she was a nurse. Mrs. Blum had given me dough to knead to keep my hands busy at first, but eventually she began to teach me for real.

I told him about the musical I starred in when I was in fourth grade, and how I stood at the edge of the stage to perform my first solo, opened my mouth to sing, and threw up all over the audience in the front row.

"You said you had a boyfriend?" DJ said. "Want me to tell *him* anything?"

"Ex," I said. "And no."

"I'd be happy to break his arms if you want."

"I thought you were a pacifist."

DJ said, "For you, just this once, I'll make an exception."

The air was definitely getting thinner. My eyes were heavy and hard to hold open. I hoped I would simply fall asleep and that would be the end. But I didn't want to die. I wanted to live even though I wasn't always sure why. I wanted to live despite my missing dad and my broken heart and all the thrown milkshakes. I wanted to live because, sure, life sucked a lot, sometimes it was unfairly horrific, but it was always worth sticking around for to see what came next.

"Noa?"

"Yeah, DJ."

"I'm really sorry."

"It's not your fault," I said, and I tried to make sure he knew I meant it.

"Someone owes you an apology for this," he said, "so it might as well be me."

"Thanks."

"And I know we've never even properly met, so you've got no reason to believe me, but I think you're wrong about love. Love isn't war. Life is the war; love is a truce you find in the middle of all that violence. And I bet there's someone out there who loves you, even if you don't know them yet."

I wanted to tell DJ he was wrong. I knew what love was and what it wasn't. If love wasn't war, then why had it hurt so badly? Why did the idea of it still give me nightmares? I had survived falling in love, and I had the scars to prove it. But this wasn't the hill I wanted to die on. DJ was trying to comfort me in my final minutes, and I appreciated that more than he would ever know.

"I wish I could've met you in person, DJ. You seem all right."

"Me too." DJ exhaled, and the sound of it over the speakers was like a breeze I could almost feel. "How much air have you got left?"

It was becoming difficult to catch enough breath to talk. "Just a few minutes. You're not going anywhere, right? You promised."

"Don't worry," he said. "I'm staying right here until the end."

QRIOSITY
KILLED THE CAT

ONE

I SAT UP GASPING BECAUSE THE LAST THING MY BODY remembered was dying. A deep ache lingered in my chest like someone had used my ribs for a trampoline, and though breathing hurt, I took one sweet breath after another, clearing the fog from my brain.

"DJ?" His name felt strange on my tongue. Strange that he was the first person I thought of upon waking, but it also felt as natural as breathing. If I strained, I could hear DJ's voice in the dark, like he was just on the other side of a door talking to me, telling me jokes to keep me from freaking out, reassuring me that everything was going to be fine with his barely-there Southern twang.

Soft blue lights flickered on. I shielded my eyes with my hand, blinking until they adjusted. The air was humid and sticky and smelled sharply of antiseptic. It reminded me of the hospital where my mom worked. For a moment, I expected her to walk through the door and tell me that I hadn't woken up in space, that the experience had been nothing more than a fever dream.

But she didn't. Because it wasn't.

I was lying on a cool white table in a sterile white room that was only slightly larger than my bedroom back home. A second table, empty, sat to my left, and there was a counter across the room that was clean except for a pile of clothes. I peeled back the silver blanket draped over me and swung my legs around to stand, but a glossy white cuff wrapped around my left bicep jerked me back. Tubes and wires ran from the cuff into a port on the wall. I touched the smooth surface, looking for a seam or a latch so that I could pry it off.

The cuff shrieked, and a gender-neutral voice with a vaguely British accent said, "Removing the MediQwik Portable Medical Diagnostician and Care Appliance while it is treating you for cracked ribs and hypoxia-related brain injury could result in complications such as internal bleeding, memory loss, and death. MediQwik, health redefined. MediQwik is a trademark of Prestwich Enterprises, a subsidiary of Gleeson Foods."

Out of all the garbage the computer voice spit out, I zeroed in on one thing. "I've got brain damage? How the hell did I get brain damage?"

"The cause of your brain damage was death."

"I died?!"

"You were clinically dead for seven minutes and thirteen

seconds before your successful resuscitation and repair. You're welcome."

I had died.

The last thing I remembered was the sound of DJ's voice. Not what he said, just the last note of it repeating on a loop until it faded entirely. I recalled no bright light. Gamma Evelyn and Grandpa Andy hadn't been waiting to welcome me home. There had been no chorus of angels, no fluffy clouds. There'd been nothing. At least, nothing that I could remember. All those years of Sunday school had been a lie.

I didn't have time for an existential crisis, so I gently set aside the question of life after death and focused on a different question. I could guess how I had died—I'd run out of oxygen and suffocated—but how had I survived?

"What happened to me?"

On the far wall, an image appeared of someone wearing one of those hideous spacesuits. I recognized the airlock. "I'm coming for you, Noa." That sounded like DJ; it had to be him.

He opened the outer airlock door, attached the tether to his belt, crouched down, and then jumped. *Out* of the airlock. The video skipped forward a minute. DJ returned, and he wasn't alone. The recording lurched ahead again. There was a body on the floor. The body was me. Someone—DJ, I assumed—had stripped me out of my spacesuit, and I was spread on the floor in nothing but a gray bodysuit. It hardly looked like me. Waxy skin, eyes wide but empty. I couldn't see DJ, but I could see his hands, one on top of the other, pushing on my chest as fast as he could.

"Please don't die, Noa. Please don't leave me here alone. I need you, Noa. Please." The recording paused and then vanished.

But DJ's urgent pleas lingered; the plaintive sound haunting me. He'd been so desperate to save me, so lost and afraid. My heart hurt for him. I remembered what it felt like to need something that badly. I wanted to crawl into the recording and tell that boy that his efforts hadn't been for nothing. That he wasn't alone. Instead, I'd have to settle for finding DJ and thanking him now. If the stupid MediQwik thing ever let me go.

"How much longer is this going to take?"

An irritating three-note chime sounded from the cuff as it popped open and hung loosely around my arm. "Congratulations! MediQwik has completed treating you for cracked ribs and hypoxia-related brain injury. Please avoid oxygen-deficient environments in the future. Additionally, drink three liters of water over the next twenty-four hours, and return to the medical suite if your urine luminesces for longer than seventy-two hours. MediQwik, health redefined. MediQwik is a trademark of Prestwich Enterprises, a subsidiary of Gleeson Foods."

There was nothing funny about the situation, but I laughed anyway. I'd done the same thing during Grandpa Andy's funeral. Busted out laughing right during Father Diaz's opening prayer. I apologized to Gamma Evelyn afterward, and she told me it was okay. That life was ridiculous and absurd, and sometimes the only way to keep it from overwhelming us was to laugh right in its face.

In the last few hours, I had woken up on a spaceship—no, not even *on* the ship. I had woken up outside a ship. A ship named *Qriosity* that was in danger of exploding. With the help of a boy named DJ, whom I'd never met, I'd repaired the ship, and then been blown into space for my trouble, where I'd apparently died.

It *was* absurd. It was the most absurd series of events that had ever happened to me, and if I hadn't laughed at them, I would have screamed and screamed and kept screaming forever.

"Your treatment is complete," MediQwik said. "You may exit the medical suite at your leisure."

When the laughter faded and my body stopped shaking, I said, "Are you programmed to diagnose mental disorders?"

"Yes," MediQwik replied.

My mom and I hadn't discussed it, but the fear that I had inherited my father's mental illness had hovered over our lives. I had to face the possibility that this was all happening in my head. "Am I sane? Have I had some kind of break with reality?"

The lights in the medical suite dimmed slightly for a moment. "According to your most recent brain scan, MediQwik has detected no physiological abnormalities that would indicate the presence of a psychiatric illness."

That *should* have been reassuring, but it wasn't. Not entirely. If this wasn't a delusion, then I'd died and been brought back to life and was still stuck on a spaceship. But if it *was* a delusion, then all I'd accomplished was having my delusion tell me that I wasn't deluded.

It was a rabbit hole I couldn't go down, or I would second-guess myself until the end of time.

"What would Mom tell me to do?"

"Your mother is not on board *Qriosity*," MediQwik replied. "Therefore I am unsure how to respond to your inquiry."

"I wasn't talking to you," I muttered.

I knew exactly what my mom would say; I could practically hear her voice. She would tell me to take it one step at a time. First step: get dressed.

My legs were wobbly and the floor was cold. It took me a few seconds to find my balance before I was able to cross the room to the pile of clothes, which turned out to be a revolting tan onesie with the name "Nico" stitched across the chest. Under normal circumstances, I wouldn't have considered wearing it, but these were not normal circumstances. Besides, step two was to find DJ, and I wasn't about to explore the ship in my underwear. I doubted they were even *my* underwear. I never would have deliberately chosen to wear a pair of dingy white briefs with a saggy ass. The whole outfit was sad with an I-dressed-myself-from-the-lost-and-found-box vibe, but it was better than nothing.

I approached the door, expecting it to slide open, but it remained firmly shut, forcing me to open it manually. "Seriously, what kind of spaceship doesn't have automatic doors?" No one replied.

Harsh yellow-tinged lights cast the corridor outside medical with a sickly glow. One of the guys my mom had dated for a while had tried to score points with me by taking me to the Naval Undersea Museum when I was nine. It hadn't worked; the guy had smelled like sauerkraut and thought "Pull my finger" was the funniest joke ever invented. Anyway, *Qriosity* reminded me of those submarines I'd toured. The steel beams, the rivets, the pipes running overhead. And whoever had chosen the color scheme should've been tossed out the airlock without a suit. The tan and green were dire and depressing.

For my first spaceship, it was disappointing.

"DJ?" I stood at the junction of three corridors, unsure which way to go. I wanted to find DJ and thank him for saving me, but I also didn't want to wander around the ship looking for him while he was wandering around the ship looking for me. The smart choice would have been to return to the medical suite and wait for DJ, but a pounding sound caught my attention, and I decided to follow it.

The thumping grew louder as I walked, and I thought I heard a voice as well. I paused and turned my ear to listen. Yeah, someone was definitely shouting, "Let me out of here!" at the top of their lungs.

I picked up the pace, not paying attention to where I was going, and when I finally reached the source of the noise, it was coming from behind a door with the word "Head" stenciled on it. I pulled the lever and opened the door.

"Let me—" A young woman spilled out and punched me in the shoulder. We tumbled into the wall and hit the floor in a tangle of arms and legs and profanity, not all of it mine. The girl seemed to take a second to realize she was free, and then she scrambled to her feet, stepping on my hand in the process, and backed away from me.

"Who are you, and why did you lock me in the toilet?" The girl was shorter than me, which most people were, with shoulder-length rust-red hair, a haphazard dusting of freckles across her fair nose and cheeks, and wide, dreamy eyes. She was wearing black pants, a gray shirt, a fitted, high-waisted black jacket, thigh-high boots, and a murderous scowl. She also looked to be about my age.

"Hello?" she said, snapping her fingers in the air. "What were you planning to do to me? It better not have been sex stuff. I know Krav Maga." She held her fists out in front of her in a manner that made me suspect she absolutely did *not* know Krav Maga.

"Ew, no," I said. "I didn't lock you in there, and I wasn't planning to do *anything* to you." I was feeling a bit abused by my treatment so far, but she had been locked in a restroom, so I tried to give her the benefit of the doubt. "I heard you banging for help and opened the door. That's all."

She relaxed slightly but kept her fists up. "Oh. Well, I hope you don't need to use the toilet. There's no paper and the sink doesn't work."

"I'm good," I said. "How long have you been in there?"

The girl shrugged. "Long enough that I was beginning to weigh the pros and cons of drinking toilet water."

"Gross." I stuck out my hand. "I'm Noa."

"Jenny." She ignored my hand and twisted her hair around her finger. "Are you sure this isn't a sex thing?"

"Positive."

"Then where am I and what is going on?"

I wasn't sure how Jenny was going to take the knowledge that she was on a ship called *Qriosity*, or how I could explain it without her laughing in my face. The only reason I'd accepted that I was in space so quickly was because I'd been floating in it.

"Noa?" I heard DJ's voice a moment before he jogged around the corner. I recognized it because it had been all I'd had to cling to in the darkness, and I felt dizzy with emotions that crashed into me too quickly to process.

DJ looked nothing like I expected. He was thick, with broad shoulders, wavy blond hair, ruddy cheeks, and blue eyes brighter than any star. I knew we'd never met before, and yet he had one of those faces that seemed instantly familiar. It was like remembering someone from a past life. "Noa!" DJ broke into a goofy, toothy smile that was flanked by these impossible dimples before he rushed me and wrapped me in a strong embrace, squeezing the air from my lungs and throwing me further off guard. I tensed and stood motionless with my arms pinned to my sides. I wanted to hug him back, to relax into his chest, but I also wanted to shove this stranger who was touching me away. Instead, I froze and waited for DJ to let go.

I cleared my throat. "So, I guess that answers whether you're a hugger." I tried to back away and put some distance between us without it looking obvious. DJ had saved my life, and I owed him more than I could ever repay, but I didn't want to risk remaining within reach of another impromptu hug.

"I'm sorry I wasn't there when you woke up," DJ said.

The spaces between his words were practically nonexistent. "MediQwik said you were going to live, and I figured I might as well try fixing the ship while the ship was busy fixing you."

DJ's neutral expression seemed to be stuck on shame. Like he was waiting to be scolded for doing something wrong even if he didn't know what he'd done. But he also possessed a sincerity that was so visceral and real it must have hurt. He didn't just wear his heart on his sleeve; he held it in his hands and presented it to anyone he thought might willingly take it. Right at that moment, he seemed to be offering it to me. I couldn't take it. I didn't want it. And if DJ had known me, he wouldn't have considered letting me anywhere near it.

"Hi. I'm Jenny." Jenny wedged herself between us. "I was locked in the toilet."

I coughed as DJ frowned. "She doesn't know where we are," I said.

"Like, she doesn't know—"

"Anything," I finished.

"*What* don't I know?" Jenny asked. "Someone needs to tell me where I am right now. I'm starting to get violent, though that might just be low blood sugar."

"We're on a spaceship, Jenny." No one had eased me gently into the knowledge. Why should Jenny's introduction be any different?

Jenny pursed her lips, her eyes darting between me and DJ like she was waiting for one or both of us to laugh and tell her we were joking. When neither of us did, she folded her arms over her chest and said, “Yeah, I’m going to need to see that to believe it.”

I was about to tell her where she could find a spacesuit and the airlock, but DJ spoke first, which was probably for the best.

“We should go to Ops. You can check out everything from there.”

“Maybe we can finally get some answers,” I muttered.

But DJ glanced at me with that sad puppy-dog look and said, “I wouldn’t hold your breath.”

TWO

DJ WAS WEARING JEANS THAT SHOWED OFF HIS BUTT and a gray T-shirt that highlighted his broad shoulders. It wasn't fair that DJ was forced to wear jeans and a T-shirt and Jenny woke up in that gorgeous jacket, while I woke up in an ugly tan onesie with someone else's name on it. And of all the things to be bothered by, not looking cute was a weird one to fixate on, but the more I thought about it, the more it infuriated me.

Plus, as if being ugly and unfashionable wasn't bad enough, the stupid jumpsuit didn't even fit properly. It was too short and kept riding up and giving me a wedgie.

These were the thoughts that occupied my brain as DJ led me and Jenny through *Qriosity*. I had no idea where DJ was taking us, nor did I care. The only place I wanted to go was home.

"How're you holding up?" DJ walked beside me, but he'd maintained a respectable distance since his surprise hug earlier.

Clearly I hadn't hidden my discomfort as well as I thought I had.

"Fine, considering I died." I wasn't sure whether it was talking about dying that was making me nervous or talking to DJ. Our conversation had flowed so much easier when he'd been a voice in my helmet rather than an actual person who gave me the most inconvenient stomach flutters when he glanced shyly my way. "Thanks for making sure I didn't stay dead."

"It was nothing," he said. "I only did it for the cake." DJ tried to hold a straight face, but he broke into a laugh almost immediately, then kept laughing like he didn't realize it wasn't that funny. But he had a cute laugh, so I let it go.

"Well, I don't care why you did it. I'm glad you did."

"Me too." DJ's smile was so earnest it hurt, and I finally had to look away.

"I can't wait to get home so that I can have the total breakdown I deserve. There'll be ugly crying and ice cream for days."

"Yeah," DJ said. "Home. Sounds good." He stopped at the bottom of a set of steps that led to a door labeled with the word "Ops." "We're here."

Ops—which was like the bridge or the command deck or the place where qualified people would have flown the ship from if there had been any of those on board—was separated into three distinct stations. Each had its own console covered with screens and knobs and blinking buttons, and each had its own chair. The equipment looked both technologically advanced and antiquated. Rundown and shabby in a way that didn't inspire confidence. The consoles were worn at the edges, and the chairs' cushions looked lumpy—one even had stuffing poking out of the side where the stitching had come undone. It totally figured that my first spaceship would be a dump.

"Whoa! Are you seeing this? Look at all those stars!" Jenny shoved past me and made her way to the enormous wraparound viewport that dominated the front of Ops.

"Oh, I've seen them," I said, averting my eyes so that I didn't have to see them again.

Jenny pressed her face and hands to the glass. "Is this real?"

"It's real," DJ said. "We're on a spaceship called *Qriosity*."

"Supposedly," I added.

"You don't think we're actually on a ship?" DJ asked.

I took a seat at the nearest station and ran my hands over the console, looking for a convenient button marked "Home." There was not one. "I'm not saying we're *not* on a ship." I leaned back in the chair, which was more comfortable than it looked. "But I don't think we should take it for granted that we are either."

DJ's eyebrows knit together while he tried to work through what I'd said. Mostly, I was just trying to sound confident because it was better than sounding afraid.

"Why is nothing working?" Jenny had finally gotten bored of the stars, though she'd left prints of her face and hands smudged across the glass, and joined the conversation in progress. She motioned at the consoles, which did appear mostly powered down.

"We shut off the reactor," I said.

Jenny frowned at DJ and me like we'd admitted to eating rocks. "Why would you do something ridiculous like that?"

"Well . . . ," DJ began. I feared he was going to recap what we'd been through in excruciating detail, and I wasn't in the mood to relive dying, so I cut him off.

"It's a long story," I said. "The short version is that the ship was going to explode and we stopped it. No thanks necessary."

DJ hiked his thumb at me. "Yeah. That."

"Great," she said. "That explains literally nothing."

DJ rested his hand on my arm, and I jerked away. "Noa, maybe we should—"

"We shut off the reactor; what more is there to explain? Should we draw a cartoon? Maybe perform an interpretive dance?"

Jenny squeezed her eyes shut and flapped her hands in the air. "I just want someone to tell me what's going on!"

Brightly colored lights swarmed into Ops from vents near the ceiling like an army of tiny fairies and began to coalesce in the center of the room. They were beautiful because they were sparkly, and terrifying because I had no idea what they were going to do to us.

"They look like fireflies." Jenny moved toward them like she was going to try to catch one, but DJ pulled her back. "What are they?" she asked.

"Don't know," DJ said.

"They could be anything," I said. "A security system that's going to irradiate us and then leave us to die as our skin slowly sloughs off."

Jenny laughed. It was a sharper sound than DJ's laugh, and it made me wince. "Oh, I get it. You're an optimist, aren't you."

"I'm optimistic that we're probably going to die."

The lights did not, thankfully, attempt to kill us. Less than a minute after appearing, the tiny stars solidified into a surprisingly well-defined hologram of a middle-aged woman wearing a fashionable periwinkle suit. Her perfectly styled wavy auburn hair hung to her shoulders, and her smile, which remained fixed in place until each dazzling photon reached its position, was both beautiful and predatory. It was the kind of smile that said, *I'm so happy you're here! I'm dying to murder you and sew your skins into an oversize tunic.*

I looked at DJ to see if he had any idea what was happening, but he was staring at the hologram with a slack-jawed expression that said he was just as clueless as me. I nudged his arm, but before he could speak, the hologram woke up.

"Hi! I'm your host, Jenny Perez, whom you probably remember as the precocious kid detective and bestselling author Anastasia Darling on the award-winning mystery entertainment program *Murder Your Darlings*."

"I'm sorry," I said, "but what the actual—"

DJ waved me quiet. "Hush."

"Don't hush me."

"If you're seeing this holographic message, then something's gone horribly wrong aboard *Qriosity*. Is it murder? Sabotage? A mysterious illness? I don't know; I'm a hologram, silly. But on the bright side, *Qriosity*'s emergency beacon will have initiated the moment the ship detected you were in trouble, and a rescue team is probably on the way."

Only about a third of what came out of the hologram's mouth made sense, and I was having trouble processing even that. "Probably?" I said. "What's that supposed to mean?"

"When will rescue arrive?" DJ asked, glossing over the whole "probably" part.

Initially, I thought the hologram was a recording and wouldn't answer, but it stuttered after DJ asked his question and then said, "Due to the current limitations of space travel, rescue may arrive in six to nine months. Sorry about it!"

Six to nine months couldn't be right. There was no way I was going to accept being trapped on a rundown spaceship, or any ship for that matter, for that long. I was, apparently, not the only one.

"Nine months my ass," Jenny said. "I don't know what the hell is happening, but I want to go home right now!"

The hologram waved her finger in the air. "A good junior detective never uses profanity. Let's see if we can come up with a better word together."

Jenny snorted. "I've got a couple of words for you."

I buried my face in my hands. How was I supposed to survive six months in space when I hadn't survived the first hour? Space was going to find a way to kill us, and there was nothing I could do to prevent it. This was a nightmare wrapped in a disaster glazed with a catastrophe.

DJ, who seemed to be taking the news of our extended

captivity relatively well, cleared his throat loudly enough that Jenny stopped harassing Jenny Perez. "We had to shut down the reactor to keep *Qriosity* from blowing up. Will we be okay without it?"

Jenny Perez paused to think, or whatever holograms do, before answering. "In the event that you've been forced to shut down the Cordova Exotic Particle Reactor, *Qriosity*'s Quazar High-Density Batteries will continue to power essential ship's systems for up to twelve months. Essential systems include basic life support, obviously, *Qriosity*'s oxygen farm, your Freshie Stasis Fridge, and me! Your Emergency Jenny Perez Holographic Help System. Lucky you!"

"Yeah," I said. "Lucky us."

"However," the hologram continued, "all non-essential systems will remain offline to conserve power until the Cordova Exotic Particle Reactor is reactivated. Non-essential systems include: environmental comfort controls, hot water, and galley prep stations. Better get used to cold showers! But don't worry about food because *Qriosity* is stocked with enough Nutreesh meal replacement bars to feed the entire crew for a full ten years. Nutreesh! Put some in you!"

Jenny had sunk to the floor during the hologram's speech and was sitting cross-legged, staring blankly into space. "I preferred being locked in the toilet."

"We're in hell, aren't we?" I looked from DJ to Jenny to Jenny Perez, waiting for one of them to answer me. "Right? This has to be hell."

While Jenny was basically catatonic, and I was on the verge of snapping, DJ had managed to remain calm. He'd done the same thing when I'd been blown into space. Maybe that was his superpower. It was impressive, but also kind of annoying.

"Where's the crew?" DJ asked. "Why're *we* here?"

"How come I can't remember how I got here?" I threw out there, not actually expecting an answer. I wish I'd kept my mouth shut.

"There is a teeny, tiny chance that you may be experiencing short-term memory loss due to the use of your Trinity Labs Quantum Fold Drive," Jenny Perez said. "That's perfectly normal and *should* be temporary. However, if any member of the crew experiences memory loss concerning events further back than seven days, recurring jamais vu, cryptomnesia, rectal bleeding, onycholysis, overactive reflexes, loss of fingerprints, or the unusual secretion of milk, please consult a Trinity Labs medical advisor immediately. But don't panic; I'm sure you'll be fine."

Jenny's head jerked up. "Did she say 'rectal bleeding'?"

This was not happening. I refused to believe that we were going to be trapped on this spaceship for six months, and that we wouldn't even have hot showers. Honestly, I was surprised I'd held it together as long as I had. "What are we supposed to do now?!" I shouted at Jenny Perez.

DJ reached for my arm. "Noa . . ."

I almost allowed him to calm me down. Even though we'd only just met, DJ didn't feel like a stranger, except that he was. And the moment he touched me, I jerked away. I didn't want to be calm. I didn't want to listen to reason. I wanted to go home, and if I couldn't have that, then I wanted to yell. "How are we supposed to survive? I can't do this! I can't!"

"All evidence tells me that you *can* do it!" Jenny Perez said. "And you'll be back on Earth in six to nine months. Twelve at the most. Unless you've suffered an unforeseen calamity, have resorted to cannibalism, or have gone mad due to boredom and murdered each other. But that's only happened on one other ship, so I'm sure you have nothing to worry about."

Jenny Perez pulled a magnifying glass from her pocket and held it in front of her eye. "Be good, junior detectives. I'll be watching you!" The hologram exploded in a burst of light and disappeared.

THREE

DJ SHOULD HAVE LET ME DIE IN SPACE.

I didn't mean that. Mostly.

Fine, there was a part of me that meant it, but it was the part that was tired of wedgies and wearing someone else's clothes, and wasn't looking forward to six months on a spaceship with two strangers and no hot showers.

"It could be worse," DJ said.

Jenny fixed him with a murderous glare. "How?" she demanded. "How could this possibly be worse?"

DJ shrugged. "I was signed up to take the SATs on Saturday. Dodged a bullet there." He looked from me to Jenny and then back to me. "Did you really have anything that exciting happening on Earth anyway?"

Maybe DJ had a point. It wasn't like I'd been happy. It wasn't like I hadn't been dreaming of stealing a car and driving to a city where no one knew me. I would've had to learn how to drive first, but that was a minor detail. Still, my mom had to be worried sick about me, and Mrs. Blum had gotten an order the day before I disappeared for two hundred fondant fancies for a bridal shower that she would never finish on time without my help. I couldn't just shrug off being in space and forget about them. And I didn't understand how DJ could either.

Jenny huffed. "Sorry if I'm a little bothered by the fact that I'm stuck on a dirty rocketship with two strange boys, one of whom may or may not have roofied me and locked me in a toilet."

"No one roofied you!" I said.

"Someone might've," DJ said. "They might've roofied us all."

Jenny stuck her tongue out at me. "At least I put up a fight." She held out her sleeve to show us the blood staining her cuff.

Unable to remain still, I stood and paced around the cramped room. Ops might have been designed for three people, but it still felt too small. "What do we do now?" I asked. "I'm not giving up on home just because a sassy hologram said to."

"We should search the ship," DJ said.

Jenny tapped her nose and then pointed at him. "There might be people imprisoned like I was."

"But were you really imprisoned?" I asked. "Imprisoned is such a harsh word. Maybe the lock got jammed. You went in to take care of your business, and the lock malfunctioned and you were trapped. It happens."

"To who?" Jenny asked.

"People."

"Has it ever happened to you?"

This was getting us nowhere. "Well, no, but—" Besides, searching the ship was probably a good idea. "Fine, let's go exploring."

Jenny hopped to her feet, energized now that she had a mission. "Great! We should split up. I'll start at the top and work my way toward the middle."

I was shaking my head before she reached the door. "No way. Splitting up never ends well. Don't you watch horror movies?"

DJ frowned. "I can't stand horror flicks."

But Jenny smiled sweetly. "The only thing you should be afraid of on this ship is me."

"I am," I said. "And we're still not splitting up."

Jenny tilted her head to the side like she was thinking and then said, "Right. You're not the boss of me, and I don't have to do what you say. You boys can stick together if you'd like, but I'm going. Scream like you're being murdered if you find anything. Or, I suppose, if you're actually being murdered."

"I'm not—" I began to say, but Jenny was already gone. I couldn't decide whether I liked Jenny or not, but I did kind of admire her.

"I guess we should go?" DJ was standing by the door with his hands in his pockets, waiting for me to make up my mind. This day had been awful enough, and I was reluctant to do anything that might make it worse. But I also couldn't sit in Ops while DJ and Jenny explored the ship without me.

"Fine." I brushed past DJ as I left.

DJ and I roamed around *Qriosity* until we reached the lower levels, but all we found down there were service tunnels, a cargo bay with no cargo in it, and the massive water storage tanks.

"Hey," DJ said. "Wanna hear a joke?" It was the first time he'd spoken since we'd left Ops, and his voice was jarring in the silence.

"Not really." I was still annoyed by Jenny Perez refusing to give us any actual answers, and at Jenny for taking off on her own.

"Oh."

"We're the joke," I said. "Three teenagers wake up on a spaceship." I frowned. "Or are we the punch line?" I shook my head and walked to the end of the corridor. I stood by the ladder leading to the next level and waited for DJ to finish searching each room. "I thought this was a good plan, but maybe it's a waste of time."

"I don't know," DJ said. "We might not find the crew, but we could still stumble across something that might help us survive out here."

"Or the ship might be full of clever traps designed to kill us like the murder hotel of H. H. Holmes."

DJ's optimistic smile slipped. "Uh, yeah. I guess it could be that, too."

I grabbed the nearest rung to pull myself up, stopped, and turned to DJ. "How are you so calm about what's going on?" I didn't give him the opportunity to reply before going off again.

"I mean, here we are in space—*in space*—and you're just rolling with it like, whatever. Are you a robot or something? You look like the type of person who punches things when he gets pissed off. Or do you break things? Why aren't you throwing things across the room or smashing stuff with your giant fists?"

It felt good to blow up. If I hadn't let out a bit of the pressure that had been building inside me, the explosion later would have been so much worse. At the same time, I felt like a jerk. DJ hadn't done anything wrong. He'd saved my life. I should have been kissing his ass and massaging his feet.

DJ lowered his eyes, and his chin dipped to his chest. "It's just . . . you're messed up about what we're going through, and I don't know what Jenny's deal is, but she doesn't seem real stable, so I figure one of us has got to keep it together. Might as well be me."

"Well, isn't that responsible of you," I said. "For the record, I don't need you to look after me. I'm usually pretty okay at looking after myself." DJ opened his mouth, but I already knew what he was going to say. "Yes, fine, I did almost die earlier, but that wasn't really my fault, was it?"

When I finally shut up long enough for DJ to speak, he either had nothing to say or chose to keep whatever he was thinking to himself. I didn't know what I was hoping would happen. That he'd argue with me? That he'd yell so that I could yell back and we could really go at it? For him to sling his arm around my shoulder and tell me he had a plan to get us home and that everything was going to be okay? Hell, maybe he was waiting for *me* to reassure *him*. He would be waiting a long time if that was the case.

Eventually, the moment passed, and we climbed the ladder to the next level. We kept the talking to a minimum as we continued our pointless search. Deck two was slightly more interesting than deck one had been. We found a couple of rooms containing what appeared to be lab instruments, a machine shop that DJ said was probably for repairing and fabricating parts for the ship, and a gym with workout equipment that looked older than me. But no people. Nothing to indicate that there had ever been people on *Qriosity* other than us. I was ready to give up when I found a room marked "Storage." DJ was investigating a locked door at the end of the corridor, so I went in without him.

The storage room was filled with shipping containers each about the size of a steamer trunk and labeled across the front with a barcode and a name.

"DJ! Check this out!" While I waited for DJ, I attempted to pry open the container belonging to J. Winters, but it was sealed tight, and I didn't see a slot for a key or a pad to enter a code into.

DJ was breathless when he dashed into the room, and his cheeks were flaming red. "What's wrong?"

"I think I found the crew's personal belongings." I stood aside so he could see the container in front of me.

"Really?" he asked. "Are you going to open it?"

"Nah. I thought I'd caress it gently and sing it a lullaby." I rolled my eyes. "It's locked."

"Oh."

I looked around the room and read off the names on the other containers. "A. London, C. Dietrich, P. Stamper, R. Douglass, A. Sass, K. Jackson, C. Roehrig. These must belong to the crew—"

"But then where's the crew?"

I ignored the question and focused my attention on the chest. "Why won't you open?" I slammed my fist on the lid and swore when it resisted my attempts to break into it.

DJ cleared his throat. "Maybe we should leave them be. Besides, they might be full of personal stuff."

"So what? Were you a Boy Scout or something?"

"Well, yeah," DJ said. "But I don't see how—"

I stood and posed for DJ with my arms held out. "Do you see this outfit? I look like I'm about to service your car, and I'm wearing underwear with someone else's skid marks in them. So if there are better, *cleaner* clothes in these trunks, I'm going to get to them one way or another."

"I get it," DJ said. "*I* think you look fine. Good. I mean, you look nice." He was blushing hard, and he wouldn't look me in the eye. "Besides, we're probably all of us wearing someone else's underpants. I woke up wearing boxers, and I *hate* boxers."

I covertly pinched my arm to keep from imagining DJ in nothing but boxers, but the more I tried to avoid the mental image, the more detailed it became. "Whatever. I just want to wear something that doesn't smell like my grandparents' bathroom. Is that too much to ask?"

DJ cocked his head and flashed those dimples at me. "How

about we finish searching the ship, and then we'll come back and figure out how to crack these open?"

I shoved my hands in my pockets. "Fine."

"Hey, I promise, okay? I keep my promises, remember?"

I should have been grateful, but DJ's patience only got on my nerves. "Why are you so nice to me?"

DJ shrugged. "I guess because I've got no reason not to be."

"I saw what you did," I said. "That MediQwik thing showed me how you saved my life."

"CPR's easy—"

"No, I saw everything. You put on a suit and jumped out of the airlock to rescue me. You don't even know me and you risked your life to save mine, which means you're either a superhero or a super freak."

"I only did what needed to be done." DJ's shoulders bowed inward like he was trying to make himself small. "Besides, you wouldn't have needed saving if I'd waited for you to get into the airlock before shutting down the reactor."

"I said it was okay. I don't blame you, and you shouldn't blame yourself." The last thing I needed was DJ following me around like a puppy, trying to make up for some imagined wrong.

"It's not a big deal," DJ said. "And you would've done the same."

I lashed out with a trenchant laugh. "I most definitely would not have."

DJ glanced up at me through his lashes. "When you're in the moment, you find yourself doing things you never thought you could. I think you're capable of more than you know."

"Maybe that's true," I said. "But I still wouldn't have jumped out of the ship to save you or Jenny or anyone." DJ couldn't hide the hurt on his face. Every word was a knife wound, and I hated hurting him, but I couldn't stop. "It's got nothing to do with you. You're cute and sweet, and if I saw you sitting alone in a bookstore, I'd maybe engineer some way to accidentally run into you so that we could talk and exchange numbers and go out . . ." I stopped and coughed. "I guess what I'm saying is that I like you well enough, it's just that I like me more."

It was an awful thing to say, especially to someone who had leaped into danger to rescue me, and I didn't know why I felt the need to tell him. I convinced myself that DJ deserved the truth and that he had a right to know where he stood, but I think it was just easier to push him away than to admit that there was a small part of me that was maybe glad I'd woken up in space. That, dying aside, meeting DJ was probably the most alive I'd felt in a long time.

I expected DJ to hate me. I expected him to call me selfish, to storm off, to even take a swing at me, despite his claim that he was a pacifist. I wouldn't have blamed him. It would have hurt, but he would've been justified. What he did was so much worse, though. He nodded slowly, looked at me, smiled, and said, "It's cool; I get it."

"DJ, I—"

"Just so you know, I don't regret saving you, and I'd do it again." DJ left to finish searching the ship, and it was a long time before I followed.

FOUR

I WAS THINKING THAT DJ AND I HAD MADE A MISTAKE preventing *Qriosity* from exploding, and then we found the galley. I loved it so much that I considered dragging in a mattress from the crew quarters and sleeping there. There were two massive ovens, an induction stovetop, and wide, expansive counters where I could spread out while I baked and never worry about not having enough space. And it was outfitted with every piece of equipment I could possibly need, including some whose function was a mystery but that I desperately wanted to play with.

On the other side of a half wall was a dining area that was dominated by an oval table surrounded by six chairs. Unlike in other rooms, the scruffy, ramshackle quality of the mismatched chairs and the table's chipped paint gave the galley a warm, homey, comfortable vibe. Whoever had crewed *Qriosity* before us had congregated here. I could practically smell the meals that had been cooked and hear the laughter that had soaked into the walls.

For a moment, I nearly forgot that I was stranded on a ship far from home. But only for a moment.

Jenny found me and DJ in the galley not long after we'd arrived, and we decided it was as good a place as any to sit down and share what we'd discovered.

"There's a recreation room with couches and some type of game system called Mind's Eye," Jenny was saying. I was only partly listening because I was busy watching DJ tear the wrapper off a meal replacement bar he'd found.

"You're not going to eat that, are you?" I asked, interrupting Jenny.

DJ froze like he'd been caught with his hand in a stranger's pocket. He tilted the bar he was holding so that I could see the word "Nutreesh" written on the metallic wrapper in an eager serif font. The bar itself looked like a hamster turd. "Yes?"

"You have no idea what it's made from," I said.

DJ sniffed it and shrugged. "Put some in you."

"I'd rather put cyanide in me." I watched DJ bite off the end, and figured it was a good sign when he didn't immediately drop dead.

"Well?" Jenny asked. "Is it any good? I'm hungry."

"Depends." DJ finished chewing, swallowed, and chased it with a gulp of water. "Have you ever eaten paper?"

"No," Jenny said.

"Want to?" DJ held up a second bar and waved it in the air.

"Hell no," I said at the same time as Jenny said, "Why not?"

The horror I felt must have been plain on my face as DJ slid the Nutreesh bar across to Jenny because he said, "What? We've got to eat something, and this is technically food."

"I don't want to eat food that looks like it might have once been roaches."

Jenny, who'd barely gotten the wrapper off before taking her first bite, licked the crumbs from her lips. "Definitely not roaches."

I suppressed a shudder. "I seriously don't want to know how you know that."

"It's got a nutty flavor," she said, ignoring me. "With a hint of ginger." Jenny touched the tip of her tongue to the uneaten portion of the bar. "Cinnamon, too. And something else I can't quite place."

"Roaches," I said again. "Either way, I'm not eating it."

DJ finished his Nutreesh and folded the crinkly wrapper into a tight square before slipping it into his pocket. "You might have to."

"I'll barbecue and eat one of you before I eat whatever that crap is." I had been trying to avoid thinking about how long we were going to be stuck on *Qriosity*. While it might have been possible there was someone hiding on the ship who could help us, there was as much chance of that as there was of Nutreesh *not* being roaches.

"You should eat me first," Jenny said with her mouth full. "DJ looks like he'd be tough, and you barely have any meat on you at all."

"If you're volunteering—"

DJ looked horrified. "Maybe we could talk about something other than who we're gonna eat first."

"I was joking." I threw a mournful glance at the galley. "None of the equipment works anyway. Apparently, it's all *non-essential*."

"Anyone want to talk about why we're here?" Jenny asked. "Who kidnapped us? What do they want with us?" She shoved the last bite of Nutreesh into her mouth. "I bet we've been kidnapped by aliens to be part of their intergalactic zoo."

"It's not aliens," I said.

"It might be," Jenny said. "They might want to study us or cut us open and see what our insides look like."

I threw up my hands. "Why does it always have to be extermination or gruesome experiments when it comes to aliens? Why can't the aliens ever want to hang out and smoke a bowl?"

DJ said, "I'm with Noa," and offered me a supportive smile. "Besides, why would aliens abduct us and give us a ship?"

Jenny twisted her hair around her finger. "Maybe the aliens saw that Earth was going to be hit by an asteroid capable of obliterating humanity, so they kidnapped us to give us a chance to find a habitable planet to settle on where we could repopulate the species."

"No offense, Jenny," I said, "but I'm not having babies with you."

"I wasn't offering." Jenny motioned at DJ. "But the flirty eyes DJ's been giving you since I got out of the toilet tells me *he* might be willing to give it a shot."

DJ's face was strawberry red to the tips of his ears, and he kept stumbling over his words, trying to get them out. "Could we please stop talking about anyone getting anyone else pregnant?"

"We're talking about saving the human race," Jenny said. "And your babies would be so pretty."

"They really would be, as long as they don't get my ears." I shrugged at DJ. "I'm willing to give it a go if you are. You know, for humanity or whatever."

I kept my face straight for as long as I could before I lost it laughing, and Jenny joined in, making a noise that sounded like what I imagined a baby elephant being tickled might make. DJ was the only one not laughing, and I wouldn't have believed it was possible for anyone's face to get that red if I hadn't seen it myself. He looked like he was going to have a stroke.

"Ha ha," DJ said, cutting through our giggles. "But now that we've saved *Qriosity* from blowing up and searched it from top to bottom, what's our next step?"

I raised my hand. "I vote we figure out how the ship works, turn it back on, and go home."

"You heard Jenny Perez," DJ said. "We can't."

"Have you tried?" I fixed him with an unblinking stare, all the laughter and mirth from before now gone.

DJ wore a wounded expression, like it pained him just to look at me. "There's still so much we don't know, Noa. Like, how long have we even *been* on *Qriosity*?"

"The hologram that stole my name said our memory loss

shouldn't go back more than a week, so we can't have been here longer than that." Jenny looked back and forth from me to DJ. "Right?"

DJ pursed his lips. "It takes at least three days to reach the moon, between five and ten months to get to Mars. I'm willing to bet we're not in our own solar system anymore, so . . ."

He let the thought trail off, but he didn't need to finish it. If he was right, we might have been gone months, possibly years. I imagined those first few days when I didn't come home. My mom would've gone off the rails with worry. Posting flyers up and down 45th, checking in with Becca and Enzo and anyone she thought I might have talked to, to see if they'd heard from me. I pictured her having to go back to work after a month even though she didn't want to. Coming home at the end of her shift, rushing right to my room to see if I was there, her hope crushed each time she saw my empty bed, still unmade the way I'd left it. Her heart breaking into smaller pieces every night when she sat down to eat dinner alone.

Even if we could have turned *Qriosity* around and returned to Earth that second, everyone we knew might've already been gone.

DJ rested his hand on mine. His skin was warm and soft. "Hey," he said. "We'll get home."

"It's not even about going home." My voice was low, almost a whisper. "I mean, it is, but it's also that we don't belong here, DJ. I'm not just going to accept that this is my life now and make the best of it. I can't."

Even as I said it, something about DJ tugged at me, and I

wanted to give in to the moment we were in rather than holding on to the past. I wanted to stop fighting and embrace my new normal. It would have made my life so much easier.

I pulled my hand out from under DJ's and dropped it into my lap, watching as he folded in on himself, as he grew smaller right before my eyes. I kept hurting him. He'd put himself out there, tried to be nice to me, and I'd fashioned his good intentions into weapons and wounded him with them.

"We never should have shut down the reactor," I said.

"What's stopping us from turning the reactor on again?" Jenny asked.

I didn't have an answer, but it was a good question. I looked to DJ to get his opinion and, instead, saw a swarm of organized twinkles flowing from the vents and assembling on one side of the table into the hologram of Jenny Perez.

"Not again," I said. Apparently, the ship had heard Jenny's question and decided to respond. It was creepy to think that *Qriosity* was listening to every word we said. An invasion of privacy, no matter how helpful it tried to be.

"Hi! I'm your host, Jenny Perez, whom you probably remember as the precocious kid detective and bestselling author Anastasia Darling on the award-winning mystery entertainment program *Murder Your Darlings*. If you're seeing this holographic message, then that means you've asked about restarting the Cordova Exotic Particle Reactor."

"Does she have to say that every time?" I muttered. "We know who she is."

"The answer is yes!" the hologram said. "I'm contractually obligated to repeat the standard greeting each time I'm initiated. Sorry about it!"

Jenny unwrapped another Nutreesh bar. "Well, that's silly."

I agreed, but I didn't want to get sidetracked. "How do we restart the Cordova reactor thing?"

"I would advise *not* shutting down the Cordova Exotic Particle Reactor," Jenny Perez said in a painfully cheery tone.

"Too late," I said at the same time as DJ said, "We didn't have a choice."

"That's a shame," Jenny Perez said. "It really would have been better if you hadn't shut it down."

I threw my hands in the air. "Okay, but we did, so can you tell us how to turn it back on or what?"

Jenny was busy putting more Nutreesh in her, but I caught DJ looking at me, and when I did, he said, "Try not to get so worked up. You were dead only a couple of hours ago."

I understood that DJ was trying to help, but if there was ever a time to get upset, it was now. It bothered me that DJ and Jenny were still so calm. I wanted to throw things while they were chatting with a hologram and eating their roach bars.

"I don't need you to look after me. I can take care of myself."

Jenny was motioning at us with her half-eaten Nutreesh. "I'm sensing some serious sexual tension here."

Gritting my teeth to keep from saying something I might regret later, I gave the hologram my full attention. "Just tell us how to restart the damn reactor, okay?"

Jenny Perez flickered momentarily. "So you want to restart the Cordova Exotic Particle Reactor." She paused and smiled like she was trying to get us to sign her petition to save the snails or to join her cult that she promised totally wasn't a cult. "Reinitializing the Cordova Exotic Particle Reactor after an unplanned shutdown requires rebooting *Qriosity*'s main computer, a Nexus Systems Quantum Cluster Advanced Logic Engine—whew! That's a mouthful!—a bleeding-edge system designed specifically for use aboard *Qriosity*. Capable of performing the one hundred sextillion simultaneous calculations required by the Trinity Labs Quantum Fold Drive for instantaneous travel through space, the Nexus Systems Quantum Cluster Advanced Logic Engine should only be rebooted by a qualified Nexus Systems technician."

I clenched my fists and stood. "Do holograms feel pain?" I was seriously considering trying to strangle it. I felt like it was taunting us when all I wanted was a simple answer. The more Jenny Perez droned on, the angrier I became.

DJ gently tugged on my sleeve, pulling me back to my seat. "We don't have a Nexus technician," he said to the hologram. "We're still in high school."

"That sounds even stranger when you say it out loud," Jenny said, mostly to herself. She wasn't wrong, though. I should have been in class, sleeping through Mr. Wilkes's lecture on the French Revolution, not sitting on a ship, listening to a lecture about reactors and computers from a hologram. It was surreal in a way that I hadn't had time to process yet. I felt like I was on a roller coaster that had taken off before I'd gotten strapped in, and it was whipping around corkscrews and flipping upside down, and I was barely managing to hold on. If I loosened my grip for even a second, I would plummet to my death.

But Jenny Perez didn't seem to care how old we were. "In the event that your Nexus Systems technician is missing, incapacitated, or dead, and a reboot of the Nexus Systems Quantum Cluster Advanced Logic Engine is absolutely necessary, please be advised that there is a one-in-five-million-three-hundred-fifty-thousand chance that the quantum states within the computer will collapse, irrevocably damaging the system and leading to the total loss of *Qriosity* and everyone on board."

"That would be bad," I said.

"Very bad," DJ agreed.

"There's a fractionally higher possibility," Jenny Perez continued, "that rebooting the Nexus Systems Quantum Cluster Advanced Logic Engine will result in the system reverting to its default operating parameters. However, the likeliest scenario is that the Nexus Systems Quantum Cluster Advanced Logic Engine will reboot without issue, allowing you to reinitialize your Cordova Exotic Particle Reactor."

Finally. I waved my hand dismissively at the hologram. "Good. Go away." Only, Jenny Perez didn't disperse. She remained standing at the table with her hands on her hips like she was waiting for one of us to ask her for an autograph.

"Did either of you understand anything she said?" Jenny asked. "I consider myself an extremely intelligent person, and that was like, 'What are you even saying?'"

"It means we can restart the reactor." I looked at DJ, who was drawing on the table with his finger. "Right, DJ?"

DJ coughed nervously. "Well, I mean, she also said rebooting the computer could break it *and* the ship."

"But the odds were like one-in-five-million-something. That's a really low percent, right?" I held out my hand, palm up. "Who's got a calculator?"

"Point-zero-zero-zero-zero-one-eight-six-nine percent," DJ said.

My eyes grew wide. "Did you do that in your head?"

DJ shrugged. "Told you I was good at math."

I was impressed, seeing as I could barely do simple multiplication without help. "The point is that the chance is small."

"But it's not zero," DJ said, surprising me.

"Wait, you're saying we *shouldn't* reboot the computer?" I thought I had to have misunderstood him because there was no way that could be what he'd meant.

"I know you want hot water and food that isn't bar-shaped," DJ said. "But if there's a chance rebooting *Qriosity*'s computer could kill us, I don't think we should risk it."

"You're actually serious," I said. I turned to Jenny. "What about you?"

Jenny said, "I'm way too invested in finding out who did this to us—so that I can slowly torture and then brutally murder them—to die for a hot shower."

"Who cares about the shower?!" I yelled. "I'm talking about going home! We reboot the computer, get the reactor online, and then figure out a way to return to Earth!" I felt like they were pranking me. Like this was an elaborate hoax they were playing. This decision should have been easy, and I didn't understand why they were making it so difficult.

DJ folded his hands on the table, his voice calm and diplomatic like he was debating with a toddler. "Right now, we're safe. We've got air and water and food—"

"Nutreesh isn't food!"

"And we shouldn't risk doing anything to jeopardize that."

Jenny chimed in, making me feel like they were ganging up on me. "We literally woke up on this ship a few hours ago, and before that I didn't even know ships like this existed. I want to go home as badly as you do, but I don't want to die in the process because I was messing with stuff I didn't understand."

It wasn't even about going home. Mom was back home, and Mrs. Blum and Becca. But Billy was there too, and I didn't care if I ever saw *him* again. It was that I refused to sit on *Qriosity*, where I'd been brought against my will, and accept my fate. I had to do something, and I was baffled by how easily Jenny and DJ were willing to give up.

"You think if we do nothing that we'll be safe?" I asked. "Bad things happen all the time. We could do everything we've been told to do, sit around and wait for rescue, and we still might die because of some danger we never anticipated."

"Exactly," DJ said. "So why risk making the situation worse by messing with stuff we don't understand?"

"Jenny?" I said, pleading with her. "Come on. Nothing bad is going to happen. Your odds of being killed by a shark are one in four million. Being killed by a tornado, one in five million."

"What about a shark *in* a tornado?" Jenny asked.

"I don't know, but it's still probably more likely than the odds that rebooting the computer will fry it."

For a second, I thought I was getting through to her. I could see the wheels turning behind her hazel eyes, and I thought she was finally willing to listen to reason. But then she said, "The only thing I know about computers is that they can catch fire if too much cat hair gets trapped inside them, so . . ." She shrugged. "Sorry, Noa."

"I should've left you locked in the restroom."

"Don't be like this," DJ said.

I rounded on him. "And you should've left me to die in space. At least it would've been quicker and less painful than being here with the both of you." I stormed out of the galley, ignoring their calls to return.

FIVE

I STOOD AMONG THE TREES AND LOOKED UP AT THE clear blue sky. A cool breeze danced across my skin, carrying the scents of a hundred different plants and flowers that I didn't recognize. I closed my eyes and tilted my face toward the sun, letting its warmth embrace me.

Of course, it wasn't real.

The garden was real. I'd passed rosebushes and gardenias and palm trees and flowering plants in a thousand different colors, some of which might not even have originated on Earth, but the sky overhead was an illusion. A dome made to look like the sky.

I'd stumbled upon the oxygen garden after leaving DJ and Jenny. I hadn't known where I was going, only that I needed to go. The ship, which had seemed so massive before, had already begun to feel too small. I had barely been trapped on *Qriosity* for a day—how was I going to survive six months or more?

The thought expanded within me like a toxic cloud, and just when I thought I would explode, I stopped in front of the door tagged "O2 Garden." It was exactly what I needed, right when I needed it. Even if it was a lie.

Once inside, I'd followed a stone path carved through the dense flora, which led me on a circuitous trail to a small pond ringed with benches. As I sat, a bee zipped around in front of my face. I tried to swat it away, but it darted out of my reach and then hovered near my nose. In actuality, it was a tiny machine that looked like a bee. I'd never seen anything like it, but instead of being fascinated by the miraculous tech, it only served to remind me that we were in so deep that we couldn't even see the surface anymore.

"Hey, loser." Jenny exited the bushes at the other side of the pond, and seemed surprised to see me. "I guess you found my secret hideout. I *had* hoped to keep it to myself for longer than an hour, but . . ."

I stood. "Sorry."

Jenny rolled her eyes. "Sit down. Unless you think I'm going to give you cooties."

"I got my cootie shot in third grade." I moved to the end of the bench to make room for her.

"That's a relief." Jenny flopped down beside me unceremoniously, spreading out to take up as much of the bench as she could. She already seemed more at home here than I did. More relaxed. "Just so you know, Noa; I want to go home too."

"Then why did you take *his* side?!" I let out a guttural sound that was half growl, half sigh. "DJ's ready to give up and wait to be rescued, but I'm not interested in waiting around to be saved. I mean, this whole situation is—"

"Ridiculous?"

"Totally absurd," I said.

"Bonkers."

"Bananas."

A look of unrestrained longing spread across Jenny's face. "Do you know how many people I would kill for a banana right now?" She fished a Nutreesh bar from her jacket pocket.

"How many of those have you had?"

"I stress-eat, Noa," she said. "And, frankly, I don't appreciate your judgment."

I held up my hands. "I'm not judging you for eating; I'm judging you for eating *that*. Seriously, how much of that crap are you going to put in you?"

Jenny bit off the end with a vicious tear. "As much as I damn well please. Any other questions?"

Fighting was the last thing I wanted to do. Actually, a fight might have been a nice way to work out the seething knot of frustration that had grown in the back of my head, but I didn't want to fight with Jenny. She scared me.

"I don't suppose DJ changed his mind about rebooting the computer?" I asked, though I already knew the answer.

Jenny shook her head.

"Any chance I can convince you to switch sides?"

"I'm not on DJ's side either." Jenny stretched her legs and kicked off her boots. "I'm on *my* side."

"Okay, but—"

Jenny cut me off. "You've got opinions, I get it. And, like I said, I'm with you on wanting to go home, but DJ seems a lot smarter than you."

"Hey!"

"I'm sure when it comes to baking or dreary poetry, you're a genius, but I have to go with my gut. It's not personal." Jenny finished with a smile that made it difficult to stay angry at her. She was also right. Even about my love for melancholy poets with cold, black hearts, but I wasn't ready to quit.

"Let me see if I understand your position," I said. "You want to go home, but you don't want to die in the process."

"Exactly!" Jenny said.

"And you'd rather wait for rescue because it's the safer of the two options."

Jenny patted my arm. "I knew you were more intelligent than you looked."

I couldn't help laughing. "Okay, but how do you know rescue is coming?"

"Because the chatty hologram told us so."

"And you're just willing to take it on the word of a computer program?" I asked. "How would the hologram know whether the distress signal was broadcast or not?"

Jenny's eyes narrowed. I had planted the seeds of doubt. Now I needed to water them.

"*Qriosity* was minutes from exploding when I woke up, and we still don't know what caused that damage. Isn't it possible that our long-range communications might also be compromised?"

"I guess," Jenny said carefully.

"Rescue might not be coming. But we won't know until months from now when it either arrives or doesn't. By then, it will be too late." I'd done the best I could. I had no clue if anything I'd said was true, but it sounded plausible, and that's what mattered.

"Do you know what the last thing I remember is?" Jenny asked.

"Tell me." This was the longest Jenny and I had spoken. DJ and I'd had time to get to know each other while I was floating in space, waiting to die, but Jenny had been locked in the restroom, and since meeting, we hadn't slowed down long enough to talk.

"I was reading a book. The sequel to a series I'd been waiting to get my hands on for over a year because the first book's cliffhanger was . . ." Jenny clenched her fists. "It was a lot. But now I might never know what happens. Do you know how frustrating that is?"

"Extremely?"

"I would easily sacrifice you or DJ for another copy of that book," she said.

I laughed, hoping she was joking. "Where are you from?"

"Warwick, Rhode Island."

"You don't have an accent."

Jenny shrugged. "My parents move a lot for their jobs. We've only been there a year."

"Do you like it?"

"I've tried not to like or dislike any of the places we've lived. It makes them easier to leave." Jenny spoke about it with an ease that felt practiced though not necessarily sincere. "As long as I have my kitties and my books, anywhere is home."

"Is that why you're not as freaked out about our situation as I am?"

Jenny threw me a frown. "Oh, I'm freaked out. At the same time, I'm used to being dropped into unfamiliar places and situations and having to make it work. Waking up on *Qriosity* wasn't the same as waking up in Warwick, Rhode Island, but they're both basically outer space."

Knowing more about Jenny hadn't exactly helped me understand her cautious approach to the reactor or how I could change her mind, but it did make her slightly less scary. "I'm sorry you're stuck out here with me and DJ."

"Could be worse," she said. "At least you're both pretty."

I laughed in spite of myself. "Wow. Thanks?"

"Have you seen DJ's butt?" She grinned. "Of course you have. How could you not? It's too bad you have no ass to speak of, but your face makes up for it."

"Way to objectify me, Jenny." I winked. "You're not wrong, but I *am* more than just a devastatingly handsome face."

Jenny patted my shoulder. "Sure you are."

I sighed heavily, feeling slightly better about Jenny but still frustrated by my inability to convince her I was right. "What are we going to do?"

Jenny pulled her legs onto the bench and retrieved another Nutreesh from her pocket. She seemed to have a never-ending supply of the things. "Here's what *I'm* going to do. I'm going to sit by this serene little lake, in this weird garden that defies all explanation, and contemplate the impossible nonsense that's happened to me over the last couple of hours. After that, I might take a nap."

"What about me?"

"Don't know," she said. "Find DJ and tell him what you told me. Maybe you can change *his* mind, though you might try being a little nicer. You've been kind of a dick. Either way, I don't have the patience for you right now. I need some Jenny time."

I envied Jenny's ability to ignore the crisis to focus on her own immediate needs, and I wished I could fix my own problems with a meal-replacement bar and a nap. Sadly, there was only one solution to my dilemma, and I was going to have to go through DJ to reach it.

SIX

I SEARCHED *QRIOSITY* FOR NEARLY AN HOUR BEFORE I finally found DJ standing at a console in Reactor Control with his back to the door. He didn't notice me when I walked in.

"So this is the reactor?" I said. "I was expecting something with a little more flash." The center of the room was dominated by a massive dark cylinder that had dozens of pipes and tubes running into and out of it. It had an industrial quality to it. Like equipment that belonged on an oil rig instead of on a spaceship.

Startled, DJ turned around so quickly that he lost his balance. "Noa? Where'd you come from?"

"Seattle," I said. "Didn't we go over this already?"

"I meant—"

I rolled my eyes before I thought better of it. "I know what you meant. I came looking for you so we could talk."

DJ hung his head like he expected me to yell at him. "I don't want to fight, Noa."

"Neither do I." There was nowhere to sit in the reactor room, so I flopped down on the floor and leaned against the wall. DJ shrugged and joined me. "Can we just discuss our options?"

"Of course."

I held up a finger. "Okay, if we do nothing, you think that someone will rescue us in a few months."

"Right," DJ said.

"Why?" I asked. "Because a hologram told you? We don't actually know if an emergency signal was sent."

To his credit, DJ listened to my questions and seemed to consider them before replying. It probably helped that I wasn't shouting at him. "Okay."

"Jenny Perez said our batteries will last about a year. If the signal didn't go out, it might be too late by the time we realize help isn't coming." While I'd been searching the ship for DJ, I'd spent my time working out what I'd say to him.

"That's true too," DJ said.

"Additionally, who's coming for us? NASA? NASA doesn't have ships like this. The truth is that we don't know if rescue is ever going to arrive and, if it does, we don't know who they'll be or whether we'll want their help."

DJ nodded slowly. I didn't know if he was coming around, but he hadn't dismissed my argument either. I didn't want to admit it out loud, but DJ probably was smarter than me when it came to science stuff. "What about our other option?"

"Reboot the computer," I said. "Crank the ship back to life and use it to get ourselves home."

"Then you know how to fly a spaceship?"

His question caught me off guard. "Well . . . no, but—"

"Because *I've* got no clue how to fly one, and I'm betting Jenny doesn't either." DJ gained no obvious satisfaction at pointing out a detail I hadn't considered, which made him a better person than me.

"Fair point," I said. "Maybe we can learn, though. And the worst-case scenario is that we have real food and hot water while we're waiting for rescue to arrive."

DJ shook his head. "The worst-case scenario's that we die, Noa. That's what I keep trying to get you to understand."

"Then we die!" I said. "But we can't just do nothing!" I was losing my hold on my temper. I stood and paced the room. "We were kidnapped, DJ. You get that, right? Someone or some*thing* stole us from our lives and is holding us against our will."

"I *do* understand—"

"Do you?" I asked. "This isn't a spaceship; it's a prison. I don't know why we're here or what they want from us, but I can't do nothing!" I was having difficulty breathing. I pressed my hand to my chest. "I can't just be a victim!" My knees gave out. The bones in my legs vanished. I hit the deck. Pain radiated up through my thighs.

And then DJ was there. He wrapped his arms around me and whispered, "It's going to be okay," over and over until my heart slowed and my jelly legs felt strong enough to support me again.

"Sorry," I said, feeling foolish. At the same time, I felt safe in a way I hadn't since waking up in this nightmare. I wanted to lean into him, dissolve into DJ's chest. But his closeness threatened to suffocate me, and the warmth of his body grew stifling.

"Okay," DJ said.

I disentangled myself from him, trying not to seem ungrateful for his help. "Seriously. I didn't mean to lose it like that."

"Okay," he said again. "Let's do it."

I backed away. "Do what?"

DJ took a deep breath. "Reboot the computer." He motioned at the console he'd been working at when I arrived. "I was considering doing it anyway. Thinking it was wrong to stand in your way of going home." He shrugged. "Anyway, all we have to do is hit that button, and it'll restart everything."

I punched DJ in the arm, and I wasn't sure which of us it hurt more. "Why didn't you tell me straightaway instead of letting me ramble like that?"

"Figured it couldn't hurt to talk it out one last time." DJ moved toward the console. "So are we gonna do this or what?"

A large button labeled "Reboot?" on the touchscreen blinked from a neon yellow to a dull mustard. I reached for it and hesitated. I wasn't having second thoughts, but now that we were going to do it, I felt the weight of the decision.

DJ stood beside me, waiting. I gave him a terse nod, and we pressed the button together.

The screen went blank.

I counted the seconds, hoping for the best. I hit twenty and was going to ask DJ if we'd made a mistake, fearing that our worst-case scenario had come to pass, when a steady vibration ran through the floor. Consoles around the room flickered to life. A light from within the cylinder in the center of the room began to glow and swirl. It looked like it was filled with bioluminescent jellyfish swimming madly, faster and faster until they were nothing but a polychromatic blur.

Eventually, the shaking settled into a low, steady thrum that I could hardly feel.

DJ smiled at me, flashing those dimples. "Looks like we did it."

"Are you sure?" I asked. The screen on our console showed graphs and readouts far more complicated than what had been inside my hud. I couldn't make sense of any of it, but it *did* seem like we had restarted the reactor.

"We didn't blow up."

"Yet," I said, smiling cautiously. "Thanks for not being the kind of person who was too stubborn to change his mind and admit he was wrong."

"I mean, I wasn't wrong to be cautious."

I patted his shoulder. "Everyone makes mistakes, DJ. It's not your fault you're not as smart as me. Few people are."

DJ laughed, and I thought everything was going to be okay. Even if we couldn't figure out how to fly the ship right away, we'd work it out eventually. Together.

"Warning!" shouted the ship over the speakers. "Trinity Labs Quantum Fold Drive will initialize spatial tear in five minutes. Warning!"

And then *that* happened.

The blood drained from DJ's face.

"That sounds bad," I said. "What does it mean? DJ?"

"I think we need to go to Ops." I barely had time to register his reply before he sprinted out of the room.

I chased DJ through the ship to Ops and was out of breath by the time I caught up. He was standing at one of the stations, staring at the viewport, at a pulsating fissure in space where there had been nothing but stars before. The rip crackled with energy, and it made me feel dizzy.

Jenny was already there, standing in front of the viewport. "What is happening?" she yelled over the sound of the alarm.

Photons surged into Ops, forming into the shape of my least favorite hologram.

"Hi! I'm your host, Jenny Perez, whom you probably remember as the precocious kid detective and bestselling author Anastasia Darling on the award-winning mystery entertainment program *Murder Your Darlings*. If you're seeing this holographic message, then you've initiated your Trinity Labs Quantum Fold Drive."

"We did?" Jenny asked.

"No we didn't!" shouted DJ.

"Sure you did," Jenny Perez said in a tone that managed to be simultaneously cutesy and condescending. "These things don't initialize on their own."

"How do we stop it?" I asked. My heart was ramping up again. I had to lean against the back of the nearest chair for support.

"Warning! Trinity Labs Quantum Fold Drive will initialize spatial tear in three minutes. Warning!"

Jenny Perez flickered. "It seems that you've recently rebooted your Nexus Systems Quantum Cluster Advanced Logic Engine, which should only be done by a certified Nexus Systems technician."

I stared bullets at her. "Have you ever investigated your own murder?"

"Actually, yes!" Jenny Perez replied. "In episode seven of season four, Anastasia Darling—"

"What's restarting the computer got to do with the fold drive?" DJ said, cutting her off. Whatever calm he'd had earlier had fled.

"Rebooting the Nexus Systems Quantum Cluster Advanced Logic Engine has initiated the Phone Home protocol."

"We're going home?" Jenny asked.

A small flicker of hope ignited within me. Jenny Perez quickly snuffed it out.

"Under normal circumstances, *Qriosity* would return to Earth upon the initiation of the Phone Home protocol. However, the navigational system is unable to determine *Qriosity*'s current coordinates, which are required for plotting a course."

"So the drive *did* initialize on its own," DJ said. "I knew we didn't do it."

"Who cares about that right now?" I said. "Are we going home or not?" I didn't understand what Jenny Perez had said, though it sounded like she'd implied we were lost.

"Without origin coordinates," the hologram replied, "*Qriosity* will select a destination at random in an attempt to reach Earth, though the chances of doing so are infinitesimally small."

"That seems silly," Jenny said at the same time as I shouted, "Make it stop!"

"I'm trying," DJ said, though I hadn't been talking to him. "Nothing works. I'm locked out of the computer."

Jenny Perez continued talking as if I cared what she had to say. "The Trinity Labs Quantum Fold Drive creates a tunnel through space-time, connecting two points, allowing for near-instantaneous travel between destinations millions or even billions of light-years apart. Isn't that neat?"

"No!" I said. "Shut it down!"

"Sorry, Charlie," Jenny Perez said. "Once initiated, the Phone Home protocol cannot be terminated. The Trinity Labs Quantum Fold Drive will engage every nineteen hours until *Qriosity* successfully reaches Earth. Sorry about it!"

"Warning! Trinity Labs Quantum Fold Drive will initialize spatial tear in thirty seconds. Warning!"

"DJ?"

DJ shook his head. Tears rimmed his eyes.

"What is going on?" Jenny asked. "I don't understand what's happening."

If rescue had been coming, they'd find no trace of us when they arrived. Once we passed through that rent in space, we would be lost forever.

I fell into the chair, my arms limp, my heart broken, and my soul exhausted.

The tear pulsed and grew brighter. *Qriosity* spasmed.

"Warning! Trinity Labs Quantum Fold Drive initializing spatial tear. Warning!"

A final convulsion shook *Qriosity* as blinding light filled the viewport. I covered my eyes and when I looked again, we were somewhere else. I couldn't tell the difference between where we were and where we'd been—the stars looked the same as before—but it didn't matter. We were never going home.

A countdown clock appeared on the screen at my station. **18:59:59**.

Tears ran freely down DJ's splotchy cheeks. "Noa, I'm sorry. I can fix this. I can—"

"Forget it," I said. "It doesn't matter anymore."

WHERE NOA HAS GONE BEFORE

ONE

QRIOSITY'S MEDIA LIBRARY CONTAINED 330 EPISODES of *Murder Your Darlings*—including a mercifully short season that skipped ahead a few years to follow Anastasia Darling as an adult—and I was determined to watch every single one.

In the week since we had rebooted *Qriosity*'s computer, which had resulted in the ship, and us along with it, being sent skipping randomly through the universe, I had done absolutely nothing but sit on the overstuffed couch in the rec room and watch the worst program ever created. *Murder Your Darlings* had run for thirteen seasons, but it should have been suffocated after thirteen episodes. Anastasia Darling was obnoxious, her parents were oblivious and had no business raising a child, I easily guessed who the murderer was within the first five minutes of each episode—it was nearly always the guest star—and the only person worth rooting for was Dominique Lavoie, Anastasia

Darling's nemesis-slash-cousin. And yet, undeterred by the show's terrible acting and predictable plots, I spent my every waking hour on the couch watching it.

I didn't shower or brush my teeth. I ate Nutreesh bars, which tasted like an old book that had been left to soak in a mud puddle, I drank coffee, and I only got up when I needed to pee. I attempted to sleep in my quarters during the day, but the persistent noise of DJ and Jenny pleading with me to come out made that difficult. When I *did* sleep, I dreamed of falling. There were no stars, no *Qriosity*. I just screamed and fell. Fell and screamed. Forever. And every nineteen hours when *Qriosity* vibrated as it prepared to fold space, I sat alone and cried. Each new location we jumped to was as devoid of light and life as the last. No sun, no planets. No hope.

Between watching *Murder Your Darlings,* not sleeping, and avoiding DJ and Jenny, my schedule was full. DJ had been especially persistent in his attempts to cheer me up. At one point, he sat outside my door for four hours, talking at me. I almost broke during that time; I almost got out of bed and let him in. Five more minutes and I would have. I told myself I was proud for outlasting him, but there was definitely a part of me that wished he'd stayed.

The rec room on *Qriosity* could have been a living room in any one of a million homes on Earth. There were a couple of reclining chairs to use while wearing the Mind's Eye virtual reality devices, which I hadn't tried yet, a sagging couch with lumpy cushions, and a projector for watching the ship's catalog of movies and programs, and the room smelled like old sweat and feet. That last part was mostly my fault.

DJ flopped down on the couch beside me and let out a dramatic sigh.

I fought the urge to look at him. I kept my eyes straight ahead, my attention on Anastasia Darling. Not that watching the show required much brainpower. Some programs were better if you gave them your full focus. You picked up on nuances and details that casual watchers might miss. *Murder Your Darlings* was not one of them. I'm pretty sure paying attention made the show worse.

"Noa—"

"Shush. I'm busy."

I expected DJ to leave, but he remained sitting beside me, quietly watching Anastasia solve the murder of her favorite librarian's prized cockatoo. Spoiler alert: the murderer was a library patron angry about a late-return fee.

"How can you watch this?" DJ asked at the end of the episode.

"It's the only program in *Qriosity*'s library." I refused to look at him. I was not going to be distracted by his bright blue eyes or his impossible dimples. "There are also a bunch of movies starring or co-starring Jenny Perez, but I haven't dipped my toes into that pool yet. There are a couple that don't look terrible. They don't look great, either, but we have to make do with what we've got, right?"

The next episode began, and DJ sat with me while Anastasia, who was on a plane, traveling to Europe with her parents, discovered the pilot dead.

DJ shifted on the couch, probably trying to find a comfortable position, and it groaned each time he moved. "Come on, Noa. Shut this off and talk to me."

"No."

"You can't ignore me forever."

"I don't see why not," I said. "Now hush. The copilot's about to be murdered and I don't want to miss it."

"The copilot?" DJ said. "But then who lands the plane?"

"I'll give you three guesses, but you won't need them."

DJ peeled his attention from the show and turned to me. "You smell, Noa. Bad."

I stuck my nose in my armpit and breathed in. "I'm fragrant." I turned up the volume to drown out whatever insults DJ might fling at me next.

DJ got up, and I thought he was finally going to leave, but he blocked the screen instead. "I know this sucks, Noa, but you're not the only person it's happening to."

I avoided his gaze like he was Medusa. I'd be fine if I didn't look directly into his eyes. Because the truth was that I wanted to look at him. I wanted to lean into him for support. For friendship and warmth. I wanted to pull him down onto the couch with me and laugh with him about how bad *Murder Your Darlings* was. I wanted to leave with him and explore the galley. Sing silly songs while baking a cake. DJ had some kind of pull on me, and I didn't quite understand it. I wasn't sure I wanted to understand. I just wanted to embrace it. Embrace him. But I didn't.

"Do you want me to beg you to leave this room and stop watching this show? I will if that's what it takes."

"I want you to leave me alone," I said.

DJ stared at, into, and through me, but I did not relent. I kept my eyes fixed firmly past him as if he wasn't blocking my view. As if he wasn't there at all. After a few seconds, DJ marched out of the room.

I'd won another round in our pointless war, but I didn't celebrate. I didn't feel good about it. I wasn't angry at DJ or Jenny. I was angry at everything. At the whole damn universe. I didn't understand why DJ and Jenny weren't sitting on the couch beside me. We were on a ship we didn't know how to control, lost in space with no hope of finding home. We were never again going to see the people we loved, never going to get the chance to say goodbye. DJ was acting like I'd given up, but you can't forfeit a game that you've already lost.

Anastasia Darling was searching the plane for clues while the flight attendants attempted to keep the passengers calm, when the projector died.

"What the hell?!" I felt around for the remote and tried turning the screen back on, but nothing worked. A moment later, DJ charged back into the room, took one look at the screen, and nodded.

"Did you do this?"

"You're going to talk to me, Noa." DJ stood at the edge of the couch with his arms folded across his broad chest.

DJ finally had my attention, and I was going to make him

regret it. "Who do you think you are? You're not my mom. You're not the captain of this busted ship. I don't know you, and I don't owe you anything." I often slouched a little to avoid drawing attention to my height, but this time I stood tall.

DJ was not cowed. He squared his shoulders and took the full brunt of my anger. "I'll turn the screen back on when you agree to talk to me."

I didn't care how cute his dimples were; I hated him right then. I wanted to punch him in the nose and then kick him while he was down, over and over until he hurt as badly as I did.

"Stay if you want," I said. "I'm leaving." I headed for the door, but DJ blocked my path. I might have been taller, but he was a cement wall. "Move."

"No."

"Move!"

DJ walked me backward, and I fell onto the couch. "Not until you talk to me," he said.

I was a ball of compressed rage, a coiled spring of anger. I bounced back and pushed DJ as hard as I could, screamed at him to get the hell out of my way. Spit flew from my mouth, and tears wetted my red-rimmed eyes. And in the face of my fury, DJ hardly moved a centimeter.

"Why won't you just leave me alone?" I sank onto the couch and buried my face in my hands.

The couch squeaked when DJ sat beside me. "Because you promised me cake."

"Bake your own damn cake."

"I tried," DJ said. "It didn't go real well. And Jenny's more useless in the kitchen than I am. But at least we found out the fire suppression systems work."

A high-pitched, angry laugh leaked out of me. "So that's what this is? You don't care about me, you're just hungry?"

"Can't it be both?" DJ rested a hand on my shoulder, but I shook him off. "Do you think Jenny and I like being on this ship any more than you do?"

"I don't care about you or Jenny. I care about me."

"You've made that obvious," DJ said.

"Clearly I haven't because you keep coming around."

DJ's face hardened for a moment like he was going to yell, but he didn't. He sighed and said, "I know this situation's bad, but we're never going to get out of it if we don't work together."

"We're never going to get out of it, period," I said. None of this was DJ's fault. I was the one who'd pushed him to reboot the computer. But if I'd kept my mouth shut and trusted his instincts, we'd just be in a different awful situation. We'd been screwed before we rebooted the computer, and we were screwed after. The only difference was the manner in which we were screwed.

"Noa—"

"What do you want from me, DJ?"

"I want you to quit moping," DJ said. "I want you to get off this couch and stop watching this silly program. I want you to take a shower. Please. You really do smell like day-old horse manure."

"And then what? Bake cakes and play starship with you and

Jenny?" My hands were trembling. I couldn't stop them. "We're trapped, DJ! We're going to die on this ship! I wish you had let me die in space so that I didn't have to face the prospect of a long, slow death here."

Tears tracked down DJ's cheeks. "Please don't say that. I regret a lot of stuff, but rescuing you isn't one."

DJ's tears made me pause. I was that person. I'd made him cry. And why? Because I was pissed I was stuck on this ship and was determined to make everyone as miserable as I was? I felt like a prick, but instead of apologizing like a normal human being, I lashed out. I wanted him to fight me. I wanted DJ to feel as angry as I felt. "Give me time and I'll change your mind."

DJ ignored my comment, refusing to take the bait. "If you and Jenny and I work together, we can learn how to fly *Qriosity*. We can stop the ship from jumping around. We can go home." He wiped his eyes with the back of his hand. "But only if we *all* work together."

I squeezed my eyes shut. "Please leave me alone."

I could tell DJ was still sitting beside me, but he was quiet for a few moments. I wondered what was going through his mind. Finally, he said, "You're not the only one missing folks, Noa. Jenny's got family she cares about. And I . . . I had someone too. Someone I cared about. I wish he was here instead of you, but he's not."

Of all the things DJ had said, that one hurt. But it's not like I didn't deserve it. If our positions had been reversed, I wouldn't have wanted me around either.

The couch groaned as DJ stood. "When you were drifting in space, thinking you were gonna die, you made me promise not to leave you alone, and I didn't." DJ's voice was soft. His anger gone. "And now I'm asking the same of you. Please don't leave me alone, Noa. This ship needs you. *I* need you."

The door opened and then closed again. The projector powered back on, and the episode I'd been watching resumed right where it had cut off.

TWO

IT TOOK AN HOUR STANDING IN THE SHOWER, LETTING the near-scalding water run over my head, to wash away the stink of despair that followed me around like a toxic cloud.

Nothing had changed. We had still been abducted and dumped on a spaceship we didn't know how to operate, we were still lost, and I was still salty about it. DJ would probably believe it was his little talk that convinced me to clean up, but it was actually a scene from *Murder Your Darlings*. Anastasia had been upset because the exchange student she'd had a crush on had been murdered, and she didn't want to go to the Valentine's Day dance alone. The advice Mrs. Darling had given Anastasia reminded me of something my mom had said to me after Grant Choi broke up with me in seventh grade.

"What do life and a large sausage and mushroom pizza have in common?" she'd asked.

"They're both a little oily?"

"You can't finish either if you quit when things get rough."

"Is this your way of telling me you ordered pizza for dinner?"

My mom grinned in the way she did when I was being a smart-ass. "Yes, but also that life goes on. Don't let it go on without you, Noa."

My mom might have been thousands of light-years away, but she was still with me. She would always be with me, and I took comfort in that.

I scrubbed and washed and rinsed. I brushed and flossed a week's worth of Nutreesh gunk from between my teeth, shaved my patchy stubble, and tamed my wavy hair. Feeling somewhat more human, I raided the crew storage containers—which, thankfully, someone had unlocked—for clean underwear, a pair of jeans that mostly fit, and a hoodie. I planned to incinerate Nico's onesie at the first opportunity.

DJ was sitting at the table when I strolled into the galley. He couldn't hide his surprise, but he kept his mouth shut. Jenny stood behind the counter, trying to cook. Her hair was piled on her head in a messy bun, and her face and clothes were smudged with flour.

"Out," I said.

"I was making—"

"A mess." I pointed to the table and didn't budge until she removed her apron, handed it to me, and left. I wasn't sure what Jenny had been making, but I had everything I needed to whip up some pancakes.

DJ and Jenny whispered amongst themselves while I cooked. I didn't know what they were discussing, though I imagined it was me. I was jealous of the bond that they'd seemingly formed while I was hiding in the rec room. I'd wasted a week getting to know Anastasia Darling when I could have been getting to know the people I was probably going to spend the rest of my life with. It was enough to make me consider running back to my quarters and never leaving again. But I didn't. I stayed and finished cooking.

When I was done, I carried a plate stacked with soft, fluffy pancakes to the table and set it down in the center.

"Dig in." I caught DJ's eye and added, "I'll bake your cake later."

"You don't have—"

"You're not the only one who keeps his promises, DJ."

Jenny hardly waited a second before grabbing a couple of pancakes. Then, to my horror, she unwrapped a Nutreesh bar and crumbled it on top before covering the whole mess with syrup. I might've puked in my mouth a little.

"These are delicious, Noa," DJ said.

I shrugged. "They're adequate. I'll be able to do more when I've had a look inside that Freshie thing."

"Everything's fresher in a Freshie," Jenny sang. When she caught me and DJ staring at her, she said, "What? It says that every time you walk inside. Every. Single. Time. It's stuck in my head now and forever."

We didn't talk while we ate. The only noises were the scraping of forks and the happy sounds Jenny made each time she took a bite. There was a kind of normality to the meal that was relaxing until reality reminded me that we were on a spaceship.

"Seeing as we're all together," I said, "I guess we should discuss what happens next."

"Then we're not going to talk about how you spent a week stewing in your own sweat and depression?" Jenny asked.

"Not if you want me to continue cooking," I replied.

"Hey now," she said. "I'm the reason you've got clean clothes to wear."

"You cracked the locks on the crew storage containers?"

Jenny beamed. "It wasn't even that hard."

"Clearly, you two have been busy."

DJ quickly said, "Well, we were trying to learn what we could about *Qriosity*, though we weren't going to do anything without discussing it with you first."

"Definitely not," Jenny added with her mouth full.

I understood that I'd made an ass of myself, and DJ and Jenny were tiptoeing around to make sure they didn't set me off again, but I was embarrassed enough as it was and just wanted to skip past the awkwardness.

"It's fine," I said. "Did you learn anything?"

DJ set his fork down and pushed his plate aside. "Here's where we stand: communications work, but there's no one out there. Someone, somewhere, might get our messages eventually, but since *Qriosity* only sticks around one place for nineteen hours—"

"It's useless to us," I finished.

DJ nodded reluctantly.

"Sorry about it," Jenny muttered.

"We also found a small shuttle that looks like it was designed for short-range travel," DJ said.

I snorted. "Too bad we don't have a pilot on board."

Jenny raised her hand. "Actually . . ."

"You can fly a spaceship?"

"No," she said. "A Cessna 172. My mom was teaching me how to fly. I looked at the shuttle's controls, and I think I might be able to figure them out. Maybe. I won't know until I try."

Learning that Jenny knew how to fly a plane and maybe *Qriosity*'s shuttle definitely came as a shock, though maybe that said more about me than about Jenny. Either way, I wasn't sure how useful flying would be since we didn't have anywhere to fly to.

"The rest of the ship seems to be working," DJ said. "Except for navigation."

DJ and Jenny were passing a look between them that I couldn't translate. But whatever was going on, it was making DJ anxious.

"What does that mean?" I asked. "Is that why we're jumping all over the place?"

DJ nodded. "Think of it like *Qriosity*'s version of GPS. It's trying to map us a way home, but it can't do that until it figures out where we are."

I wanted to call DJ out for explaining it like I was five, but it was actually helpful. "So if we fix it, we can go home?"

"Theoretically," DJ said. I expected him to be a little more excited, but he looked like he was going to vomit.

"What?" I asked. "What aren't you telling me?"

Jenny threw up her hands, looking at DJ in disgust. "It's outside the ship," she said. "You have to go outside to fix it. It's a two-person job, and there's no way you're getting me into one of those spacesuits. It will never, ever happen. Which means that you have to do it. You and DJ. But DJ's been afraid to tell you because of what happened last time. He even tried to go out there by himself, but I stopped him."

DJ scowled at her. "She put laxatives in my morning smoothie. I don't even know where she got them from."

Jenny laughed so hard she spit pancake. "Kept you out of the airlock, didn't it?"

"Because I couldn't leave the bathroom for longer than ten minutes!"

While Jenny and DJ argued like siblings, I sat with my hands folded on the table and tried not to panic. The mere suggestion that I go outside the ship again made my stomach clench. The pancakes I'd eaten might as well have been hot needles. I had nightmares about what I'd been through in space, but I hadn't thought I'd ever need to go out there again. That was silly, of course. The longer we remained on *Qriosity*, the more likely it was that systems were going to malfunction. Systems like the coolant conduit that could only be repaired from the outside. I'd been a fool to think I'd never have to leave the ship.

But how could I? How could I put on a suit and step out of the airlock? I literally died last time. I stopped breathing and my heart stopped beating and my brain starved for oxygen. If DJ hadn't rescued me, my body would still be floating among the stars. So how could they ask me to go out there again? How could I consider doing it?

Because I only had two options. The first was to help DJ fix the navigational array. The second was to return to the rec room, put on another episode of *Murder Your Darlings*, and remain on the couch until I pickled in my own juices.

"I'll do it," I said.

DJ stopped speaking mid-sentence and turned to face me. "You don't have to. We'll find another way."

I had a fist-size lump in my throat as I spoke. "If we fix the navigation thing, will it tell us where we are?"

"It should." I didn't care for the uncertainty in DJ's voice, and he must have realized it because he said, "Nothing's a sure thing, Noa, but it should work."

It wasn't the reassuring optimism that I was looking for, but if DJ had believed strongly enough it would work that he'd been willing to attempt to repair it alone, then it would have to do.

"Good enough," I said. "We should get started." I pushed back my chair and stood.

"What?" DJ asked. "Now?"

"Why not?"

"Zero-G on a stomach full of pancakes?"

"Yeah," Jenny added. "That seems like a bad idea."

DJ and Jenny were probably right, but I didn't want to wait. I couldn't wait. Already, a voice in the back of my mind was whispering that this was a mistake and that I was going to die if I left the ship. The longer I listened, the more likely it was that I would lose my nerve.

"We do this now or not at all."

DJ shrugged with his hands and gave me a weak smile. "Yeah, Noa, okay. It's your call."

The antechamber where the spacesuits were stored was shaped like an octagon with a locker in four alternating faces. But I couldn't stop staring at the inner airlock door. It was shaped like an iris, round like a camera's shutter. I imagined it opening, the air inside the room blasting out at the speed of sound, dragging me and DJ with it.

"Something wrong with the hatch?" DJ asked.

I had to tear my eyes away. "I've never seen it from this side."

"Oh."

I wished I hadn't mentioned it. DJ was treating me the way my mom treated the Christmas china, looking at me like a sneeze could shatter me. I appreciated his concern, but it was making me more anxious instead of less. Finally, he lowered a bench from the wall and pulled off his sneakers.

I opened the nearest locker. Each piece of the suit was secured to the inside, and there was a gray stretch garment hanging on the back of the door.

"What am I supposed to do?" I asked. DJ looked at me,

confused, so I added, "I woke up in the last one, but I don't remember putting it on."

"Oh," DJ said. "Yeah, right." He pointed at the door. "The bodysuit goes on first, then the bottom section, top, boots, gloves, helmet. In that order. I can help you with the chest piece since it's a little complicated."

I frowned skeptically at the stretch suit, which looked like it was sized for a small child. When I turned to ask DJ how I was supposed to fit into it, he was standing in his underwear.

"Wow," I said. "You are *white*. Are you sure you're from Florida?" I hadn't meant to catch DJ undressed, and it flustered me a bit. DJ was built like a Greek statue, with a broad chest, thick muscles, and a little pudge around his belly. He had a scar that ran along the bottom of his ribs on the left side.

DJ tried to climb into his bodysuit so quickly that he stumbled into the wall. "I don't tan," he mumbled. "I burn and peel."

"Sorry," I said. "It slipped out. You have a very nice body. Not that I was looking. I mean, obviously I looked—I do have eyes—but I wasn't ogling you. Not purposely. I'll shut up now."

DJ kept his gaze lowered as he zipped up his suit. "You should get undressed," he said. "Dressed. You should get into your suit."

"Are you trying to get me out of my clothes? You figure I've seen you, so now you should get to see me?" A memory surfaced, and I snorted. "Except, you've already seen me out of my clothes."

"I didn't—"

"Someone undressed me and lifted me onto that table in the med suite."

"You were dead," DJ said. "I wasn't thinking about that stuff." Whatever embarrassment he'd felt before evaporated. "Come on. The faster we do this, the faster it's done."

I nodded, but I couldn't stop thinking about the video. Seeing myself. My body. Dead. DJ trying to pump my heart. "I really hope I come back alive this time."

I hadn't meant to say it out loud, but I had, and DJ had heard it.

"Me too," he said.

THREE

"WHAT DO YOU MEAN WE'RE NOT USING THE TETHER?" I stood on the hull, outside the airlock, with my hands on my hips, studiously avoiding looking *out there*.

"You don't have to yell," DJ said. "I can hear you just fine." He tapped the side of his helmet.

I kept forgetting that DJ couldn't see my facial expressions. How would he know that I wasn't joking around if he couldn't see the utter terror in my eyes? We'd managed the first time, when I initially woke up in the suit, and I was sure we'd figure it out again, but it wasn't easy.

"You still haven't answered my question."

DJ made a motion in the air, and an image of *Qriosity*, complete with a blinking green dot at the rear and a red dot at the front, appeared on my hud. "The green dot's us," he said. "The red dot's where we have to go. The tether isn't long enough."

"But—"

DJ patted his belt. "When we reach the navigational array, I have tethers for us to use while we work. Our boots will keep us secure while we're walking."

"Yeah." I laughed derisively. "My mag boots kept me real secure last time."

"That was a fluke."

"But what if it happens again?"

"It won't."

"But it might!" I said.

DJ rested his gloved hand on my shoulder. I could only feel the subtle weight of it through my suit, but it helped. "I swear on my life that I won't let anything happen to you, Noa."

The boy was a mystery to me. Protecting me wasn't his job. Rescuing me wasn't his job. Yet he treated both like they were. When he said he wouldn't let me come to harm, I believed that he would throw himself into danger, no matter what it was, to keep that promise. And I didn't know why. But I was grateful for it.

"All right," I said. "Let's go. But if I get blown into space again, I'm taking you with me."

DJ unspooled the tether on his belt and attached it to me. A length of a couple of meters hung between us. When he was done, he said, "Where one of us goes, we both go."

Walking was a slow, laborious process, and I was happy to let DJ lead the way so that I didn't have to worry about him seeing me struggle. DJ didn't seem to have any problem, but I was huffing and breathing heavy after only a couple of minutes. I did a lot of walking back home, seeing as Mom wouldn't let me drive, but this was like trudging through mud.

"Thank you for doing this," DJ said. "It can't be easy for you being out here after you died last time."

"It's not, and I'd appreciate talking about literally anything else." I kept my head focused on DJ's back so that I didn't have to look at the stars, but that didn't stop me from knowing that they were out there waiting to kill me.

"Like what?"

"I don't know," I said. "Did you learn anything else about *Qriosity* while I was researching the murder mysteries of Anastasia Darling?"

DJ snorted. "Is that what we're calling what you spent the last week doing?"

"Yes."

The mics in DJ's helmet were sensitive enough that they picked up his laughter despite him trying to hide it. "It seems like *Qriosity* was meant to have a crew of at least twelve. That's how many storage containers Jenny and I counted."

"I wonder where *they* are."

"Jenny's got a couple of theories about that," DJ said. "She took an inventory of the ship's supplies, and she said there were at least four spacesuits missing."

"Missing?"

DJ's helmet moved a little, and I figured he was shaking his head, though I couldn't be sure from the back. "She thinks some crew might've been in their suits when whatever catastrophe happened to us occurred." DJ held out his hands. "But that's just speculation. We still don't know anything more about what happened to us or why we're here than we did a week ago."

It was too much to hope that DJ and Jenny had unearthed the secrets to everything while I sat on the couch and wallowed in self-pity. "What do you do all day?"

"I don't know what Jenny does," DJ said. "But I've been using my time to study *Qriosity*."

"And?" I asked. "What have you discovered so far?"

"It's a ship."

I laughed loudly and then slapped my helmet while trying to cover my mouth. Wearing it took some getting used to.

"I wish I had more to tell you," DJ went on. "But it's like every scrap of information that might help us is gone. *Qriosity*'s entertainment library is full of programs starring Jenny Perez, and the database has repair manuals for every system on the ship, but anything relating to the crew or their mission is gone. And not just gone, but deleted. I can see the holes where those files are supposed to be."

I wished that surprised me. It seemed we'd been given everything we needed to survive but not much else. "What about cameras? When I asked MediQwik how I'd died, it pulled up video of you performing CPR on me in the airlock. Maybe there are some earlier recordings."

"The recordings begin the moment we woke up," DJ said.

"Figures."

I wanted to scream. Our past was hidden from us; our future was on autopilot. Even trying to fix the navigational array felt futile because I was sure that, even if we succeeded, we'd run into another complication. And then another, on and on forever.

"I'm glad you stopped being sad," DJ said. "Jenny really is an awful cook. She tried making lasagna, and it somehow came out raw and charred at the same time."

Jenny's voice piped into my helmet. "You know I can hear you, right?"

"Now I do," DJ said. "But you have to admit that lasagna was a crime against humanity."

"Fine," Jenny said grudgingly. "It was terrible. But, in my defense, I warned you that it would be. If you need someone to beat a difficult level in a video game, I can do that. If our lives depend on answering trivia about aquatic mammals, obscure anime, or eighteenth-century Russian history, you'll want me on your side."

"Don't forget your unexpected lock-picking abilities," I said. "Without which, I would still be stuck wearing a onesie that didn't fit."

"That was luck," Jenny said. "And boredom."

I happened to look up and caught an eyeful of stars. A sea of lights out there waiting to swallow me. An inky ocean, vast and hungry. I wavered, and my heart rate alarm went off.

"Hey, Noa. What do you think you'd be doing right now if you were back on Earth?" DJ's voice cut through the terror and nausea. It pulled me back from the abyss.

My voice was shaky when I replied. "What time is it?"

"A little after ten," DJ said. At the same time, Jenny said, "Does it matter? The way we measure time is a construct. A fiction that we agreed to share."

"Uh, sure," DJ said. "But how about for the sake of the discussion, we pretend it's ten in the morning?"

Jenny sucked in a breath like she was definitely going to argue the point, so I quickly said, "I guess I'd be in Mrs. Ahmed's class for AP English."

"Of course you're an English nerd," Jenny said.

"Stories put me to sleep," DJ said. "Math on the other hand—"

"I can't do math," I said. "The numbers get jumbled in my brain."

"Dyscalculia."

"What?" Jenny and I said at the same time.

DJ cleared his throat. "Dyscalculia. It's like dyslexia, but for numbers."

I'd never heard of it before. "My teachers have always blamed it on me being lazy."

"You're not lazy," DJ said. "Your brain just functions differently. There are tricks you can learn to make it easier to work with numbers. I can show you a couple sometime."

"Thanks." In all the years I'd struggled with math, DJ was the first person to suggest that the problem was something other than me not trying hard enough. "What about you? What are *you* awful at?"

"Singing," Jenny blurted out, which made me laugh. When DJ tried to argue, she added, "I can hear you when you're in the shower."

"I'm not *that* bad," DJ said.

"I hate to agree with Jenny . . ."

"Wow," DJ said. "You've only been out of the rec room for a few hours, and you're already ganging up on me."

"You brought this on yourself," I said.

"Speaking of ganging up on something," Jenny said. "Unless you need me, I'm going to go gang up on the rest of those pancakes."

DJ stopped walking and turned to look at me. The reflective glass made it difficult to see his face. "Noa?"

I couldn't think of any reason we might need Jenny in the immediate future. "Enjoy second breakfast."

DJ and I continued walking. We had only covered half the distance to the navigational array, but I felt like we'd been out there for days. DJ might have been enjoying our spacewalk, but every second we were out there reminded me of dying. Talking seemed to help.

"You said you had someone back home?" I said.

DJ grunted. "We should stay focused on what we're doing."

Clearly DJ didn't want to discuss it, which made me even more curious. "Come on."

"It's real complicated," he said. "You don't want to hear about it."

"Oh, I absolutely do. Besides, you owe me for making me

come out here." It was a dirty trick, and I owed DJ *way* more than he owed me, but I was hoping he wasn't the type of person who kept score.

The silence stretched on long enough that I feared DJ was going to let it go on forever. When he finally spoke, there was a hitch in his voice. "I . . . we were in love. The kind of love that I think only comes around once in a lifetime."

"Love's not real," I said.

"You don't believe that."

"I'm pretty sure I do." I felt like a jerk as soon as the words left my mouth. I'd pushed DJ to talk about this, and then I'd ripped into him for it. "Sorry," I mumbled. "You said you *were* in love. What happened?"

I wouldn't have been surprised if DJ had decided to quit talking to me for the rest of the walk. But he didn't. "One day he looked at me like he didn't know me anymore—like our entire history together had been erased—and there was nothing I could do about it."

I wanted to hug DJ and tell him that it would be okay, but it wouldn't. When you fall in love, pain isn't just a risk, it's a guarantee.

"What about you?" DJ asked. "You said you had an ex."

"I don't want to talk about him."

"Well, that's not fair," DJ said.

"Life's not fair," I shot back.

"Fine." Judging by the harshness in DJ's voice, it was *not* fine.

Bringing up Billy, thinking about him, was almost as bad

as thinking about drifting through space. They both made my heart race wildly like a car without brakes. They both made me want to vomit. They'd both embraced me and nearly killed me.

"I met him on the bus." I started talking before I thought about what I was doing. The words tumbled out. "I didn't usually take the forty-four bus, but I did that day. I was reading some fantasy novel, I can't remember which, and I noticed this boy watching me. For five stops, every time I looked up from my book, he was staring at me. Finally, he sat beside me and told me I should read better books. I told him he should mind his own business. And then he spent the next ten stops rattling off every book he thought was better than the one I was reading."

DJ said, "He sounds like a jerk."

"Yeah," I said. "We kept arguing, and I didn't even notice I'd missed my stop, so I got off to catch the bus the other way, and he followed me. He said he was supposed to meet a friend, but that I was the most interesting person he'd talked to since moving to Seattle to attend UW, and he wasn't going to leave me alone until I gave him my number. So I did. That was the start of everything."

Billy's face floated in my mind. His brown eyes and his chipped front tooth and the three freckles beside his nose. The way he smiled and made me feel like I was the only person in the world.

"It was also the beginning of the end."

DJ had slowed down to walk beside me. "He hurt you?"

"You have no idea."

"But you still loved him."

"Yeah."

DJ touched my arm and pulled me to a stop so that he could face me. "Hearts break to remind us we have hearts *to* break."

"Like I told you," I said, "I was born with mine broken, so whatever. Besides, I'm never falling in love again. It's not worth it." I turned away from DJ and continued walking.

We didn't talk again until we reached the navigational array. It was a box that looked like a power transformer. Near it, a cluster of antennae rose about fifteen meters into space.

"Tell me what you need me to do," I said.

True to his word, DJ immediately clipped our tethers to the hull, and as soon as I was securely fastened, the tension riding in my neck and shoulders eased back. I still wanted to finish the job as quickly as possible so that we could return to the safety of the ship, but at least I knew I wasn't going to fly off the hull while we fixed the array.

My main job consisted of handing DJ tools when he needed them, preventing the tools he wasn't using from floating away, and standing idly while DJ typed slowly on a keyboard that had slid out of the junction box.

"Do you know what you're doing?" I asked. I was awed by the confidence he exuded as he scrolled through the lines of code, changing bits here, deleting bits there.

"The computer's feeding me instructions through my hud," DJ said.

"But you still have to have some clue what to do. You really are a computer genius, aren't you?"

"You can bake."

"Anyone can learn to bake," I said. "What you're doing is on a whole other level."

DJ's laugh filled the emptiness. It was quickly becoming my favorite sound. "I'll teach you about computers and you can teach me to bake."

"How is that a fair trade?" I asked. "Baking is fun."

"And fixing computers isn't?"

"No."

"That's only because you've never done it," DJ said. "There's a rush that comes from solving a problem that's like nothing else."

"You are such a nerd." DJ's enthusiasm was endearing. I still had no desire to learn how to tinker with computers or write code, but I could've happily listened to DJ talk about it all day.

"I'm serious!"

"Oh, I know you are," I said. "But you should stay focused on what you're doing." I pointed at the screen.

Maybe this isn't so bad. Spending time with DJ and Jenny, laughing and telling jokes. I was smiling before I realized it. And then the horror of what I'd been thinking hit me. The idea that this could be normal, that I could get used to living on a spaceship, was revolting. I'd toss myself out of the airlock before I let *Qriosity* become my new normal.

"You done yet?" I asked, getting impatient.

"Almost."

"Good," I said. "The faster we flip on the GPS and go home, the better."

FOUR

FIXING THE NAVIGATIONAL ARRAY TOOK TWO LONG hours. I had plenty of oxygen left, according to the readout in my hud, but I walked as quickly as I safely could back to the airlock, determined to get out of the suit.

"What's the hurry?" DJ asked.

"I want to see if it worked." I was winded, but I didn't want DJ to know.

"Do you hate it here so much?" DJ asked. "It's not like you get the chance to explore space every day."

"Are you serious?" I stopped, and DJ stumbled into me from behind. Instinctively, I crouched down and grabbed hold of something to make sure I didn't fly off, but my mag boots held tightly to the surface. When I was sure we were secure, I stood.

"I was mostly serious," DJ said when we were walking again.

"I was kidnapped and brought aboard *Qriosity*, DJ. There's

nothing fun about it." It was driving me mad that DJ couldn't seem to get that through his head.

"But what if this doesn't work?" DJ asked. "What if we get stuck out here for a long time?"

"That's not going to happen."

"What if it does?" DJ pressed.

"Do you *want* to stay out here?" I asked. "Did you hate your life so much that you're willing to ignore how seriously disturbing it is that someone put three teens who don't know anything about running a ship in charge of one?" I shook my head, not caring that DJ couldn't see me do it. "I'm not playing their game, DJ."

DJ's voice was calm despite my anger. "So if you don't get your way, you're going to give up? That seems like a real terrible way to live your life."

I rounded on DJ and yelled, "You don't know the first goddamn thing about my life, okay?" I was vibrating with anger, but DJ didn't respond, so I took off walking, not caring if he followed.

DJ caught up to me as we neared the airlock. "I'm not trying to be a jerk, Noa. I'm just worried about losing you again."

"Losing me again?"

"You know," DJ said. "To the couch. To depression and Anastasia Darling."

I tried to throw up my hands in frustration, but it didn't have the same effect in a gravity-free environment. "Why did we come out here if you've already decided it's not going to work?"

DJ sighed. "There are so many things that could go wrong. We might've fixed navigation, only to discover something else is broken. Or we might get back to Earth and find that nothing's the way we left it."

"None of that is going to happen," I said.

"But it might."

"It won't!"

"You don't know that, Noa!"

DJ and I didn't speak again until we were inside the airlock and the outer door was secured. We were stuck in the tiny space together for two minutes while it pressurized, making him difficult to avoid.

"Sorry for yelling," he said.

I began to apologize too, but I wasn't sorry. "I didn't ask to be here. I'm not the kind of person who can shrug and accept that this is my life now. And I don't know what will happen if fixing the nav array doesn't work. I can't even think about it because if I do, I might sit down in this airlock and never get up again. It just has to work. There's no other option, okay?"

DJ looked at me, and I could practically hear the speech he'd composed about how I was stronger than I thought I was and how we could face anything if we faced it together or some other nonsense. There were entire monologues written across his face that I never got to hear. Because when he finally spoke, just as the airlock chimed and the inner door opened, all he said was, "Okay, Noa."

Jenny was sitting at the starboard station with her feet

propped on the console when DJ and I reached Ops. "Good, you're back," she said. "I tried calling you, but neither of you answered, so I assumed you were dead."

"And you look absolutely broken up over it," I said.

Jenny shrugged. "You, at least, have been dead before. I figured it might not stick."

DJ slid behind the nearest console and began to work. I stood over his shoulder, trying to follow along, but I was immediately lost. DJ navigated the system like he'd been working on it his entire life. The only difference I noticed was that the status lights that had been red before now shone green.

"It worked," I said under my breath. We'd fixed the array. The countdown clock on the screen said we had four hours and fifty-three minutes until our next jump, which meant we could be home in under five hours. My skin felt hot and itched. I was sure that if I'd been in the spacesuit, the hud would be warning me to practice deep breathing.

DJ and Jenny, for whatever reason, didn't seem to feel the way I did about *Qriosity*. DJ viewed it as an opportunity to explore the stars like a hero from a science fiction book, and I couldn't get a read on what Jenny thought of our situation, but she didn't seem terribly troubled by it so long as she had a steady supply of Nutreesh. For me, though, *Qriosity* was a prison. There might not have been jailers, and we might have been able to travel freely from one end of the universe to the other, but the ship was still a prison and we had been sentenced to life.

"Here goes," DJ said. "I'm asking *Qriosity* to scan for our current location." He tapped a button on the console and then sat back, folding his arms across his chest.

My entire body tensed while we waited. It seemed like forever, but a moment later a message appeared on the screen: **Location scan in progress. Location scan will take approximately thirty-one hours and twelve minutes.**

I stared at the words, reading them over and over. And then I began to laugh. I fell into the nearest chair and held my belly as laughter ripped out of me. As tears welled in my eyes. Because of course scanning for our current location would take thirty-one hours. I had been a fool to believe there could be any other outcome.

DJ touched my arm. "Noa . . ."

I jerked away from him. "Nope, I get it. This is my life now. I live on *Qriosity*. I'm going to die on this ship. We're all going to die here. Are you happy? Of course you are! This is your dream." Another laugh escaped, deformed and grotesque. "Your dream and my nightmare."

"Is someone going to tell me what's going on?" Jenny asked.

In a tired, defeated voice, DJ said, "The computer needs thirty-one hours to calculate our current coordinates, but the fold drive initiates every nineteen hours."

"So we're *not* going home?" Jenny asked.

DJ tried to answer, but I beat him to it. "Nope. Sorry, Jenny, we're stuck out here. Get used to breathing stale air, drinking recycled piss, and eating Nutreesh bars, because we're never getting off this ship." I stood and headed for the door.

"Where're you going?" DJ asked.

I paused, looked him in the eye, and shrugged. "To pick up where I left off. Season four, episode thirteen. The one where Anastasia Darling finds a boy who's gone missing. Someone on this damn ship deserves a happy ending."

FIVE

JENNY FLOPPED DOWN ON THE COUCH BESIDE ME, opened a Nutreesh bar, and proceeded to devour it. Crumbs tumbled onto her shirt, and she smacked her lips as she ate, which made me want to scream.

"I expected DJ."

"Expected?" Jenny asked. "Or hoped for?"

I rolled my eyes, ignoring what she was implying. "Seeing as he can't stop sticking his nose where it doesn't belong and you don't seem to care about anything but food . . ." I shrugged.

Jenny scooted around to face me. "I'm betting you didn't have any friends back on Earth."

"I had friends."

"You couldn't have," she went on like I hadn't spoken. "Because I can't imagine anyone putting up with your selfish ass for long without sticking a knife in you."

I gave her the finger. "I'm not selfish."

Jenny snorted. "And I'm not full of Nutreesh right now."

"What do you want?" I asked, my patience frayed.

Jenny folded her arms across her chest and stared at me. Her eyes were narrow and she flared her nostrils. "I get it; you're sad. You want to go home. The universe is a cruel, desolate place, no one loves you, and nothing matters because existence is meaningless." She paused. "Get over it."

"I didn't ask for this!"

"And you think I did?" Jenny asked. "You think I wanted to be trapped on a ship with one boy who's got his head up his ass and another who hardly knows I exist because he's so worried about you?"

"DJ's not worried about me."

Jenny slapped my arm. Hard. "Are you really that dense? That boy has it *so* bad for you. And I don't know why. You're okay-looking, I suppose, but your personality is somewhere between raw broccoli and a rabid raccoon having an existential crisis."

I didn't know what Jenny was going on about. DJ had no interest in me, and even if he had, I had no interest in him or anyone. "Sorry I'm not living up to your expectations."

"You're hardly living at all," she said.

"Do you want me to cook? Is that what this is about?"

"No," she said. "I mean, yes, that would be nice. But I also want you to find a reason to get your broody ass off this couch. I want you to find a reason to get out of bed every day and keep going."

"I . . ." I had planned to recite my list of reasons to get up in the morning, but my list was blank. I eyed Jenny thoughtfully for a moment and then asked, "What keeps *you* going?"

"Revenge."

"On whom?"

Jenny shrugged. "I don't know yet. I've been scouring *Qriosity* for clues. I think there's more happening here than we realize, and I'm going to uncover the truth. When I do, I hope it will lead me to the people who kidnapped us."

"And when you find them?"

"I'm going to cut off their balls," she said. "If they have them. If not, I'll devise a suitably painful alternative."

"You've been investigating our kidnapping this whole time?"

Jenny nodded. "And I don't need a sidekick."

"I wasn't offering."

"Good," she said. "You've got to find your own thing. DJ's found his."

"What?" I asked. "Being perfect?"

"You." Jenny looked at me like it should have been obvious. "Taking care of you, trying to get you home. If you asked him to capture you a comet, he'd try to find a way to do it." She shrugged. "We all need a hobby, and you, inexplicably, are his."

What was I supposed to do with the knowledge that the only thing that kept DJ from joining me on the Couch of Misery was his desire to help me? Maybe that's just the kind of person he was. He saw someone in pain and needed to fix them. It was sweet, but also unsettling.

"You know it doesn't work that way, right? You can't tell me to stop being sad. I can't flip a switch and shut off my emotions."

Jenny took my hand and offered me a sympathetic smile. "You don't have to stop being sad, Noa. I have cried myself to sleep every single night since you found me."

"You have?" I didn't mean to sound so surprised, but Jenny didn't strike me as the type who would readily admit to crying.

"Yes," she said. "And I overheard DJ having a full-out argument with himself in the Freshie. He blames himself for everything that's happened to us. We're all hurting, Noa."

I felt embarrassed. Jenny and DJ were going through the same thing I was, but they had kept moving forward, despite their pain, while I'd watched TV.

"What do I do?" I asked. "You've got your mystery and DJ's got me, I guess. What should I do?"

"Hell if I know. Maybe you should ask the hologram." Before I could stop her, Jenny said, "Hey, Jenny Perez, get out here. Noa's got a question for you."

As the sparkling photons gathered into the form of Jenny Perez, Jenny stood and took off.

"Hi! I'm your host, Jenny Perez, whom you probably remember as the precocious kid detective and bestselling author Anastasia Darling on the award-winning mystery entertainment program *Murder Your Darlings*. What can I help you with today?"

I was about to tell her to go away, but I stopped. I sat up on the couch and pulled my legs under me. Jenny Perez stood in front of the screen wearing a hopeful, slightly devious expression that I'd grown familiar with over a hundred episodes of her award-winning mystery entertainment program. I'd spent more time with her since waking up on *Qriosity* than with DJ or Jenny.

"If you have a problem," she said, "I would love for you to give me a clue so that we can solve it together."

"Okay," I said. "Here's one. How do I go on when everything seems hopeless?"

I didn't expect an answer from Jenny Perez. She was, after all, a hologram. So I was surprised when she sat down on the ottoman in front of a leather chair, sighed heavily, and said, "It wasn't always easy growing up in front of an audience the way I did. Some days I thought about setting fire to my entire life and walking away."

"But you didn't," I said.

Jenny Perez shook her head. "No, I did not. Why is a long story. Would you like to hear it?"

"Yeah," I said. "I've got the time."

THE BODY IN THE GALLEY

ONE

I SAT IN FRONT OF THE VIEWPORT IN OPS AND STARED AT the stars. I was so close to the glass that I could touch it, but I kept my hands in my lap. There were a million million *million* stars out there. Some had planets around them. A few of those planets probably supported life. Maybe one of them had intelligent life sufficiently advanced enough to help us. But they would never know we existed. Even if someone looking through a powerful telescope happened to see us, we'd be nothing more than a blip to them. There and gone again.

"I didn't expect to find you here."

DJ's smiling face was reflected in the viewport, and I waved perfunctorily but kept my eyes trained on the stars. "I'm engaging in a kind of exposure therapy."

"Exposure to what?"

"Space," I said. "This is as close as I can get to it without suiting up, and I am *not* doing that again anytime soon."

DJ grunted and sat at his station. I say *his station* because it was the one he spent most of his time at, but each of the consoles had access to the same systems. DJ was a creature of habit, I'd come to learn. He thrived on routine and order. He ate the same thing for breakfast each morning, jogged around *Qriosity* immediately after waking up, and dropped by Ops to check if the computer had somehow managed to calculate our coordinates while he slept. It never did.

"Wait," I said. "Is it morning?"

"Have you been here all night?"

I turned around and leaned against the viewport. "I guess I have."

"Noa . . ."

"Don't start."

This was part of DJ's routine too. Make sure Noa gets enough sleep, make sure Noa is eating, make sure Noa isn't slipping into a debilitating depression from which he will never escape.

"I'm just looking out for you," he said. "If you want to stay up all night looking at the stars, I can't stop you, but I don't think it's healthy."

"You should be happy I'm not watching *Murder Your Darlings*." I was, in fact, still watching the show. I'd seen every episode and was working my way through it for the second time. But DJ didn't need to know that.

"I am," he said. "But—"

"I'm trying, DJ."

DJ's stern expression softened. "I know you are. I just wish you didn't have to try so hard."

"You and me both." I hugged my knees to my chest. My exhaustion was starting to catch up to me. I could've shut my eyes right there and fallen asleep. "It's a struggle, you know? I had no idea what I was doing with my life on Earth, but I was surrounded by people who had their own ideas, and I could let them tell me what to do."

"If you need someone to tell you what to do," DJ said, "I've got a list of repairs—"

"That's not enough, DJ, and you know it."

"It might have to be."

Maybe he was right. If nothing changed, *Qriosity* could be my entire universe for the rest of my life. I could die here without setting foot on a planet or seeing another living soul other than DJ or Jenny. And, somehow, I was going to have to make peace with that. I just didn't know how.

DJ was looking at me, a curious expression on his face. "What?" I asked.

"You remind me of someone."

"Who?"

DJ shook his head. "No one. It doesn't matter."

"How come you never talk about home?" I asked. Usually when the conversation turned to home, DJ got quiet or suddenly had somewhere else to be. He probably thought I hadn't noticed.

"What's the point of talking about a home we can't go back

to?" he asked. "My life is here, with you and Jenny. Everything else is just someplace I'll never see again."

"You don't believe we'll *ever* get back to Earth?"

DJ took a moment to answer. I liked that about him. I liked that he didn't fire off the first words that popped into his brain the way I often did. "We might," he said. "I hope we do, Noa. Honest. But that's tomorrow, and I've got to live in today."

"I wish I was as strong as you."

"You are," he said. "You're stronger."

That was a load of crap if I ever heard it, and I was about to say so when Jenny's voice crackled over the comms. "DJ? Noa? Anyone? I think you'd better come to the galley. I've got a real emergency here."

I rolled my eyes. "Ten bucks says the emergency is that she ate the last of the croissants I baked yesterday."

DJ laughed. "No way I'm taking that bet." He raised his voice. "We're on our way, Jenny."

"Hurry," she said. "There's been a murder."

TWO

THE BODY LAY SPRAWLED FACEUP ON THE FLOOR OF THE galley in front of the table.

Jenny paced around the body babbling, and DJ tried to calm her down enough for her to explain what happened. I couldn't take my eyes off the body, its blue lips and its wide-open eyes, staring into nothing. Off the jumpsuit that looked like the one I'd been wearing when I woke up. The one with someone else's name on it. The name on her suit was Kayla. It looked like it fit better than mine had.

"I already told you!" Jenny said. "I was eating a croissant and reading when the aft door opened and this girl came stumbling in. As soon as she saw me, she reached out and tried to speak."

"What'd she say?" DJ asked.

I looked up in time to see Jenny shake her head. "I don't know. She collapsed right where you see her and died."

I knelt beside the body and pressed my fingers to her neck the way I'd been taught in my CPR class. Her skin was still warm, but there was definitely no pulse.

"Why do you think she was murdered?" I asked.

Jenny glared at me like she couldn't believe I was asking such a ridiculous question. "Because people don't just drop dead."

"Sometimes they do," I muttered, but Jenny ignored me.

"Where'd she come from?" DJ asked. "We searched every room and crawlspace on *Qriosity*."

"Obviously, we missed something," Jenny fired back.

I felt like we were missing something now. And then it hit me. "MediQwik."

Jenny and DJ turned to look at me. "What?" DJ asked.

"MediQwik!" I grabbed the body's arms. "Come on! We have to get to medical!"

"What're you doing, Noa?" Jenny asked. "She's *dead*."

I started trying to drag the body toward the door, but it was heavy and I had the kind of muscles that came from lifting books and burritos. "So was I, and MediQwik brought *me* back!" They kept looking at me like I was speaking a language they didn't understand. "Damn it! Someone help me!"

Finally, DJ grabbed the body's legs, and we carried her through the ship. When we reached medical, I was completely winded and my arms felt like jelly. Without needing to be asked, Jenny stepped in and helped DJ lift the body onto the table, while I fitted the MediQwik cuff around her arm. The lights in the room dimmed briefly.

"Thank you for choosing the MediQwik Portable Medical Diagnostician and Care Appliance. This patient appears to be suffering from death. Would you like me to attempt emergency revival?"

"Yes!" I said.

"Attempting emergency revival. There is a thirty-nine percent chance of success. MediQwik, health redefined. MediQwik is a trademark of Prestwich Enterprises, a subsidiary of Gleeson Foods."

We stood around the table in silence. I wasn't sure if I could call her "the body" anymore. Not when MediQwik was attempting to heal her. Her name might not have been Kayla any more than my name had been Nico, but I didn't know what else to call her. She looked about our age, and she seemed like the kind of person who had smiled a lot when she was alive.

"I can't sit here," Jenny said.

"Where are you going?" DJ asked.

"To figure out where she came from." Jenny marched out of the room like she was on a mission. I didn't know whether she'd left because she needed to learn where Kayla had been hiding or because she couldn't stand to be so near to death.

I walked around and hopped up on the other table. DJ paced the room, chewing on his thumbnail.

"You don't have to stay," I said. "You can help Jenny if you want."

DJ shook his head. "It's not that. It's just that this reminds me . . ."

"Oh."

The last time DJ had been in the med suite had been when

he'd carried *my* lifeless body from the airlock. Only, he'd had to carry me alone.

"What percentage did MediQwik give me for revival?" I asked, though I wasn't sure I wanted to know.

"Noa—"

"I'm alive. What's the big deal?"

DJ looked at Kayla and then at the floor. "Thirty-three percent," he said. "But only a twelve percent chance that you would be revived without permanent brain damage."

A shiver ran through me. I'd done everything I could to avoid thinking about being dead since MediQwik had fixed me, but I hadn't been able to escape knowing that I *had* died. I just hadn't realized how close I'd come to remaining dead.

"What was it like?" DJ asked.

"What was what like?"

"Death." As soon as he said it, he caught my eye and added, "Forget it. I shouldn't have asked."

Part of me was glad he had asked, though. I'd avoided thinking about it, not because I didn't want to face it, but because I didn't want to face it alone. Talking about it with DJ made it less scary.

"There was nothing," I said. "It was like I didn't exist in the moments between when I died and when I was revived."

DJ touched the wall, and a bench folded down for him to sit on. "Nothing at all? Maybe you just don't remember."

"Maybe," I said. "But I don't think so. There was . . . nothing."

"What do you think it means?"

"My mom worked in a hospital, in the ICU, so she dealt with death a lot. We weren't religious or anything, and one time I asked her what happened to the people who died. She told me about the law of conservation of energy and how energy can't be created or destroyed, so the energy that makes us who we are has to go somewhere."

DJ frowned out of one side of his mouth. "I don't mean to disrespect your mom, but I don't think it works like that."

"Obviously," I said. "She totally made it up so that I wouldn't be scared of death. I think when we die, we just die."

"That's it?" DJ said. "We just stop being anything?"

"Yeah. I mean, if there's something else after this life, I sure as hell didn't see it. And if this is all there is, then nothing we do matters, does it?"

DJ furrowed his brow, looking confused. "Of course it does. Everything we do matters."

I felt myself slipping again. If MediQwik hadn't revived me, the universe wouldn't have cared. Life would have gone on without me. DJ and Jenny would have continued without me. Everyone I knew and loved on Earth was moving forward without me. Even Becca. Even my mom. They would be sad, they might struggle, but they would keep living, and eventually no one would remember that I had existed.

I slid off the table. "I have to go."

"Noa—"

"You stay with the body," I said. "I'm going to help Jenny." DJ called my name again, but I was already out the door and gone.

THREE

I HEARD JENNY BEFORE I SAW HER, AND I THOUGHT, AT first, that she was arguing with herself.

"But *why* can't I see a map of the entire ship?"

"Because such a map doesn't exist, silly."

"You mean to tell me that there are no schematics or drawings of *Qriosity* anywhere in its library?"

"That is *exactly* what I'm saying. You catch on quick, which makes you my number one junior detective."

"I hate you so much."

There was only one person on the ship who could provoke that kind of anger in Jenny. As soon as I turned the corner, I spotted the hologram of Jenny Perez standing in the corridor. She was smiling like a psychopath, and Jenny looked like she was going to claw the hologram's eyes out.

"What's going on?" I asked.

If my sudden appearance had startled Jenny, she didn't show it. She stood with her hands on her hips and turned to look at me with the contempt she'd been directing at Jenny Perez. "What're you doing here?"

"Looking for you."

Jenny's expression softened. "Is she . . ."

I shook my head. "MediQwik is still working."

It might have been none of my business, but I was curious what I'd walked in on. "What were you and the precocious kid detective and bestselling author Anastasia Darling from the award-winning mystery entertainment program *Murder Your Darlings* talking about?"

Jenny Perez beamed when I mentioned her. Jenny looked less thrilled. "Sometimes I use her to bounce ideas off of. Plus, she helps me interact with *Qriosity*'s computer. I can't figure out the operating system, so I just get *her* to do it."

I hadn't known that was something we could do, and I was kind of impressed Jenny had figured it out. Though I wasn't sure the tradeoff was worth it, seeing as it meant having to listen to Jenny Perez.

"Why were you asking about a map of the ship?"

Jenny pointed at a door off the corridor. It wasn't labeled, but it looked like every other door on the ship. "Scuff marks," she said. "That girl had been limping, so I followed the scuff marks left by her boots from the galley to here. Thankfully, *Qriosity*'s cleaning bots hadn't gotten to them yet."

Qriosity's fleet of rarely seen cleaning robots kept the ship from getting too gross, though they refused to pick up my clothes off the floor of my quarters, which made them kind of useless to me.

"What's inside?" I asked.

"That's the second problem," Jenny said. "The door is locked."

"What's the first problem?"

"I would swear this door wasn't here yesterday."

"Seriously?" I asked. Jenny didn't look like she was joking, but her sense of humor was often bizarre.

Jenny said, "Yes!" and fired off an exasperated sigh. "My quarters are one deck up, and I walk this way to reach the garden at least once a day."

"Maybe you never noticed it before."

But Jenny glared at me and said, "I notice everything. There are two labs, three empty crew quarters, a storage closet, and three service tunnel access doors between my room and the oxygen garden. This door was *not* here yesterday."

Jenny seemed so certain that I found it difficult to doubt her. If I'd learned one thing in our time together, it was that Jenny had a good memory. She could remember things I'd said to her that even I'd forgotten. But it didn't make sense that a door to a room appeared out of nowhere, and I wasn't the only one who thought so.

"I'm sorry, but this door *was* here," Jenny Perez said. "It has always been here."

"Then show it to me on a map!" Before Jenny Perez could answer, Jenny said, "I know, I know. You don't have a map. Because you're useless. Go away now."

The figure of Jenny Perez burst into a swarm of dazzling lights and vanished into the vents.

I stood in front of the door and pulled on the latch, but it didn't budge. When I turned around, Jenny was watching me.

"All the doors on this ship can be locked from the inside," she said, and I knew it was true from experience. If I hadn't been able to lock the door to my quarters, I never would have been able to keep DJ or Jenny out. "But they can also be locked and unlocked by voice command."

"They can?"

Jenny nodded. "If you lock a door, you're the only person who can unlock it." She must have seen the confusion in my eyes because she added, "You spend a few hours locked in a toilet and see if it doesn't make you obsessed with finding out how the door locks work."

"Fair point," I said. "But if the scuff marks led you here—"

"Then the girl in medical is probably the one who locked this door. Which means she's the only one who can unlock it."

"You really are turning into a good detective," I said. "I've watched every episode of that stupid show, and I wouldn't have thought to do what you did."

Jenny managed to look both insulted and flattered at the same time. "Don't take this the wrong way, Noa, but you're not very observant."

She wasn't the first person to tell me that, and she wasn't wrong. Becca used to say that I couldn't find a clue with a map, a compass, and GPS.

"But, while I definitely want to know where this door came from, what's behind it, and who the girl in medical is," Jenny said, "the questions I most want the answers to are: Did somebody kill her? And, if so, who?"

FOUR

I SAT IN MEDICAL WITH KAYLA'S BODY WHILE JENNY showed DJ what she had discovered. I didn't want to be alone with the person who might have been murdered, but DJ thought someone should stay with her in case she woke up. It was sound logic that I couldn't argue with.

Not much had changed since I'd left. Kayla remained still; her eyes were closed. But her skin looked a little warmer than it had before. If I hadn't known she'd been dead a couple of hours earlier, I would have guessed she was sleeping.

There were more questions than I knew what to do with swirling about in my mind, but there was one that I kept returning to.

"MediQwik? What can you tell me about death?"

"Death occurs at the cessation of the body's biological functions."

"I was dead, right?"

"Correct.

"But you revived me the same way you're attempting to revive the patient on the table now."

The lights in the room dimmed for a moment before MediQwik said, "The method by which your body's biological functions were restored is different from the methods currently being employed due to the unique nature of your injuries."

I shook my head. "That's not . . . I just meant that we were both dead and you revived us."

"The current patient has not yet been revived."

"Right, but I was," I said, trying not to get annoyed. "I was dead and then I wasn't."

"Correct."

I took a deep breath before asking my next question, not sure what I wanted the answer to be. "Where did I go when I died?"

This time when the lights dimmed, they remained so for nearly sixty seconds, and I thought I might have broken the computer. Eventually, they returned to normal. "According to available data, your biological processes ceased to function at a location outside *Qriosity*. Your destination, extrapolated from your trajectory, was airlock three on deck two."

I laughed at the answer because it was technically correct but also ridiculous. "Okay," I said, trying again. "Do you know what consciousness is?"

"Consciousness is a being's state of awareness of its own existence."

I wasn't sure how accurate the definition was, but it sounded good enough. "What happened to my consciousness when my biological processes ceased? What happened to *me* when I died?"

"MediQwik is a Portable Medical Diagnostician and Care Appliance, not a philosopher, and is not designed to dispense psychological care."

It had been silly of me to expect a computer to know what happened to me when I died. I'd been able to put the experience out of my mind until this stranger had had the bad luck to show up dead. Now it was the only thing I could think about.

Maybe we were no different from machines. When my body shut down, I simply ceased to be until MediQwik turned me on again. The thought of being dead wasn't as terrifying as the thought that I was little more than an accidental blip in the history of the universe. When my body was beyond repair, the soul of who I was would simply stop existing. I had come from nowhere, and I would return to that abyss when I died.

I stood over the body on the table. "Are you in there? Can you hear me? Of course you can't. You're still dead. Mostly dead, I guess. I don't even know anymore. This is stupid."

I screamed when Kayla's eyes opened. She sat up and grabbed me by the front of my shirt. She was surprisingly strong. "You're supposed to be dead. You should've died."

I shoved her hand away and stumbled back. "Who are you?" I asked. "Who tried to kill you?"

Her eyes were wild. I wasn't sure she had heard me. She said, "They're watching you," and then she collapsed.

FIVE

THE LIGHTS IN MEDICAL FLIPPED TO RED AND BEGAN TO flash.

"Please step away from the patient in Bed A. MediQwik is attempting emergency lifesaving measures. MediQwik, health redefined."

Despite the warning, I moved toward Kayla. Her back arched. She convulsed. Rails rose from the side of the bed to prevent her from falling off. Her back arched again.

"What did you say? Who's watching us? Why am I supposed to be dead?" My voice cracked.

She didn't answer. Kayla's eyes were open, pointed at the ceiling but looking at nothing.

The red lights faded and the blue lights returned.

"MediQwik is sorry to inform you that revival of the patient in Bed A has failed."

"What does that mean? You have to wake her up! I need to know what she was trying to tell me!"

"The patient has expired. Revival efforts have ceased. We are sorry for your loss. MediQwik, health redefined. MediQwik is a trademark of Prestwich Enterprises, a subsidiary of Gleeson Foods." The cuff beeped and popped open on Kayla's arm.

I tried to push the cuff closed again, but it wouldn't lock. "Bring her back!"

I needed DJ. He'd know what to do. I tore out of the room, calling DJ's name as I ran. "DJ!"

Finally, DJ answered. He and Jenny were outside the cargo bay. I was out of breath.

"Noa? What's wrong? What's happening? Is she awake?"

"Spoke," I said. It was all I could get out. I started coughing because I couldn't breathe.

"What the hell is going on?" Jenny asked.

"Give him a second," DJ said.

I bent over and rested my hands on my knees. When I was able to talk, I said, "She's dead. But she sat up and said *I* was supposed to be dead and that *they* were watching us."

"Who's watching us?" Jenny asked.

"Can MediQwik bring her back?"

I shook my head at DJ and said to Jenny, "I don't know. She died again as soon as she said it, and MediQwik said it couldn't revive her." I grabbed DJ's wrist. "Come on. We have to go."

"Go where?" DJ asked.

"You can fix it. You have to. I have to know what she was trying to tell me."

DJ pulled his hand back. "Wait, Noa. If MediQwik says she's dead, I can't change its mind."

Why was he arguing with me? I wanted to punch him until he quit talking and did what I told him to. "I don't know, but can't you just try?"

DJ looked to Jenny, who shrugged. "All right," he said. "Let's go. But I'm not promising anything."

"Fine. Whatever. Just hurry." I walked as quickly as I could back to medical without running, annoyed that DJ and Jenny were only barely keeping up. I kept replaying what Kayla had said. The fear in her eyes. I didn't know what she'd meant, though, and I needed to.

I knew something was wrong when I saw the door open to medical. I hadn't left it open. I rushed ahead to get inside. Bed A was empty. Nothing remained to prove that Kayla had ever been there.

"Noa?" DJ said, crowding into the room. "Where is she?"

"She was here!" I said. "And she was dead!"

DJ's eyes widened slightly. "You said she woke up. Was she sick? Did she have any mucus coming out of her?"

"What?" I asked. "No! I told you, she said I should have died and that they were watching us!"

"Most dead bodies don't get up and walk away," Jenny said. She was still outside in the corridor and seemed reluctant to enter. "MediQwik? What happened to the patient you were trying to revive?"

"We have no record of any such patient." MediQwik's neutral voice sounded tinny to me. Like I was hearing it through a tunnel.

"She was right here!" I yelled.

The lights dimmed and then MediQwik said, "The last patient we treated was suffering from acid reflux."

DJ raised his hand. "That was me. It was the night you made mac and cheese and I had four helpings."

"I didn't imagine her!" I looked to DJ and then Jenny, but neither seemed to know what to do. "You both helped me carry her here."

"No one's doubting you, Noa," DJ said. "But maybe MediQwik *did* revive her and she's lost somewhere and confused. We should look for her."

"Agreed," Jenny said. "I don't want a stranger wandering around my ship."

"Fine," I said, "but this time we are *not* splitting up." I pointed at Jenny. "Please don't argue with me on this."

Jenny held up her hands. "There's either a stranger, a zombie, or a killer somewhere on *Qriosity*. Possibly all three. I am totally okay with sticking together."

We started on the top deck and methodically searched the ship, going into every room, checking every service tunnel, opening every hatch. *Qriosity* had seemed so big in the beginning, but I'd spent enough time in it that I didn't think there was anywhere for someone to hide where we wouldn't find them. Someone had, though, and that was scary.

I was about to suggest we try Ops, see if there was a way to scan the ship for the missing girl, when Jenny, who was a little farther down the corridor, shouted, "It's open! The room is open!"

I pushed past DJ and ran to where Jenny was standing in front of the room that had been locked earlier. Sure enough, the door stood wide open.

"Hello?" I peeked my head in, and there she was. The girl, Kayla, was lying on a narrow bed, her knees bent to her chest, so obviously dead that anyone could have seen it. Her eyes were glassy and her skin was chalky. "She's here," I said, quietly like I was scared to wake her. "She's in here."

SIX

I DON'T KNOW IF HER NAME WAS ACTUALLY KAYLA. IF I had died the moment I woke up and DJ and Jenny had found my body, they might have thought my name was Nico. But without our having another name to call her by, Kayla stuck.

We moved Kayla's body back to the medical suite and locked the door this time to make sure that she couldn't get out. Then we returned to Kayla's room to see what we could discover about her.

"She liked Nutreesh almost as much as you do," DJ said to Jenny.

"Funny," Jenny said. Seemingly to spite DJ, she whipped a bar out of her pocket and unwrapped it, eating noisily.

Kayla's room was twice the size of my quarters, but it still felt small. Nutreesh wrappers littered the floor. They filled and overflowed the trash can.

"You don't think she was trapped in here the entire time?" Jenny asked.

"Couldn't have been," I said. When DJ and Jenny both turned to look at me, I added, "You can't live on Nutreesh. She would've needed water, too. And she had to go to the bathroom sometime."

Jenny shivered. "That means this strange girl was wandering around *Qriosity*, living here with us, and we didn't know it."

"Maybe we're the interlopers," DJ said. "We don't know which of us was here first, so to her we might've been the strangers living on *her* ship."

"How many other people are living on this ship that we don't know about?" I asked. DJ looked away, and Jenny was quietly going through Kayla's belongings. Neither had an answer.

It was morbid searching a dead person's room to try to get to know them, but we didn't have much choice. I kept hoping to find a journal where Kayla had written her innermost thoughts or the answer to every question I was carrying inside me. Who kidnapped us? What did they want with us? Why was I supposed to be dead?

I found nothing like that, though. Her room was spartan. Some clothes, a projector and screen, an entire case of Nutreesh. I was ready to give up when Jenny pulled something out from under the bed.

A sketchbook. Jenny set it on top of the mattress and opened it to the first page. Inside were watercolor paintings of the most beautiful landscapes that I had ever seen. Landscapes that could not have existed on Earth. A field of violet trees with a blue sun overhead. An ocean of starry night. Mountains cloaked by velvet orange clouds that rained fire.

"Good imagination," DJ said. "I wish I could paint like that."

"How do you know these aren't places she actually visited?" I asked.

DJ tried to speak but stumbled over his words until he finally spit out, "I guess I don't."

"They were special to her," Jenny said. "She wouldn't have hidden them otherwise."

"Hidden them from who?" I turned to the last page. It was the first and only painting that wasn't a landscape. Staring back at us was the unmistakable image of Jenny Perez. "What do you think it means?"

"We should ask her," Jenny said. I wasn't sure it was the greatest idea, but Jenny was already saying, "Hologram! Get out here. We've got a few questions for you."

Seeing the hologram's photons assemble from nothing hadn't yet grown so commonplace that it didn't fill me with awe. But the wonder always vanished as soon as Jenny Perez began to speak.

"Hi! I'm your host, Jenny Perez, whom you probably don't remember from a show that no one watched because it was awful and so am I. Sorry about it!"

DJ busted out laughing, and Jenny said, "That's a scarily accurate impression, Noa."

"Imitation is the sincerest form of flattery," Jenny Perez said.

"In this case," I said, "it's not." I nodded at Jenny. "This was your idea."

Jenny cleared her throat. "Did you know this room existed?"

"Of course, silly. This room was created exactly three hours and nine minutes ago."

"Created?" I asked. "How could—"

Jenny held up a finger to silence me. "And were you aware there was someone other than the three of us living aboard *Qriosity*?"

Jenny Perez cocked her head to the side. "There is? I detect no human beings other than my junior detective and her two perky sidekicks."

"Sidekick?" I wasn't sure how I felt about the hologram viewing me as Jenny's sidekick, but it also wasn't the time to argue.

DJ said, "How's it possible that there's been someone living on this ship since we woke up and you didn't know about it?"

"It's not," Jenny Perez said. "Therefore you must be mistaken."

"We've got a dead body in medical that says we're not," Jenny said.

Something had been nagging me, and it finally clicked into place. "She wasn't part of the crew." The others, including Jenny Perez, turned to look at me. "She couldn't have been. There was no storage container with her name on it."

Understanding dawned on DJ's face. "Which means she was like us."

"Not exactly like us," Jenny said. "She was hiding here. She could have come out and talked to us at any time, but she didn't."

"I'm more concerned about how she was able to hide on the ship without the super detective over there knowing," I said. "How many more people are secretly living on *Qriosity* that we don't know about? Is one of *them* a murderer?"

"We don't know for sure she was murdered," DJ said. "We won't until MediQwik completes its autopsy."

Jenny Perez, who'd been standing quietly with her trademark smile plastered on her face said, "MediQwik has finished the autopsy of the unknown deceased human in the medical bay. Would you like the results?"

"Yes!" Jenny said

"MediQwik has determined that the cause of death for the unknown deceased human was heart failure due to a ventricular septal defect, a common congenital heart defect."

"So she wasn't murdered?" I asked.

Jenny Perez said, "MediQwik suggests the probability that death was caused by factors other than the heart defect is less than one percent. Looks like there's no case here, junior detectives. Sorry about it!"

"I guess we should be glad there's not a killer on board," DJ said, but he wasn't smiling. None of us were.

SEVEN

WE STOOD OUTSIDE THE INNER AIRLOCK DOOR. KAYLA'S body, wrapped in a shroud, lay inside the airlock, which was visible to us via a screen on the wall. Nothing in Kayla's room had indicated what religion, if any, she followed, so we were left to muddle through. I hoped we did right by her.

"Anyone want to say anything?" DJ asked. He'd been hovering near me all afternoon like he wanted to be nearby in case I needed him, but the closer he got, the farther away I wanted him to go.

"Sorry you died," Jenny said.

I just shook my head. I wasn't going to pretend I knew her. I wasn't going to pretend I'd miss her. I wished she wasn't dead, but even my reasons for that were selfish. I only wanted to know what she'd been trying to tell me. I wasn't sure if that made me a bad person, but I certainly didn't like myself much right then.

DJ clasped his hands in front of him. "I'm real sorry you felt like you had to hide from us, and I wish you hadn't died alone. Hopefully, you'll find peace now." DJ pressed the button on the touchscreen that opened the outer airlock door. Kayla's body was hurled into space, frozen forever.

I was sitting in Ops, in front of the viewport, when DJ found me later. I hadn't exactly been avoiding him and Jenny, but I hadn't wanted to see them either. DJ sat beside me, and I could feel the warmth of him. I scooted away.

"Why do you do that?" DJ asked.

"Do what?"

DJ pursed his lips and eyed the space between us I'd created. "Move when I get near you, flinch or pull back when I touch you?"

"Maybe I don't like being touched. Have you ever considered that?" My words had the bite of a frigid winter wind. "Anyway," I added. "I don't *always* pull away."

I could feel DJ wanting to argue with me, but he kept what he was going to say to himself and we sat in silence for a while. It was nice to just be there with him. I wasn't completely oblivious. I knew DJ was into me, but he didn't ask for more than I was willing to give, which, in my limited experience, was a rare quality.

"She said I was supposed to die," I said after a while. "That's what she told me, DJ. That I should be dead."

"But you're not."

"I was." I couldn't see Kayla's body. Even if the fold drive hadn't already engaged and skipped us to some new section of the galaxy, it would have been too small. But I imagined I could still see it tumbling through the stars. "That could've been my body you spaced."

"But it wasn't," he said. "You're alive, Noa."

"Then why does it feel like I'm not? Why does it feel like I'm still dead?"

"Noa—"

I turned to face DJ. "I died, and that was it. There was nothing waiting for me. Just like there's nothing waiting for her. And I don't know what I'm supposed to do with that. If there's nothing after this, then nothing matters. And if nothing matters, then what the hell is the point of anything?"

Tears welled in DJ's eyes. "Everything matters, Noa."

"Not if there's nothing waiting for us when we die."

"You're wrong," he said. "That makes our lives matter more." DJ struggled to find the words, but he finally said, "I don't know whether there's anything after we die. I guess I won't know until it happens to me, so I have to focus on what's important. On what's right in front of me."

"She said I should have died—"

"She was wrong!"

I turned to the viewport again. No matter how many times we skipped through space, I couldn't tell one patch of stars from another. They were all the same to me. "How can something be filled with so much light and yet be so empty and dark?"

"You'll get through this, Noa. We'll get through this together." The anguish in DJ's voice hurt, and I hated that I was the cause.

"All that darkness, all that emptiness, all that *space*. It's not just out there, DJ." I took his hand and pressed his palm to my chest. "It's in here, too."

"Then let me help you," DJ whispered.

I let go of DJ's hand, the warmth of him quickly forgotten. There was some part of me that wondered what would happen if I accepted DJ's offer. If I tried to fill that infinite, spacelike void in my chest with his laughter and Jenny's intensity, and made an honest attempt to build a life on *Qriosity*. But that would've required forgetting the entirety of my life before I woke up on the ship. It would've required giving up on going home. And, to me, that felt like a kind of death too.

"You can't," I said. "I don't think anyone can." I could feel DJ readying his argument, and I didn't have the strength to fight him. "I'd like to be alone for a little while, okay?"

DJ paused, probably considering whether he should leave me alone, and then nodded. "Yeah, okay." He stood and headed for the door. But before he left, he said, "For what it's worth, I don't think death is the end. Not for Kayla, and not for us."

I chuckled, thinking back to the first time I saw DJ's face. "When you found me and Jenny outside the head that first day, I thought you seemed familiar."

"You did?" His eyebrows rose and he seemed surprised by the admission.

"My mom went through a phase where she believed in

reincarnation, and she said that recognizing a stranger is a sign you knew each other in a past life." I shrugged, mostly because my mom had dipped her toe into a lot of different religions but had never committed fully to any.

"Do you think it could be true?" I asked. "Do you think we might have been friends in another life?"

DJ was looking at his feet. "I guess I think anything's possible."

"I hope it's true." I liked the idea that maybe DJ and me ending up on *Qriosity* together wasn't random. That there was an invisible hand guiding us.

"But, Noa?" DJ said. "Whether we knew each other in the past or not doesn't change how important your life is in the present. Jenny needs you . . . and so do I."

THE END OF A VERY LONG DAY

ONE

THE TIMER I'D SET BEGAN TO BLARE AS I OPENED THE oven door. The moment the air hit it, the soufflé collapsed in the middle. It caved in more when I pulled it out of the oven. The whole disaster resembled a delicious chocolate sinkhole.

"Damn it!"

"Problems in the kitchen?" Jenny was sitting at the table, playing with a device the size of an apple that was composed of interlocking triangles. The metallic faces lit up different colors—red and blue and orange and green—as she twisted them into various positions.

"I can't get this soufflé right. I think something must be wrong with the ovens." I dipped my finger into the creamy, spongy, molten-hot mixture. "Son of a—" I ran my burned finger under cold water. It hurt, but I didn't think it would blister.

"Or maybe you're not good at making them."

"Maybe." I took off my apron, tossed it on the counter, and sat at the table across from Jenny. "Mrs. Blum tried to teach me, but I couldn't get it right then either. She said I was impatient."

Jenny snorted. "You are."

I stuck my tongue out at her. It'd been a few weeks since Kayla had stumbled out of her hidden room, died, briefly come back to life, and then died again, and I'd fallen into a routine. I spent my mornings running simulations with DJ and Jenny. The tutorials were intended to teach us how to operate *Qriosity* without destroying the ship. When we weren't busy with those, I spent my free time working out with DJ in the gym, using Mind's Eye to visit the virtual recreation of Bell's Cove, the fictional town where most of *Murder Your Darlings* takes place, or hanging out in the galley, baking. My life was uneventful except for the part where I was living on a spaceship that randomly skipped around the universe every nineteen hours.

"What is that thing?" I motioned at the object Jenny was playing with.

"I don't know," she said. "I found it in one of the science labs. I think it's a game. That I'm meant to twist the pieces around until the faces light up the same color."

I watched Jenny play with the device. The way the faces shifted made my head feel tight, like I'd spent too much time in the sun and was dehydrated. "Do you think you should be messing with it?"

Jenny shrugged. "It hasn't killed me."

"Yet," I muttered.

Jenny ignored me. "What's with all the baking, Noa?"

"What do you mean?"

"You've been spending more time in the kitchen than usual," she said. "Not that I'm complaining."

"Of course not," I said. "I noticed the chocolate croissants I made yesterday are already gone."

"I only had one!"

"They didn't eat themselves."

"Maybe they did," Jenny said.

It wasn't worth arguing about because I honestly didn't care who'd eaten them. Besides, Jenny wasn't wrong about how much time I'd been spending in the kitchen, and my devotion to baking had little to do with her voracious appetite.

"Waking up and getting out of bed every day is hard, Jenny," I said. "Making it through the day is a choice I have to make over and over and over. And you'd think it'd get easier, but it never does because everywhere I look is a reminder that I didn't choose this." I shrugged. "The truth is, baking is the one thing on *Qriosity* that makes me feel normal."

Jenny nodded solemnly, her hands idly twisting the puzzle. "When you first let me out of the toilet, I thought this was a nightmare. Nothing seemed real to me. I was a girl trapped on a spaceship with a couple of guys, which sounds like the start of a weird story or a low-budget porn."

I snorted.

"Eventually, you and DJ and *Qriosity* began to feel more real to me than my life on Earth."

"Doesn't that scare you, though?" I asked. "Doesn't it piss you off?"

"Yes." She paused. "I used to hate my parents every time they dragged me to a new school in a new state where I had to start over again. But hating them didn't change anything." Jenny's face softened. Not pity, but not quite sympathy, either. "This is our life now, Noa. You don't have to like it, but you do have to live it."

"I know," I said with a sigh. "And I'm doing my best. I really am—"

"But some days are harder than others?"

I nodded. "Days like today."

"Why don't you go find DJ, then? He usually puts a smile on your face." She winked suggestively.

I rolled my eyes. "There's nothing happening between me and DJ. Nothing is *ever* going to happen between me and DJ."

"Uh-huh," Jenny said.

"I'm serious. We're friends. That's all."

Jenny's devious grin did not waver. "You keep saying that."

"Because it's true," I said. "Anyway, it's complicated. There was a guy on Earth—"

"Billy," Jenny said. "You've mentioned him. Please tell me you're not still hung up on a boy you're never going to see again."

"No!" I said it so loud that I startled Jenny, causing her to drop the game. It hit the floor and broke into a dozen pieces. Jenny gathered them together and laid them on the table. "Sorry about that."

"Whatever. Now it's a different kind of puzzle." She set about trying to fit the segments back together. "So you were shouting about how you're absolutely, positively not hung up on your ex?"

"I'm not," I said. "But, at the same time—"

"You can still love someone who hurt you."

"Can you love someone you hate?"

Jenny nodded emphatically. "Definitely yes. Is that why you won't give DJ a chance?"

"Jenny—"

"If we never get off this ship, DJ may literally be the only available human male you see for the rest of your life."

"DJ's nice and all, Jenny. Really nice. And sweet and cute and brave. But I don't want to wind up hating him." I didn't want to peel back his layers and find something awful I couldn't unsee. I wanted to always smile when I thought about him, and I wanted to look at him and believe he was a good person. Mostly, though, I didn't want him to wind up hating me.

Jenny tapped her fingernails on the table as she leveled a serious stare at me. "That Billy really hurt you, didn't he?"

"You have no idea."

"Tell me."

I considered it. Part of me wanted to. I'd never told anyone, and I knew that the longer I held on to it, the more it would fester inside me. "Maybe another time." I pushed my chair back and stood. "Speaking of DJ, he asked me to meet him in the garden."

Jenny raised her eyebrow.

"To help him clean the recyclers," I said. "It's a two-person job, and he said you already refused."

"Sure." She dragged out the word, and was still grinning obnoxiously when I left.

I made my way through the ship to the oxygen garden. I thought back to that first day. Waking up in medical and getting lost while trying to find the source of the noise that had turned out to be Jenny. Now I could navigate the ship with my eyes closed. I could barely remember what sunlight smelled like, but I knew the smell of the air recyclers when they needed to be cleaned. I couldn't remember the sound of the city, but I was familiar with the almost imperceptible hum that ran through *Qriosity* in the minutes before the fold drive engaged. I still thought of Earth as home, but *Qriosity* was my home now, and I hated how easily the change had occurred.

Jenny was right. I didn't have to like this life, but I did have to live it.

I knew something was off the moment I walked into the garden. The first clue was the sky. No matter what time of day the ship said it was, the fake sun of the garden's dome always hung overhead in a blue sky with gentle clouds that occasionally drifted by. It was always mid-afternoon and summer in the garden. Yet, as I pulled the heavy door shut, I noticed the long shadows cast by the innumerable plants and trees surrounding me. The dome was no longer pale blue. Orange fire blended into the red of an ember that faded into a soft, gentle pink.

The second clue was that the air was cooler than normal. Not cold—*Qriosity*'s computer kept the temperature within the optimal range for the plants in the garden to thrive—but not the tropical heat I was accustomed to.

"DJ?" I followed the path that wound through the garden, reaching out instinctively to touch the flowers as I passed, ignoring the tiny bee-shaped pollinating drones that buzzed near my fingers, attracted by the pollen that had attached to my skin. "DJ?"

"I'm over here, Noa!"

Sound traveled strangely under the dome. "Over here" could have been anywhere, but the recyclers were submerged in the pond, so I made my way there, expecting I would also find DJ.

"Did you change the sky?" I called.

"Yeah. To sunset."

"It's beautiful. I haven't seen a sunset in . . ." I hadn't seen a sunset since being abducted from Earth. And though I tried, I couldn't remember exactly how many days I had been gone. "DJ?"

"Hurry up," he said. "I got something to show you."

"How many days have we been on *Qriosity*?"

Before DJ answered, I reached the pond and found him standing at the edge, wearing a tan suit that didn't quite fit properly. The jacket was tight across the shoulders, his chest looked like it was straining the buttons, and he'd had to roll up the cuffs of his pants. But he was smiling, and his hair was combed off his forehead, and he was holding a delicate yellow flower in one hand.

"What . . . uh . . . what's going on, DJ?"

DJ flashed his dimples like he didn't know how utterly dangerous and disarming they could be. "I thought, maybe, since you always do the cooking around here, you might like it if someone cooked for you."

I hadn't noticed before, but there was a blanket spread out

on the grass, set with plates and glasses. "That was nice of you," I said. "Should I get Jenny?"

DJ coughed. His smile slipped, and the hand holding the flower trembled. "You see, Noa, I was kind of hoping it could just be you and me."

"Like a date?"

"Not *like* a date," he said, sounding unsure of himself.

I didn't know what to say. DJ had rendered me speechless even as a couple of things clicked into place. I would've bet money, if money had mattered aboard the ship, that Jenny had known about DJ's plan. She'd probably helped him organize it.

"I practiced cooking after you went to bed, and I'm not as good as you, but I made some spaghetti and garlic bread and a salad. It's not much, and I didn't mean to spring it on you, but I thought you'd like the surprise. This doesn't have to be a big deal. Just dinner. We spend a lot of time together, but we don't hang out much." As DJ kept talking, sweat beaded on his forehead and upper lip. It rolled down his temples and was probably soaking his back.

"Will you just say something, Noa? Yell at me for tricking you or smile or something."

I held up my hands and backed away. "No thank you." I turned and ran out of the garden. DJ's voice calling my name followed me as I threw open the door and headed to my quarters. I reached them and locked myself in. I crawled into bed, shut off the lights, pulled my pillow over my head, and closed my eyes.

TWO

THE TIMER I'D SET BEGAN TO BLARE AS I OPENED THE oven door. The moment the air hit it, the soufflé collapsed in the middle. It caved in more when I pulled it out of the oven. The whole disaster resembled a delicious chocolate sinkhole.

"Damn it!"

"Problems in the kitchen?" Jenny was sitting at the table, playing with a device the size of an apple that was composed of interlocking triangles. The metallic faces lit up different colors—red and blue and orange and green—as she twisted them into various positions.

"I can't get this soufflé right. I think something must be wrong with the ovens." I went to dip my finger into the creamy, spongy mixture, but before I touched it, I had a memory of being burned. I stood staring at the mess in the dish, feeling like I'd done all of this before.

"Jenny?"

"Yeah."

"Didn't the hologram say something about the fold drive causing déjà vu?"

Jenny said, "Jamais vu."

"What's the difference?"

"Jamais vu is not remembering something you know you've experienced. Déjà vu is remembering something you know you haven't. Why?"

I pulled my apron over my head, tossed it onto the counter, and joined Jenny at the table. "After I took the soufflé out of the oven, I was about to stick my finger into it to taste it when I was overcome with this memory like I'd done it before and had gotten burned."

Jenny had set aside the game she'd been playing with, but I kept stealing glances at it because there was something familiar about the device. Everything about this day was familiar. "How long did you work in Mrs. Blum's bakery?"

"A few years."

"I imagine you burned yourself a couple of times there."

I held out my hand to show her the faded scars on my fingers and wrists. "More than a couple."

Jenny nodded like that was the answer she had expected. "See? So you're probably confusing a time you got burned in the bakery with today." She picked up the device and began twisting it around. The triangle's faces changed colors as she shifted the pieces.

"I remember that, too." I pointed at the puzzle. "What is it?"

"I think it's a game; like a Rubik's cube," she said. "I found it in one of the science labs this morning."

"Oh." I buried my face in my hands. "Maybe I'm losing my mind. Being stuck on this ship for weeks has finally broken me, and I'm going quietly insane."

"Doubtful." Jenny patted my arm. "But if you're worried, get MediQwik to check your brain."

"I did that after I died," I said. "I was worried because of my father's history, you know?"

"You told me."

"MediQwik said I was fine." I let out a manic laugh. "But it didn't make me feel much better."

Jenny sighed. "Because if you were sick, you could get help. You're not sick, though. You're just—"

"Here. Yeah."

"Is that why you've been baking so much?" Jenny wasn't the sensitive, caregiving type. If I tripped and fell, she'd definitely offer to help me up and would ask if I was okay, but only after she finished laughing. So if she was concerned about me, she must have been more worried than she appeared.

"I feel like my life is on pause. Ever since waking up on *Qriosity*, it's like I've been stuck in this space between moments." I felt like I wasn't explaining it well. "Have you used Mind's Eye to explore Bell's Cove?"

Jenny nodded. "There's a cat café in town called Barista-Cats—"

"Of course there is."

"Sometimes I go there to hang out and play with the kitties." Tears welled in Jenny's eyes. "I miss August and Teeth."

"Your cats are named August and Teeth?"

"Shut up," she said. "You were the one who brought up Mind's Eye."

We'd gotten off track, and I had to think back to what we'd been talking about. "Right. Anyway, so you know how when you pause the simulation, the entire world freezes?"

Jenny covertly wiped her eyes on her sleeve. "It's creepy. The air gets still, the ambient noises disappear. Even the smells vanish."

"That's sort of how living on *Qriosity* feels to me. Like my life is frozen and I'm never going to move forward."

"But this *is* your life."

"Rationally, I get that. I really do. But there's a part of me that's still waiting to wake up in my own bed at home. To pick up where I left off with my mom and my friends."

Jenny bit her bottom lip like she was debating saying something. Finally, she said, "There's a psychologist in Bell's Cove."

"Dr. Kim," I said. "Yeah. Mr. and Mrs. Darling send Anastasia to see her in the fourth season because they're worried about the psychological damage being involved in so many gruesome murders might be causing."

Jenny hesitated again. "I've talked to her. Like, as a patient."

"You have?"

"Yes," Jenny snapped back. "And, no, I won't tell you why."

I held up my hands. "I wouldn't dream of asking." I sat quietly for a moment, thinking about Jenny seeking help from Dr. Kim. There was nothing wrong with needing help. In fact, asking for help is one of the bravest things a person can do. I guess I just hadn't thought about how our situation on *Qriosity* might be affecting her, and I should have. "Did it help?" I asked. "Talking to Dr. Kim?"

"A little," Jenny said. "You know how the characters can get when you talk about stuff they don't understand."

"Yeah."

Jenny went back to playing with her puzzle. She twisted and rotated the pieces, causing different parts to light up. I didn't understand what she was trying to get it to do. I wasn't sure she understood either.

"Well, I should go meet DJ," I said. "I promised I'd help him clean the air recyclers in the garden since you already refused."

A sly, suggestive grin crept onto Jenny's face. "Have a good time," she said in a singsong voice.

I gave Jenny the finger as I left the galley and made my way toward the garden. Maybe it wasn't such a bad idea to visit Dr. Kim in Bell's Cove. It was fine talking to DJ or Jenny, but I also had to live with them. There were things I hadn't told them, things I didn't want to tell them, that it might be beneficial to discuss with someone else. That was one of the reasons I visited Bell's Cove. To escape *Qriosity*. To see people other than DJ and Jenny, even if those people ultimately weren't real.

The first thing I saw when I opened the door to the oxygen

garden was the sky painted the colors of a crane lily. The ground fell away, and I wavered on my feet. Stumbled into the bulkhead and managed to stay upright, but only barely. Impossible memories filled my brain. DJ was going to be standing at the pond in a tan suit, holding a yellow flower. He never intended for us to clean the air recyclers. He'd invited me to the garden for a surprise date. And Jenny had helped him arrange it.

I couldn't catch my breath. I pressed my hand to my chest and fought for air. As the memories that had assaulted me began to settle, the dizziness receded. That couldn't have been déjà vu. That had been violent, as if someone had cracked open my skull and forced the remembrance of something I'd never experienced into my brain.

Slowly, I followed the path deeper into the garden. I remembered this, too. I called DJ's name. He called back. I found him at the pond. This time I remained quiet as I walked. As I grew closer to the end of the path, I prayed DJ wouldn't be there. Or that he would be wearing the overalls he usually wore when he planned to do particularly filthy work and not an ill-fitting tan suit.

"Hey, Noa."

The yellow flower. DJ held it out to me and smiled. God, he was so handsome, and there was a moment, brief and fleeting but real, where I considered taking the flower from him.

"This is a date, isn't it?" I said. "You lied to me about cleaning the air recyclers so that you could get me here." I pointed at the food containers sitting on the blanket on the grass. "Spaghetti, bread, and salad."

DJ stared at me like I'd unzipped my skin. "I mean, yeah. It wasn't really a lie, though. You could look at it like it was, I suppose, but—"

I ran from the oxygen garden, not bothering to listen to the rest of his explanation. I'd been right. How could I have known? Maybe I could have read subtle body language from Jenny. At best, though, that would have given away that DJ was planning *something*. Not what he was planning. Not what he was wearing. I'd known down to the way he'd cuffed his pants because they were too long. I shouldn't have. It should not have been possible.

I opened the door to medical, tugged off my shirt, and snapped the MediQwik cuff around my bare arm before hopping onto the table.

"Thank you for choosing the MediQwik Portable Medical Diagnostician and Care Appliance. How are you injured?"

"I don't know. But there's something wrong with me. I'm remembering things that I shouldn't be able to remember."

"Your heart rate is currently one hundred and seventy-five beats per minute, and your respirations are abnormally high. You appear to be suffering from panic-related tachycardia—"

I slammed my fist on the table. "I don't care about that! What's wrong with my brain? Why am I able to remember things before they happen?"

The door opened, and DJ, face flushed and sweaty, ran in. He was the last person I wanted to see, but I was also grateful he was there because maybe he could convince MediQwik to do its damn job.

"Noa?" DJ moved cautiously like he was afraid I might bolt again. "What's wrong?"

I laughed and laughed. "You wouldn't believe me if I told you."

DJ inched closer. "Try me."

"Fine," I said. "It started with the soufflé. I was going to taste it after I took it out of the oven, but when I did, I burned my finger. Except, I hadn't touched it yet. I only *remembered* burning my finger. But how could I remember something that I hadn't done yet? And then there was this conversation with Jenny. It went differently last time, but I remember the game she was playing with. You were the same, though. You made the dome look like a sunset, and I said I hadn't seen a sunset in a long time, and you said it was a date, and I said 'No thank you' and ran off because . . . well, that's not important."

DJ licked his lips and swiped his hand through his hair. "It's good you came here."

"It would be if MediQwik would follow my commands." I tapped the cuff with my finger. "What's wrong with my brain?"

"Your heart rate and respiration are dangerously high. Probable diagnosis is that you are suffering from a panic attack. Would you like to begin treatment?"

"No!" I said. But DJ said, "Yes, he would."

"I absolutely do not!" I told him.

"Immediate treatment is recommended," MediQwik said.

"I don't know what's going on, Noa, but you're not making sense, and I'm worried about you. Let MediQwik help you and then we can figure out what's happening together."

"You're not listening to me!" I tried to pry the cuff off my arm, but it let out a harsh beep, and the lights flashed red.

"MediQwik is initiating patient override protocol. Administering treatment directly. MediQwik, health redefined. MediQwik is a trademark of Prestwich Enterprises, a subsidiary of Gleeson Foods."

"DJ?" A cool sensation spread through my limbs, and the world slowed to a blur.

DJ approached and helped me lie back. "You're gonna be okay, Noa. I promise."

My eyelids grew heavy. What was I worried about?

"I'll be here when you wake up." DJ took my hand. It felt like he was touching me through two inches of foam rubber.

The drugs invaded my blood, they drowned my brain, but I fought the darkness. I clawed for the light. I felt helpless and alone even with DJ by my side. My eyes slid shut and I screamed soundlessly.

THREE

THE TIMER I'D SET BEGAN TO BLARE AS I REACHED FOR the oven door.

"Wait," I said. "It's not ready. The soufflé will collapse if I take it out now."

"Talking to yourself again, Noa?" Jenny called from the other side of the galley.

I remembered. I'd done this before. More than once. I walked around to the table and flopped down in the nearest chair, my mind in a daze. Jenny was playing with a familiar object. A game or puzzle. It was the first time I'd seen her with it, but I *knew* without a doubt that I had watched her twist and turn the pieces while trying to get the faces to light up the same color.

"Noa?"

I blinked and looked at her. "Call DJ and tell him to come here."

Jenny frowned. "Aren't you supposed to meet him in the garden?"

"To clean the air recyclers," I said. "But it's a trick. When I get there, he's going to be wearing a tan suit that doesn't fit well, and he'll be holding a yellow flower." I caught Jenny's eye. "Just get him here."

When DJ walked into the galley, Jenny's mouth fell open. She stared at DJ, then turned to me. "How did you know?"

DJ looked from me to Jenny, confused. I didn't blame him. "What's going on?"

There was no easy way to explain what I was experiencing because no matter what I said, they were going to think I was sick or delusional. I still had to tell them, obviously, so I just went for it. "I think I'm stuck in a loop. Like *Groundhog Day*. I'm repeating the same day over and over."

DJ pulled out a seat and fell into it like his bones had liquefied. "I know it feels that way sometimes, but—"

I shook my head. "Not a metaphorical loop. I'm pretty sure I'm literally reliving the same day. This is the third or fourth time. The first time, I burned my finger on the soufflé—damn!" I ran back into the kitchen, pulled on gloves, and grabbed the soufflé from the oven, but it was too late. The top was blackened and charred, and it had still collapsed in the middle. I dropped it on the counter and returned to the table, where DJ and Jenny were whispering to each other. I only caught the tail end of what Jenny was saying.

"—knew you were wearing *that* exact outfit," she said. "He mentioned a yellow flower, though."

"You had a yellow flower, and you had somehow changed the sky dome to mimic a sunset."

DJ nodded slowly. "I did have a flower, a yellow dahlia, and I changed the dome too."

I needed them to believe me. "You set up a picnic by the pond. Spaghetti, bread, and salad."

"Did you tell him?" DJ asked Jenny.

Jenny held up her hands. "I swear I didn't."

"I knew," I said, "because I'm repeating this day."

"Maybe we should go to the med suite." Jenny was speaking to me but looking at DJ. "MediQwik—"

"No!" I yelled. "There is no way in hell I'm putting on that cuff again." The memory of MediQwik drugging me, of my inability to fight, was fuzzy around the edges, but the terror I'd felt was as sharp as if it had happened only a moment ago.

Jenny's eyebrows rose. "No one's going to force you."

"Have we done *this* before?" DJ asked.

I shook my head. "I changed things when I asked Jenny to call you here."

"Demanded," Jenny said under her breath. She'd set aside the puzzle before DJ had arrived, and was eating a Nutreesh bar.

"Then let's talk this through." DJ bit his thumbnail. "Where does the loop start?"

"Here." I pointed at the kitchen. "Actually, in there. I'm standing at the oven, about to take out my soufflé."

"And where's it end?" he asked.

"Different places." I furrowed my brow, trying to remember

each loop. "I think it resets when I lose consciousness. Once, I fell asleep. Last time, MediQwik sedated me against my will."

Jenny looked surprised. "It can do that?"

"Can and did."

DJ said, "Have you noticed anything abnormal?"

I started to laugh, but neither DJ nor Jenny joined in. When I caught them watching me like they were thinking maybe they *should* take me to medical, I said, "Everything on this ship is abnormal."

"He's not wrong," Jenny said.

"Yeah." DJ sighed. "Why you, though?"

"I ask myself that question every single day."

"What I mean is why are you the only one of us who remembers?" DJ looked handsome in his suit, even if the shirt buttons did look like they were going to pop off. I shouldn't have been thinking about him, but I couldn't help myself.

"Why am I on *Qriosity*?" I asked. "Why did I survive death when Kayla didn't? I don't know. I'd love the answers, I'd give anything for someone to tell me, but things continue to happen on this ship that I have a feeling I'm never going to get a satisfactory explanation for."

"Calm down, Noa," DJ said.

I hadn't realized I'd stood. That I was leaning over the table, yelling. But I didn't want to sit down again. I didn't want to discuss what was happening to me like there was any chance we were going to be able to fix it. Each time something went wrong and we tried to make it right, we screwed up our situation even more. I didn't know how much worse my life could get, but I was sure *Qriosity* would be happy to show me.

Without another word, I left the galley, ignoring DJ and Jenny calling my name. I made my way to Ops and sat at my station. The simulations DJ, Jenny, and I had been running had made me a little more familiar with the console and how to work the computer, and I scanned the area around the ship for abnormalities. I wasn't surprised when the computer returned nothing out of the ordinary. The answer was never going to be that simple.

I recognized DJ's heavy footsteps approaching Ops. That boy couldn't have snuck up on a coma patient.

I barely spared him a glance when he sat at the station beside mine. "You doing all right?" When I half turned to glare at him, he quickly added, "Stupid question. Sorry for asking."

"Why is this happening?" I whispered. I wasn't expecting him to answer.

"I don't know," he said. "But maybe you could look at this as an opportunity."

"Are you serious?"

DJ nodded. "Do you know what I'd do if I had an infinite number of days?"

"Math."

"No," DJ said.

"Liar."

"All right, I might work on the Riemann hypothesis or P versus NP if I had that much free time." He probably didn't even realize he was smiling. He always smiled when he talked about math. "That's not the point, though."

"What is?"

DJ turned his chair to face me. "You can do anything you want. If you're really trapped in a loop, then your options are limitless. You could spend every day trying to solve the mystery of why you're repeating this day; you could learn every single thing there is to know about *Qriosity*; you could waste a million days doing absolutely nothing and still have a million more waiting for you after that."

Leave it to DJ to try to find the bright side. "It sounds exhausting, actually," I said. "This could be a fluke, though. Some weird side effect of the fold drive."

"Then let's test it scientifically."

"How?"

DJ tapped his chin. "Why not try going to sleep?"

I looked around Ops. "Here?"

"Why not?" he asked. "The worst thing that happens is you wake up in a few hours with a stiff neck. If you *are* stuck in a loop that resets when you lose consciousness, then you'll open your eyes in the galley."

There was definitely something appealing about the idea of unlimited do-overs. No matter how badly I messed up, I could go to sleep and reset the entire day. I wasn't thrilled that DJ and Jenny wouldn't remember and that I would need to explain the situation to them every time, but it was a small price to pay. Either way, I needed to know for sure, and I couldn't think of a good reason not to try DJ's idea.

"I can't sleep with the lights on."

DJ dimmed the lights, leaving the room lit by only the soft glow of the viewport and our consoles. "Do you want me to stay with you?"

"Would you?"

"Of course."

FOUR

THE TIMER I'D SET BEGAN TO BLARE AS I REACHED FOR the oven door. A smile slowly spread across my face.

NINE

I FLIPPED HEAD OVER FEET, LANDED AGAINST THE bulkhead, bent my knees, and pushed off toward the center of the cargo bay, crowing as I soared through the air. This was nothing like being in space because in the cargo bay I didn't have to wear the suit and there was plenty of oxygen to breathe. Here, I could fly.

"Why have we never done this before?" DJ asked, shouting from overhead where he was holding on to the ceiling cross-beams. He dove and pulled his knees to his chest, spinning like a pinwheel.

"This is amazing!" Jenny wasn't doing tricks. She was content to float in the currents created by the air recyclers.

"Because I only recently discovered that I could shut off the RealGrav plating here without shutting it down throughout the rest of the ship."

DJ caught the ladder and turned to look at me. "When did you become an expert on the artificial gravity system?"

"Today."

"You are so weird," DJ said.

I shrugged like this was old news. "Nice suit, by the way." I didn't always tell DJ and Jenny that I was stuck in a loop. Each time the day reset, so did they. Explaining the situation when all I wanted to do was have fun was a waste of time. DJ usually seemed a little annoyed when I spoiled his secret plans, but he never mentioned the date, so neither did I.

"Just trying something new," he said.

"It suits you." I winked at him. "Pun intended."

"It's too bad about your soufflé," Jenny said from behind me. "That would've made this day absolutely perfect."

DJ landed on the deck and pushed off toward me. He was red-faced and panting, but he was grinning like a fool, wearing his dimples loud and proud. "Nah. Today's perfect just the way it is. I don't think anything could make it better."

A grin slowly spread across my face. "Well, now, that sounds like a challenge."

SEVENTEEN

I DRAMATICALLY PULLED THE CLOTH AWAY TO REVEAL the spread I'd prepared. "Popcorn, of course. Individual lemon cakes, pretzel bites and cheese to dip them in, nachos—"

"What is all this?" DJ asked. He and Jenny were standing beside me in the cargo bay that I'd transformed into a movie theater. It had been easy to convince Jenny to give up her plans for the day, but convincing DJ to come along, without letting on that I knew he'd been planning a surprise date in the garden, had been more challenging.

"How on earth did you get the couch in here?" Jenny had targeted the snacks and was moving in for the attack. I loved that about her.

"I thought we could use a movie day," I said, answering DJ. "As for the couch, I lowered the gravity between the rec room and the cargo bay."

DJ eyed me suspiciously. He'd been giving me similar looks ever since I'd convinced him to abandon his surprise. "What brought this on?"

"Who cares?" Jenny asked through a mouthful of pretzel bites.

"Exactly," I said. "Can't I do something nice for literally the only two people in my life?" I stood with my hands on my hips, smiling at DJ. These past few days had been more fun than I'd had in a long time, even if I was the only one who remembered them.

"I guess," DJ said, but I wasn't sure I'd convinced him.

"Well, I hope you like movies starring Jenny Perez, because that's all we've got."

DJ climbed over the back of the couch to settle in. "Just as long as it's not a scary movie."

EIGHTEEN

"I HOPE YOU LIKE MOVIES STARRING JENNY PEREZ," I said, "because that's all we've got. I thought we'd go with a movie from her short-lived phase as an action hero since I know you don't like horror flicks."

DJ climbed over the back of the couch to sit. "Just as long as nobody's dog dies," he said. "I refuse to watch movies where dogs die."

NINETEEN

"I HOPE YOU LIKE MOVIES STARRING JENNY PEREZ." Before DJ could open his mouth, I added, "I chose one of her comedies since I know you hate horror films and movies where dogs die."

DJ climbed over the back of the couch to sit on the opposite side from Jenny. He glanced at me and smiled. "How'd you know that?"

"Because I'm stuck in a time loop and this is the third time we've had this conversation."

"What?" DJ said at the same time as Jenny said, "Huh?"

"Just kidding," I said. "Anyway, don't get your hopes up about the movie. It's a romantic comedy in which Jenny Perez plays a cat named Snowball who's been transferred into the body of a human woman. She then proceeds to fall in love with a man who's had the consciousness of a dog named Biscuits transferred into him. It's called *Purrfect Ten*."

Jenny clapped her hands. "I love this film!"

"Of course you do." I lowered the lights and started the show, wriggling into the open seat between DJ and Jenny.

The movie was objectively terrible. Worse than terrible. It was quite possibly the worst movie that had ever been made. If hell had a movie theater, *Purrfect Ten* would've been on the marquee every day. Despite how bad it was, DJ, Jenny, and I spent nearly two hours laughing, though not at the parts we were meant to find funny, and, for a while, life felt nearly normal.

During the scene where Jenny Perez's character crashed a funeral while wearing a cat costume, DJ scooted closer to me—so close I could feel the heat from his lips as he whispered into my ear, "This was a really great idea, Noa. Thank you."

When he pulled away and retreated to his side of the couch, I found myself wishing that he hadn't.

THIRTY-FOUR

I WAS SITTING IN OPS WITH MY FEET PROPPED ON THE console, eating the remnants of my failed soufflé while alarm Klaxons blared in the background and the computer issued dire warnings.

"Warning! *Qriosity* will self-destruct in one minute. Warning!"

"What're you doing, Noa? Shut it off!" DJ slammed his fist on the screen. His entire body shook and his face was splotchy and red, but he really did look good in that suit.

"No can do," I said. "And don't even think about trying to override it. You need my authorization code, and I'm not giving that up. Honestly, I thought activating the self-destruct would be a lot more difficult."

"Why?" DJ begged. "Why are you doing this?"

"Warning! *Qriosity* will self-destruct in thirty seconds. Warning!"

I licked the back of the spoon, trying to get every bit of chocolate. "You know what? I don't even think I like soufflés."

"Noa?! Please tell me what's going on!"

The anguish and betrayal in DJ's voice hurt my heart, but in less than thirty seconds he wouldn't remember it. He never remembered. He didn't remember the movie or learning to swim or when I'd accidentally overloaded the reactor while trying to shut it down. No matter what I did, DJ would forget everything when the day reset and began anew.

"You want to know what's going on?" I said. "I'm repeating the same day. This day. I've *been* repeating it for . . . I don't know. A long time. It was fun at first, but now I'm bored, DJ, and I want it to end. I *need* it to end. But it never does. It never, ever ends."

"I don't understand, Noa. Something's wrong with you. Let me help you. Please."

"Maybe next time, DJ."

FORTY-EIGHT

I WATCHED *QRIOSITY* DRIFT AWAY. I MUTED JENNY'S voice in my helmet calling me names and saying I'd lost my mind. I'd disabled the suit's remote controls so that DJ couldn't force me to return to the ship.

I should have died out here that first day. Maybe this time my death would stick. Maybe that's what all of this had been about. The universe was angry that I'd escaped death before, and it was punishing me by freezing me in amber and preventing me from moving forward.

My fingers fumbled at the latches on my helmet, but I finally worked them open and pulled my helmet free.

The stars were so beautiful with nothing between us. Space wasn't so scary after all.

FIFTY-THREE

DR. KIM POLK WAS A GRANDMOTHERLY WOMAN WHO walked with a slight hunch, smelled like peppermint tea, and wore enormous glasses, hanging from a chain around her neck, that made her eyes look huge.

"That's quite a story, Noa." Dr. Kim had been taking notes on a fresh yellow legal pad while I'd been talking, but she'd never once broken eye contact with me. I wasn't sure how she was interpreting what I'd told her—and I had told her *everything*—because the limitations of the Bell's Cove recreation in Mind's Eye made it so that the non-player characters often ignored anything that didn't fit into the narrative of their reality. I hoped Dr. Kim would be different.

"It's true," I said. "Every word of it."

"Then it sounds to me as if you need a physics professor rather than a psychologist." Dr. Kim's laugh accentuated the lines around her eyes and mouth.

I didn't laugh because I didn't find anything about my situation funny. I wished I *had* been able to laugh. I wished I'd been able to find the humor in what I was going through. It might have made my experiences slightly less painful. "What do I do?"

"I'm not sure I'm qualified to answer that."

"Great." I threw up my hands. "This has been a super waste of time."

I stood, but Dr. Kim waved me back down. "My son Louis is grown with children of his own now, but when he was younger and sprouting an inch a day, it seemed, I used to wish I could freeze him the way he was, prevent him from aging one single day more. But I would have been an awful mother if I'd kept Louis from changing. We become who we are by accepting the past for what it is, letting go of it, and moving forward." She took off her glasses and let them hang against her chest. She fixed her eyes on me and said, "You need to move forward, Noa."

"How?" Tears threatened to well up in my eyes. I could feel the pressure building. Feel the frustration of the countless days I'd spent trapped in one unending loop growing dense inside me, threatening to collapse under its own weight like that stupid soufflé I couldn't get right. "I've tried everything."

"Have you?"

"Yes!" My voice cracked. "I've scoured *Qriosity* searching for the reason I'm stuck in this looping day. I've run every emergency simulation in the database at least ten times. I've blown up the ship; I've blown up myself; I even blew up the shuttle trying to learn to fly it. During one loop, I stayed awake so long that I began to hallucinate that I was being chased by a monster that had already eaten DJ and Jenny. I ended that loop screaming, trying to dig through the floor. No matter what I do, I eventually fall asleep or die, and the day starts over again."

Dr. Kim put her glasses back on and scanned the notes she'd written on her legal pad. She tapped a line near the top with her finger. "Tell me about the first day you remember."

That first day seemed so long ago. For everyone else, it was still just one day, but for me, weeks had passed. Maybe months. "I already told you. I talked to Jenny; I went to the garden, where DJ was waiting with his picnic; I left and went to my quarters, where I fell asleep."

"Have you considered remaining in the garden?"

"With DJ and his surprise date?"

Dr. Kim let out a breezy laugh. "It's a date, Noa, not a death sentence."

I rolled my eyes. "Going on a date isn't going to help me escape this day. I'm beginning to think nothing will."

Dr. Kim watched me for a few moments. She wasn't even real, yet the intensity of her gaze was unnerving. She was definitely different from the other characters I'd interacted with in Bell's Cove. Finally, she said, "You keep insisting that you have tried everything, but you haven't."

"Still, I don't—"

"What could it hurt to try?" Dr. Kim asked. "If it goes badly, the day will end, he will forget, and so will I."

I chewed the inside of my cheek, trying to think of a reason why Dr. Kim's suggestion was ridiculous. "What if I—"

"Noa," she said in a firm but kind voice. "How can you expect to move forward if you never stop running away?"

FIFTY-FOUR

THE TIMER BEGAN TO BLARE, BUT I CANCELED IT AND set it for another five minutes.

"Smells good in there," Jenny called from the table where she was playing with the familiar puzzle. I peeked my head around the corner while I waited for the timer to go off again.

"Soufflés never work for me," I said. "But I'm hoping this will be the one."

Jenny shrugged, her attention on the game.

"What is the point of that?" I asked.

"To get all the lights to turn the same color?" Jenny glanced at me and crinkled her nose. "I only found it this morning and I'm already bored. I'm terrible at these puzzles." She held it out to me. "Wanna try?"

"Can't," I said. "As soon as my soufflé's done, I've got to meet DJ in the garden."

A smile crept across Jenny's face. "Oh really?" she asked, trying to sound innocent. "Whatever for?"

"It's a date," I said. "He thinks that I think I'm helping him clean the air recyclers, but it's a picnic by the pond."

Jenny's smile deflated slightly. "It's supposed to be a surprise," she said. "He's been planning it for days, so don't you dare ruin it."

"Why do you think I'm making the soufflé?"

I stopped by my quarters to change before going to the garden because there was no way I was going to show up to our surprise date wearing ratty jeans and a T-shirt with a hole in the armpit while DJ was wearing a suit. I didn't have a suit that fit, but I found nice pants and a collared shirt that weren't wrinkled. Balancing the soufflé dish in the crook of my elbow without burning myself while I opened the door to the oxygen garden was tricky, but I managed without dropping anything, which was kind of a minor miracle.

I stood on the path and took a deep breath. "This is ridiculous," I said to myself. "Why am I doing this? Because a computer program told me to? She's not a real therapist." But I couldn't deny that Dr. Kim was right. This was the one thing I hadn't tried. Not that I expected it to change the outcome.

"Noa?" DJ's voice seemed to be coming from everywhere at once, but that was just a trick of the dome. I knew exactly where he was.

"It's me," I said.

"Hurry up," he called back. "I've got something to show you."

I took the long way to the pond, dragging my feet even while I was anxious to reach DJ and get this over with. And then there he was. DJ, standing at the edge of the water by a picnic blanket laid out on the grass, wearing that tan suit with his hair brushed back. I'd seen him in that suit a dozen times, but this was the first time I really saw him. The slightly green cast to his skin, the sheen of sweat on his forehead. He was terrified. He was as scared as I was. Maybe more.

"What's that?"

I held up the dish. "A chocolate soufflé." The top had risen to form a perfect rounded dome. "I've never had one come out before. I thought it would go well with dinner."

DJ's mouth fell open, but no words escaped.

"I know this is a date, DJ."

"Jenny told you, didn't she?"

I shook my head. "Call it a feeling." I set the soufflé down beside the containers that held the rest of the food DJ had prepared. "You look nice."

DJ blushed furiously and plucked at the suit. "It's too small. And too big." He cleared his throat. "We should eat. Are you hungry? I'm hungry. There's spaghetti and garlic bread and salad. It's nothing like you would've made, but I managed to do this without setting the galley on fire."

"It looks great, DJ," I said. "Really."

DJ served dinner and we sat on the blanket to eat. Both of us seemed intent on keeping our mouths stuffed with food so that we didn't have to speak. The garden was filled with the sounds of the drone bees buzzing and the splashing of the small waterfall at the other end of the pond.

"I thought you might like the sunset," DJ said when he'd finished eating. He'd gotten a dribble of marinara sauce on his jacket, but I didn't bother to tell him. It was kind of cute.

"It's beautiful. How'd you do it?"

DJ shrugged. "It was easy, actually. I can change it to night, too. Or make it so that it keeps time with the same twenty-four-hour cycle that *Qriosity*'s running. I think it's always daytime to maximize the amount of light the plants receive."

"Makes sense." I leaned back and stared up at the smudges of color smeared across the dome. "I like it this way."

"Me too."

I caught DJ watching me. "What?"

"Tell me how you knew I was planning this," he said. "Did you see me cooking? I tried to do it while you were asleep—"

"It's not important right now."

"Oh." DJ picked at a blade of grass, pulling it up and tying it into a knot. "I wasn't sure you'd be happy with me for doing this. I was scared you'd run away."

Thankfully, I'd also finished eating or I might've choked. "Run away?" I forced a laugh. "Why would I do that?"

DJ cocked his head to the side and fixed me with a knowing frown. "I'm just going to take it as a good omen that you're still here and that you brought dessert."

"Speaking of dessert." I dished up the soufflé, which was still moist and warm inside. The chocolate was rich and decadent, and I didn't think I'd be able to eat much, as full as I was after dinner, but I ate every spoonful.

"Will you think badly of me if I lick my plate?" DJ asked.

"I'd think badly of you if you didn't."

DJ laughed, but he was seriously eyeing the remains of the soufflé stuck to the inside of the dish it had been baked in. I might have fought him for it, but I didn't think I could eat another bite without vomiting.

"How about a walk?" DJ asked. I agreed, and he helped me to my feet. We strolled through the garden, admiring the various flora that lined the path.

"Do you think all of these are from Earth?" I asked. "I recognize some, but others I'm not familiar with."

"I don't know. It's weird to think we might be wandering among alien flowers."

"Would it be any stranger than anything else we've experienced?"

DJ pursed his lips as he thought. "I guess not."

"I keep wondering why us," I said. "Like, why us specifically. There has to be something about you and me and Jenny that made someone kidnap and keep us here, but I can't figure out what it could be."

"Me neither."

"Did we do something wrong? Are we being punished for crimes I can't remember?" I stopped in front of a curtain of vines hanging from the catwalks overhead and breathed in the scent wafting from the orange flowers. It was like honey but with a salty undertone. When I turned to walk again, DJ was giving me a queer look. "What?"

"You think this is punishment?"

"Feels like it sometimes."

"Oh." His shoulders slumped as he walked ahead.

I caught up to DJ and nudged him with my elbow. "What?"

"Nothing," he said. Then, "It's just that this, being here with you, sure doesn't feel like punishment to me. It feels like maybe I did something all right in a past life that I'm finally being rewarded for."

"Liar."

"I'm serious!" DJ said. He took my hand and pulled me to a stop so that he was facing me. "I like you, Noa. You probably already know that because I'm not real good at hiding my feelings, but in case you don't know, I think you're amazing. I like how your smile reaches your eyes and how your nostrils flare when you get really serious. I like that you're stubborn and that not even dying can stop you. I like that you're brave—"

"I'm not brave."

DJ snorted. "If what happened to you the day we woke up here had happened to me, I never would've put on a spacesuit again. But you did."

"Out of necessity."

"Doesn't matter," DJ said. "You're brave, Noa. And stronger than even you know."

I shut my eyes and sighed. This was why I had walked away

that first day. Because I didn't want to do this. "You only like me because there are no other guys on *Qriosity*. If we were on Earth—"

"I'd be too intimidated to approach you."

"You are so full of crap," I said.

"It's okay if you don't have feelings for me, Noa." And like with everything else DJ said, he meant it. He would be hurt, but he would survive.

"It's not that."

"Then you *do* like me?"

"DJ . . ."

DJ pulled me closer. He leaned forward to kiss me, but I pushed him away. I didn't mean to shove him hard, but he tripped over a root protruding from the earth and fell. He hit the ground hard, knocking the wind out of him.

"I'm sorry!" I said. "I didn't mean . . . See? I screw everything up."

DJ stood, brushing himself off. "I'm fine, Noa. It's okay."

"It's not okay!" I marched back the way we came until I'd reached the pond. I took off my shoes and socks, rolled up my pants, and dipped my feet in the cool water. I heard DJ approach, though I wished he'd taken the hint and left. I couldn't wait for this day to end so that DJ would forget this had ever happened.

"What did I do, Noa?" DJ asked. "Whatever it is, I'm sorry."

"It's not you."

"Then what?" he asked. "Sometimes I feel like you might want more from me, but every time I get close, you push me away. Literally."

DJ was right. There were times, like while we were watching the movie in the cargo bay, when I'd felt like I wanted to be closer to him. There were moments when I looked at him and it was like I was seeing someone I'd known my entire life. Someone I never wanted to spend a second without. But then the past came rushing in, and I couldn't get away from DJ quickly enough. Maybe it wasn't DJ I was running from, though. Maybe it never had been.

"I met Billy on the bus. I was fourteen; he was eighteen and a freshman at the University of Washington. He smiled at me in a way no one had ever smiled at me before. In a way that made me feel visible.

"That was Billy's magic, really. When he looked at you, you were the sun around which everything orbited. I could hardly believe he wanted to talk to me. That he wanted to go out with me. This skinny, awkward, bookworm with big ears and acne."

DJ sat beside me, though he kept his feet out of the water. Not that I blamed him. I hadn't taught him how to swim in this loop. He sat close enough to hear me tell my story, but left enough distance between us that I didn't feel crowded.

"I didn't tell anyone about Billy. Not my mom or Becca or any of my friends. Billy belonged to me, and I belonged to him. We went to movies and out to dinner, and we sat around coffee shops arguing about books. Every moment I spent with him, I fell a little more in love.

"And he never pressured me to have sex with him. He knew I hadn't been with anyone, and he was cool about it. He told me we could wait until *I* was ready, which I thought I might be, even though I definitely wasn't.

"One night, after we'd been together a couple of months, he invited me to a party. I lied to my mom, said I was spending the night at Becca's, and snuck out of the house. I'd never done anything like that before. It's not who I was. My mom and I had an understanding, but I was worried she wouldn't understand this. I was afraid if I told her, she wouldn't let me go, and I didn't want to disappoint Billy.

"I was so excited. I was going to a college party with my college boyfriend, where everyone would be discussing literature and art and philosophy. The reality turned out a little different than I'd imagined. It was a party, but there were more keg stands than intense arguments about the deeply rooted damage caused by American colonialism. I didn't care, though. I had a couple of drinks. Billy introduced me to his friends, and he didn't seem the slightest bit embarrassed to tell them I was younger and still in high school.

"Whatever happened next, I don't remember much of it. I opened my eyes in a dark room. My head was swimming and someone was hurting me. I heard their grunts in my ear and felt their breath on my neck, and my pants were bunched around my ankles."

Tears ran down DJ's cheeks, but I kept talking because if I stopped now, I knew I would never work up the strength to start again.

"I was confused at first, but it didn't take long to understand what was happening, what Billy was doing. I knew it was him; I recognized the smell of his citrus body spray and the shape of his hands pressing into my back. I used to love the way his hands felt against my skin, but that night they were cold and callous.

"Maybe I should have struggled, maybe I should have cried out, but I just lay there like I was dead. Waited for him to finish and roll over and pass out.

"The second Billy started snoring, I got dressed and ran. My mom caught me sneaking back into the house, looking like I'd been mugged, and she smelled the alcohol on my breath, but I didn't tell her what had happened. I still felt the weight of Billy on top of me, and I was terrified if I tried to speak, all I would do was scream and scream and scream and never stop. So she grounded me. Took away my phone, which I was actually grateful for because it meant I wouldn't have to avoid Billy's calls or pretend to not read his messages. And he sent a lot of them.

"A week later, when my mom returned my phone, I read what Billy had written. Just seeing his name on the screen brought back the smell of his breath and the sounds he'd made as he'd pushed into me. But that wasn't the worst of it. Billy had been texting me like nothing was wrong. Like he was genuinely confused about why I was ignoring him. Like the party had been amazing and he hadn't done to me what he'd done.

"I threw my phone away and changed my number and stopped riding the bus line I'd met him on. I got tested for STDs. But none of that helped because I still loved him. I loved him and I trusted him, and he fucked me."

DJ didn't speak, and I thought I never should have told him because now he knew the truth and he hated me for it. And the longer it took DJ to say something, the more certain I became that DJ regretted bringing me on this farce of a date. He deserved better.

Finally, DJ said, "You have nothing to be ashamed of, Noa. You get that, right? You didn't do anything wrong."

"I didn't say no. I didn't try to stop him."

"You shouldn't have had to."

"Maybe."

"Why didn't you tell someone?" he asked. His voice was choked with tears. I could hardly look at him.

"Because as soon as I did, people would have stopped talking about how I showed up to the eighth-grade Halloween dance dressed as Ursula from *The Little Mermaid*; they would've stopped telling the story of the time I fell asleep during Mr. Martin's class and snored so loudly that everyone, including Mr. Martin, recorded it on their phones for a laugh. They would've stopped telling those stories and would've only told the story of how I was raped. And maybe I didn't want that to be the only story anyone told about me."

DJ knuckled the tears from his eyes. "Telling your story doesn't make you a victim. It doesn't signal that you're this one thing and nothing else. Telling your story in your own words shows the world that you're here. That you are *still* here, and that you're not going anywhere without a fight. It tells others who haven't reached a place where they feel safe that they're important too. You're not a story, Noa. You're a storyteller."

I wanted to believe DJ. I wanted to believe that every time he looked at me, he wasn't going to see what had happened to me. I wanted to believe that DJ was as honest and real as he seemed, and that he wasn't a liar like Billy had been.

I wanted to believe. But I didn't.

FIFTY-FOUR

"NOA?" DJ'S VOICE WAS CAUTIOUS. TENTATIVE AND soft. "Can you maybe come out of the airlock?"

I turned around. "It's not what you think. Trust me." I reached for the button to shut the airlock door.

"Wait!" DJ rushed forward and hit the touch panel on his side, which opened the door again. "What are you doing?"

"Look," I said. "I know what this looks like—"

"It looks like you're trying to end your life!"

"I'm not. I mean, kind of but not technically." I reached for the panel again. There had to be a way to override DJ's commands.

DJ jumped into the airlock with me before the door shut.

"This won't change my mind," I said.

As I moved to hit the button that would cycle the airlock, DJ shoved his body between me and the touch panel. "You're not doing this."

"Get out of the way, DJ."

"No!"

I tried to push DJ, but he was a brick wall, and I didn't have the strength to overpower him. "You think I'm planning to end my life, but I'm just resetting the day. It's going to happen no matter what I do. Popping open the airlock is just quicker than trying to fall asleep."

"What is wrong with you, Noa?"

"Nothing's wrong with me," I said. "Something is wrong with the universe." I tried to get past him again, but DJ's hand shot out and grabbed my arm. "Don't touch me!"

DJ yanked his arm back. "I'm sorry! But I'm not letting you do this."

"We're stuck in a loop, DJ. Don't you get it? This day repeats over and over." I waited a second to see if he understood, but he was still staring at me with that look of utter confusion and fear. "How do you think I knew you'd planned a picnic? How do you think I knew to bring dessert and to change into something nicer than what I was wearing? Because every time I fall asleep or get knocked unconscious or die, the day starts over. Every single thing resets right back to where it was. I'm in the galley, Jenny's at the table, and you're waiting for me in the garden."

There was no way I was going to get past him, but I also didn't think I could convince him I wasn't delusional. The best I could do was try and hope for the best. So I began at the beginning. I told him about every version of this horrible, unending day. By the time I finished, we'd moved out of the airlock and were sitting in the changing room, though DJ remained between me and the airlock door.

"How many times?" DJ asked.

I shrugged. "Fifty? Maybe a hundred. I lost track. And some days ended quickly, so I'm not sure if they count."

"And you have no idea why this is happening?"

"None."

DJ was shaking his head, but I didn't know why. "What?" I asked.

"Nothing," he said. "Except I don't think you actually want to stop the loop."

I was tempted to make another try for the airlock. "Of course I do."

"Do you? Because for someone who claims to want to move forward, you seem real determined to go back." I spluttered and tried to tell him he was wrong, but he kept going. "I understand how difficult it was to tell me about what Billy did to you, and I know it made you feel vulnerable, but what was the point if you're going to jump out of the airlock and make it like it never happened?"

"Yeah, well, it didn't happen to you." I crossed my arms over my chest.

"You're not the only person in the world who's been hurt, Noa. You're not the only one who's scared. Do you think it's easy for me to put my feelings out there knowing you might stick *them* in the airlock and blow them into space?"

"Of course not—"

"I care about you," he went on. "As a friend first. I was hoping for a chance to see if there might be more, but maybe I was wrong about you."

I snorted and laughed. "We're on a spaceship, DJ, we're lost, I'm stuck in a time loop, and you're worried about our relationship?"

"This isn't worth it anymore," DJ said. His shoulders relaxed and he hung his head low. He stood up and moved out of the way of the airlock. "You wanna jump? Jump. You wanna spend the rest of your life watching *Murder Your Darlings*? I won't stop you. But I can't keep trying to make you happy, Noa. I can't keep begging you to be part of this crew. To be part of our lives. I don't want to live the rest of my life on *Qriosity*, but I may have to. So I'm going to make the best of it. With or without you."

Then DJ did the one thing I never expected. He gave up.

"Wait!" I said when he reached the door. "You promised you weren't going to leave me alone?"

DJ looked over his shoulder. "Can't leave someone who's already gone." He turned around. "What're you waiting for? You wanted to start the day over. I'm not in your way anymore." He paused before adding, "Do me a favor next time?"

"What?"

"Don't come to the garden," he said. "That picnic was my last-ditch effort. I promised myself if you didn't come or if you got there and weren't into it that I was going to let it go." DJ sniffled and wiped his nose with the back of his sleeve. "What you did today, giving me hope and then snatching it away . . . I don't want to go through that again, okay?"

I felt like the air was being sucked out of the room even though I hadn't opened the airlock door. I tried to speak, but even if I'd had the words, even if I'd known *what* to say, I couldn't.

DJ left, and I was alone.

FIFTY-FOUR

I FOUND DJ IN THE GALLEY. HE WAS SITTING AT THE table, examining the puzzle I'd seen Jenny with earlier. As soon as I walked in, DJ pushed back his chair.

"Please don't," I said. "Please don't leave."

DJ didn't stand, but he didn't relax either. "Decided not to jump?"

I sat at the table, but I couldn't look him in the eye. "I miss home," I said. "I miss my mom and my friends and the Indian takeout place nearby that does the most amazing samosas. I even miss the things I hated like waking up early for school and people who spit on the sidewalk and late buses and rain."

"I get it," DJ said. "You hate it here and you wish you were home."

He was angry, and he had every right to be. "You feel like home to me, DJ. From the first time I heard your voice in my helmet, there's something about you that makes me feel like I want to be anywhere you are. And that scares me."

DJ sat up a little straighter. "Why?"

"Because if home is where you are, then what's back on Earth? By telling you what I told you about Billy, by admitting that I have feelings for you too—that I think *you're* the bravest person on this ship—then I'm letting go of the past. I'm giving up on ever seeing that home again."

"No you're not," he said. "We can make the best life we can here and still try to find our way back to Earth. It doesn't have to be one or the other."

"And I'm scared—" I stopped, paused. Took a deep breath. "No, I'm terrified that you're going to hurt me."

DJ leaned across the table and rested his hand on my chest. It was warm and strong and, for the first time, I didn't flinch. I didn't want to pull away. "You think it's empty in here, you think there's nothing but darkness, but you're wrong. There's more light in here than from all the stars in the universe combined."

I wanted to believe him, but it wasn't easy. I couldn't simply ignore the wound that had been festering within me since the night with Billy. I couldn't just decide everything was better and pretend I'd never been hurt before. I wasn't sure if it was even possible. There was only one thing I knew for certain. "I don't know what happens now, but I don't want you to forget." I rested my hand on top of DJ's and held both of our hands to my heart.

"Neither do I."

Of course Jenny chose that moment to walk in. I don't know what would have happened if she hadn't, but I knew what I was hoping would happen. I knew what I'd dreamed about from the first time I saw DJ's face. That had been déjà vu as well. Like meeting an old friend from a past life.

"Don't let me bother you," she said. "I was just looking for my game." Jenny grabbed the device from the table and turned to go.

"Wait," DJ said. "Where'd you get that?" The way DJ asked the question got me thinking.

"One of the science labs." Jenny was idly twisting the pieces.

"You think *that's* what's causing this?" I asked.

DJ shrugged, but he wore a determined expression. "Tell me exactly where you found it and when," he said to Jenny.

Jenny rolled her eyes and said, "I found it in the lab on deck three. The one near where we found the crew's storage containers. It was in the back of a drawer just sitting there. It looked interesting, so I grabbed it. I forgot it was in my bag until I was sitting here. The pieces looked like they moved, so I twisted them. That's when faces lit up. Then Noa's alarm started going off for his soufflé." She scowled in my direction. "Which I never got to try, by the way."

"The day always starts with that timer going off," I said. "It can't be a coincidence, can it?"

DJ turned his attention to Jenny. "Have you ever solved it?"

Jenny shook her head. "I *think* I'm supposed to make all the lights the same color, but I'm not sure."

"It's worth a try," I said. "Do you think you can do it?"

"Only one way to know." DJ held out his hand. "May I?"

Jenny passed him the puzzle. "Have fun."

DJ turned it around and around, examining it from every angle, before he tried manipulating the faces. Finally, he began to rotate and turn them. He muttered and mumbled to himself while he worked, and I'd never seen him concentrate so hard on anything.

After twenty minutes, Jenny got bored and ransacked the kitchen for Nutreesh, leaving me alone with DJ. "Maybe this—"

"I've almost got it," he said. "Are you sure you want me to finish?"

Did I want him to? What if it worked? Everything that had happened would stick. I would be free of this loop, finally able to move forward, but I would have to face the consequences of what I'd told DJ in the garden during our date. I couldn't pretend it had never happened. It wouldn't be fair to him, and it wouldn't be fair to me.

"Do it," I said.

DJ made two more turns. The faces of every triangle lit up cobalt blue. The device let out a chime like a meditation bell and then went totally dark.

"That's it?" DJ asked. "Did it work?"

I didn't know, but I felt like something was different. I was different. DJ took my hand when I held it out to him. "Let's go finish our date," I said. "We'll know if it worked soon enough."

ALIENS ATTACK!

ONE

I COULD FEEL DJ BREATHING. MY HEAD RESTED ON HIS stomach as he slowly inhaled and exhaled—in and out—and I was sure there was nothing more relaxing in the entire universe than this. I was reading one of the *Murder Your Darlings* spin-off novels, *More Murder with the Darlings: Knock, Knock. Who's Dead?*, in the garden while DJ napped. Tried to nap.

"I can't believe how bad this book is!"

"Then why are you reading it?" DJ asked.

"What else am I going to do?"

"I can think of a few things." There was a playful, suggestive quality to DJ's voice that made me grin because I knew that if I looked at him, he would be doing the same.

The past couple of weeks had been mostly boring. Nothing had exploded; none of us had become trapped in temporal anomalies; no strangers had appeared on the ship and then died.

DJ, Jenny, and I spent a couple of hours each day running simulations so that we could become comfortable operating the ship as a team, and we usually ate breakfast and dinner together. When Jenny left to do whatever it was she did when she wasn't with us, DJ and I took advantage of the time we had to be alone. We went on dates in Bell's Cove; we watched movies in the rec room; we relaxed in the garden and talked until Jenny found us and told us it was morning. We were getting to know each other, and I was enjoying every second.

The time I'd spent trapped reliving the same day had begun to blur together in my memories. My mom had told me once that the reason doctors give kids lollipops at the end of a visit is because what we remember of an experience is usually an average of the entire thing, with greater weight given to the end. It's the same reason why a woman will swear *during* childbirth to never again go through the pain and agony of it but will, after holding the baby and seeing its beautiful face, often convince herself that the suffering she'd endured hadn't been that bad.

I sometimes woke in the middle of the night, drenched in sweat, from a nightmare where I was trapped in a single minute of time, but despite my fears, the days did go on. Morning became night, night became day. Time passed, even if it sometimes *felt* like it didn't.

"What's your favorite color?" DJ asked. "I just realized we've been on *Qriosity* for a few months and I don't know what your favorite color is."

"Do I have to pick just one?"

DJ's belly shook. "I'm not sure you'd be you if you did."

"Are you insinuating that I'm difficult?"

"Pick a color, Noa."

I huffed playfully. "Fine. A tree-lined street on the first day that feels like spring has finally arrived."

"I wouldn't know anything about that," DJ said.

"Say what?"

"Florida," he said. "Remember? Land of perpetual summer?"

It was strange to me that there were places that didn't know the joy of emerging from hibernation at the end of winter and watching the world come to life. Places that never experienced the shift from summer to fall when the world curled in on itself to sleep during the dark months of cold and rain. Places like *Qriosity*, where nothing ever changed.

"I'm guessing your favorite color is green," DJ added.

"Yeah," I said. "But it's more than a color. It's the smell of life waking up and stretching its limbs, it's the feeling of turning a corner, a light at the end of the tunnel that's suddenly close enough to touch."

"Do you actually understand the concept of colors, Noa?" DJ was laughing when he said it.

"I'll show you colors." My book forgotten, I attacked DJ with a flurry of tickles that had him squealing for me to stop. Tears ran down his cheeks, and snot dribbled out of his nose. It wasn't pretty, but I refused to relent. And then DJ went on the offensive, and we were rolling in the grass, each one trying to gain the upper hand. DJ had the advantage of size and strength, but I was a slippery eel with fast hands.

DJ rolled on top of me and was leaning over me. His eyes were a blue break in the clouds, his cheeks the warm promise of sunrise.

"Hey," he said.

"Hey," I whispered back.

DJ plucked grass from my hair and used it to tickle my nose. "You know what my favorite color is?"

I shook my head, unable to speak.

"You."

"And I'm the one who doesn't understand the concept of color?" I tried to make a joke, but my voice was strained.

"You're my favorite color, Noa. And my favorite sound. You're my favorite part of the day, my favorite flavor, and my favorite program." DJ leaned in closer.

"DJ, I—"

Immediately, DJ reversed course. The reassuring weight of him on top of my chest lessened as he rolled off me. I hadn't meant for him to go. I hadn't meant to push him away. I wished I could explain it to him. I was trapped in that liminal place where everything I did with DJ was both a painful reminder of the past I was trying to move beyond and a promise of the future I could have if I were only bold enough to accept that I deserved it.

I wanted to tell DJ that the last couple of weeks had been *my* favorite everything, and that I had him to thank for it. That I was still scared of taking the next step, whatever that might be, but weren't we all afraid of moving forward? Weren't we on the roller coaster, poised at the apex of the drop together? I might not have been holding my hands in the air—I might have been white-knuckling the safety bar and trying not to vomit—but I was still on the ride, ready for the plunge.

I wanted to pull DJ back toward me, but I hesitated and he noticed.

DJ stood and brushed the grass off his pants. He held out his hand to help me up. "Come on. We were supposed to meet Jenny fifteen minutes ago."

"Can't we skip it?"

"Probably better if we don't," he said. "I'd spend every second with you if I could, but we can't exclude her. It's not fair."

"I guess you're right." I squeezed his hand, trying to use the contact to tell him that I didn't want to go. That I didn't want this moment to end. To tell him what I had failed to say with words.

I didn't know what was happening between me and DJ, but I didn't want to screw it up, and I was terrified I was going to.

TWO

JENNY WAS ARGUING WITH JENNY PEREZ WHEN DJ AND I strolled into the galley.

"But *why* are the cameras malfunctioning?" Jenny asked, drawing out the "why" like she was talking to a child. "You freely admit that you're recording everything that happens on *Qriosity*, which I still contend is deeply creepy, yet you never have recordings of the times or locations that I need."

I had never seen the hologram Jenny Perez look annoyed before, but she was currently doing a pretty fair imitation. "Unfortunately, I don't have an answer for you. But you're a superb junior detective, so I'm sure you'll figure it out."

"I'm not a junior—"

DJ cleared his throat, causing both Jennys to look our way.

"Finally," Jenny said. "You're late."

"We lost track of time," I said.

Jenny Perez's smile returned. "You seem to have organic matter in your hair."

Jenny busted out laughing. DJ quickly said, "It's grass."

I rolled my eyes and headed to the kitchen. "Leave it to the hologram to put it in the most ambiguously suggestive way." While Jenny and the hologram continued to argue, I looked around for something to snack on. Wrestling with DJ had made me hungry. "Hey," I called. "Did one of you eat the last of the lemon cake I made yesterday?"

"I'm a hologram," Jenny Perez said. "I lack the tangibility to consume actual food."

"No one asked you."

DJ called, "I had a slice last night, but there was still plenty left."

"It wasn't me," Jenny said. "And that's one of the things I was trying to get this useless hologram to show me."

Disappointed, I wandered back to the table. "Someone had to have eaten it."

"Exactly." Jenny motioned for us to sit. "I think there's another stowaway hiding on *Qriosity*."

"That's what this is about?" I asked. "We've been over this ship multiple times—"

Jenny raised her eyebrow sharply. "Talk less, listen more."

"My junior detective has collected some compelling evidence."

"I don't need your help," Jenny said to the hologram.

I was daydreaming about returning to the garden to roll

around in organic matter with the boy I had conflicted feelings about, when he said, "Why don't you tell us what you've got."

Jenny closed her eyes, inhaled, held the breath, and then exhaled and opened her eyes again. It was very dramatic. "It started with the blood on my jacket. The one I was wearing the day this nightmare adventure began. I wasn't injured, so I was fairly certain the blood wasn't mine, but I suspected that it might belong to whoever had locked me in the toilet." Jenny looked from me to DJ knowingly.

"Wait? You thought it belonged to one of us?" I said.

"Initially," Jenny said. "But I gathered DNA from each of you and asked the computer—"

"That's me!" Jenny Perez said.

"—to compare the samples."

DJ grimaced. "DNA samples?"

"Hair," Jenny said. "You both shed like dogs."

I wanted to protest, but Jenny wasn't wrong. My mom had complained about it too. "You said 'initially,'" I said. "Does that mean we weren't a match?"

Jenny nodded. "Correct."

"Were you able to test Kayla's DNA?" DJ asked.

"Not a match either." Jenny waved her hands around, flustered by our questions. "Which means someone else put me in the toilet."

Jenny had told me she was investigating, but I'd assumed it would be like the time I decided I was going to learn French. I downloaded a language program, signed up for a free online class, spent a couple of hours Googling pictures of handsome French boys, baked a dozen croissants, and then forgot about it and moved on.

"You could've gotten that blood on you before you boarded the ship," DJ said.

"Possibly, but that's not my only evidence." Jenny took another deep breath. "*Someone* wrote Noa the note in his hud for him to see when he first woke up in space, and they left you instructions as well, didn't they, DJ?"

"Yeah, but—"

"However, that doesn't prove someone else is on the ship. Whoever abducted us could have arranged the notes before leaving." Jenny rolled on confidently, and I wondered if there was a room where she'd taped our pictures to the wall and used bits of string to connect the various clues.

"Kayla proved that it was possible for someone to live on *Qriosity* without us knowing. We never saw her, and there's *conveniently* no video of her."

"How can that be?" I asked.

Jenny looked pointedly at Jenny Perez. "That's what I was trying to find out."

"Sorry about it!"

"I don't think you are," Jenny said.

Everything Jenny had laid out was odd, but odd on *Qriosity* was pretty much the norm. I didn't see how she thought there was still someone hiding on the ship. "How do you know Kayla wasn't the one who locked you in the toilet?"

Jenny glared at the hologram one last time. "Like I said, the blood wasn't a match, but I also don't think she ever left that room."

"She had to use the bathroom sometime," DJ said.

"Yes. She did." Jenny waved her hand in the air, and Jenny Perez projected a three-dimensional image of Kayla's quarters onto the table. "While you boys were picnicking, I searched that room one square millimeter at a time. Know what I found?"

I glanced at DJ. "I'm really hoping it wasn't gallon jugs of urine."

DJ snorted, earning me Jenny's ire.

"Show them the recording," Jenny said.

The image wasn't an image at all. It was video. And it began to play. On the recording, Jenny walked into the room and began crawling around on the floor, looking beneath the bed, pulling the furniture away from the walls. We watched as she found a Nutreesh bar under Kayla's pillow and began to eat it.

"You can skip ahead," Jenny said.

The video flashed forward, and suddenly Jenny was standing in front of the wall directly opposite the door with her hands on her hips and her head cocked to the side. After a few moments, she pressed her palm to the wall, and a door appeared that absolutely had not been there before. Jenny pushed it open and stepped inside. The recording ended there.

"Was that—"

"A bathroom, Noa," she said. "Complete with a shower and everything. It's the only private bathroom on *Qriosity* that we've found."

"Restrooms and showers are no-no zones for surveillance," Jenny Perez said.

"That's reassuring," I muttered.

DJ's mouth was hanging open. "A secret room with its own secret bathroom?"

"I know," Jenny said. "I'm totally blowing your mind right now."

"A little."

"But how does this prove there's someone else on the ship?" I asked. "The only thing this proves is that Kayla was trapped in that tiny space until she died." Thinking about her locked in there alone made me feel awful for the complaining I'd done. At least I'd had the whole ship to mope around in.

Jenny dismissed the recording. "That's where the mystery of the vanishing food comes in."

"Vanishing food?" DJ asked. "I didn't realize food was disappearing."

Jenny nodded. "There's the lemon cake that I swear I didn't eat the last of."

"The chocolate croissants," I said. "I accused Jenny of eating them during the repeating day from hell. When she said it wasn't her, I assumed someone was waking up in the middle of the night with the munchies."

"Wasn't me," DJ said. "At least, I don't think it was me."

"I don't believe it was any of us." Jenny waited until we refocused our attention on her before continuing. "Food only seemed to go missing when it was left out in the open, so I placed some treats in random locations before I went to bed. In the morning they were gone. But it still could have been one of you, so I repeated the experiment with Nutreesh because—"

"I would eat my own toenails before eating Nutreesh," I said.

"Exactly. And in the morning, they were also gone."

DJ turned to Jenny Perez. "How about video of that? Did you see who took the Nutreesh?"

"Unfortunately, there appears to have been a malfunction in *Qriosity*'s monitoring system during the requested period. Sorry about it!"

Jenny gave the hologram the finger. "See? I tried to go back to different instances where food went missing, and there was a *malfunction* every damn time."

I didn't know what to say. Neither, it appeared, did DJ or Jenny. It was a lot to wrap my mind around, and the truth was that DJ was the only mystery I was interested in unraveling. We could search the ship again, but we'd done that multiple times and hadn't found anything.

Jenny Perez coughed to get our attention. "I don't mean to interrupt, but there seems to be a problem with the water filtration system."

"What kind of problem?" I asked.

"A fairly wet one."

THREE

DJ SPRINTED TO THE LOWER DECKS WHERE THE WATER storage tanks were located. Jenny and I caught up a few seconds after. The doors to the room were shut, and DJ was heaving on the handle to force them open. The hologram hadn't told us what we might be walking into, and I wasn't convinced rushing in was the best idea. No one had asked me, though.

When DJ finally wrenched the doors open, lukewarm water streamed into the corridor.

"This seems bad," Jenny said. Again, she wasn't wrong.

Together, we sloshed into the room and immediately spotted the problem. A pipe as wide around as DJ's torso that ran from one of the enormous tanks into the wall was spewing water into the air like a fire hydrant. The sound of it was deafening.

DJ was shouting, but I couldn't hear him over the geyser. I had a pretty good idea what he was saying, though. We needed to shut the water off. The tanks were huge, and *Qriosity*'s water filtration system was exceptionally efficient, but we couldn't afford to have gallons of water spilling into the ship and going to waste.

I pointed at a valve on the tank, and DJ pointed at another where the pipe ran into the wall. We didn't know whether the busted pipe was carrying water into or out of the tank, so we needed to shut both valves to be sure.

We slogged through the ankle-deep water to reach the valves. I gripped the wheel in both hands and tried to turn it clockwise, but it refused to budge. I hoped DJ was having better luck than me. Jenny appeared with a crowbar, which she shoved through the spokes of the wheel. Then we each grabbed one end and used the additional leverage to turn the valve. Even with both of us, it was difficult, but the flow of water from the busted pipe slowly began to recede until it was nothing more than a dribble.

"Well, that was fun," I said.

"You needed the shower anyway." Jenny pinched her nose.

I shoved her playfully, and she pushed me back. Jenny felt like the sister I'd begged my mom for when I was little. Before I understood where babies came from or why my father was never around. Either way, I was glad she was on *Qriosity*.

"Uh, Noa? Jenny?" DJ sounded more serious than usual. "I think you should check this out."

DJ was standing over the busted pipe. There was a hole the size of a basketball in it, and the edges of the thick metal looked like they had been eaten through.

"I've never seen anything like this before," DJ said.

"I have."

Jenny and DJ turned to look at me.

"The day I died," I said. "There was a hole like this in the coolant conduit. Conduit F-519." No matter how hard I tried, I couldn't forget the details of that day. They were like the seam of a sock poking my toe inside my sneaker, irritating and impossible to ignore. The darkness of space, the sound of my own voice in my helmet. I remembered everything, right down to the taste of the air in my suit.

"That can't be a coincidence," Jenny said. "Right?"

I was starting to think that Jenny's theory about there being another person living on *Qriosity* might not be as far-fetched as I'd initially believed. Worse, though—that person might be a saboteur.

"What could do something like this?" DJ asked.

"I don't—" I stopped, and my eyes shot up to meet his. "Wait, we're thinking this is a what? Why not a who?"

"Whom," Jenny said.

The blood had drained from DJ's face. The last time I'd seen him that scared was in the video when he was pumping my chest in the airlock, trying to bring me back to life.

DJ sputtered, "I mean, I don't know, I guess. It might not be a what—"

Jenny ran her fingers over the ruined section of pipe. "No, I think you're right. Feel how the edges are pushed up?"

I traced the border of the hole. The metal felt rough and

jagged. It did not feel like damage caused by someone burning a hole into it from the outside.

"Are you saying that you think something came *out* of the pipe?" DJ asked.

But she didn't need to answer. Jenny, DJ, and I pressed ourselves together. The room took on a sinister quality. The receding water, which was less than a couple of centimeters deep now, could have been hiding anything.

"We should talk about this somewhere—"

"More secure," DJ said, finishing Jenny's thought.

"Ops?" I asked. "Maybe we can rig the scanners to turn inward and check the ship."

"Good idea," DJ said. "We should definitely do that."

A wave of déjà vu washed through me, and my knees nearly buckled. "Not again."

"What?" DJ grabbed me under my arms to help keep me upright.

"I've done this before."

"This?" Jenny asked. "You're stuck in another loop?"

I shook my head, trying to sort reality from my confused memories. "No, I don't think so."

DJ kept us moving toward the door. "Let's talk about it when we get to Ops."

But the feeling was growing stronger. "There was one loop where I tried to stay awake for as long as possible because I wanted to see what would happen. There had been a monster chasing me, but I assumed it had been a hallucination. I'd been awake for days by that point."

Jenny's voice was trembling when she said, "What happened?"

It might have been better if I hadn't said anything, but I couldn't keep it to myself now that I'd brought it up. "It ate you and DJ, and then it eventually got me, too."

"But it was probably a hallucination," DJ said. "You don't know for sure."

"Great," Jenny said. "We're being stalked by a monster that's got a taste for human flesh and lemon cake, and we're all out of lemon cake."

"Let's not panic." The way DJ managed to remain calm awed me. No matter what mess we stumbled into, he rarely let it fluster him. "We're going to—"

"Warning! Magnetic containment of Cordova Exotic Particle Reactor is failing. Total failure will occur in four minutes and seven seconds. Warning!"

DJ's calm vanished. Without a word, he dashed into the corridor at a dead run.

"Wait!" Jenny called. She turned to me. "Where's he going?"

"Reactor Control," I said. "Probably. Come on!" I took off after DJ, running as fast as I could. Climbing the ladders recklessly. There might have been a dangerous monster on the ship with us, but that wouldn't matter if the reactor's containment failed and *Qriosity* exploded.

I was running so fast that I nearly missed the door to Reactor Control. Jenny had fallen behind, but I could hear her cursing me for not slowing down, DJ for taking off without saying why, and *Qriosity* for not having an elevator.

DJ was standing at a console, tapping the screen furiously. As I entered the room, a metal shield lowered around the core and the doors slammed shut behind me. "Warning! Radiation exposure protocol has been activated. Warning!"

Jenny banged on the doors even as I yanked on the latch to open them. "DJ? Noa? Are you in there?" The doors were too thick for her voice to travel through. I was hearing her over the comms. "I can't get in!"

"We're in here!" I yelled back, though I wasn't sure she could hear me. "What the hell is going on, DJ?"

DJ didn't reply. He didn't even look up from what he was doing.

"Noa?" Jenny called again. "Oh! Oh God, I think there's something out here! Open the door! Noa, open the damn door!"

The lights flickered once and then died, plunging the room into darkness.

A loud clang like a bell echoed through the room.

Jenny screamed.

FOUR

I CALLED JENNY'S NAME. I CALLED DJ. NEITHER answered. I would have given one of my ears for light to see by. I didn't know why the power had failed or why the loss hadn't triggered the emergency lights. I had no idea if Jenny was alive or why DJ wasn't responding. Anything could've been hiding in the dark. Anything could have been waiting for me to move within reach of its grasping limbs so that it could snap my neck and eat me in peace.

"DJ?"

If DJ had answered, he would have told me that everything was going to work out. That we were safe. But I didn't feel safe. The current crisis reminded me of the sci-fi flick starring Jenny Perez, *Project Vortex: In the Beginning*. The movie's premise is that an alien infiltrates a deep space vessel, the ENS *Eden*, stalks, and kills the entire crew except for Jenesis Paine, the ship's medic played by Jenny Perez, who survives by putting on a spacesuit and luring the alien monster out of the ship, where she wrestles it into submission and then flings it into a nearby star. I'd seen the movie six times, and I'd given up expecting it to make sense.

I'd been in Ops when the fold drive had last engaged; the nearest star to *Qriosity* was over ten light-years away, so we wouldn't be doing that.

The emergency lights flickered on, filling the room with an ominous red glow that made me feel like we were definitely trapped in hell. But hell was better than nothing. I scanned the room and spotted DJ crumpled on the floor in front of the console he'd been working at earlier.

"DJ!" I crawled across the floor to him. Blood stained his face from a gash on his forehead. His eyelids fluttered when I rolled him over, and he turned to the side and vomited. The sharp tang triggered my gag reflex, and I tugged my shirt over my nose and turned away. As soon as DJ had emptied his stomach, I dragged him to the other side of the room.

"DJ? Talk to me. Are you okay?" I pulled off my shirt and pressed it to DJ's head to stanch the bleeding. There was so much blood, but my mom had told me once that even superficial head wounds bled a ton, often making the injury seem worse than it was.

"Ow." DJ tried to touch his forehead, but I batted his hand away.

"You hit your head pretty bad. You're bleeding and probably have a concussion, so take it easy." I wasn't sure how DJ had hurt himself, but everything on *Qriosity* seemed like it was designed to kill or maim us, so it could have been anything. "Do you know what happened to the lights?" I asked. "Did the reactor shut down again?"

"No." DJ spoke slowly as I cradled his head in my lap, keeping pressure on the wound. "The magnetic shield around the reactor was fluctuating. I shunted power from non-essential systems to shore up containment."

"Good thinking."

DJ smiled weakly. "Where's Jenny?"

I'd been so busy being scared of the dark and then worrying about DJ that I'd forgotten about Jenny. She was out there alone. No, she wasn't alone. She'd said there was something in the corridor with her. "She was right behind me, but the doors shut and I couldn't open them, and she was screaming. DJ, we have to get out of here so we can find her."

"Help me up."

I lifted DJ gently out of my lap, stood, and tried to pull him to his feet, but he clutched his head and doubled over, moaning in pain. I lowered him back to the floor. "Yeah, that's not going to work."

"I'm sorry, Noa. I'm sorry." DJ repeated it over and over, his voice thick with tears.

I smoothed back his hair, combing my fingers through it and whispering to him that it was okay. DJ tried to close his eyes, but there was an episode of *Murder Your Darlings* where Marco had suffered a concussion while helping Anastasia solve the case of a serial murderer who targeted brown-haired baristas. He'd gone undercover at the Happy Bean and had been assaulted while emptying the spent coffee grounds into the compost bin. When Anastasia had found him, she'd told him that he shouldn't fall asleep with a concussion or he might not wake up.

I doubted the show was a useful source of sound medical advice, but I refused to take risks when it came to DJ.

"Eyes open, DJ." I gave his arm a gentle squeeze. "I need you to talk me through how to fix this mess. We've got to unlock the doors. Jenny might be in trouble."

DJ opened his eyes wide and blinked like he was trying to convince his body that he didn't want to sleep. I peeled back my shirt, which was now soaked through with DJ's blood. The wound was still bleeding. I hopped up and grabbed the first aid kit from the other side of the room. I dug out the tube of InjureEZ Wound Sealant and squeezed the gray paste across the gash. Almost immediately, it spread to cover the cut, and DJ's face relaxed at the same time.

"How does that feel?" I asked after I'd wrapped gauze around his head.

"Little better."

"Do you think you can help me?"

"I'll try," he said through clenched teeth.

I hated that he was hurting, and I wished I could take him to medical so MediQwik could work its science magic, but I couldn't unseal the doors without him. I took my bloody shirt and spread it across the vomit puddle by the console so that I didn't have to look at it, but the smell was overpowering. My stomach lurched.

"Doors first, okay?" I said.

"Yeah." DJ might've had a concussion, and he might have been a little sluggish, but he was still the smartest person I knew. If anyone could get us out of the reactor room, it was him. "What's the screen say?"

The terminal was filled with readouts of the various systems, most of which I was unfamiliar with, but a flashing alert at the top of the screen caught my attention. When I tapped it for more information, the floor dropped out from under me.

"There was a radiation leak, DJ. That's why the doors sealed shut." I immediately began imagining my hair falling out and my skin sloughing off. Tumors bursting from my skin. Of all the ways I'd nearly died aboard *Qriosity*, radiation was my least favorite.

"How much radiation?" DJ asked, sounding infinitely more calm than me.

"This doesn't say," I told him. "It only says that we'll reach fatal exposure in four hours."

"Four hours is plenty of time." DJ had scooted into a sitting position and was watching me patiently. His face was covered in blood, he had a concussion, and we were both being irradiated to death, but he looked like he had everything under control. Like we were still in the garden arguing about colors.

"What about Jenny?" I asked.

"We can get the comms working," DJ said. "Then the reactor."

I stood over the console completely certain I had no idea

what I was doing. How was I supposed to fix anything when there might be a monster loose on the ship? When Jenny might be fighting for her life? When *Qriosity* might explode?

"How do I do this?" I hadn't meant to say it out loud.

"I'll talk you through it."

"That's not what I meant," I said. "How do I do *anything* right now?"

"You just do it. You do it because not doing it could be the difference between surviving and not. You do it because no one else can."

DJ's pep talk didn't make me less terrified, but it did get me moving. "What do I do first?"

One step at a time, DJ walked me through how he'd diverted power from secondary systems to the magnetic containment field that shielded us from the reactor core, and explained how to return power to the communications system.

"Will we lose containment again if I do this?" I asked. "I don't want to dump more radiation into the room."

DJ shrugged. "Probably not. Internal comms aren't a big drain on the system."

"You're guessing, aren't you?"

"Maybe a little," he said.

"How often do you do that?"

DJ looked away sheepishly. "It's an educated guess. I didn't have time to calculate exactly how much power the containment system needed, so I threw everything at it just to be sure."

I laughed out loud, letting the sound fill the room with

madness. "We really are one stupid mistake away from death out here. We're kids playing with stuff we don't understand."

"Noa—"

"It's a miracle we haven't blown up *Qriosity* yet." I chose to believe the numerous times that I *had* blown up the ship during my time loop didn't count.

When my laughter faded, DJ said, "Either we give this a try or we abandon Jenny. You know what she would do."

"Leave us and save herself?"

"Not a chance," DJ said. "She loves your baking way too much to let you die."

I said a silent prayer, held my breath, and redirected power back to comms. I waited for an alarm to warn me that containment was failing again, but a minute passed and nothing changed. The computer said we were still four hours from dying of radiation poisoning. I tried the comms.

"Jenny? Jenny, can you hear me?"

I waited again. Waited for Jenny to respond. She should have been able to hear me no matter where she was.

"Why isn't she answering?"

"I'm sure she's safe," DJ said. "She's too smart to die."

"But she said something was out there with her, and she sounded so afraid, and then she screamed—"

"Take a breath, Noa, and let's see what we can do to open the doors."

DJ's first suggestion was to attempt to override the radiation containment protocols. The work went slower than it would have if he'd been the one doing it instead of having to explain it to me, but I tried my best, and he was patient. The computer, however, refused to cooperate.

"Damn it!" I said. "I think this means there's still radiation leaking from the core, but I barely understand any of this nonsense."

"It's okay," DJ said. "We'll just have to fix the radiation leak. We can do that."

I turned around and leaned my head back, raking my fingers through my hair. "Why does everything on *Qriosity* have to be so difficult? I miss home."

I expected DJ to tell me that home was far away and we had to focus on the problems we could solve, but instead he said, "I miss the ocean."

"Even though you don't know how to swim?"

"Sometimes I would stand at the edge of the water and stare at the horizon. It reminded me how small I was. How I was to the world what a grain of sand was to the beach." DJ didn't talk about home often, and I was surprised to hear such a deep sense of loss and need in his voice.

"I miss my phone."

"I miss having music to listen to while I run," DJ said.

With a laugh, I said, "You could listen to Jenny Perez's albums, though I'm not sure they qualify as music."

DJ wrinkled his nose. "I tried. Her singing was . . . not good."

"You know what I miss? The lasagna at Machiavelli's." My mouth watered as I thought about it. "They're a tiny restaurant that doesn't take reservations, so my mom and I would arrive right at opening to make sure we could get a table."

"*Your* lasagna's pretty good," DJ said.

"It's dog food compared to theirs. There's something about their sauce, and I could never figure out—"

"Noa? DJ?" Jenny's quavering voice spilled into Reactor Control through the speakers. "Is anyone there?"

"We're here!" I shouted. "Jenny, are you okay? Are you hurt? We're trapped in—"

"We were right," she said. "There's a monster on the ship. It almost—" Her voice cracked, and it sounded like she was fighting back sobs.

"Tell me you're safe, Jenny. Are you injured?"

A couple of seconds passed in silence. I threw DJ a worried look. His body was tense like he was going to attempt to stand and pry open the doors with his bare hands.

"I'm . . . I'm fine," Jenny said. "Just my leg. But, Noa, the monster, it's horrible. You have to help me."

"Where is she?" DJ whispered.

"Where are you?"

"I'm in—" Jenny broke off, leaving us hanging on her last word. When she finally returned, she whispered, "It's here! I have to go. Please hurry!"

FIVE

I FELT UTTERLY USELESS. DJ TALKED ME THROUGH repairing the magnetic shielding, which prevented more radiation from leaking into the room, but Jenny was out there alone being hunted by a monster and we were still dying of radiation poisoning. I was doing everything I could, but it wasn't enough.

"That's it," DJ said.

My mind had been working on autopilot. Following DJ's commands without actually paying attention to what I was doing. "We still can't open the doors. Why can't we open the doors?"

DJ had me help him to the console. He was looking worse. His skin was pasty, and his eyes were empty hollows. "The radiation cleanup protocols have kicked in. As soon as the levels are low enough, the doors will open on their own."

"Meanwhile we just sit here and let it kill us?"

"I don't see any way to override them." DJ shuffled back to sit against the wall. "It'll be okay, Noa. MediQwik should be able to fix us right up when we get out of here." I wished I could borrow a little of his confidence. Even a thimbleful would have been better than what I had.

With nothing left to do but wait, I sat beside DJ and rested my head on his shoulder. "What else do you miss from home?" I asked.

DJ shifted and cleared his throat. "I don't know, Noa. Lots of stuff. Why do we have to talk about it?"

"You always do that when I bring up home," I said. "Either you change the subject or you shift the focus to me. Anything to avoid talking about your past. Is it your parents? Were they awful to you?"

"No," DJ said. "My folks were fine. Kind of clueless, but I think most adults are. Some are just better at pretending than others."

"Was it him?"

"Who?"

"The guy you told me about," I said. "Your ex?"

"Noa—"

"I'm not jealous." At least, that's what I told myself. "How am I supposed to get to know you if you keep parts of yourself locked away?"

"Because those parts are in the past."

"Doesn't the past make us who we are? Aren't we just the sum of our memories?" DJ tried to interrupt, but I hushed him.

"If he hurt you, I understand if you don't want to talk about it."

DJ said, "He didn't hurt me. More like the opposite."

Sometimes knowing when not to speak is as important as knowing when to speak. I could sense DJ's trepidation, his fear, but I could also feel that he wanted to talk. That maybe he needed to. And that he would if I gave him some space.

"He was so stubborn." DJ began slowly, his voice soft. "When he got an idea in his head, nothing could change his mind. Telling him something couldn't be done was a sure way to make certain he tried to do it.

"He never gave up either. Not ever. He could have been the last person on the planet, facing down a horde of bloodthirsty monsters, and he would've shrugged and said he liked those odds."

Once DJ started, the words poured out of him. I had convinced him to open the floodgates, and I was beginning to regret it.

"His sense of humor was wicked. I never laughed so much as I did when we were together. But behind the sarcasm and the jokes was someone who was kind and compassionate. He always made sure to laugh with people instead of at them."

How could I compete with someone like that? How could I compete with a ghost? I had to wall off the jealousy that seethed within me; I had to remind myself that I had pushed DJ into this conversation.

"You miss him a lot, don't you?" I asked.

"Yeah."

"Do you think you'll ever see him again?"

"No," DJ said. "He's gone, and I won't ever get him back."

"But if you could," I asked.

"Noa—"

I shifted my body away from DJ. "I mean, he sounds great. I can see why you miss him. What I can't see is why you'd want anything to do with me."

"You're completely different people, Noa."

"That's obvious," I shot back. "He's brave, I'm a coward. He's funny, I'm basically the human equivalent of Valium. He never gives up, I give up at the first bump in the road."

DJ slid his hand into mine and laced our fingers together. "None of that's true and you know it."

"But if you could have him over me, you'd take him, wouldn't you?" I shook my head. "No need to answer. I already know. Hell, I'd take him over me."

"He's my past, Noa, but you're my future. I hope." DJ took my chin in his hand and turned my face toward his. He leaned in to kiss me. His lips barely grazed mine. I wanted to close my eyes and fall into it. I wanted to fall into him. Instead, I flinched. My body seized and I pulled back.

DJ lowered his eyes. "Sorry—"

"No, DJ, I didn't mean—"

"Noa? DJ? Are you there?"

I was annoyed at Jenny because now DJ was going to think I had flinched because of him. At the same time, I was grateful to her for saving me from embarrassing myself further.

Reluctantly, I let go of DJ's hand. "Jenny? We're here. Where are you?"

Jenny sounded more composed than she had last time. Less consumed with panic as a result of being stalked by something that was going to eat her. But only just barely. "I'm hiding in the shuttle."

"Are you hurt?" I asked. "Where's the monster? Is it a monster?"

DJ squeezed my knee and threw me a look that was like, *Give the girl a chance to answer.*

"It's definitely a monster." Jenny was breathing hard. I couldn't imagine what she'd been going through. "It grabbed my leg and secreted some kind of juice that burned me pretty bad. I can still run, though."

My heart dropped. Jenny was out there, hurt and alone, and DJ and I were trapped and couldn't help her.

"I don't know what the hell it is, Noa, but it's big."

"Tentacles?" I asked.

Jenny stifled a horrified laugh. "No. But it's got teeth. Lots and lots of teeth."

"Jenny?" DJ said. "Can you stay in the shuttle? Are you safe there?"

"I'm safe for now." Jenny paused. "But I don't know for how long. It burned through the door to the cargo bay. I only escaped because I've searched the ship so many times that I know where every service tunnel is."

What the hell could burn through a two-inch-thick pressure

door? If the monster got tired of chasing Jenny and tried to get through the door to Reactor Control, it could flood the entire ship with radiation. And also kill us.

"Any chance I could get some help from you guys?" Jenny asked. "I could really use it."

"We're trapped in Reactor Control," DJ said. I mentally added, *Slowly dying from radiation exposure*, but kept it to myself because Jenny had enough problems to deal with.

"You're working on escaping, though, right?"

"Yeah," DJ said. "We're doing our best, but I don't know how long it's going to take. Just stay—"

"It's here!" Jenny's voice dropped to a whisper again. "I have to go."

DJ and I waited for Jenny to come back, but the comms remained silent.

SIX

THE SHIP WAS TOO BIG AND THE ROOM WAS TOO SMALL, and Jenny was out there fighting for her life while DJ and I were trapped and unable to do anything to save ourselves except wait. Despite that, despite the desperate circumstances in which we were imprisoned, I couldn't stop thinking about DJ's lips as I paced the room. About kissing his lips. About what they would feel like pressed against mine—would they be warm? Would they be dry or soft or smooth?—about what they would taste like, about how it might feel to be touched by someone with the lights on and whose face I could see.

"How're you feeling?" I asked.

It had been maybe an hour since we'd last heard from Jenny, and I imagined a million different scenarios, each worse than the last. In one she was strung up from the ceiling in a web of alien mucus, frantically trying to free herself as the monster crept closer, its jaws widening so that she could see each of its razor-sharp teeth. In another, the alien paralyzed her but left her conscious so that she would remain awake while it slowly devoured and digested her, unable to move. Unable to scream. I tried to turn my thoughts to more productive tasks, but there was little I could do that I hadn't already done. Thinking about DJ was the only thing that took my mind off Jenny, and I felt guilty as hell about it.

DJ had managed to stand and was working quietly at the station farthest from where he'd emptied his stomach. "Head still hurts," he said. "But it's not too bad."

"Maybe you should sit." I stopped pacing. "My mom told me this story about a guy who hit his head and thought he was fine because he seemed fine, but then he dropped dead a few hours later because it turned out his brain had been bleeding and eventually the pressure built up so much—"

"My brain's not bleeding."

"You don't know that."

DJ turned around. "You're right. I don't." He returned to his work.

I peeked over his shoulder and tried to figure out what he was up to, but no matter how much I learned about *Qriosity*, DJ knew more. "What're you doing?"

"Trying to use the ship's sensors to scan inside *Qriosity* like you suggested before this mess started," he said. "We might not be able to reach Jenny, but we might be able to help her stay one step ahead of the monster."

"You remind me of my mom," I said. "In a good way. She's cool in a crisis and so are you. You could be a firefighter or a nurse or a doctor." I paused and thought about what I'd said. "Could've been, I guess. We don't need nurses or doctors as long as we have MediQwik, do we?"

DJ swore under his breath. It was the first time I'd ever heard him cuss, which I took as a sign that things were not going well. He sighed and leaned over the console. "I'm not calm," he said. "And I'm not good under pressure either."

"Then you're a hell of an actor."

"Yeah." DJ waved at the console. "I can't scan the ship. I might be able to reroute the systems from Ops, but we can't get there." He threw up his hands. "Jenny's on her own."

"She's resourceful," I said. "That monster should be scared of her."

DJ eased himself back to the floor and leaned his head against the bulkhead, closed his eyes. "I'm not going to sleep," he said as I was opening my mouth to remind him he shouldn't.

I resumed pacing. Back and forth across the room. I couldn't see the radiation that was poisoning me, but I swore I could feel it invading my cells, killing them slowly. Killing me. And what if MediQwik couldn't save me this time? What if there was a limit to how many deaths MediQwik could reverse, and I had exceeded mine? Death was how the universe reminded us we were unimportant, but DJ was important to me—he had become important slowly, sneaking into my life one smile and kind word at a time—and I didn't want to die without letting him know.

"I'm sorry," I said. The words burst out of me like an accusation rather than an apology.

"For what?"

"Being me. For not being him. For pushing you away every time you try to—"

DJ frowned. "Noa, I don't want you to be anyone but you. Not ever." His face softened, and my knees nearly buckled. "As for pushing me away, I'm the one who's sorry. I made you uncomfortable, and I should've been more considerate."

I sat across from him, pulling my legs under me. "It's not you, DJ. It's him. It's my past. It's the memories that I can't escape."

"Hey," DJ said softly. Gently. "You told me you didn't want that to be the only story folks told about you, right? Well, memories are just stories we tell ourselves to make sense of the past, so don't let that one memory become the only story *you* tell about yourself. Who we were isn't who we are; it doesn't limit who we can be."

I tried to imagine what Becca would've said if she were there. Or what advice my mom or Mrs. Blum would've given me. Mrs. Blum's advice was usually something like, *Go to the gym. You can't knead dough with noodles like those*. But even she probably would have agreed with DJ. The problem was that it was easier to know what to do than to actually do it.

"You don't under—"

"He died, Noa. He's gone." DJ's expression was solemn, his voice flat. "I watched him die. I *watch* him die every night when I sleep."

"Oh, DJ—"

DJ held up his hand to stop me. "Watching him die broke me in ways I didn't know a person could be broken. And now you're here, and I've got these feelings for you because you're this moody, complicated, selfish, smart, beautiful, weird person that I can't wait to keep getting to know." He sat up on his knees, scooted closer to me. "This ship is death, Noa. It feels like every day it comes up with a new way to try to kill us, and I'm terrified it's going to succeed and that it'll take you first. That I'll have to watch someone I care about die again."

"Why didn't you tell me?" I whispered.

"Because it's not gonna stop me from having feelings for you. I'm not going to sacrifice one second of the present to my fear of repeating the past." DJ bit his lip. "We're the storytellers, Noa." He pointed from me to him. "And this is the story I want to tell."

I trusted DJ, but I had trusted Billy, too. When he had told me he was willing to take it slow, to wait for me, he had been as sincere as DJ was being now. I didn't know what to do.

"I can't just forget what happened."

"You don't have to," he said.

I got on my knees and inched closer to DJ. "Do you promise to never hurt me?"

DJ shook his head. "I promise to never hurt you like he did, and I promise I'll try to never hurt you, but I'm going to make mistakes."

A small laugh bubbled out of me. "I'm sure I will too."

"I'll do my best, though," DJ said.

I leaned my forehead against his. He rested his arms on my shoulders. One of the last messages Billy had sent to me, one of the last I'd seen anyway, had said, No one will ever love you. You're going to die alone. It hadn't been a wish. He hadn't said he *hoped* I would die alone. It had been a prediction, and I'd believed it. I had believed I would never be loved. I had believed I didn't deserve it.

Maybe he was right. DJ could have been telling me the things he thought I wanted to hear. He could have been lying to me. Preying on my fears. Using me.

But what if he was wrong? What if I did find love? What if I deserved to find it? What if the opportunity was kneeling right in front of me?

There was only one way to find out.

"You can kiss me if you want."

DJ said, "What?"

"I won't flinch this time."

"Noa, I—"

I didn't wait for DJ to kiss me. I kissed him. I reached my arm around his neck and pulled him to me and kissed him like the room was filled with radiation and we were going to die. I kissed him in the present and I kissed him in the future, and I left the past behind me.

We might die. Radiation might kill us, a monster might eat us, the ship might explode and scatter our atoms across the void, but this moment belonged to us. I was lost in DJ, except I wasn't really lost at all. I had finally been found.

Just because I had been born with a broken heart didn't mean I had to die with one.

DJ and I were so caught up in each other that neither of us heard the door open. Nor did we notice Jenny standing over us, dripping with ichor and blood. Not until she cleared her throat and said, "No, it's fine. I'll just do everything myself."

SEVEN

I SAT ON AN EXAM TABLE IN MEDICAL, A MEDIQWIK CUFF around my arm, receiving treatment for acute radiation poisoning. DJ sat on the other table, also receiving treatment. I wished I didn't have to be so far from him, but another hour and all Jenny would have found when she opened the door to Reactor Control was our corpses.

"So while you boys were making out, I was killing an alien monster that was trying to eat my face." Jenny sat on a bench in the corner. She'd wound a bandage around her leg to stop the bleeding until she could get time in a MediQwik cuff, and she was covered in an algae-colored mucus. The odor wafting off her was like rotting meat mixed with spoiled milk. It was, quite possibly, the most vile smell that had ever assaulted my nose.

"How did you manage to kill the alien?" I asked. I kept stealing glances at DJ, and I wanted to hold his hand, but the tubes and wires connected to the cuffs wouldn't reach.

"That was the easy part," Jenny said. "I was hiding in the shuttle, and the monster was trying to get inside, so I opened the bay door and launched the shuttle." She wrinkled her nose. "It's not *exactly* like the planes my mom was teaching me to fly, but it was close enough. I only dinged the outside a little. I'm sure the damage is fixable."

"So you blew the alien out the airlock?" DJ asked.

Jenny shook her head. "It clung to the shuttle and tried to use its nasty acid to burn through the hatch. So I flew a safe distance away and performed some extremely unsafe maneuvers. Eventually, it let go." She was grinning, looking so proud of herself. And she had every right to be. I wouldn't have had the nerve to do what she'd done. If Jenny had been trapped in Reactor Control with DJ, and I'd been the one running from the monster, I would have wound up alien food.

"You're amazing, Jenny," I said.

"It was nothing." Jenny was actually blushing. I couldn't remember ever seeing her embarrassed before. But I'd been serious in my praise. She had saved her life and ours.

DJ motioned at Jenny's clothes. "What is that all over you?"

Jenny's smile vanished. "The less said about it, the better. But the picture book was right. Everyone poops. Aliens too."

THE SCHOOL AT THE EDGE OF FOREVER

NOW

DJ LOOKED LIKE A FAIRY-TALE PRINCE. HIS BLACK TUX was tailored perfectly, hugging his shoulders and his hips; his blond hair was brushed up and back into a stylish wave; his dimples were on display and causing trouble; and his blue eyes shone like binary stars, so bright they were visible from the other side of the galaxy. He stood outside the Beta Cephei High School gymnasium waiting for me. My prince. Which, I suppose, made me a princess.

"What?" DJ asked. "Do I have something on me?" He checked his pristine white shirt for stains. "I haven't been eating anything, and—"

"You are so handsome."

DJ lowered his eyes and blushed a deep scarlet. "No . . . I mean, I guess I am. But not like you. You're . . . look at you," DJ stammered as he tried to string words together. It was adorable.

I spun a graceful pirouette to give DJ the opportunity to

absorb every exquisite detail of my blue suit. The jacket was cut higher than a regular tux, and the slacks were so tight that I could barely breathe, but I was definitely feeling cute.

DJ caught my hand and pulled me to him. Wrapped his arms around me and kissed me like tomorrow was a dream and we were its dreamers.

A cold metal appendage, belonging to a Teacher, wedged itself between our chests and forced us apart. In an effete mechanical voice, it said, "Please keep your genitals in your trousers," before moving away to ruin the fun of other students who were trying to share a moment.

When Teacher was far enough away that it probably couldn't hear me, I collapsed against DJ's chest, laughing. "Is this really happening?"

"I think so?" DJ squeezed my hand. "Come on. Let's go in. Jenny and Ty are waiting." He led me to the gymnasium's entrance and handed the Teacher guarding the doors our tickets.

Teacher scanned the barcodes printed on the passes with its single, bulbous red eye. "Noa North?"

"That's me." I clung to DJ's arm, hardly able to believe that this was real.

Teacher turned its cyclopean gaze to DJ. "Then you must be DJ Storm."

"I am."

Teacher stood aside and motioned for us to enter. As DJ pulled me into the gym, I said, "Wait. So we're seriously not going to talk about the fact that your full name is DJ Storm?"

THIRTEEN HOURS EARLIER

JENNY'S MOUTH HUNG OPEN SO WIDE I COULD HAVE counted her fillings, and her eyes bulged like a tree frog's. Behind her, stars filled the viewport, same as always. The universe was beautiful and deadly and dreadfully empty. I didn't know how many times the fold drive had engaged since our misadventure had begun—I was sure DJ could have told me if I'd cared enough to ask—but the view never changed.

"Well?" Jenny said. "Are you going to tell me how it went or am I going to have to yank out your fingernails?" She dug a Nutreesh bar from her pocket to snack on, spilling more crumbs on her station.

"It was nice."

"Nice?"

"Do you want the play-by-play or something?"

Jenny threw up her hands. "Yes! Why else would I be talking to you?"

I leaned back and propped my feet on my console. DJ hated when I did that, but he was asleep and would never know. Jenny and I had stayed awake to talk. Also, the fold drive was scheduled to engage soon, and we figured we might as well stick around to monitor it. Not that it was necessary.

It had been a few weeks since our alien invasion adventure, and life aboard *Qriosity* had returned to some semblance of normality. Jenny was still following clues, DJ had thrown himself into repairing the damage to the shuttle caused either by the alien trying to get inside or Jenny's attempt to fly it, and I was baking my way through *Mokatines and Murder: Eighty-Three Recipes Inspired by Murder Your Darlings*. DJ and I had spent as much time together as we could while also doing our best not to desert Jenny. We'd tried to keep our dates a secret, but she somehow always knew and hounded me for details.

"It was good," I said. "Really good. Dinner was fancy. I had the best lobster bisque I've ever tasted in my life, DJ ordered an appetizer without knowing what it was and ended up eating fish eyeballs, the primo uomo two tables over was murdered during the entrée, and DJ and I shared tiramisu for dessert."

Watching Jenny clench her jaw so hard that she looked like she might crack her teeth was quite possibly as delicious as the tiramisu had been.

"I don't care about any of that," she said. "Get to the good stuff."

I furrowed my brow in confusion. "I told you about dessert."

"The *other* good stuff."

"You don't really expect me to kiss and tell, do you?"

Jenny snorted. "I absolutely do."

"We walked around Bell's Cove," I said. "We sat on the pier and talked until the sun came up. I got cold and DJ gave me his jacket." I painted the date in broad strokes for Jenny because the particulars belonged to me and DJ alone. The feel of his cheek under my thumb; the way he smiled after every bite like each forkful was a special gift just for him; the unholy screeching sound he called singing; and the way he refused to believe he couldn't carry a tune. Every second I spent with DJ, my appreciation of him deepened. He was exactly who he appeared to be—courageous and thoughtful and kind—but he was also more. There were depths I would need a lifetime to explore.

"How am I supposed to live vicariously through you when you're courting like a couple of Puritans?" Jenny took out her anger on the last of her Nutreesh, chomping forcefully.

"We're taking things slowly—"

"Glacially."

I was trying to keep in mind that DJ and I were lucky to have each other, but my patience with Jenny was wearing thin. "Sorry," I said. "I'm not jumping into bed with DJ to keep you entertained. Our relationship isn't for you."

Jenny hung her head, looking dejected. "I need *something*, Noa."

"What about Bell's Cove? I'm sure you can steal Marco away from Anastasia for a little fun. I know it's not real, but . . ." I let Jenny's imagination fill in the blanks.

"Been there, tried to do that," she said.

"Marco's choosy. You might have to—"

Jenny cut me off. "Not what I mean. Snatching Anastasia's boy from her was cake. He was making out with me thirty seconds after breaking up with her."

I had never seen this side of Jenny, and I was intrigued. "Then what's the problem?"

"Kissing is as far as it went," she said. "That's as far as it can ever go." I must have looked confused, which I was, because she added, "Have you ever tried to get anyone from Bell's Cove naked?"

I laughed at first, thinking she was joking, but the angry glint in her eye told me she was not. "Wait. I have so many questions."

"There we were, me and Marco, in his room. His parents were gone, and I was ready to get some. But when I took off his pants, do you know what I found?"

I shook my head.

"Another pair of pants. Khakis, actually."

"Seriously?"

Jenny looked like she was going to flip a table, thinking about it. "And when I took those off, more pants. Pants, shorts, pajama bottoms, capri pants. It was pants all the way down, Noa."

"Maybe it's just a glitch with Marco's program."

Jenny flared her nostrils. "Obviously, I hooked up with Anastasia, too. She's a better kisser than Marco, but it was the same situation. Dresses under pantsuits under cute skirts and blouses. There's just no way to get to the center of that Tootsie Pop."

I really did have questions, but I was afraid of the answers.

Thankfully, Jenny kept talking. "I dug into the Mind's Eye software and found the templates for the character models. They're all rated 'I' for 'I'm never getting past second base again.'"

"Sex isn't everything," I said. "You could enjoy cuddling with Marco or Anastasia."

Jenny wound her hair around her finger. "I love a good cuddle, don't get me wrong, but I also love sex. I get and appreciate that it isn't always necessary for a healthy, fulfilling relationship, but it is for me."

This was quite possibly the strangest conversation Jenny and I had ever had, and the last thing we'd discussed had been aliens. "Maybe you can ask DJ to make changes to the models so that you can . . ." I couldn't finish the sentence because there were so many things wrong with the suggestion. It wasn't the idea of Jenny having sex with a simulation, though I tried to keep the mental image of Jenny having sex with anyone far from my mind. It was everything else. They might have been virtual characters, but they were virtual *underage* characters who were based on real people. How virtual were the characters? Could they consent? Did they have any type of free will? The characters populating Bell's Cove were digital assets in a computer program, but that didn't mean we could or should treat them like objects. It was possible that the actors had made the deliberate choice to prevent Mind's Eye users from having sex with their characters, and I didn't think I could allow DJ or Jenny to alter those parameters. Fortunately, Jenny didn't seem keen on reprogramming the characters either.

"Or," Jenny said, "you and DJ could hurry up and get it on

and then describe the entire encounter to me without omitting a single detail."

"That's never going to happen, Jenny."

"But why?" she whined. "What if you let me watch you make out? I'll sit quietly in a corner. You won't even know I'm there."

It was bad enough knowing *Qriosity* and its ubiquitous cameras were there. And Jenny's suggestion earned her a down-the-nose glare. Sometimes I didn't know if I would have been friends with Jenny if we weren't trapped on a spaceship together. Yet, I couldn't imagine life aboard *Qriosity* without her.

"Were you with anyone back on Earth?" I asked, trying to change the subject.

Jenny shrugged. "I didn't really do relationships. It was easier to not get attached, seeing as my parents kept us moving around all the time. Besides, people are messy, and I hate messy."

"Sex isn't messy?"

A slow grin spread across Jenny's face. "It can be if that's your thing." Her smile faded. "I'm not saying I wish I was home, but I do miss parts of it. Other parts, not so much." She laughed ruefully. "I certainly never thought this was what I'd be doing with my life."

"What did you think you'd be doing?"

"I figured I'd graduate high school—become an assassin or go to college and apply to the FBI."

Of the many career paths Jenny might have taken, FBI was not the one I would have guessed. Assassin felt like a better fit. "You really wanted to be an FBI agent?"

"I like solving puzzles."

"Then maybe you're exactly where you belong." I motioned around us. "*Qriosity* is one giant puzzle."

The ship began to vibrate, cutting short our conversation. The countdown clock on our screens hit two minutes, and Jenny and I slipped on our seat belts.

There was something hauntingly beautiful about watching *Qriosity* tear a hole in the fabric of space and time. It shouldn't have been possible, yet we did it every nineteen hours. The process was like getting on a bus in Seattle, sitting down, driving ten feet, and exiting in London or Portugal or the Antarctic. Jenny Perez had attempted to explain the science behind the fold drive to me, but it still looked like magic.

When the countdown hit zero, a brief flash filled the viewport. It was over. The stars had changed position, but everything else looked the same. Just like always.

"Um, Noa?" Jenny was staring at her console, her nostrils flared. "There's something out there."

"I'm sorry, what?"

"The computer says there's something out there." Even Jenny sounded like she didn't quite believe it. "It's small and shaped like a dome, but it's there."

"Can you put it on the viewport?"

Jenny zoomed in on the object, allowing *Qriosity*'s sensors to resolve the image before enlarging it again. At first, I didn't see anything. But as the unknown object grew in the center of the viewport, I realized Jenny was right. Whatever was out there looked sort of like a snow globe. There was green under the dome. And buildings.

"Does that look like a football field?" Jenny asked.

"Zoom in more," I said, pointing at a section. "There's something written on the side of that building."

Jenny continued enlarging the image, zeroing in on the writing. When it was finally large enough to read, I sat silently for a while, unable to process it.

"I'm hallucinating, right?" Jenny asked.

"If you are, then I am too." I scrubbed my face with my hands. "We'd better wake DJ. He's going to want to see this."

Though it defied explanation, written on the building in block letters were the words: BETA CEPHEI HIGH SCHOOL.

TWELVE HOURS EARLIER

"WHY IS THERE A HIGH SCHOOL IN THE MIDDLE OF space?" DJ must have jumped out of bed and sprinted to Ops the second Jenny and I had called him on the comms and told him we'd discovered something strange. When he'd arrived, his face was flushed and he was breathing heavily and he was only wearing his boxers. I'm not saying I wished he'd taken the time to get dressed, because I did enjoy looking at him, but it was distracting.

Jenny shrugged. "Hell if I know. But we're going to check it out, right?"

"We have to," I said. "There might be people down there who can tell us where we are. We could go home." The idea of home no longer felt as distant as it used to. I still missed my mom and my friends and Mrs. Blum, but home was here, on board *Qriosity* too.

DJ frowned out of one side of his mouth. "I don't know. This could be a trap."

"Of course it could be a trap," Jenny snapped. "But it's also the first thing we've run into since you rebooted the computer and sent us jumping randomly through space."

DJ winced. It had been a while since anyone had brought that up. "How would we get there?"

"Shuttle," Jenny said. "Duh. The computer says we can reach the school in a couple of hours."

"Are you sure you can fly it? I just finished repairing the damage from the last time you piloted it."

"Screw you, DJ," Jenny said.

I leaned against DJ and slipped my arm around his waist, stealing a bit of his warmth, and trying to defuse the tension. DJ's concerns felt valid and real, but I understood Jenny's frustration as well. She had been stuck on *Qriosity* with me and DJ for months, and we might continue to be her only companions for a long time. If there were real people in that snow globe, we couldn't deprive her of the opportunity to talk to them.

We spent an hour arguing back and forth, moving our conversation to the galley so we could eat. Jenny remained insistent that we go, and DJ continued advising caution. He seemed more wary than usual. I mostly sided with Jenny, but I didn't want DJ to think we were ganging up on him.

Eventually, though, after we'd run out of different ways to say the same things, I said, "We've got eighteen hours until the fold drive skips us away from here. I think going is worth the risk."

"But—" DJ said.

"We should still be careful," I continued. "But we either take the shuttle to the surface or we don't. I vote we go."

Jenny raised her hand. "I'm with Noa."

DJ sighed and shrugged. "Looks like we're heading back to school."

NINE HOURS EARLIER

JENNY DIDN'T CRASH THE SHUTTLE. IN FACT, JENNY WAS a damned good pilot. We departed *Qriosity* without incident, flew to the high school in the middle of nowhere, and then Jenny set us down in a copse of what appeared to be fir trees at the edge of the football field.

"Sorry for what I said earlier about your piloting," DJ said as we were landing. "You're really good."

"Apology accepted."

I was so anxious that I could hardly wait for the shuttle doors to open. The moment they did, I dashed out, fell to my knees on the grass, and laughed. "It's real!"

"Real*ish*," Jenny said.

The grass was dewy and soft. The sky overhead was filled with fluffy clouds and sunshine. The ground had that soft spring to it that not even the oxygen garden had managed to replicate. If

I hadn't flown through the dome a few minutes before, I could have been fooled into believing I was on an actual planet instead of on an island floating on the edge of forever.

DJ held out his hand to help me up, and the three of us crossed the field toward the buildings. I felt safe with DJ. Like I could handle anything.

"What do we do?" I asked as we left the grass and stepped onto the sidewalk. "Check in at the main office? Do you think we'll get detention for being late?"

"We have to be careful," DJ said. "At the first sign of trouble, we get back to the shuttle and take off, okay?"

"It's school, DJ," I said. "How much trouble can we really get into?"

As we passed between the buildings and entered a large open quad that was decorated with trees that looked like they were from Earth and had picnic benches arranged in a ring around the center, we were startled by a mechanized voice that spoke with an unplaceable and slightly pretentious accent. "Welcome, new students."

I turned around and screamed a little. DJ squeezed my hand. Lurking behind us was a machine. Possibly a robot. In place of legs, its upper body was supported by what appeared to be a gyroscope. Its torso was like plate armor, out of which sprouted four appendages that were probably arms, and the majority of its head consisted of a single, pulsating red eye the size of a grapefruit. It definitely wasn't creepy or menacing at all.

"Um, hi?" DJ said. "Could you tell us where we are or what *you* are?"

"I am Teacher. You are unregistered students." Faster than any of us could react, Teacher's appendages whipped around and stabbed each of us in the shoulder with a pneumatic injector, shooting something under our skin. It was over before I had a chance to protest.

"You have been registered," Teacher said. "Congratulations, you are now students of Beta Cephei High School. Your schedules can be accessed by looking at your palms. First period is currently in session. It will end in three minutes. You are expected to attend second period. Absence or tardiness will result in punishment. Profanity, consumption of food during classes, physical violence, or the sharing of bodily fluids will also result in punishment."

"What kind of punishment?" Jenny asked.

"The bad kind," Teacher said, then rolled away, disappearing into a nearby building.

I didn't know what to make of what was happening. I rubbed the lump under my skin on my shoulder through my shirt.

"What do you think?" I asked.

Jenny was holding her hand in front of her face. "This is wild." I didn't understand until I held up my own hand. A schedule, superimposed over my palm, appeared before my eyes. Second period was highlighted, indicating where I was supposed to go next. Whatever the robot had injected us with must have made it possible. It was cool in a way that was also incredibly intrusive and disturbing.

"You have got to be kidding me," I said.

"What's wrong?" DJ asked, pressing closer to me. He was a reassuring presence. I don't think I would have handled the situation as well without him.

I didn't even want to say it. "My next class."

Jenny grimaced. "I've got mitochondrial bioenergetics, whatever that is."

"Pottery," DJ said.

I glared at my hand, checking my schedule again to make sure it hadn't changed. And, of course, it hadn't. "PE," I said. "I'd rather bleed from every orifice."

"Maybe that's what punishment is," Jenny said.

DJ squeezed my hand and pulled me into a circle of two. "We don't have to do this. We can return to the shuttle and fly back to *Qriosity*."

Jenny punched him in the shoulder, and there was nothing playful about it. "Like hell we can."

"Jenny—"

"If you boys want to hide in the shuttle and suck face, you have my blessing, but I need to spend some time with people who aren't you." Jenny took off toward the other side of the quad. "We'll meet up at lunch!"

"Should we go after her?" DJ asked.

The idea of being forced to play space dodgeball or whatever made me want to vomit, but DJ and I didn't have the right to deny Jenny this opportunity. Besides, we were at a high school floating in space, and I was curious to know more.

"Nah," I said. "She'll be fine."

"She's really excited about school, isn't she?"

I shook with silent laughter. "I think she's more excited to spend time with people her own age who are anatomically correct." When DJ wrinkled his nose, I added, "Don't ask."

"I won't."

A chime sounded, and a few seconds later, students poured out of the classrooms, filling the silence with their discordant symphony of voices. They looked like people I could've gone to school with. They also acted like people I could've gone to school with in that none of them paid attention to me.

DJ scanned the crowd. "Robot teachers but human students?"

"Apparently."

"Weird." DJ was a master of understatement.

"So I guess we should find our classes?" I said without enthusiasm.

"You might have fun."

"Trade me, then. You go to PE and I'll make a ceramic vase."

DJ kissed me gently on the lips, and I hated that it felt like a goodbye. I knew it wasn't—I knew I'd see him again—but I didn't want to spend any time apart from him that I didn't have to. "Three periods until lunch," he said. "And if you hate it, we'll lure Jenny back to the shuttle with Nutreesh."

"Deal."

DJ took off, leaving me alone.

I had spent hours and days wishing to be anywhere other than *Qriosity*, and now that my wish had been granted, *Qriosity* was the only place I wanted to be.

"Excuse me," I said to no one in particular. "Can you tell me where the gym is?" I had kind of shouted my question into the mass of students in the hopes that one of them would answer, but the most they did was side-eye me as they walked on.

I was about to pick a direction at random when I spied a familiar face. A face that couldn't exist. "Kayla?" I shoved through the crowd, forcing my way upstream to reach her. "Kayla!" I hadn't really known her, but I'd spent enough time with her dead and dying body that I'd memorized her face. Her round cheeks and crooked nose. Her black hair and long neck. It had to be her. It couldn't be her.

She peeled off from the group she was with and entered one of the buildings. I followed her inside. I jogged to catch up and get her attention. "Kayla?"

"Sorry," she said, seeming annoyed at being stopped. "You got the wrong person."

But I was so certain. "Is your name Kayla?"

She shook her head. "Talley."

"Are you sure?" I asked. "Do you remember *Qriosity*? It's a spaceship."

"Uh, pretty positive, and no." She turned up her nose at me and motioned for me to move, which I did. I didn't know what to do or think. She wouldn't have known me because she'd spent the majority of our time together dead. And it couldn't have been Kayla anyway because the last time I'd seen her was when we'd committed her body to the stars.

My mind was playing tricks on me. Everyone has a doppelgänger, right?

The bell chimed again and an alert flashed on my hand, warning me that I had two minutes to get to class or I would be punished. The warning was followed by a map showing me the fastest route to the gym. I ran the entire way, but I couldn't outrun the doubt that followed me.

NINE HOURS EARLIER

ALL THE ROBOTS WERE CALLED TEACHER. THAT WAS THE first thing I learned when I ran, huffing and wheezing, into class as the final bell rang. The second thing I learned was that gym uniforms are universally hideous. The one I was given consisted of blue shorts that were borderline indecent and a mustard-yellow shirt with "Beta Cephei High School Stellar Fragments" printed on the front. I refused to wear it until I was threatened with punishment. After I changed, my class of thirty students was broken into four teams and sent to play volleyball. The only game I hated worse than dodgeball was volleyball.

I wish I could properly convey how deeply strange it was to be playing indoor volleyball with a group of students I'd never met before, all of whom attended a school with robot teachers on a domed rock floating in the middle of space that I had accidentally traveled to in a spaceship that had torn a hole in the fabric of the universe. At the same time, it was also so aggressively normal. The way the students looked faintly uncomfortable in their ugly gym uniforms while trying to pretend they weren't; the uncoordinated students flinging eye daggers at the athletic students; the undercurrent of whispered conversations, each student assuming everyone who wasn't talking to them was talking about them. It was comforting to know that, even on the other side of the universe, high school locker rooms smelled like sweaty crotch and cheap body spray.

If I ignored the robots with the murdery red eyes, it could have been home.

"Hey." It took me a moment to register that the boy standing next to me had spoken. He was long-limbed and gangly, like he'd grown two feet overnight and was still trying to figure out how to move without falling on his face. "I'm Thao."

"Noa," I said. "I'm awful at this game, by the way."

"Me too."

I heard someone laughing, not like they were having fun but like they were about to make someone else miserable. The sadistic kind of laugh usually heard from psychopaths or children in horror movies. And then a volleyball smashed into Thao's face. He crumpled to the polished maple floor as blood spurted from his nose.

"Heads up!" shouted a guy from the other team, probably the same one who'd spiked the ball at Thao's face. He was tall and fair with messy auburn hair and the kind of grin that said he'd definitely pulled the legs off grasshoppers when he was a kid.

I scrambled to help Thao stand. "We should get you to

the nurse or infirmary or whatever you have here."

Thao's eyes widened in terror, and he tried to use his sleeve to wipe away the blood. "I'm fine."

"Your nose could be broken."

Teacher rolled toward us, its bulbous red eye fixed on me and Thao. "You are leaking."

I hiked my thumb at the guy who'd started this. "I'm pretty sure he did this on purpose. Aren't you going to punish him?" I hated bullies. I hated them more than dodgeball and only fractionally less than volleyball.

Thao whipped off his shirt, ignoring the laughter from the other students, and pressed it to his nose. "It's fine. *I'm* fine. I need to sit is all. The bleeding will stop on its own."

Teacher's eye pulsed once. "You may be absent this game. If you can't return at the conclusion, you will report to Nurse."

Thao said, "Thank you," in a way that was too eager to be normal. He turned to go, stopped, and said, "Can the new kid come with me? The teams will be uneven otherwise."

Teacher took a moment to process the request. "Yes," it said, then rolled away.

I followed Thao to the bleachers.

"I'm sorry about your nose."

"You didn't do it." Thao's voice was nasally, which made sense, seeing as he probably couldn't breathe well.

"But I'm benefitting from it," I said. "I really hate playing volleyball, so you getting hit in the face is the best thing that's happened to me since class began."

Thao laughed, but it was more of a snort that sounded like he was choking. "It's cool."

I looked back at where we'd been playing. The athletic guy who'd started this and some of his friends were scowling in our general direction. "What's his deal? Did you do something to piss him off or is he just genetically predisposed to being a dick?"

"Clayton?"

"Is that his name?"

Thao nodded. "You're on the new kid track, right? So you should probably avoid him or you'll get drawn into his bully nonsense, which sucks unless you're angling for a revenge or redemption arc."

I fully understood, individually, each of the words that had come out of Thao's mouth, but they didn't make sense to me as a sentence. "Say what again?"

"Are you funny?" he asked. "You have a good look for being the funny guy. Where are you from?"

"Earth."

Thao frowned and rolled his eyes. "Yeah, but where are you *really* from?"

I felt more lost than normal. It's what I imagined it would've been like if I'd been able to travel back in time to when my mom was in high school and everyone wore flannel shirts and listened to grunge and no one had a cell phone.

"What's your deal?" I asked. "What's the deal with this school?"

"I don't know what you're talking about." His eyes flicked

past me. I followed his gaze to where Teacher was watching us with its big, red eye.

"Come on. None of this is right. Where are we? Do you know?"

Thao's face changed in an instant. Gone was the plucky nerd who'd been bullied by aggressive jocks and was happy to have a new friend. In its place was someone feral and terrified. "Shut up!" His voice was a whisper, but sharp.

Teacher rolled toward us slowly.

"Maybe I can help you," I said. "I came here with friends. We have a ship—"

Teacher reached us and rested one appendage on Thao's shoulder. "You are still injured. You must report to Nurse."

"He's fine," I said. "We were just talking."

Thao shook his head. He peeled the shirt away and said, "See? I'm not bleeding anymore. I can play."

But he *was* still bleeding. It was a slow ooze rather than a gush, but the flow ran from his nostrils, down his lips and chin.

"I'll take him to the nurse," I said.

Teacher pointed at the volleyball court I'd left earlier. "You will return to the game now." It lifted Thao up, and I wasn't sure whether the kid would have been able to stand on his own. He was trembling.

"What the hell is going on?" I asked.

The other students were still playing, but their attention was fully on us.

"You will go to Nurse," Teacher said to Thao. "You will return to the game. Obey or face punishment."

Thao was crying freely. His shoulders slumped and his head bowed. “I’ll go.”

Teacher released Thao and then patted his back three times. “There. There. Nurse will correct you.”

Nothing made sense. I didn’t understand why Thao was so scared to go to the nurse’s office, but I felt like it was at least partially my fault and that I should try to help. “I could—”

“Leave me alone.” Thao slouched toward the exit, accompanied by Teacher.

I didn’t see that I had any choice other than to rejoin the game. I moved into the first empty spot. It was near a young woman with blond-streaked hair pulled back in a ponytail. I tried to ask her what had just happened, but before I could speak, she said, “Oh my God, do you watch *Murder Your Darlings*? It’s only my favorite program ever. Anastasia Darling is my idol.”

It wasn’t *what* she said that made me suspicious—though it would have been enough, seeing as no person who had seen *any* other show would have chosen *Murder Your Darlings* as their favorite—it was the way she said it just loud enough for Teacher to hear.

Something was going on that I didn’t understand, and until I did, it seemed the best course of action was to play along.

“Yeah,” I said. “Anastasia’s the best.”

EIGHT HOURS EARLIER

I WAS DISGUSTING AND SWEATY BY THE TIME TEACHER dismissed us to shower and change before our next class. The girl with the encyclopedic knowledge of Anastasia Darling had been the only person willing to talk to me after Thao had left, and even she had seemed nervous. I hoped my next class, finite element methods for partial differential equations, involved less blood.

The shower nozzles lined the walls, and steam filled the air. I wasn't thrilled by public showers, but I also didn't intend to spend the rest of the day stewing in my own fragrant juices. I grabbed a towel, which I hoped had been boiled in bleach, and went in.

I didn't notice the other boys were clustered together on one side of the showers until I was rinsing shampoo from my hair and caught them staring at me. It made me nervous because I was naked and vulnerable, and there was nowhere to run. I considered ignoring them. If they wanted to be weird, I should let them. But I was tired of letting things go.

"What?!" I said.

Clayton was already at the front of the group. His cocky swagger had evaporated. In the showers, he looked as scared and defenseless as the rest of the boys. He crossed the space between us, stopping when he was less than a meter away. "Quit asking questions."

I was proud of myself for not backing up or flinching. There was something of Billy in Clayton. I'd noticed it when he was laughing after smacking Thao in the face with the ball, but I saw it even clearer without his cloak of arrogance.

"You do get how creepy this is, right?"

Clayton moved nearer. I pushed him back.

"Have you never heard of personal space?"

"They can't watch us here," Clayton said, his voice low. "But Teachers sometimes stand by the door and listen."

"Is this a joke? Some kind of hazing thing you do to all the new students? Because it's not funny." Even as I said it, I knew none of the kids were talented enough actors to fake the fear radiating off them. "What happened to Thao? Why was he so—"

"Stop asking questions!" Clayton's voice was still low, but it was harsh. Strained.

I'd rinsed the shampoo out of my hair, and had no further reason to stay. "If you're not going to tell me what the deal is here, then we're done talking." I shut off the shower. "Excuse me."

Clayton flared his nostrils but stepped aside. As I passed, he grabbed my arm, his fingers tight around my bicep. "All you have to do around here is go along to get along, okay? If you can't do that, at least try not to take anyone down with you."

I yanked my arm free and walked out, ignoring the rest of the boys, each of whom stared at me like I was infected with a virulent disease. I had no idea what we had stumbled into, but I was ready to leave.

FIVE HOURS EARLIER

DJ, JENNY, AND I SAT IN A CIRCLE UNDER THE EXPANSIVE shade of an oak tree and ate our lunches. Jenny was the only one who was happy about it.

"Nutreesh? Really?" I turned up my nose at the bar I'd been given along with a bottle of Hydrophoria, which was just water, and a banana. We hadn't been offered a choice; it was the standard-issue lunch everyone had received. At least we'd been allowed to spend the hour outside.

"This place is a prison," I muttered.

DJ leaned in and kissed my cheek. "High school always feels that way."

"No," I said. "I mean, yeah, but this place is worse."

"I'm with Noa," Jenny said. "There was a kid in my xenobiology class who wouldn't stop talking, so they sent him to the office. I've never seen someone cry like that over being kicked out of class. This school is freaky."

DJ leaned against the tree and tried to scan the area in a way that looked casual. It wasn't. There were other students outside, clustered together in groups, each of whom was watching us the way we were watching them. Teachers patrolled the perimeter of the grassy knoll, and herded students toward the center if they wandered too near to the edge.

I had told DJ and Jenny about Thao and Clayton and my experience in gym class, but they hadn't been able to make any more sense out of it than I had.

"What do we do?" DJ asked.

"Leave," I said. "When the bell rings, we make a run for the shuttle and get the hell off this rock."

"Are you sure?" DJ asked. "We might be giving up the chance to find a way home."

I slipped my hand into DJ's. Maybe my feelings were the result of chemicals, but the more time I spent with DJ, the more time I *wanted* to spend with him. "I'd rather live the rest of my life on *Qriosity* than here."

Jenny made barfing sounds into her napkin.

"Besides," I continued, "I feel like the longer we stay, the more at risk we are. For all we know, this could be a Nutreesh processing facility, and we're about to learn that Nutreesh is made from rebellious high school students."

Jenny looked at her empty wrapper. "I thought you said Nutreesh was probably roaches."

"Well, now I'm saying it might be people."

"Nutreesh isn't people."

"Are you sure?" I asked. "Are you certain enough to keep putting it in you?"

DJ wedged himself into the conversation before Jenny and I really got going. "We've only got two classes left after lunch. It'll probably be easier to sneak away after that."

It was a good point, and I was about to say so when Jenny said, "Well, actually," in a dramatic fashion, and then waited for us to give her our full attention. "There's a dance this evening. The Equinox Formal."

"Okay?" I said.

"I've been asked to go," she said. "Officially."

I didn't mean to snort. It just happened.

Jenny slapped my arm. "What? I'm a catch."

"I would've thrown you back." I winked at Jenny, and she hit me again.

DJ said, "Staying for another class is one thing. But a dance? I don't know."

Jenny shrugged. "And I don't care. A living, breathing person who thinks I'm attractive has asked me to attend a social function as his date, and there is no way in hell I'm not going."

"It's dangerous," DJ said.

As soon as DJ and Jenny began to argue, I tuned them out. Mostly because the sound made me want to stuff my ears full of Nutreesh. Over the past few months, Jenny had helped carry my emotional baggage, discovered an intruder, fought aliens, and been forced to endure unwanted isolation due to my and DJ's burgeoning relationship. Jenny had had to smile and be happy for us even as we pulled away and left her alone. If she wanted to spend a couple of hours slow dancing to cloyingly sweet songs while her date worked up the nerve to try stick his tongue in her mouth, then I felt like I'd be a jerk to stand in her way.

"We should stay for the dance."

I don't know who looked more surprised by my decision, DJ or Jenny.

"Really?" DJ said.

I nodded. "You heard Jenny: she's got a date. Besides, we have ten hours until *Qriosity* leaves."

Jenny laughed. "I love how I'm the only one of us who can fly the shuttle, but it's *your* decision."

"There's also that," I said. DJ opened his mouth like he was going to raise another objection, but I stopped him. "It might be fun to live normal lives for a while."

DJ motioned at the nearest Teacher. "How's *that* normal?"

"Sure, there are robot teachers and this is a space school filled with Stepford students—"

"Just agree to stay, DJ," Jenny said. "You'll feel much better when you do."

DJ threw up his hands in surrender. "Fine. I guess we're staying."

Jenny's scream of joy caused heads to turn, students' as well as Teachers', and I wasn't entirely comfortable drawing so much attention to ourselves. But it had been a long time since I had seen Jenny so happy. She wasn't the only one excited about the dance, though. I might have been slowly adapting to my role aboard *Qriosity*, but I was still sixteen, and I was looking forward to doing something where the stakes weren't life and death.

"The dance could be the perfect opportunity to break into the school's computer system and see what we can learn," DJ said.

"That's a good point too." I was disappointed that DJ only saw the dance as an excuse to sneak around, but I tried to hide it. Not well enough, apparently.

"What's wrong?" DJ asked. Lunch had ended, and he was walking me to my next class. Jenny had abandoned us when the second the bell rang.

"Nothing."

"Liar."

I shrugged, trying to play it off like it was no big deal. "I was looking forward to the dance a little. That's all."

DJ held my hand, and we strolled across campus like we belonged there. "We're going."

"But only as cover for breaking into their computers."

DJ pulled me to a stop, ignoring the dirty looks thrown our way from the people forced to walk around us. "To potentially find a way home. Don't you want that?"

I nodded. "I did. I *do*." I sighed. "I guess I'd gotten used to the idea that we were never going home. That I'd never go to prom or graduate high school or worry about college. That I was never going to have the experiences I'd expected to have. Then we came here, and it's weird, but it's also a reminder of everything I lost."

I expected DJ to tell me I was being silly, because I was and

I knew it. Instead, he wrapped his arms around my waist and kissed me.

"No exchanging bodily fluids!" the nearest Teacher yelled, but it was too far away for me to care.

"If you want to dance all night, then we'll dance all night."

It was so tempting to give in. To enjoy a few hours with DJ as a normal high school couple. Our relationship didn't have to be complicated. We didn't have to be DJ and Noa, strangers who were abducted and stranded aboard a spaceship. I could just be Noa, the devastatingly handsome popular kid, and DJ could be my hot but nerdy boyfriend.

It would have been nice, and it would have been normal, but that wasn't our story.

THREE HOURS EARLIER

FRESHMAN YEAR OF HIGH SCHOOL, SECOND-PERIOD English, I was seated next to a new kid by the law of alphabetical order. Mrs. Forrester had us team up to work on a project. The new kid's name was Victor, and he was kind of cute. I wouldn't say I had a crush on him, but I definitely wanted to impress him. He was telling me about his life—how his family traveled the world because his mom was a famous photographer—and I made up a story about my dad being an actor. It was a ridiculous lie, but it spilled out of me before I could stop it. Victor learned the truth—I should have known he would because I'd been going to school with most of the same kids since first grade—and he told everyone what I'd done.

I thought my life had ended. I felt like the entire universe had imploded. How was I going to return to school? How was I going to face anyone now that they knew I was a liar? Every decision

I made during high school felt monumental. Every mistake I made was the end of everything.

As I sat through my last class, having lived on a spaceship where I'd been forced to make life-altering decisions, where the choices I'd made had led to my actual death, I realized how small and inconsequential high school was. There was a bigger world beyond high school, and an even larger universe beyond the world. That lie I had told and the other mistakes I had made, none of them mattered beyond my high school walls, and I was beginning to doubt that they had mattered much there, either.

At the end of last period, DJ and I waited in the quad for Jenny so that we could plan our next move. Jenny arrived a few minutes later, dragging behind her a tall, handsome, freckle-faced boy in a letterman jacket and very tight jeans.

"Meet Ty," she said. "He plays football."

Ty was nearly a head taller than Jenny. He waved at us and flashed a charming, easy smile. "What's up? You must be Noa and DJ." He spoke with a lazy, lackadaisical style in a voice that sounded like an ocean wave.

I pointed at myself. "Noa."

"DJ."

"Cool," Ty said. He was too pretty to be real. His eyes shone like smoky quartz, his skin was ivory and smooth, and he had the broad shoulders and narrow waist of a doll. Next to him, I felt like a troll. Like my face was covered in pustules on the verge of bursting and my mouth was filled with foul, green, crooked teeth.

I wondered if DJ was feeling as suddenly inadequate as I was. If so, he didn't show it. "What now?" DJ asked. "We've got some time to kill before the dance, right?"

Jenny said, "Ty's going to show us where we can get clothes. We can't show up looking like this. Apparently, it's where everyone goes shopping."

"Yeah," Ty said. "The Underground."

The Underground, as it turned out, was both the name of the place and a literal description. As in the mall was literally underneath the school. I stood at the top of a long escalator and looked down.

"It's a mall," I said.

Ty was grinning and, of course, he had a perfect smile full of straight white teeth. "Awesome, huh?"

I rolled my eyes but kept my face turned so that only DJ could see. "Yeah. Totally."

Jenny and Ty got onto the escalator, and DJ took my hand and pulled me on behind them. From the top, I could see everything. We were in a pastel-and-neon underground mall with a huge fountain in the center and fake palm trees lining the promenade. The stores had names like "Dankworth & Fernsby," "Eternally Eighteen," "Munch," and "Illicit Syzygy." The most surprising part was that it was crowded with teenagers. The entire school must have been there.

I couldn't remember the last time I'd been to a mall. And I certainly never went there to hang out. That was something my mom had done when she'd been sixteen, which I knew because

I'd seen the pictures. Her permed hair held back from her face with something she called a scrunchie. She and her friends trying to look disaffected and cool, crowded at a table in the food court. The Underground was a paradox. A futuristic anachronism. But I was willing to overlook that if I could find something decent to wear that also fit well.

DJ was characteristically quiet as he took the scene in, but I wondered what was going through his mind.

When we reached the bottom, Jenny pulled Ty off the escalator and said, "I don't know what F and G is, but those dresses in the window are gorgeous. I'm going in."

Before Jenny could drag Ty away, DJ said, "Why don't I go with you? That way Ty won't see your dress until the dance."

Jenny's eyes lit up. "Perfect! I love that idea!"

"I don't know . . ." I wasn't keen on being left alone with Ty, but DJ was wearing a determined look that made me suspect he was actually suggesting that I spend time with Ty to pump him for information.

Ty motioned toward the other end of the mall. "We can check out Chainsaw. They have killer suits."

DJ kissed my cheek and whispered, "Be careful." And I wanted to shout at him that sending me off with a stranger had been his idea, but he and Jenny took off, and I was lured away by the promise of shopping for suits.

Insert montage of me trying on every article of clothing in the entire store. With a name like Chainsaw, I had expected generic, bland clothes for men who still thought colors were gendered, but I was quickly proven wrong. The store presented me with such a vast array of choices, any of which could be quickly tailored by a Sales Associate to fit, that I nearly broke into tears. Sales Associates were exactly like Teachers, but their job seemed to be making sure I found the perfect outfit for the dance.

"What do you think of this?" I walked out of the fitting room wearing an iridescent tux, with a banded collar, that made actual whooshing sounds when I spun around.

"Dope," Ty said. He wasn't my ideal shopping partner. He responded to everything with one-word replies that were either "dope," "rad," or "meh." Ty's lack of verbal skills was probably the main reason Jenny liked him. If I hadn't been occupied trying to find a suit that would melt DJ's knees, I would have been bored. He certainly didn't seem to know anything about the space school.

I held out my arms and turned to get a better view of the back. The shiny suit definitely made a statement, but I wasn't sure if I liked what it was saying. "I should try the blue one on again."

I was in the fitting room, hanging the shirt I'd just taken off on its hanger, when Ty opened the door and ducked inside. The tiny space was barely large enough for me, and Ty had to press against me to fit.

"Whoa," I said. "You're cute, but I'm with DJ." I paused. "I think." It wasn't a conversation we'd had. We'd made out, and we'd gone on dates, but we hadn't exactly defined our relationship.

Ty clamped his hand over my mouth. "Jenny told me you arrived here in a shuttle." His voice was barely loud enough for me to hear, but his tone was razor-sharp. Gone was the dopey, goofy jock Jenny had introduced us to, and I didn't know how to react. A familiar dread seized me, and I froze. "You have to take me with you when you leave."

I refused to be intimidated by him. Sure, Ty could have folded me into a neat square and tucked me into his back pocket, but that didn't mean I had to give up. I pried his hand off my mouth. "Why would we do that?"

"There's no time to explain," he said. "Just promise you'll take me."

"I'm not promising anything until you tell me why."

Ty clenched his jaw. "Because you need me. You'll never escape without my help."

A Sales Associate knocked three times on the door. "Fitting rooms are designed for single occupancy."

I reached past Ty to open the door, but he grabbed my arm. He mouthed, *Please.* His palms were damp, and there was genuine fear in his eyes.

This wasn't a decision I wanted to make alone. DJ would have known what to do, but I didn't. What would be the repercussions of allowing Ty to come with us? What would happen if I said no? Would Jenny want Ty living on *Qriosity*? This was a decision that the three of us should have made together, as a crew. But there was no time.

"If one of you does not vacate the fitting room immediately, I'll be compelled to call Manager."

Ty squeezed my arm harder. I gave him a terse nod, hoping I

wouldn't regret it. Ty sighed with relief, let me go, and opened the door. "No need," he said to Sales Associate. "We're good."

But I wasn't so sure we were.

I tried to find other ways to talk to Ty, but a Sales Associate always seemed to be lurking nearby. Later, when we met up with DJ and Jenny, I tried to get DJ alone, but couldn't manage that, either. If I hadn't seen Ty's transformation for myself, I wouldn't have believed it.

Eventually, the mall began to clear out as the time of the dance neared. We made our way back to the surface and then to the quad in front of the gym. Ty had chosen a white tuxedo with tails while DJ had picked up a traditional black tux. After much debating, I'd settled on the most amazing blue suit. It was dramatic and modern. I'm not saying I wanted to die, but it was definitely an outfit worthy of dying in.

Jenny was the star of the show, however. She arrived wearing an elegant strapless aubergine sheath dress. Her hair was piled on her head in a cascade of ringlets, and it glittered like a million stars. If Jenny didn't steal Ty's heart, then he was probably a robot.

Despite knowing that DJ and I weren't really there for the dance, I did my best to pretend we were. To live in the moment and enjoy the evening. Jenny and Ty went inside first. DJ and I followed after the Teacher at the door scanned our passes and stood aside to let us in.

"Wait," I said. "So we're seriously not going to talk about the fact that your full name is DJ Storm?"

NOW

THE GYMNASIUM HADN'T BEEN TRANSFORMED SO MUCH as shoddily disguised in the hopes that none of the students would notice. Fairy lights hung from the walls, paper streamers dangled from the ceiling, and a mirror ball spun over the section of the floor designated for dancing, but the stink of shame, rubber, and BO remained.

It was perfect.

"What were your parents thinking? Does DJ stand for something? Let me guess: Django Johannsen?" DJ and I were making our way around the room. He was scoping out the exits while I tormented him.

"What? No. DJ doesn't stand for anything. I think they just liked the name."

"Okay, but 'DJ Storm' sounds like they expected you to grow up to be either a B-movie action hero or a literal deejay."

I motioned at the front of the gym, where a Teacher stood behind a soundboard, spinning what I supposed passed for music in this part of the galaxy. The song playing had a generic but infectious beat that tugged at my brand-new dancing shoes.

And I wasn't the only one itching to move. Though it was still early, twenty or thirty students were on the floor dancing like no one was watching. The rest were seated at tables or clustered in impenetrable cliques.

Teachers were situated at the edges of the gym, their menacing red eyes seeming to look everywhere at once.

"I count eleven Teachers," DJ said. "We'll wait until more students get here before we try to find somewhere more private."

I grunted to let him know I understood. While there were no Teachers immediately nearby, they were robots and we had no way of knowing if they could hear us. We had to be careful what we said. It was why I hadn't yet told DJ about Ty and my promise that we'd take him with us.

"Did I tell you I thought I saw Kayla?" That topic seemed safe.

DJ stopped and threw me a strange look. "Impossible."

"Obviously, but I was so sure it was her that I chased her across campus. It wasn't her, but you wouldn't believe how similar they looked. Identical almost." I craned my neck to see if I could spot her so I could point her out to DJ.

"It's probably guilt making your brain play tricks on you," DJ said.

"Guilt?"

"I mean, not guilt exactly, but something." He squeezed my hand. "You watched a girl die. A girl who'd been locked in a room on our ship for weeks."

There was still a voice in my head insisting that the girl I'd seen was Kayla, even though I knew it couldn't have been. "Whatever. If I see her, I'll show you."

DJ just shrugged.

"What now?" I asked.

DJ raised my hand to his lips, kissed it, and bowed. "Noa North, would you dance with me?"

It was so corny that I nearly laughed, but it was also straight out of a fairy tale. I really did feel like a princess. In that moment, I belonged to DJ. I would have gone anywhere with him and done anything for him. I had been born with a broken heart, and Billy had shattered the pieces into tiny fragments, but DJ seemed determined to put it back together.

I let DJ lead me to the dance floor, slipping between the other students. Just as we reached the center, the hyper pop song that had been playing faded into a romantic ballad. I draped my arms around DJ's waist and rested my forehead against his as we swayed to the unfamiliar music. I dissolved into him. Nothing else mattered. Not Jenny, not Teachers, not Ty. Not *Qriosity* or Jenny Perez or finding a way home.

During that song, I realized something. The universe was vast and cold and empty and would try to kill me if given the chance. But it would never succeed. With DJ near, I would never be cold; with him holding my hand, I would never be alone; with him, the universe was wherever we were together. That was my story. Our story. A love story, set in space.

"What do you think?" DJ asked.

"It's magical," I said. "I mean, the gym reeks, the music is crap, and I have no idea who any of these people are, but I'm here with you."

DJ opened his mouth to speak, but I didn't want him to. Not yet.

"I thought, after Billy, that's just the way things were. I thought every guy I met would be like him, and I was afraid to get close to you. I gave it a shot, though, because I figured if I was going to get screwed again, I could at least do it with my eyes open.

"But you're not him. You're you, and you're the kindest, bravest, most wonderful person I've met."

DJ shook his head.

"You are," I said, "and I love that you won't even admit it. I love the way you look in this tux; I love the way you think you can sing even though you really, *really* can't. I love every second I get to spend with you, and I never want it to end."

By the time I finished pouring my heart out, DJ's cheeks were crimson and he was sweating. "Right, but I was asking . . . I mean, I meant to ask what you thought about the plan? Which door do you think will be easiest to sneak out of unnoticed?"

"Oh. Right. The door by the corner that leads to the locker room." I backed away, horrified. "Ignore everything else I said."

DJ grabbed my wrist to keep me from leaving. He kissed me

softly but quickly because the moment our lips touched, a dozen red eyes turned our way. He leaned close to my ear and whispered, "I would jump out of a thousand spaceships for you."

"I really hope you don't have to."

The music changed to something faster and frenetic, but DJ and I ignored it. We were dancing to our own music, and aside from my momentary mortification, everything was perfect. I was with someone who genuinely cared about me, no one was trying to kill us that I knew of, and nothing was threatening to explode. If I were ever going to be trapped in another time loop, this was the moment I would have chosen. This would have been my happily ever after.

But this wasn't the end. Of us or our story.

NOW

JENNY FAKED A FIGHT WITH TY, THOUGH I'M NOT SURE *he* knew it wasn't real, providing DJ and me the distraction we needed to slip out of the gym through the locker rooms and make our way to the main building.

The hall lights were dim, giving the school a creepy vibe that made the hair on the back of my neck stand on end. And it was too quiet. There should have been students shouting over one another as they moved in herds from one class to the next. The lack of chaos was unnerving.

"Where do you think the students go when school is out?" I asked.

DJ and I checked classrooms on opposite sides of the hall. We were looking for a computer with network access that DJ could use, though I was worried we weren't going to find one. What use were computers to Teachers? They *were* computers.

"No idea," he said. "Let's stay focused, okay?"

I said "Sure," but I couldn't stop my mind from picking away at the problem of the impossible school. "It's weird, though, right? They've got an underground mall. Maybe there's another level below that with houses. And how come all the adults are robots? Where are the actual adults? Where are the parents?"

"Got something!" DJ ducked into a classroom containing a dozen workstations organized into two neat rows. He slipped into a seat behind the nearest computer and got to work.

"I'll keep an eye out," I said, remaining near the door. "But maybe hurry up. I have a bad feeling about this."

DJ's fingers danced across the keyboard; his eyes were fixed on the screen. My only real regret about the time I'd spent looping through the same day is that I hadn't become a computer genius. I suppose I was lucky I had DJ.

"I'm really glad you were on board *Qriosity* when I woke up," I said. "Jenny too, but you especially."

"Same," DJ said.

"Think of all the people I could've been stuck with. My French teacher, Mr. Hoosier? What a dickbag. Gerald, my neighbor who moved away when I was ten. He used to throw rocks at me because he thought it was hilarious, and I'm ninety-nine percent certain he's going to grow up to be a serial killer. Could you imagine being trapped on the ship with a psycho killer? The only thing worse would have been waking up alone."

"Isn't being stuck with Jenny bad enough?" DJ asked, quickly flashing his dimples.

I snapped my fingers as a thought occurred to me. "I couldn't tell you before, but when Ty and I were shopping, he barged into my fitting room and begged me to take him with us on the shuttle when we left."

DJ glanced at me with pursed lips. "What was he doing *in* the fitting room with you?"

"You're cute when you're jealous," I said. "Kidding. Jealousy is gross. It wasn't like that. But you should have seen him. There was a moment when he became a totally different person."

"Weird," DJ said, his attention back on the computer.

"I told him he could come because I didn't have a choice." I bit my lip. "But we're not going to do it, are we? Take Ty, I mean. It would change our whole dynamic."

"If he wants to leave, and you promised he could come, we have to take him."

"What if everyone wants off this rock? We can't take them all." There were easily a few hundred students at Beta Cephei High, and while we probably had space for a hundred if we crammed them into the cargo bay, we'd quickly run out of food and water. But the bigger problem was that we only had space for four on the shuttle. With more time—

"I think I got it," DJ said.

"Our coordinates?"

"Access to their network."

DJ sounded excited about it, but before I could congratulate him, Klaxons began to blare. Red lights in the hallway flashed like lights on a fire truck. "Alert! Intrusion detected! Alert!"

"That's bad, right?" I asked.

"Damn!" DJ slammed his fist on the keyboard and then stood so quickly his chair fell backward. "They locked me out." Fear was etched onto his face. He looked more scared than when we'd been waiting to die from radiation exposure. "They know I was trying to penetrate their system."

Whatever else happened, we needed to return to *Qriosity* before the fold drive engaged. "Forget it, then. It's time to go."

DJ shook his head, undeterred. "I can still get in. We just have to find a computer connected directly to—"

I took DJ's hand and smiled. "Hey. It's all right. We'll find another way home. This isn't the end of the world."

"I'm sorry, Noa."

I kissed his palm and I kissed his cheek and I kissed his lips, and I wished I could keep kissing him until the end of time. But the alarms were incredibly distracting. "Come on. Let's find Jenny and get the hell out of here."

DJ and I dashed into the hallway. He was looking the wrong way and didn't see the three Teachers blocking the path we needed to take to reach the gym. The Teacher in the middle raised one of its appendages, and a bright flash of light erupted from the center. Time moved like honey. My brain registered the threat before I did. The middle Teacher had fired a weapon at us. At DJ. With every ounce of strength I possessed, I shoved him to the linoleum. The blast from the Teacher struck my thigh, and the pain was blinding. I screamed as DJ dragged me down the hallway and away from the Teachers.

My leg was on fire. It was molten lead.

"What were you thinking?" DJ asked. He had pulled me into a classroom and was kneeling beside me.

"Must not have been."

DJ tore open the hole in my trousers, which caused me more pain than actually being shot, and said, "It's not too bad. You're not bleeding." Tears streamed down his cheeks, though he was trying to hide them.

"Hey," I said. "What is it?"

"You're not supposed to do that!" he said. "You're not supposed to risk your life for me. You said you'd never do it, and I . . . I don't know what I'd do without you."

I thought back to the day I had told DJ I wouldn't have put myself in danger to save him the way he'd done for me. So much had changed since then. "I'm fine, DJ. You said so yourself. And I still don't know if I'd have the courage to jump out of a spaceship for you, but I'm not about to lose you either."

DJ sniffled and wiped his tears with his sleeve. When he'd pulled it together, he peeked out the door. "Three Teachers are still blocking the path, but they're not coming for us."

"There has to be a way out," I said. "But I'm not sure about walking." Just the idea of standing sent a surge of pain through my leg.

DJ ran to the other side of the classroom. He returned with a first aid kit and set about applying some type of bandage to my thigh. A cool sensation spread through my leg, and the pain grew distant.

"Do you think you can walk now?" he asked.

With DJ's help, I stood and slowly put weight on my injured leg. It hurt, but I could manage it. "I won't be running."

"You didn't do much running before," DJ said with a smirk.

I gave him the finger and then kissed him.

DJ's face grew sober. "Here's what we're going to do. I'm going to run for it. Distract the Teachers. Then you find Jenny, and the two of you get to the shuttle."

"Nope," I said. "We are *not* splitting up."

DJ cupped my chin in his hand. "They'll never catch me."

"We go together."

"I can do this," he said. "And we'll be together back on the shuttle. I promise."

There had to be a better plan. Something that didn't require DJ to put his life in danger so that I could escape. I even tried to think of what Anastasia Darling would've done, but she would have marched into the hallway and given the Teachers a long-winded speech that would have somehow reprogrammed them to be her friend or caused their robot brains to explode. I doubted that would work for me. I lacked Anastasia Darling's oratorical prowess and her writers.

I had to trust DJ. I *did* trust him.

"Be careful," I said.

"I'll try."

"Don't take this the wrong way," I said. "But I'm going to need you to do a hell of a lot more than try."

DJ kissed me, and then he was gone.

NOW

I COUNTED TO TEN AFTER DJ LEFT BEFORE PEEKING MY head out of the classroom. All three Teachers were gone. The hallway was empty. Over the sound of the alarms, DJ's footsteps echoed as he led the Teachers, who seemed to have no qualms about shooting students with lasers, away from my hiding place.

Not wanting to waste a single second DJ had bought me, I limped back to the gym. The throbbing in my thigh grew more intense with every step, but I forced it out of my mind. My only goal was to reach Jenny and get to the shuttle.

When I emerged from the locker rooms into the gym, the scene made me stop and wonder if I'd slipped and fallen into a vat of hallucinogens at some point in the evening. Everyone was dancing. Everyone but the Teachers. The tables were empty; there were no groups hugging the walls. Every single student was in the center of the gym, dancing. It was like some seriously weird choreographed routine that I did not have the time or patience to deal with.

I scanned the crowd for Jenny and found her in a small group, dancing with Ty and trying valiantly to keep up. She clearly had no idea what she was doing, but she was doing it pretty well. The girl had moves.

The second the song ended, the students splintered off, and I darted toward Jenny.

Jenny's brow was damp with sweat, and she looked a little frazzled, but she smiled when she saw me. "Did you see that?" Her smile flipped. "How did you tear your pants? What's wrong with your leg?"

I held out my hand. "We have to go."

"Did you find—"

"Now, Jenny."

Thankfully, she realized the seriousness of our situation because she didn't argue. Jenny turned to Ty. "This was fun. Deeply, deeply weird. But fun." She grabbed his face and kissed him. It looked and sounded sloppy, and it was awkward to watch, but I also couldn't look away. When she finished, she said, "Later!"

Jenny tried to pull me toward the door, but Ty was pleading with me with his eyes to keep my promise. I wasn't sure I felt bound by what I'd said, seeing as he hadn't given me a choice, but I thought about what DJ would do.

"You need me," he said.

"Oh, Ty," Jenny said. "We had a nice night, but I'm just not that into you."

"I told him he could come with us, Jenny."

Ty leaned in and held out his hand. He was holding a device that looked like a cell phone. "I can help. You won't make it to your shuttle without me."

"What is that?" Jenny asked.

"I've been planning my escape for quite some time," Ty said. "The only piece missing was a ride."

We didn't have time for this. DJ had said he would meet us at the shuttle, and I was going to get there no matter what. "He's coming."

Jenny eyed Ty up and down and finally shrugged. "Yeah, okay. Whatever."

"Let's go," I said.

The second we headed toward the exit, the nearest Teachers turned their red eyes our way. We walked faster, as fast as I could on my injured leg. The Teachers advanced, moving quickly enough to keep up with but not overtake us.

"Keep calm," Ty said.

"Just so you know," I warned them, "those things have lasers."

Jenny dug her nails into my arm, which actually did a fair job of taking my mind off my leg. "Say what now?"

"They're no matter." Now that Ty had dropped his goofy jock routine, he was more secret agent than frat boy. He held the door open for me and Jenny, but a Teacher was waiting for us outside.

"The Equinox Formal does not end for another fifty-seven minutes," Teacher said. "Please return inside and continue to dance." Its eye smoldered, pulsing like a heartbeat.

"No thanks," I said. "I'm all danced out." I limped forward. Teacher rolled back but didn't move out of my way. Three more Teachers emerged from the gym and formed a ring around us.

"You will dance and make merry," the Teachers said in unison, "or you will be punished."

Jenny let out a loud cackle. "I'm so scared. What're you going to do? Give us detention?"

"Did you miss the part where I said they have lasers?"

Ty, Jenny, and I crowded together as the Teachers tightened their circle. "Whatever you're going to do," I said to Ty, "now would be a good time."

"On it." Ty held up the device so the Teachers could see it, and pressed a button on the side. "School's out. *Forever*."

All four Teachers collapsed as if they were puppets and Ty had snipped their strings. Even the light of their red eyes died.

Jenny kicked the nearest Teacher. "How's that for punishment?"

"Did you kill them?" I asked.

Ty shoved the device into his pocket and shook his head. "The EMP's range is short, and it will only take them a few minutes to reboot. We should leave immediately."

He didn't need to tell me twice. We took off in the direction of the shuttle as quickly as my injured leg would allow. Jenny had to help me when the pain grew too great. Thankfully, we didn't encounter any other Teachers along the way, and DJ was waiting for us in front of the hatch. I crashed into him and hugged him like I was never going to let him go.

"You made it!"

DJ laughed. "Why does it sound like you were expecting I wouldn't?"

Instead of a snarky reply, I just kissed him. It felt like the right thing to do.

Ty cleared his throat, and I reluctantly pulled away from DJ. "Hey, DJ," he said.

Jenny pushed past us and buckled herself into the pilot's seat. "Ty's coming with us. This tripartite is now a foursome."

"She's the pilot?" Ty asked, his voice low and skeptical.

"Oh yeah," I said.

Jenny wasted no time preparing the shuttle for launch. She fired up the engines, and we shut the hatch and secured ourselves in our seats. I felt a little sad leaving Beta Cephei High, but I was also eager to return to *Qriosity*. It wasn't home, but it was familiar and safe. Well, safe*ish*. At least it didn't have robots with lasers trying to shoot us.

We reached *Qriosity* with ten minutes to spare, and we crowded into Ops to watch the fold drive tear a hole in the universe. When the countdown clock reached zero, the floating school vanished and was replaced by another empty patch of space in the middle of nowhere.

Jenny gave Ty a tour of the ship, DJ and I made out while MediQwik repaired my leg, and eventually we met up in the galley, where I made French toast. I even crumbled Nutreesh on top of Jenny's.

When we'd had a chance to eat a little, Jenny said, "So are

you going to tell us what that school was or not?"

Ty hadn't said much since boarding *Qriosity*, which I figured was due to the stress of our escape and his relief at finally being away from that place. I kind of expected he'd be a little reluctant to talk about it, but that he'd eventually tell us. I was surprised when his lips twisted into a cruel half smile.

"Why don't *you* tell *me*?" he said. "Or better yet, why don't you tell *them*." Ty motioned at me and DJ.

Jenny had just stuffed French toast into her mouth; syrup dripped from her bottom lip. "What?"

"Enough with the games," Ty said. "I know what you are." He reached into his jacket pocket and pulled out what looked like a pistol. He aimed the deadly end at Jenny.

She swallowed. "What are you talking about?"

Ty sneered. "If you won't tell them, then I'll show them."

I screamed. DJ leaped across the table. But we were too late.

Ty pulled the trigger.

Jenny's chair flew backward. She hit the floor.

DJ tackled Ty, and I rushed to kneel beside Jenny as a quickly spreading pool of blood ruined her beautiful dress.

BACK IN TIME

NOA

JENNY SLEPT IN A MEDICALLY INDUCED COMA WHILE MediQwik repaired her injuries. DJ was napping in the corner. A ribbon of drool ran out of the side of his mouth, and he made little piglet snorts every few minutes. I should have woken him so that he could shower and change out of his ruined tux, but he'd had a long day and needed the rest.

According to MediQwik, Jenny had a 73 percent chance of survival. The projectile had torn her aorta, and she had technically died from blood loss. DJ had scooped her up and carried her to the med suite quickly enough for MediQwik to revive her, but she was now part of a club of which I'd been content to be the only member.

Quietly, so that I didn't wake DJ, I sneaked out of the room and followed the congealed drops and splatters of blood down the corridor to the galley. Mostly eaten French toast had cooled into a sludgy mess on our plates. The sickly sweet smell of butter and syrup and blood hung heavy in the air.

If I left it alone, cleaning bots would do as they were programmed and the mess would disappear, but I couldn't bear to wait. I cleared the table and washed the dishes. Then I found a bucket and hot water and soap and set about scrubbing the blood off the floor and the walls. Drops had splattered onto the table and the chairs. The galley had been my favorite place on *Qriosity*, but now it would always be where Jenny had died.

Anger bubbled in my chest like a geyser on the verge of bursting through the surface. Before I knew what I was doing, I found myself marching through the ship. Standing in front of the head where I had initially found Jenny. Opening the door to stare down at Ty, his hands and feet bound. Kicking him in the stomach over and over. Ty hardly cried out. He didn't beg me to stop. I might have kept kicking him until he hurt as badly as I did, but my leg began to ache where I'd been shot.

"She's going to live," I said between breaths.

"Pity for you." Whoever Ty had been at Beta Cephei High, he was someone else entirely now. He was calculating and equable and British.

I pulled back to kick Ty again, pleased when he flinched. "If you want to live, I suggest you convince me why I shouldn't throw you out of the airlock." I had already lost my temper once, and I fought hard to keep it in check.

"Untie me and I'll explain."

An explosive laugh burst from me. "Not a chance." DJ had

taken the weapon that Ty had used to shoot Jenny. A pistol that looked like it had been cobbled together from spare bits and pieces of other devices; cruder than his EMP, which DJ had also confiscated. Even if I'd had the pistol on me, I wouldn't have trusted Ty enough to free him. And he shouldn't have trusted me, either. It was probably for the best that DJ had kept the gun.

Ty shrugged. If he felt any fear, he hid it well. Bound and completely at my mercy, he looked like he believed he was still in control. That triggered a warning voice in the back of my mind. Either Ty was an absolute psychopath or he knew something I didn't.

"Tell me why you killed Jenny," I said. Before Ty could open his mouth, I added, "This isn't a negotiation. You don't get to suggest terms. Answer my question or I'm leaving."

"You honestly haven't the foggiest idea what's going on, have you?" His laugh made me cringe inside.

"Goodbye." I backed out of the room.

"Beta Cephei High School isn't the only school like it," Ty shouted. "It's not even the first you've attended."

I paused in the doorway. "I'm pretty sure I'd remember going to a high school in space staffed by robot teachers."

Ty's smug expression slid into pity for a moment. "No," he said. "You wouldn't."

"Maybe spending a couple of days alone will make you more talkative."

"You don't remember how you arrived on this ship, do you?" Ty must have sensed my hesitation because he added, "You only remember what they want you to remember."

"Who's 'they'?" I asked. "Tell me what the hell is going on!"

Ty exhaled a weary sigh. "None of this is real, Noa. You're one of the leads on a program called *Now Kiss!* It's currently the most popular show being broadcast throughout the galaxy."

"Okay, yeah. Whatever." Ty's story was ludicrous. Sure, I'd been abducted, had woken up on a spaceship, had spent a couple of months trapped in a single day, had narrowly escaped being eaten by an alien but had nearly died of radiation poisoning, and had just broken out of a floating school with murderous Teachers, but Ty's story was absolutely bonkers.

I expected Ty to backtrack. To tell me he was joking. That he was messing with me. But he didn't. "Trillions of viewers are obsessed with you and DJ. They've been watching you from the moment you woke up, shipping you, rooting for you and DJ to survive the horrors of space, fall in love, and maybe find a way home. DJ's the sweet but resourceful soft boy who would do anything for you, and you're the stubborn hero with the gritty and tragic backstory who uses sarcasm to hide his wounded heart."

With every word that came out of Ty's mouth, my disbelief grew, and when he finally finished, I said, "Right. So you're clearly suffering from a mental disorder. I get it now. But don't worry. I'm sure MediQwik can treat whatever is wrong with you."

"I'm not delusional," Ty said.

I shouldn't have been listening to him. I should have shut the door and walked away. But I needed answers, even if they were nonsense. "Fine," I said. "Pretend I believe DJ and I are the stars of a weird program. That still doesn't explain why you shot Jenny."

Ty tried to scoot into a sitting position, but he found it difficult to move with his hands and feet bound, and gave up. "Jenny isn't who she claims she is. On the program, she plays your batty sidekick, your confidante and friend, but she's a spy for Production. Her job is to guide the story, providing a nudge to you or DJ when necessary, and to prevent you from discovering the truth."

The things that Ty was saying sounded outlandish, and yet I couldn't help wonder if any of them might be true. Had Jenny been locked in the toilet when we woke up so that DJ and I would find each other and work together to prevent *Qriosity* from exploding? Maybe not, but it was possible. And I had always thought it was strange that Jenny shared her name with our ship's hologram. Plus, I'd assumed Jenny's interest in my relationship with DJ was the result of severe boredom, but what if her motives were more sinister?

"Jenny isn't her real name," Ty said. "And she isn't your mate. She's a collaborator, and I wish you had let her die."

"Wish not granted, Ty."

Jenny, supported by DJ, limped toward us. Her face was drawn and pale, and I couldn't stop staring at the ragged, bloody hole in her dress.

"I can't believe I kissed you." Jenny stuck out her tongue and gagged.

"What are you doing out of medical?" I asked. I turned to DJ. "What is she doing out of medical?!"

DJ shrugged. "MediQwik said it was done with her, and she

demanded a shower. I was taking her to her quarters to get some clean clothes."

I hiked my thumb over my shoulder at Ty. "Did you hear the crap he was saying? That we're the stars of a show and Jenny's a spy?"

"I swear she is!" Ty yelled. "She betrayed you!"

Jenny snorted. "That's ridiculous."

"See?" I said.

"I'm not the spy," Jenny went on. "DJ is."

I looked at Jenny like she'd lost her mind. "Are you joking right now? I can never tell when you're joking. Maybe we should return to medical and get you checked—"

DJ shook his head, cut me off. He focused his gaze on the floor. "No, Noa. She's right. Jenny didn't betray anyone. I did."

DJ

THE FIRST TIME I WOKE UP IN SPACE, I PUKED. I THINK IT was about a year ago; I'm not certain. Time's tough to keep track of when you keep losing chunks of it. I wasn't on a spaceship then, but on a station named *Arcas* that was orbiting Callisto, one of the moons of Jupiter. There were twenty-five of us, and we were confused as to how we'd ended up in space. Sound familiar? It was pretty chaotic at first. A real *Lord of the Flies* situation, with folks breaking into factions and trying to take control, pretending they weren't as lost and scared as everyone else.

Arcas was old and rundown, so when we weren't fighting amongst ourselves, we fought to keep the station from crapping out. As soon as we fixed the carbon dioxide scrubbers, gravity plating would malfunction. After that it was the electrical systems, then the Freshie. Eventually, we were so exhausted from trying to stay alive that we stopped caring about who was in charge. We found an unexpected equilibrium in survival.

Then Adam got sick, and everything went to hell.

At first, it seemed like Adam had the flu—fever, joint pain, headache—so we stayed away from him, but no one thought it was a big deal. It was a big deal. Soon after, a thick, yellow mucus began to ooze out of every orifice. Then his skin slowly jellified and sloughed off. He screamed and cried from the pain, and nothing we did helped. Adam died a couple of days after he started showing symptoms. But that wasn't the worst part. The worst came a few hours later, when Adam rose from the dead desperate to do one thing: kill.

Even before the outbreak I'd kept pretty much to myself. I liked tinkering with machines, so the work of keeping the station running came naturally to me. After the outbreak, I did my best to remain apart from the others. Judy had some medical training because her parents were doctors who traveled to impoverished countries and treated those who needed it, but she was in way over her head. She couldn't figure out how the virus was being transmitted or how to treat it. And we didn't have MediQwik. I figured my only chance of surviving was to avoid everyone.

But I couldn't avoid Nico.

Arcas was an enormous station built for way more than twenty-five people, and it had an elevator that ran its length. I was silly to take the elevator in the first place. With more folks getting sick, we hadn't been able to keep up with repairs. Power outages became common. Whole sections of the station were left to freeze. But climbing from one end of *Arcas* to the other could take hours, and I was in a hurry that day. I never asked Nico why he'd risked using the elevator, and he never offered a reason.

At first, Nico and I kept to our corners, figuring the power would come back eventually. It always had before. It was probably around the second hour when he made a joke about which corner we were going to designate the official toilet corner. Come to think of it, he probably hadn't been joking. Either way, it broke the ice, and we started talking to kill time.

I'd seen Nico around plenty, so he wasn't a stranger, but I'd been on the station for weeks and he was the first person I really took the time to get to know. He was the first person I let know me.

Nico was from Baltimore, where he'd been homeschooled by his mom. He'd read more books than any person I'd ever met, and he was passionate about *everything*. He loved to argue, and he usually won. "Space," he said, "is okay, I guess. But have you ever seen the sun rise over the Atlantic from the shore of Nags Head during the summer when it paints the sky like a fever?"

I hadn't, but damned if Nico didn't make me want to.

Two hours turned into four, four into eight. We each ended up using the corner and then pretending there wasn't a puddle of urine on the floor. The power to that section never returned, and after eleven hours, we crawled out through the top of the elevator car and climbed to freedom. From then on, we had each other's backs.

I fell hard and fast for Nico. When he smiled, I forgot I was on a space station full of sick folks who died, rose again, and then hunted the living. Nico and I hid in service tunnels and air ducts. We passed the time constructing elaborate plans to escape *Arcas* and fly back to Earth. We found reasons to laugh amidst the horrors that surrounded us. We found reasons to keep living even as everyone else died. Those weeks were the best of my life. I know it sounds ridiculous, but falling in love is like falling into a black hole. There's no escaping it once you cross the event horizon, and it distorts your sense of time. Hours feel like days, and every day is a lifetime.

I spent lifetimes with Nico, and it wasn't enough.

After three months, only seven of the original twenty-five remained, including me and Nico. The dead stalked the living, and the living learned to avoid the common areas of the station. We learned to move quietly. To sleep in shifts if we had someone we trusted to watch over us, or to avoid sleep altogether if we didn't. The others left Nico and me alone, and we were happy to return the favor. I didn't want any of them to die, but my first concern was for Nico.

Food was growing scarce, and we had to range farther from our hiding places than usual to scavenge. I remembered where there was a large store of food, but we couldn't get to it without crossing through an area the dead had claimed as their own. I had the brilliant idea that I could reach the cargo bay where the food was kept if I traveled outside the station. I already had a suit. I didn't tell Nico because I wanted to surprise him. I wanted to see his face light up with a beautiful smile when I returned with something to eat that wasn't half-rotted or Nutreesh. So I told Nico I'd be back in a few hours and left.

Getting there was easy. I reached the cargo bay with no problems, and I found enough food to keep our bellies full for a month. Returning was where I got into trouble. My oxygen tank malfunctioned, and I didn't have enough air to get back. It took me nearly two days to find another tank while keeping hidden from the dead. I managed to get myself stabbed in the belly by a jagged piece of metal, and I had nothing to fix the wound with but antibiotics, glue, and prayer. The whole time, I was scared Nico would try to come find me, and get caught by the dead. It wasn't the first time one of us had been out longer than expected, but Nico could be impulsive. It was one of the things I loved about him.

When I finally returned to our room, Nico had locked the door and wouldn't let me in.

"Come on," I said. "I'm sorry I was gone so long, but I brought you chocolate."

"I'm sick," he called through the door. "I have yellow crap coming out of my eyes."

I pounded on the door. I clawed at it until my fingernails broke and bled. I screamed until my voice was raw. "Let me in!" I refused to believe Nico was sick. I refused to leave him to suffer alone. I refused to let him die.

"No," he said. "You have to get away from here."

"I'm not leaving you, Nico. I'll never leave you. Not ever."

Nico kept trying to convince me to go, that it was too dangerous to stay. He tried to be gentle, telling me he'd been worried. That he was happy he wasn't going to die wondering what'd happened to me. He tried being mean, saying he didn't love me and never had. He even begged. But I wouldn't go.

I sat in front of the door for two days, talking to him while he grew sicker. Crying silently while he screamed from the pain and begged me to kill him. I told him stories, I told him lies, I told him the only truth I knew: that I would love him forever. I stayed with him until he took his last, gasping breath.

After that, living was little more than a habit. I became lost in my grief. I got careless. I wasn't looking to die, but I didn't care much for living, either. A couple of weeks after Nico passed, I allowed myself to become cornered in an airlock. There were no suits, no spare oxygen tanks, and only one way out. I'd seen what happened to folks who were caught by the living dead, and I didn't want to die that way.

My idea was to open the hatch, blow the zombies into space without being blown out myself, and repressurize the airlock before I suffocated.

The first part of my plan worked. The second part, not so much.

NOA

WE HAD REGROUPED IN THE MED SUITE BECAUSE DYING was exhausting and I didn't want Jenny to overexert herself. "This is some bullshit," Jenny said.

"I agree." I was sitting as far from Ty and DJ as I could in the small room, trying not to stare at DJ but finding it difficult to avoid. I didn't know who he was anymore. I wondered if I ever had.

DJ held up his hands, trying to regain control of the room. "I know it sounds ridiculous—"

"The part where you were living on a space station full of zombies?" Jenny asked. "Or the part where we're all on a program and I'm not the star?"

"I promise everything will make sense when I finish, but I've still got a lot to tell you." The DJ speaking now lacked the confidence of the DJ I'd spent the last few months getting to know. But I also sensed from him a feeling of relief that he didn't have to hide anymore.

"I thought Ty was a hell of an actor," I said. "But you clearly win the award for best performance in a drama."

"Noa—"

"Was anything real? Was our whole relationship make-believe?" A thought occurred to me. The room contracted, breathing in and out. "Was that *his* outfit I woke up on this ship in? Did you dress me in your dead boyfriend's clothes?"

"Christ, DJ," Jenny said. "That's sick."

"I'm not Nico," I said.

DJ hung his head. "No. You're not."

I didn't know what to say or do. I wanted to run dramatically from the room and fling myself out of the ship, but that would have killed me and I didn't want to die. It seemed I wasn't the only one unsure what to say. Jenny was uncharacteristically quiet as well.

It was Ty who finally broke the silence. "Please don't stop, DJ. You dying was the best part of that whole maudlin story, and I must know what happens next."

"We should've gagged him," Jenny said.

I glanced at the cabinets along the wall. "We still can. I'm sure there's something in here we can use."

Jenny swung her legs over the side of the bed and came to sit beside me. She leaned her head on my shoulder. "Do you want DJ to go on? We don't have to do this now."

I caught DJ's eye. Telling the story seemed to cause him at least as much pain as it caused me to hear. So I nodded. Partly because I needed to know the whole truth. Partly because I wanted DJ to hurt.

DJ

THE SECOND TIME I WOKE UP IN SPACE, I WAS RESTING on the bottom bunk of a barracks-style room that I was sharing with at least fifty other teens. I opened my eyes gasping, struggling for breath and not understanding why there was oxygen and why I could breathe. My last memory was of suffocating. Of dying. It took a moment to realize I was no longer in a vacuum. I wasn't even on *Arcas*. I was thrilled to be alive, but confused about how. Thankfully, in that, I wasn't alone.

I got up and wandered around. The overhead lights were too bright. I stumbled into a girl, who shoved me back like I'd attacked her. Kids were shouting questions into the air and flinging accusations at one another. The smell of violence filled the room the way the sharp tang of ozone heralds an oncoming storm, propelled by confusion and fear. I began herding some of the younger kids toward the walls to get them out of harm's way.

Just when it seemed like the chaos had reached a tipping point, a sharp screech cut through the noise, and we were all suddenly too busy shielding our ears with our hands to worry about anything else. A hologram of a woman in her mid-thirties appeared at the front of the room, and the alarm stopped.

"Hi! I'm your host, Jenny Perez, whom you probably remember as the precocious kid detective and bestselling author Anastasia Darling on the award-winning mystery entertainment program *Murder Your Darlings*. If you're seeing this, then you have died. Sorry about it!"

One of the boys I'd gathered around me—he looked twelve or thirteen—broke into tears. I didn't think crying was going to do anyone much good, but I couldn't fault him for doing it. If there was ever a situation that called for crying, we were in it.

"Welcome to the Fomalhaut Processing Center. On the surface is Fomalhaut High School, where you will attend classes, dances, and sporting events, and go about your typical teenage lives, during which time you will be assessed by Production. Your performance will determine your next placement, so do your very best!

"Refusal to participate is not an option and will earn you a spot at the Jenny Perez Reeducation Arts and Crafts Camp. Rule breaking of any kind will not be tolerated and will result in punishment. Teachers will be watching at all times, and they're not nearly as pleasant as me. But if you do what you're told, and put on a great show, you just might survive.

"I'm so happy we understand each other. Now, you have one hour to clean yourselves up, get dressed, and prepare for your first day of school. Good luck, students. You'll need it!"

The hologram hadn't explained much. If anything, I had more questions after her speech than I'd had before. But punishment sounded like something I wanted to avoid, so I followed Jenny Perez's orders and suggested the others do the same. I took a shower. I found my schedule when I looked at my hand. There were clothes in my size in a footlocker with my name on it by the bunk I'd woken up in. I put on the first things I grabbed. I fell into the crowd and took the escalators to the surface for school.

It was surreal. I didn't know where I was, but it looked like Earth. Blue sky, trees, clouds. Even the school buildings seemed like they'd been lifted right out of a TV show. But this wasn't a program. Each of us remembered dying, we were all being held against our will, and our teachers were robots.

My first period was an orientation for new students where my Teacher played a video to show us what happened to anyone who broke the rules. All I'm gonna say about that is I'm glad I hadn't eaten breakfast. What they did to anyone who got injured or sick was equally bad. Instead of punishment, they were sent for reconstruction.

I was determined to stay out of trouble, especially after a kid in my second-period class lost it, and a Teacher came in and dragged her away. Jenny Perez hadn't been exaggerating.

For the rest of that day, I went to my classes, but I don't remember what happened during any of them. I couldn't help wondering if I'd died and gone to hell. The idea didn't seem less rational than anything else I could come up with.

But I wasn't in hell. I realized that when I spotted Nico on my second day as I was walking to third period. If Nico was there, maybe I was in heaven.

"Nico?"

When Nico saw me, he dropped his books and sprinted across the quad, shoving aside anyone who got in his way. He threw his arms around my neck and kissed me. I wasn't sure how much time had passed since I'd last seen his beautiful smile, but it felt like it'd been forever. I melted into Nico's arms. I cried. I sobbed so hard that other students stopped to stare.

"Hey," he said, brushing my hair back. "Hey, it's okay. We're both here. We're alive." He kissed my forehead and led me to a quiet hall. "I need you to pull it together. I've got to get to moral philosophy, and while Production doesn't mind a good crying scene, they don't care for ugly crying."

No one cried uglier than me. My face got splotchy and my eyes bloodshot. But Nico had to understand that I was crying because I was happy and because I was scared and because I'd been there when he'd died. A maelstrom of conflicting emotions was threatening to overwhelm me.

Nico kissed me again. "We are going to be okay."

I wanted to believe him. "What do we do now?" I asked. "How do we escape?"

"Quiet," Nico said. "I'll find you at lunch, but I have to get to class. You'd better go too. You don't want to be punished. Trust me." Before I could stop him, he slipped into the stream of students heading away from me and was gone.

Losing Nico had been the worst trauma I'd ever experienced, and that included being trapped on a space station with zombies. Finding him again was like finding a lost piece of my soul. I couldn't stop smiling for the rest of the morning. It was apparently so distracting that a Teacher threatened to punish me if I didn't stop.

True to his word, Nico tracked me down at lunch and told me he wanted to show me his favorite spot. He led me to the football field and under the bleachers. The moment we passed into the shadows, Nico kissed me until I couldn't breathe. He wrapped his arms around my waist and kissed me like our last kiss had only been practice. He kissed me like someone who had believed he would never see me again. And when he pulled away, he had tears running down his cheeks.

"What's going on, Nico?" I asked. "We were on *Arcas* and you died. *I* died."

Nico brushed his lips across my knuckles. "How did you go? You didn't get sick, did you?"

I shook my head. "Cornered in an airlock by zombies. I blew the hatch, figuring I could pressurize it when they were gone, but I guess that didn't work out so well." I looked around. "Or did it? Where are we?"

"I don't know *where* we are, but it's not real." Nico huffed like he was frustrated. "It's real in that it's actually happening, but it's part of a program. Sort of. Production is watching us, but only so they can decide where to use us next. They're not actually broadcasting what happens here."

Nothing Nico was saying made sense, and he was talking so quickly that I had to wait until he took a breath to speak. "What happened to us on that station felt pretty real to me."

"We were secondary characters on a program called *Outbreak on Arcas*. Our only function was to die." Even as Nico was saying it, I could tell he didn't quite believe it either. "Production keeps recycling us. We get assigned to a program. When we die or outlive our storyline, they bring us to a school where we wait for our next assignment. Then they rewrite our memories with whatever character they've decided we're going to play, and it starts all over again."

"I remember my parents," I said. "And school."

"Those aren't your memories." Nico held on to my hand like it was an anchor. "There's more." He kept going without giving me time to absorb what he'd already said. "I've been talking to people, and I think they also do something to us that slows down our aging. I heard a rumor about a student who might be in her early thirties, but they just assigned her to play a high school freshman."

My knees were too weak hold me up. I sat on the dirt, not caring what might be in it. "So this Production just wipes our memories clean and pops in some new ones?"

"It's slightly more complicated than that," Nico said. "They can't change our fundamental personalities, but they can swap out our memories with memories harvested from other students and create new backstories to make us more interesting."

"I'm not real." It was too much to process. I felt like my brain had disconnected from my body to protect itself. "None of this is real."

Nico was crouching beside me. He cupped my chin in his hand. "You're real. My feelings for you are real. None of this changes that."

"How can it not?" I asked.

"Because we are who we are now." Nico kissed my forehead, lingering. "I love you. Do you love me?"

I nodded, unable to speak.

"Then that's what matters."

My entire body shook as I fell into Nico, just holding him. He was alive, which was everything I'd wanted after he'd died. But I felt like we were in the eye of a hurricane, death and destruction swirling around us.

"What do we do?" I still had a lot of questions about the school and Teachers and who Production was and how they abducted us, but those could wait.

"I'm working on that," Nico said. "Security is tight, and I don't know where we are. I suspect we're on a planet or a very large ship. With your computer skills, we should be able to learn more. But we have to be careful. If Production catches us—"

"Punishment?"

Nico nodded. Fresh tears welled in his eyes. "I missed you so much."

"No one's ever going to separate us again, Nico. I swear it."

Over the next few weeks, Nico and I settled into a routine. We were inseparable except when we were in class. Nico had gotten to know a few of the other students and had tried to piece together the puzzle that was our lives, but there were still bits missing that we worked together to fill in.

We learned that Fomalhaut High School was a way station where students were kept when they weren't on an active program, during which time Production evaluated them for their next assignment. Every student we spoke to had come from somewhere strange. Joon had been surprised to wake up in a castle and discover she was a wizard in training, Carlos had been a rogue grim reaper, and Sophie and Lydia had been twins on opposite sides of a violent and bloody competition to be named their high school's valedictorian. But most of the students at Fomalhaut High were there because they'd died on their program. Gloria had been the girlfriend of a young woman whose best friend was a girl named Charlie, who was destined to save the world from an unspeakable evil. Gloria had been stabbed in a random act of violence. Alfie died when he fell through the ice trying to reach his best friend, Winter, on whom he'd had an unrequited crush for years. Nara had died when their car was run off the road by an assassin who had mistaken them for someone else. Then there was Lexi, who'd sacrificed her life to help a vampire regain his conscience. Most of the stories were similar. Most students had been secondary characters who, at best, had died to serve as the emotional motivation for someone else, or at worst, had died for no real reason at all.

"This is where they bury their gays," Nico said after I told him about Lexi. We were eating lunch under the bleachers because, other than the showers, it was the only place we were safe from the prying eyes of Teachers and Production. "We're disposable to them. Nothing but filler bitches."

It did seem that everyone at Fomalhaut had been a background character in someone else's story, but that wasn't my biggest concern. "Who is Production?" I asked. "How's any of this legal?"

Nico snorted. "Legal? Are you planning to demand a lawyer?"

"No, but—"

"I don't care who Production is or about exposing their big evil plan. We need to remain focused on escaping this nightmare."

Nico was right. Escape remained our primary goal, and he'd come up with a plan. I'd finally managed to gain access to a computer and had learned that we were on an asteroid. The top level was the school, with a dome to hold in the atmosphere and provide the illusion of sky; the second level contained a mall, where students socialized after classes; the third level included the barracks where we slept; and the lower level was heavily secured—students were not authorized to enter. While digging through the computer, I also found out that ships regularly docked with Fomalhaut, dropping off students who died on their programs and transporting students who'd been reassigned by Production to their new shows. Sometimes the ships remained docked for a few days. Nico figured our best chance off the rock was to steal a ship while it was empty. But that was easier said than done. Production monitored our movements, and the loading docks were located on the lower level. We wouldn't make it down the escalator before being intercepted by a Teacher. It seemed an impossible task, but Nico was undeterred.

"How are we going to do this?" I asked.

Nico leaned his head against my shoulder and sighed. "I don't know, but we're smart. We'll figure it out."

I frowned at him.

"Fine," he said. "*You're* smart."

Even if he was right, I wasn't sure I wanted to escape. Our life wasn't perfect, but we had each other and I was scared of risking that. It had been different for Nico because he'd died first. He hadn't been the one left alone on *Arcas*. He wasn't the one who'd had to listen to the person he loved suffer in agony as they died. Even when he woke up at Fomalhaut without me, he at least had the comfort of knowing that I was alive. Losing Nico had carved that fear into my bones. It had left indelible scars on my heart. I could think of nothing worse than losing Nico again.

Nico was never going to give up, though. He just wasn't wired to quit.

Besides, eventually Production would assign us to a new program, and I doubted they'd keep us together. They'd rip out our memories and fill our heads with new ones, and the next time I saw Nico, he wouldn't recognize me. I'd been serious about never leaving him again, so I redoubled my efforts and eventually found the solution.

Buried deep within the command structure of the operating system that controlled the entire facility was a maintenance program that would reboot all of the robots simultaneously. The upside was that it would clear the way for Nico and me to get to the docks, find a ship, and steal it. The downside was that we would only have two minutes to accomplish our task.

I wanted to tell some of our friends. Help as many of them escape as we could. Nico convinced me that it would be difficult enough with just the two of us, but that we'd definitely fail if we had to shepherd ten or twenty or thirty others. Our best bet was to keep the plan to ourselves, escape, and then find a way to help those we'd left behind. We only made one exception.

I'd met Karen in my third-period class, theoretical atomic, molecular, and chemical physics. She'd been on a supernatural program called *Love Craft*, about a group of teenage witches who accidentally summon a monstrous deity who offers them immense power in return for the hearts of the lovesick. Karen, who'd been quietly pining over their group's funny girl, Alethea, died a gruesome death immediately after admitting her feelings to Alethea and discovering the other girl felt the same. Karen was sullen and prone to brooding. She often wiggled her fingers at people and whispered curses at them even after she learned none of what she'd experienced had been real. But we invited her to escape with us because we needed a pilot, and she'd once boasted she knew how to fly.

The three of us spent another week working out the kinks in our plan. We decided to leave on the night of the Homecoming football game because the students and the majority of the Teachers would be attending the mandatory event. We removed the tracking devices from under our skin and planted them on other students so they would be our unwitting alibis. And then, right after kickoff, I executed the command.

We nearly escaped. Earlier that day, I'd identified the perfect ship to steal. A little cruiser. It was small, so it would be easier to pilot, and it was close to the entrance, so we could reach it faster. With the Teachers incapacitated, we raced to the ship, got inside, and fired it up. There was one thing we hadn't anticipated. We couldn't release the docking clamps from inside the ship. It had to be done from the control room. We weren't going anywhere.

The reboot sequence finished while we were still on the ship. Teachers came, took us into custody, and threw Karen into one holding cell and Nico and me into another.

"You're bleeding again," Nico said. One of the Teachers had cut a gash in my upper arm during the struggle. It wasn't serious, but it was bleeding pretty fiercely.

"It's nothing."

Nico broke down. "I'm so sorry," he said, crying into my chest. "This is all my fault."

I was scared, but I held Nico as tightly as I could. "They can scoop out chunks of my brain with a spoon, and I will never forget you."

"You're the best thing in my life," Nico said. "Even if my memories aren't real, you're real. You will always be real to me."

"I love you, Nico. Forever."

Those were the last words I said to Nico before Teachers

took him away. I waited alone in the cell for hours or maybe days. I don't know. When they came for me, I figured they were going to drag me to a room with a creepy medical chair like the one I'd seen in the orientation video. Instead, a Teacher escorted me to a cozy office where I was instructed to sit on a comfortable leather couch and wait. A few minutes later, a familiar woman entered the room.

"Hi!" she said. "I'm Jenny Perez." She offered me her hand, which I only shook to make sure she wasn't a hologram. She looked exactly like I remembered, only she was wearing a pink suit instead of blue. "You have been a naughty young man."

Jenny took a seat across from me and poured us each a cup of tea from a ceramic teapot, smiling warmly, as if we were two old friends. "Sugar?" she asked.

"Two," I said, though I had no intention of drinking anything she gave me. "What are you going to do to me? Punishment?"

Jenny Perez slid the cup and saucer across the table, and lifted her own tea to her lips. She closed her eyes as she sipped. All I'd been given since arriving at Fomalhaut had been Nutreesh and Hydrophoria, and the citrus aroma wafting from my teacup was tempting.

"That depends on you, my little chickadee."

"Me?"

"You very nearly escaped. No student has ever come as close as you did." Jenny Perez's smile was tight. "As a result, you have given the other students hope, and we certainly can't have that, can we?" She continued to sip her tea. "If I must, I will strip out your memories, stuff in a few new ones, and have you reeducated to make you more pliable. But I would rather you be punished in a way that serves as a warning to anyone else imagining they might escape. For that, I need your cooperation."

I felt a small surge of pride in knowing that Nico, Karen, and I had nearly outwitted the school. That others at Fomalhaut High knew what we had done, and that our attempt might inspire others to try. "Why would I help you if you're just going to punish me anyway?"

Jenny flicked her hand at the wall, and a screen lit up, resolving into a live video stream of Nico. He was in a room like I'd imagined ending up in, strapped to a chair, fighting against his bonds.

"Every program that's broadcast has a minder," Jenny Perez said. "A person, like you, who retains their memories and the knowledge that they're on a program. Their job is to remain in contact with Production and to steer the narrative when necessary."

"Like a spy?" I finally couldn't resist the tea anymore. I was already at Jenny's mercy. If she'd wanted to poison or drug me, she wouldn't have needed to spike my drink. It was a delicate black tea with hints of lemon and orange. It took all my strength not to gulp it.

Jenny tilted her head to the side. "You could look at it that way if you choose, though a minder's job is also to protect the others from themselves."

"Okay?"

"Production is working on a new program. A meta reimagining of *Murder Your Darlings,* the most popular program ever broadcast. The star is a young woman named Jenny—after me, of course—who finds herself aboard a ship named *Qriosity*." Jenny spoke about the show with a reverence that was strangely endearing. "Jenny, along with two young men—one her best friend, the other her rival—will travel from world to world, solving small whodunits while attempting to unravel the biggest mystery of all: where they came from and how they get home.

"Jenny will, obviously, have help in the form of the witty and clever ship's hologram—me! And each adventure will follow a similar pattern. Jenny will stumble upon a mystery; the three of you will investigate; the best friend, played by Nico, will get hurt; the rival, you, will cause problems; and Jenny will follow the clues to the solution."

This sounded like a joke, but Jenny Perez was dead serious. "So my punishment is to watch Nico get hurt over and over?"

Jenny Perez smiled gleefully. "And to be trapped aboard a spaceship with the love of your life who has no idea who you are, who has no memory of your past together, who doesn't feel about you the way you feel about him and never, ever will—we'll make certain of it."

The idea of looking into Nico's eyes and seeing a stranger was unfathomable. It was one thing to be threatened with the erasure of both of our memories, but to remain whole while Nico forgot? I didn't know if I could survive that.

"What if I say no?"

On the screen, two Teachers detached from the walls and closed in on Nico. He struggled harder against the restraints, but he would never break them. Jenny said, "We're going to rewrite his memory regardless, but if you refuse to play your role, we'll simply arrange for Nico to die tragically during the first episode—to motivate our heroine, of course—and introduce a different companion to take his place. Nico will be sent to a school far away, and you will never see him again."

I didn't want to cry in front of Jenny Perez, but I couldn't hold back the tears. I was helpless. If I agreed to her terms, I would lose Nico. But I'd lose him if I told her no too.

Asking me to choose had always been part of my punishment.

"Why are you doing this?" I wiped my nose with my sleeve. "All of this? What's it for?"

Jenny Perez laughed. "Ratings, silly."

Our program was called *A Complicated Mystery Set in Space*. Karen became Jenny Price, teen sleuth, cat fan, and Nutreesh addict whose parents moved frequently when she was a child, making her well suited to a nomadic life in space. Nico was rewritten as Noa North, a Seattle teen who loved baking, hated math, and had trust issues due to a secret trauma from his past. And I would play DJ Storm, a schemer from Florida who was constantly causing problems, and who screwed things up as often as I fixed them.

I watched them march Karen and Nico onto *Qriosity*. Except they weren't Karen and Nico anymore. They were you—Jenny and Noa. Your lifeless eyes, the way you stared without seeing me. It hurt more than I had imagined it would.

Production had decided our program would begin in the

middle of a crisis. *Qriosity* would be on the verge of exploding. I would be in Reactor Control, Noa would be in a spacesuit outside the ship, and Jenny would be in Ops, where she would seize control of the situation, tell us each what to do, and save the day.

The hologram of Jenny Perez stood over me after the Teachers left the ship. "Once *Qriosity* reaches its destination, you will need to dress Noa in his spacesuit and get him into position outside the ship. Jenny is already in Ops." She smiled at me like a predator. "I'll be watching you personally, DJ."

I was going to go along with it. Come up with a plan to free us while our program played out. But when I went to the airlock to put Noa into his suit, I realized I couldn't do it. It was really Production's fault. They had dressed Noa in an ill-fitting jumpsuit that had Nico's name on it. Just one of the small ways they meant to punish me. But seeing Nico's name on Noa's outfit reminded me that Nico wasn't really gone. His memories might've been gone, but *he* wasn't. And maybe there was a way to remind him that he had loved me.

So I changed the plan.

I put Noa in the spacesuit, but I posted a note in his hud to prevent him from panicking. I ran to Ops before Jenny woke up, and I dragged her to the head and locked her in. The cut on my arm from our escape attempt started bleeding again, and got on Jenny's sleeve, but I didn't have time to find new clothes for her. When I was done, I raced to Reactor Control just as Noa was waking up.

You lived the rest.

NOA

I DIDN'T THINK IT WAS POSSIBLE TO LOVE SOMEONE SO much, and hate them, all at once. But that's how I felt about DJ by the time he finished his story. I wanted to kiss him because I did love him and I loved him for what he had done to be with me. But I wanted to kick him for every lie and every deception. He had betrayed me so thoroughly, but he had done so only because he loved me so thoroughly. And he was staring at me, hopeful, waiting for me to tell him that I understood, waiting for me to forgive him. I didn't have the words, at that moment, for either.

Ty broke the silence. "How did you get away with it?" he asked. "Surely, Production attempted to stop you."

DJ nodded. "They planned to. As soon as the crisis on *Qriosity* was resolved, Jenny Perez was going to keep her promise to kill Noa. But Jenny Perez was the one who had said everything is about ratings, and ours were the highest for any debut in history. Viewers fell in love with me and Noa. They wanted to watch *our* story.

"So Production quickly retitled the program *Now Kiss!* and let it play out."

Ty looked somehow appalled and impressed simultaneously. "You've just been doing whatever you want this entire time?"

"No," DJ said. "I'd changed the nature of the show, and Production was *angry*. They let me know they were still in charge by cutting us down to emergency power. They invented the Phone Home protocol that sent us skipping through space to make Jenny and Noa hate me. Every single awful thing that's happened to us has been arranged by them."

"The looping day?" I asked.

"Best episode by far," Ty said.

DJ nodded but then stopped and shook his head. "Kind of. The loop was intended to torture me, but Jenny found the time device before she was meant to, and the nanites that MediQwik used to repair your brain injury after you died protected you from the loop. That's why you remembered what happened when it reset."

"What about Kayla?" I asked. "Did you kill her?"

"No!" DJ said. "She was the spare companion. The one who would take your place if Production decided to remove you. She escaped on her own. I think Production had her killed somehow."

"Is that everything?" I asked. "Are you keeping anything else from us?" The question came out harsh, and DJ flinched.

"No," he said. "That's everything."

Jenny had been quiet for a while, which was unusual. In a low voice full of icy rage, she said, "This was supposed to be *my* story? I really was supposed to be the star, and you hijacked it?"

"Jenny, I—"

"You don't talk, DJ. You don't get to talk to me at all!"

But DJ ignored her. "This was important, Jenny! You've got to see that."

"What I see is that you have been gaslighting me this whole time," she said. "You changed the results when I did the DNA test so that the blood on my jacket wouldn't match yours. You've been the one erasing the footage from cameras—"

"Production's doing that."

"With your knowledge!" Jenny yelled. "I get it! I get that you wanted Nico back, but what about *me*? What about the story you stole from me? Did you even give that a moment's thought?"

DJ opened his mouth to answer, closed it, and shook his head.

Ty cleared his throat. "Sorry for shooting you, Jenny. I'd be happy to shoot DJ if that would make amends."

"Don't tempt me," she said.

I looked up and DJ caught my eye. I could feel the questions he was dying to ask, feel the things he needed me to say. Maybe it would have been easier if I had yelled at him the way Jenny had. Gotten the anger out in the open. But I couldn't. Instead, I simply stood and walked away.

THE WEIGHT OF THE TRUTH

ONE

THE FALSE SUN OF THE OXYGEN GARDEN WARMED MY face as I lay by the pond with my eyes shut. If I ignored the subtle vibrations running through *Qriosity*, I could almost imagine I was stretched out on a blanket at the park on a summer day. That if I opened my eyes, my mom would be sitting beside me reading a book and Becca would be on the other side trying to take the perfect picture. But I wasn't outside. It wasn't summer. I wasn't on Earth. I didn't even know if Becca and my mom were real. The sun was a lie. Everything was a lie.

"I'm sorry, Noa."

I'd known DJ was there. It couldn't have been Jenny because she shuffled her feet when she walked, and there was no way DJ would let Ty run free on the ship. I kept my eyes closed because I wasn't sure if I could look at him.

"Don't you mean Nico?"

"I mean you," DJ said. He let out a low growl of frustration. "This is so confusing. Nico's gone, I know that, but he also isn't. He's still in you. At the same time, he was never real to begin with. Neither is Noa. The person I'm in love with isn't Nico or Noa. It's who you are when everything else is stripped away."

I opened my eyes and sat up, still unwilling to look at DJ. "If I'm not Noa, if I'm not real, then who am I?"

DJ sat across from me, keeping his distance. "Noa's just a name. Changing it doesn't change you." He plucked a blade of grass and held it up. "We could call this a dribble of jelly instead of a blade of grass, but that wouldn't change what it is."

He reached his hand to me, but I ignored it and he slowly pulled back. "None of this is fair, Noa. I get that. I've had months to wrestle with these questions and I'm still struggling."

The last thing I wanted to hear was how much DJ hurt when his wounds were mostly self-inflicted. "I cried myself to sleep at night, thinking about how worried and scared my mom must have been when I never came home. She's not real, though. None of them are real! Not Becca or Mrs. Blum or . . ."

"Noa—"

"Christ, DJ! Was what Billy did to me real?" I fought back a sob. "Did Production stick a memory of me being raped into my head because they thought it would make me more interesting?"

"I know how you feel."

"No you don't!"

DJ's Adam's apple bobbed. "Part of my backstory on *Arcas*, the reason I kept away from people and enjoyed fixing things more than socializing, was because I had a head full of memories about older brothers who tortured me. They locked me in a dark closet and left me there for hours. They used me as a practice dummy for tackling. I idolized them and I despised them and I was terrified of them. By the time I got to *Arcas*, I wanted nothing to do with anyone."

I finally looked at DJ. I had no reason to believe him except that I did. "Don't you see how twisted and cruel that is? We don't mean anything to Production. We're just a collection of tragedies the audience gets to watch make out."

"We're more than that, Noa. You're more."

The weight of the truth was too much. I felt like I was collapsing in on myself. "Who we were *is* who we are," I said. "Our experiences are the scaffolding for the people we become. If none of my memories are real, then nothing about me is real! Why do I love baking if it isn't because Mrs. Blum taught me? Why do I love horror movies if it isn't because my mom and I marathon-watched them every October? Why do I love reading so much if it isn't because of the summer days I spent on my apartment building's roof, soaking up the sun with my battered copy of *Brown Girl Dreaming*?"

"Those memories *are* real, Noa. They may not have belonged to you, but they belonged to someone. There is a real Mrs. Blum who owns a bakery. There is a real Billy who deserves to be in jail." DJ clenched his fists.

"So what?" I said. "They're not my memories."

"They are now," DJ countered. "They're in your head. You're

their caretaker. You have to honor the people those memories were harvested from and the pain they endured creating them."

"Doesn't that make us as bad as Production?" I asked. "They're stolen memories regardless of whether I stole them. Our audience"—just saying the word made me uncomfortable—"loves us because of who we are, but who we are is a lie. A lie appropriated from others. If I keep playing that role, then I'm complicit."

Even knowing that I had probably never lived in Seattle, that my father hadn't abandoned me, that I didn't have a best friend named Becca, those memories still felt like my life. They were mine, but they didn't belong to me. "I don't know who I am, DJ."

"You're Noa North. You're courageous and stubborn. You doubt yourself and your own worth even when everyone around you can see how amazing you are. You have a dark sense of humor, but you love making people smile."

"Did Nico like to bake?"

DJ shook his head. "Nico loved to paint. Even after people got sick, he'd sneak around the station and paint murals on the walls of sunny beaches or snowcapped mountains in the hopes that it might make someone's day a little better."

"Oh."

"You bake, he painted, but you're both kind and generous."

It was easier if I thought of Nico as a totally different person and not as someone who had inhabited my body before me. "Why didn't you tell me?" I asked. "Was it easier to manipulate me into falling in love with you if I didn't know?"

DJ looked like I'd torn open his belly with a rusty baling hook. "I . . . I swear I didn't manipulate you."

"Didn't you?"

"I promise," he said. "I did everything I could to give you your space and let whatever happened between us happen."

"What would you have done if I had never returned your feelings?"

"I would have been happy to have your friendship."

It was so difficult to believe him. How often had I believed his lies in the past? He looked sincere, but he had proven he was a talented liar.

"And I didn't tell you because I wasn't allowed," DJ said. "After you died, Production made contact through Jenny Perez. They informed me that our ratings were the only reason they weren't canceling us immediately. They warned me not to tell you or Jenny the truth."

"You could have tried," I said. "I would have."

DJ nodded solemnly. "I know. Just like on Fomalhaut. I was so scared of losing you that I was willing to do anything to hold on to what we had, even if it was imperfect."

I kept trying to sympathize with DJ, but he had lied to me. He'd betrayed me. I didn't know how to reconcile that with my feelings for him.

"Are we in danger now?" I asked.

"I honestly don't know," he said. "Production has controlled everything that's happened to us. They set the alien loose; they trapped us in Reactor Control and flooded it with radiation. We never would have arrived near the school if they hadn't wanted us to. I assumed they'd planned for Ty to join us, but now I don't think they did." He shrugged. "I've got no idea what happens next."

"Okay." It was the only thing I could say. I was heartbroken and confused. DJ was the one person I wanted to talk through my feelings with, but he was also the one person I couldn't.

"Noa, please believe me. I didn't mean to hurt you."

"I need time, okay?" I told him. "Just give me some time."

Slowly, DJ stood and turned to leave. "I wish I could tell you to take as long as you need, but we may not have much time left."

TWO

JENNY WAS ALONE IN HER QUARTERS, SITTING CROSS-legged on her bed, when I found her. I'd tried the galley first, but she was gone. Ty was gone too, and I assumed DJ had locked him up again. Not that I cared. Ty could've taken a short walk out of the airlock and it wouldn't have made much difference to me.

"Should I call you Nico or Noa?" she asked.

I shrugged. "Should I call you Jenny or Karen?"

"It's so weird to think that there was some other me wandering around in my body," Jenny said. "But from what DJ described of Karen, you boys got the better version of me."

Jenny had changed into a pair of comfy sweats and a tank top. Her ruined dress lay in a heap on the floor in the corner. I motioned at it with my chin. "How's your . . . How're you feeling?"

"I died, Noa."

"Welcome to the club."

Jenny barked out a laugh, then covered her mouth as if embarrassed at the sound. "Sorry."

"No need to be," I said. "Did you *see* anything when you were dead?"

"Like a bright light?"

"Or whatever."

Jenny pursed her lips, frowned, and then shook her head.

"Me neither." I sat beside Jenny, and she rested her head on my shoulder. "This is so messed up."

It was a few moments before Jenny replied. "My whole life, I've felt like someone's sidekick. In middle school, it was Margie Gelbwasser. She was my best friend, but she was always up to something, dragging me along for the ride. In high school, it was the same, but with a different group. I followed. I was a follower. But I had this feeling I could be more. That, if given the opportunity, I could step up; I could be the star.

"And then I had the chance, and DJ locked me in the toilet and forced me into the background again."

I leaned back and stared at her. "That's what you're pissed about? That DJ snatched the spotlight?"

"Everyone wants the chance to tell their story, Noa." I attempted to interrupt, but Jenny wasn't having it. "Do you know what I went through while you were trapped in the reactor room, making out with DJ?"

"We weren't—"

"No, you don't," she said. "Because you didn't ask. You didn't care. And neither does whoever watches our program, because the story has been about you." The more Jenny spoke, the more worked up she got. "You haven't even asked how I knew DJ was the one who'd betrayed us."

So much had happened since then that I'd forgotten Jenny had called it. "How?"

"Because I'm a damned good detective, that's how," she said. "I've been onto DJ for weeks."

"Why didn't you say anything?"

Jenny's anger receded slightly. "Well, I knew *something* was weird—he disappeared from the ship's surveillance feed a lot, and I heard him talking to himself more than once—but I didn't know exactly what it was until Ty shot me and said I had betrayed you. Ty knew one of us had to be a spy for Production—DJ told us that every program has one—and he assumed it was me because you and DJ are the stars. I didn't know about us being on a program until after Ty shot me, but I figured that if Ty thought one of us was a spy, and I knew it wasn't me, then the most likely suspect was DJ."

It hurt that Jenny had suspected DJ while I had been taken in by him so thoroughly. Also, Jenny really was a damn good detective. "I'm sorry I didn't pay more attention to what you were going through," I said. "But how can you be more upset that you're not the star of our show than about having your memories erased and being manipulated by . . . I don't even know who?"

Jenny sighed. She reached under her pillow and returned with a Nutreesh bar. "It's who I am."

"But it's *not* who you are," I said. "It's who they made you to be."

Jenny nibbled on the bar absently. "Yeah, but aren't we always who someone else made us?"

"What? No! Don't be silly."

"Someone's being silly, but it's not me." Jenny paused like she was waiting for me to contradict her, but I kept my mouth shut. "If Production hadn't screwed us up, our parents would have."

"This is different."

"But it's also not." She held up the now-empty wrapper. "The only reason I like these is because they remind me of the granola bars my nana used to keep hidden under the sink for when I would visit. Knowing that I never knew the woman in my memories or visited her house by the lake doesn't mean I'm going to stop craving them."

I understood what Jenny was saying because it was similar to what DJ had said. "The past is just backstory," I muttered.

"Exactly!" Jenny said. "And it only has to matter as much as we let it."

"Some of the memories they put in my head, though—"

"Oh yeah." Jenny clenched her fists involuntarily. "Production are a bunch of sick sadists, and I'm going to find a way to ruin them if it's the last thing I do, but I'm not going to let *them* ruin *me*."

Jenny was so much more sanguine about our circumstances than I was, and I wished I knew her secret. But she did have a point. Each of us was constantly trying to move on from the trauma and hurt of the past. Mine and Jenny's memories might not have been real, exactly, but they were real to us. I wasn't going to stop baking any more than Jenny was going to stop putting Nutreesh in her.

"On the plus side," Jenny said, "I no longer have to feel guilty about luring Claudia Pazzafini's boyfriend away from her in seventh grade. Or Josh Machado's girlfriend in ninth."

"You are such a cliché."

Jenny raised her eyebrow. "No, I'm just a person who happens to know what she wants and isn't afraid to ask for it."

"Touché." I smiled in spite of myself. And my smile turned into a laugh because only Jenny could find the bright side to having a head filled with stolen memories.

"What are you going to do about DJ?" Jenny asked.

I'd been trying to avoid thinking about him. Unsuccessfully. "What do you think I should do?"

"He cares about you, that's for sure."

"Does he?" I asked. "Or does he only care about who I used to be?"

Jenny wrapped her arm around my waist and hugged me. She said, "You remember that picnic date he set up for you?"

"How could I forget?"

Jenny snorted. "A couple of days earlier, DJ came to my room and asked me what he should do about his feelings for you. He put it all out there. How much he cared about you, and how crushed he'd be if you didn't feel the same."

"How do you know those feelings weren't for Nico?"

"Because," she said, "he wasn't talking about Nico. He was talking about you. He described, unprompted and in excruciating detail, everything that made you, Noa, special." Jenny poked the center of my chest. "That boy cares about *you*. Noa North. And I think the one thing you can trust, if you can't trust anything else, is that DJ would do anything to protect you."

"Maybe."

"Weren't you listening?" Jenny asked, looking at me like I was dense. "Production did everything they could to make you hate DJ. The memories they saddled you with were meant to prevent you from trusting him. But he earned that trust from you anyway. Isn't that worth something?"

Jenny was right. DJ might have been a pacifist, but I believed he would fight to the death to keep me from harm. It was a feeling supported by experience. Memories that Production hadn't stolen, recycled, and used to colonize my mind. Memories that I had earned, some at the cost of my life.

There was so much to unravel—too much. Was I me? If I wasn't me, who was I? What did I owe to the person whose memories I possessed? Was there someone out there with the memories of who I had been before I'd become Nico or Noa? Could I blame DJ for what he'd done when he'd done it to protect us? Could I stay mad at DJ for the choices he'd made knowing that all the choices available to him had been bad ones? It was going to take a lifetime to figure out the consequences of what had been done to me and to figure out how to move forward.

I guess I was quiet for too long and Jenny had gotten bored. "Do you think they watch us in the showers?"

My head jerked up. "What? Of course not. Right?"

"You said the boys in the locker room at BCH told you there were no cameras in the showers, and DJ said the same thing, but how do we really know?"

It was bad enough that everything I did was being recorded and edited and broadcast into the universe for trillions to watch. "Great," I said. "I'm never going to shower again."

"Please don't say that. You smell really, really bad when you don't shower."

I pinched my nose. "I'm not the only one."

"Jerk!" Jenny shoved me and we laughed.

I was about to launch a counteroffensive when a chime sounded over the comms. It was immediately followed by a familiar voice that said, "All junior detectives must assemble immediately in the galley for a special announcement. Attendance is mandatory."

"Should we go?" Jenny asked.

"Do we have a choice?"

"I think we always have a choice."

I stood and held out my hand. "Then let's see what this nonsense is about."

THREE

DJ WALKED INTO THE GALLEY FROM ONE SIDE AS JENNY and I entered from the other. He immediately dropped his eyes and wouldn't look at either of us. I hated seeing him so hurt, but I also didn't have the brain space to deal with him at the moment. What was I supposed to say? He had betrayed my trust, lied to me, kept secrets. I couldn't forget that. I also couldn't forget the sound of his laugh or the tickle in my stomach that his dimples gave me or how safe I felt when he was near—even now. I wanted to forgive him, but I didn't know how.

"Do you know why we were summoned?" I asked.

DJ shook his head.

As soon as we were seated around the table, Jenny said, "All right, you pervy voyeurs, we're here. Let's do this."

Antagonizing Production probably wasn't the best opening

move, but Jenny had earned the right to her anger, and I wasn't going to prevent her from expressing it.

Shimmering photons swirled from the vents around the room and formed into the familiar hologram of our antagonist, Jenny Perez, who took a seat in one of the empty chairs as soon as she was fully formed.

"Hi! I'm your negotiator, Jenny Perez, whom you probably remember as the helpful hologram who spent the last few months trying to keep you out of trouble."

I scoffed. "'Helpful' isn't the word I'd use."

"If you're seeing this," Jenny Perez continued, "then it means that you three have seriously screwed the pooch."

Having to share space with Jenny Perez, even if she was only a hologram, made the veins in my temples throb. I'd been planning to let Jenny take the lead, listen until I felt I had something intelligent to say. But the levee holding back my anger broke, and the words rushed out.

"Who the hell do you think you are?" I bellowed. "You kidnapped me, stranded me on a spaceship, manipulated my memories, manipulated my heart! I suffocated, I was irradiated, a robot shot me with a laser! Do you know the nightmare you put us through?" I laughed bitterly. "Of course you do! The entire universe knows because you've been exploiting us this whole time. Packaging our misery and joy and our private moments as entertainment. What gives you the right?"

I probably would have kept going if Jenny Perez hadn't interrupted. "You gave us the right."

"Back the shuttle up," Jenny said.

"Each of you is here voluntarily—"

DJ said, "I volunteered, but they didn't."

"I don't mean for this program," Jenny Perez said. "I mean for *the* program." She smiled like that explained everything, and I hated her. I was 99 percent sure I had never hated anyone as much as I hated Jenny Perez. "Now that you've finished with your tantrum, let's discuss our current predicament. It's a sticky one."

"You still haven't explained about us being here voluntarily," DJ said.

"And I'm not going to." Jenny Perez folded her hands on the table. "Time to move on. *Now Kiss!* is currently the number one program being broadcast, but viewers want a romance, not the story of a group of plucky kids who overthrow an evil empire—we already have two of those that no one is watching.

"Your audience is invested in the romantic relationship between Noa North and DJ Storm. The ratings during the dance at Beta Cephei High were phenomenal. They nearly beat *Murder Your Darlings* at its peak. Production intended to introduce Ty as a love interest for Jenny—"

Jenny stuck out her tongue like she'd bitten into rotten fruit. "He was the best you could do?"

"Yes," Jenny Perez said. "And then he would have attempted to murder you and hijack the ship, forcing you to kill him even though you loved him. His death and your grief would have strengthened the bond between DJ and Noa."

"Figures," Jenny muttered.

"But Ty wasn't meant to shoot Jenny for at least four more episodes, and he was certainly not supposed to inadvertently out DJ and his role on *Qriosity*." Jenny Perez frowned thoughtfully. "He shouldn't have known he was part of a program." She returned her attention to us. "No matter. We'll dissect him later to root out how he retained his memories. First, we must focus on getting *Now Kiss!* back on track."

I looked at Jenny, but she spread her hands, seemingly as lost as me. "DJ?" I asked. "Did you know about Ty?"

"No," DJ said. "I swear I thought he was really trying to help us."

Jenny Perez tapped her fingernail on the table; she was insubstantial, but I still imagined I could hear the sound. "None of that is important. Here is Production's proposal. You will each submit to minor rewrites—a procedure that will remove your memories of the past three days."

"Counteroffer," Jenny said. "You and Production can kiss my ass."

Jenny Perez waved her finger in the air and tsk'd reproachfully. "Your language, Jenny and Noa, has had your sponsors in quite a tizzy."

I gave Jenny Perez the middle finger. "Put some in you." And when I looked around the table, Jenny and DJ were giving her the finger too.

"Be reasonable," Jenny Perez said. "This is the best outcome for everyone."

"How do you figure that?" I asked.

Whatever patience the hologram had begun our conversation with, we had clearly exhausted it. "If you refuse to submit for rewrites, we will cancel you."

I didn't know what she meant by "cancel," but I had a few guesses.

"Can't you delete her?" Jenny asked DJ.

"Silly children," Jenny Perez said. "You have no control here. Your lives are ours. Your ship is ours. You can't even turn off the lights without Production's permission."

I looked to DJ for confirmation, and he clenched his jaw and nodded.

Jenny had been wrong. We didn't always have a choice. At least, we didn't always have a good choice. Either we submitted or Production would force us to submit.

"We would also like Ty returned to us," Jenny Perez said.

"Can we . . ." I glanced at DJ and Jenny. They looked as unsure as I felt. "Can we have some time to discuss it?"

Jenny Perez seemed to give it a moment's thought. "*Qriosity* engages the Trinity Labs Quantum Fold Drive in seventeen hours. Production will be awaiting you at your destination and will expect your compliance at that time." She pulled her magnifying glass out of her pocket. "Don't try anything silly because we are *always* watching you. And yes, that does include in the showers."

"I knew it!" I said.

The hologram scattered, leaving us alone. But we weren't really alone, and I couldn't forget that. Someone was always observing us, expecting us to perform. Every joke, every fight, every kiss would feel scripted for someone else's pleasure and consumption. Production and the audience probably knew more about me than I knew about myself.

"Jenny Perez is officially my nemesis," Jenny said. "They better change the name of this program to *Jenny's Gonna Cut a Bitch,* because I swear to God that when I find Jenny Perez, I am going to cut that bitch."

It was difficult to put my conflicted feelings for DJ aside, but we had some decisions to make. "Does this mean Jenny Perez is in charge?"

DJ wrinkled his nose and furrowed his brow, looking uncertain. "I don't even think she's real. She might think she's real, but I think she's a computer program. Maybe a digital reconstruction of an actress named Jenny Perez who might have been real at one time."

"Are you serious?" Jenny said.

"Why not?" I said. "After space schools and time loops and aliens, a fake Jenny Perez makes total sense." I turned back to DJ. "So if Jenny Perez isn't in charge, who is?"

"Production," DJ said.

"And they are?"

DJ hesitated, then spread his hands. "I don't know."

Jenny leaned back in her chair and folded her arms across her chest. "They're not taking my memories. They're mine, I made them, and I'm not giving them up."

"Same." Everything that occurred before I opened my eyes

in the spacesuit outside *Qriosity* might have been fake or might have belonged to someone else, but the memories I'd made from that moment forward were real. Those memories, not the ones from before, told me who I was and who I wanted to be. Eventually, I was going to have to reconcile the stolen memories with the memories I had created, but I refused to let Production take anything else from me.

DJ's eyes motioned toward the ceiling. "What can we do? The only weapon we have is Ty's pistol, and no matter what we come up with, Production will be ready for it."

"Actually," I said, thinking about Ty's weapon, "I might know a way we can talk privately. But we're going to need warm coats."

FOUR

A COUPLE OF HOURS LATER, DJ, TY, JENNY, AND I WERE sitting in the back of the shuttle, floating a few hundred meters off the port bow of *Qriosity*. Jenny had cut power to all systems, including heat, and the temperature was dropping rapidly.

Ty held the phone-shaped device he'd used to stop the Teachers at Beta Cephei High. "Are you certain about this?" He'd been surprised when we'd asked him to help, but not quite as surprised as DJ and Jenny had been when I'd suggested the plan.

"Why're you looking at me?" I asked, pulling my jacket tighter around my shoulders.

Jenny smacked my arm. "Because it was your idea!"

"Do it," DJ said. "The shuttle's powered down, so the EMP will only fry equipment that's still on, which includes anything Production is using to monitor us." He quickly added, "But we've only got about forty minutes of oxygen—"

"How do you know?" Ty asked.

"The cubic meters of the inside of the shuttle converted to liters of air, divided by the number of liters we each consume per minute—"

"It's math," I said. "Trust him." I was less worried about suffocating than I was about freezing, and I was already wearing two coats.

Ty activated his device, but nothing seemed to happen. It was kind of disappointing. He set it aside and rubbed his wrists where the restraints had cut into his skin. He looked uncomfortable sitting between the person he had shot and the person he meant to shoot, and I almost felt bad for him.

"Did it work?" I asked.

Jenny pinched Ty's arm and twisted the skin. "It better have."

"It did!" he yelped.

DJ cleared his throat. "This is your show, Noa. What's your plan?"

"Uh, this was it." I glanced at them. "Get to the shuttle, where we could talk without being watched. I was hoping one of you could come up with a way to keep us from having to submit to Production's memory-rewrite thing."

"Oh," DJ said. "I just thought you might've—"

Ty interrupted. "Are you certain JP said they intended to dissect me?"

With Ty's usefulness ended, I ignored him. Jenny did too. "We have to do something," she said. "I'd rather die again than let them poke around in my brain."

"Was Jenny Perez serious about us having no control over the ship?" It was difficult talking to DJ, working with him, and not acting like I wanted to hug him and hold his hand and hear him tell me we were going to solve this problem. In a way, it was like Production had already reverted us to versions of ourselves who didn't know each other.

DJ nodded solemnly. "I've been trying this whole time to crack the hold they have over *Qriosity*, but I haven't made any real progress because there's nowhere on the ship they're not watching."

"Which is gross, by the way," Jenny said. "And illegal. Isn't it illegal for them to watch us shower and go to the bathroom?"

Ty rolled his eyes. "It hardly matters. Production isn't people." When I looked at him blankly, he said, "You do understand that, right? Production is an algorithm, or an artificial intelligence, if that makes it easier to comprehend. The point is that Production isn't having a wank watching you lather up in the shower."

"We're being held captive by a computer program?" Jenny asked.

"That actually makes sense," DJ said.

Jenny threw up her hands. "On what planet?"

The shuttle was cooling off far quicker than I expected it to, and a shiver shook my body. "Can we please focus? I'm freezing."

"Maybe we can hack MediQwik," DJ said. "That's what they'll use to rewrite our memories. If we can make it fake the memory procedure, it might buy us some time."

"Can you do that?" I asked, shifting my gaze between Ty and DJ.

Ty shook his head. "I can disassemble MediQwik, but I haven't the faintest idea how to reprogram it."

"I could," DJ said. "Maybe. Fifteen hours isn't very long, though." Even though it was his idea, he did not sound optimistic.

"Is there any part of the ship that we do control?" Jenny asked. She dug a Nutreesh bar from her pocket.

"You're not seriously going to eat that, are you?" Ty wore a look of horror as he watched Jenny unwrap the Nutreesh.

"Is it roaches?" I asked. "I tried telling her it was probably roaches. Is it worse than roaches? It's people, isn't it?"

"Nutreesh isn't made from roaches," Ty said. "Or people. At least, not that I'm aware of. But Gleeson Foods is your program's biggest sponsor. Every one of those that you eat is more free advertising for them."

DJ cleared his throat to regain our attention. "Every system is controlled and monitored by Production. Navigation, communications, the reactor, Mind's Eye. Even the equipment in the kitchen. You couldn't bake a cake if Production didn't want you to."

I laughed bitterly as a thought occurred to me that I felt foolish for not realizing sooner. "We're not skipping randomly through space, are we? We're not lost."

"No," DJ said.

"What about the shuttle?" Jenny asked. "We turned off the power. Doesn't that indicate that we have control over it?"

I looked expectantly at DJ. "Well?"

"Sure," DJ said. "But the shuttle isn't connected to the ship, so I'm not sure how helpful it's going to be. It doesn't have a fold drive like *Qriosity* does; even if we stole it, we'd die long before we reached the nearest habitable planet."

"So we're screwed," I said. "Is that what you're saying?"

Jenny shivered. Ty slipped out of his jacket and hung it over her shoulders, which wasn't nearly as surprising as her letting him do it.

We sat in that cold, dark shuttle in silence, each of us lost in our own thoughts. I kept hoping that inspiration would fill the cramped space with its light, that someone would conceive of a brilliant plan to save us from the fate that we seemed on an unavoidable collision course with. But our silence only filled the shuttle with the stench of defeat.

"Nothing?" I asked, looking around. "Seriously?"

"I'm sorry, Noa," DJ said. "I'm so sorry."

FIVE

I DIDN'T WANT TO SPEAK TO DJ, BUT I ALSO DESPERATELY wanted to talk to him. So I was both annoyed and grateful when he peeked his head into the galley, saw the absolute disaster I was standing in the middle of, and didn't immediately run away.

"Noa?"

DJ's distorted reflection in the chrome cabinet doors was a misshapen blob staring back at me. "I'm not interested in shouting at you from across the room."

He turned to leave.

"What do you want, DJ?"

DJ trudged into the kitchen, his hands shoved in his pockets, his shoulders rolled forward. "You've been busy." He wasn't wrong. I'd been baking since we'd returned from the shuttle, and there wasn't a square centimeter of counter space that wasn't covered with chocolate splatter or flour or wasn't stacked with mixing bowls.

"Baking calms my nerves."

"Nothing about this kitchen says calm." DJ's eyes slid over everything but me. "It looks like a bomb detonated."

"Under the circumstances, I'm not sure what you were expecting." I was busy folding ground almonds and powdered sugar into the meringue I'd finished whipping moments before DJ had shown up. "But I suppose baking is only a coping mechanism because Production decided it should be. They chose the recipes that are rattling around in my brain."

"I told you," DJ said. "Production doesn't invent the memories. They remix them from the memories harvested from others. Everything you experienced happened to someone."

"You know that makes it worse, right?" Folding the batter was a delicate process. I had to be careful not to knock the air out of the meringue. It was probably the only reason I wasn't shouting and throwing things. "These memories belong to someone who doesn't know they're missing but probably still feels their loss. What memories am I missing, DJ? What did Production steal from me? What *else* are they going to steal from me?"

DJ approached the worktable from the other side. He didn't speak while I worked, slowly and gently folding the batter to the right consistency.

"What're you working on?" he asked.

"Macarons."

"Aren't they difficult to make?"

"Not really," I said. "They only contain four ingredients: powdered sugar, ground almonds, egg whites, and white sugar. But they're delicate and can be fussy. If one side of the oven is a degree or two hotter than the other, it could ruin the batch. If you over-fold or under-fold the batter, they won't come out properly. If you don't let them sit long enough, or if you let them sit too long . . ." I shrugged. "Okay, I guess they are difficult. But they're worth it."

DJ craned his neck to peer into the bowl where the violet mixture was just about the consistency of lava. "I don't think I've ever had a macaron before."

I laughed. "Neither have I. My brain only thinks I have." I handed DJ a piping bag to hold open so that I could spoon the batter in. Then I squeezed out little macaron blobs into the waiting trays. The first time I banged the pan on the counter, DJ gave me a strange look. "You have to do this to force the air bubbles to rise to the surface. Otherwise they'll expand in the cookie and ruin it." I motioned at the other tray.

The violence of the act was satisfying. I didn't have to be careful with this part. DJ was smiling too. After a few good bangs, I leaned over and pricked any errant bubbles with a toothpick.

"Done," I said. My back ached from bending, but the batter was smooth, the color vibrant, and they hadn't spread much after I'd piped them. Mrs. Blum would have been proud.

"You're not putting them in the oven?" DJ asked.

"They need time to form a skin." I untied my apron and hung it on the hook before leaning against the counter.

DJ stood less than a meter away, watching me. Staring at me. His eyes were glassy with tears that wouldn't fall. "I did what I did for us," he said.

"You lied to me. Kept secrets from me."

"Only to protect you." DJ inched closer, and I had nowhere to go. "I have never lied about my feelings for you."

I laughed bitterly. "Only about everything else." But since learning the truth, I'd thought back over my time on *Qriosity*, I'd scrutinized every decision DJ had made, and I'd found nothing I would have done differently if our positions had been reversed.

"I can't go back," I said. "I'm not sure about my past, but all I have is who I am right now. I won't let them take that from me."

DJ chewed on his thumbnail. "There's one other thing I haven't told you."

"Seriously?"

My incredulity tore into DJ, but he was prepared for the blow. "It's something Jenny Perez showed me when she was threatening to lobotomize you."

DJ paused, but I was done with secrets. "Get on with it," I said.

"The *Arcas* wasn't the first time we'd met. We were on two other programs before that one—a musical crime show and an apocalyptic private school drama. We were only background characters, created to die tragically; we didn't even have names. But we found each other. We met and we fell in love."

The implications of what DJ was saying were potentially huge, and I couldn't wrap my brain around them. How many times had we done this? How many times had we been created and killed? How many lives had we lived?

"Jenny Perez told me about our previous lives because she thought knowing she'd separated us over and over would hurt me, but it did the opposite, Noa. It proved to me how powerful we are together. It showed me that no matter what our names are or whose memories we have or where we are or what's trying to kill us, we *will* find each other." DJ had nearly closed the space between us.

"Do you think . . . do you think we knew each other before?" I asked. "Back on Earth?"

DJ nodded. "I do. I think I've always known you. I always will."

"What if Production separates us?"

"They won't," he said. "We're ratings gold." DJ smirked and my knees wobbled. He moved to touch me.

I pressed my hand against his chest. Pushed him away. "I can't, DJ. Not right now."

"Noa—"

"I don't know how to get past this, DJ," I said. "Living on *Qriosity* has proven that, given enough time, anything strange can become normal. So I could eventually get used to a head full of memories that aren't mine or the knowledge that I'm on some weird program. But you lied to me, DJ. How do I get over that?"

DJ raked his hands through his hair. He was so perfectly disheveled and broken. "I made you a promise to never leave you, and I kept it. I won't apologize for that, Noa."

"It's just—"

"What do you want me to do?" DJ asked. "Do you want me to get in the shuttle and give myself up to Production? If you tell me to do it, I will."

I rolled my eyes. "What? No. Don't be ridiculous."

"I would trade my life a thousand times for yours, Noa."

"What if I don't want you to?" I said, raising my voice. "How is that fair to me? You go off and die heroically, leaving me alone. Leaving me to live the rest of my life without you. I don't want that, DJ. I don't ever want to live without you." The words poured out of me, and I couldn't stop them. I didn't try.

"You're the one who jumped in front of a laser blast," DJ shot back. "How is it fair that you get to risk your life for me but I can't do it for you?"

"It's not," I said. "Deal with it."

DJ moved toward me again, and this time I didn't push him away. "I love you, Noa. I understand if you can't forgive me, and I understand if you don't feel the same way anymore. But I will never stop being in love with you. Our story never ends; our story is always just beginning."

Production had intended to punish DJ by making me bitter. By making me the boy who was born with a broken heart. By making me afraid to trust. Afraid to love and be loved. My entire history was designed to ensure that I never fell in love with DJ. And yet, I did. Against all odds, I fell in love with him, and those feelings might have been the only ones I could trust. I didn't know who I'd been, but I wanted to be the person DJ saw when he looked at me.

DJ ran his finger along my cheek and down the curve of my jaw. "I love you, Noa."

I took DJ's hand and pressed it to my heart. I let go of my anger, I let go of my fear. I let go of everything that wasn't DJ.

"Production can't watch us in the shuttle, right?" I asked.

"Well, Ty's EMP took out the monitoring equipment, but we were just there. Why do you want to go back?"

I flashed DJ a grin and pulled him toward the door. "I want to spend what little time we have left with you. And I *don't* want an audience."

SIX

DJ SNORED. IT SOUNDED LIKE THE RAT-TAT-TAT OF A machine gun, making it impossible for me to sleep. It was annoying and adorable, which pretty much described everything about DJ and why I loved him.

I lay with my head on his bare chest on the floor of the shuttle. I'd covered the front window with a tarp to make sure Production couldn't spy inside. DJ was using our balled-up clothes as a pillow.

I didn't know if this was the first time I had been with DJ, though I suspected it wasn't. Even knowing that my memory of that night with Billy hadn't happened to me, I had been scared to shed my clothes in front of DJ. I'd flinched, at first, at his touch. I wondered if the person from whom Production had stolen the memory about Billy still felt a tight knot of fear in their stomach when someone touched them, even if they didn't know why. I hated Production for exploiting someone's pain for the entertainment of others. It was disgusting and cruel.

I wondered, if Production got their way and sent me for rewrites, would someone else get my memory of the last couple of hours? Would Production extract my memory of this time with DJ, remix it, and inject it into someone else's head? Whoever the recipient was would get to feel safe the way I felt safe. They'd get to feel loved the way I felt loved. They'd know what it was like to be the only star in someone's universe. They would know, and I would forget.

It wasn't fair. I didn't want to lose this memory. I didn't want to lose *any* of my memories. There are fates worse than death, and to love and be loved and have the memory of it ripped away is one such fate.

According to DJ, this wouldn't be the first time, or even the second. How many times was Production going to tear me and DJ apart? How many times were we going to let them?

I knew if I shared my thoughts with DJ, he would keep trying to find a way to save us. That was one of my favorite things about him. No matter the situation, he put his head down and got to work. DJ wasn't flashy or showy, and he never demanded gratitude. But I could always count on him to be in the corner quietly doing the work necessary to keep us alive.

He couldn't save us this time, though. It was my turn to do the work.

I sat up, slowly and carefully. Disentangled myself from DJ. I kissed his forehead and whispered, "I won't let them take you from me again."

GOODBYE, FAREWELL AND AMEN

ONE

“WARNING! *QRIOSITY* WILL SELF-DESTRUCT IN THIRTY minutes. Warning!”

I guess when it came down to it, I’d decided I was done playing Production’s game.

Jenny and Ty reached Ops together, which was a development I was definitely not expecting.

“What’s this?” I asked, wagging my finger at them. “What’s going on here?”

“You first!” Jenny said. “The ship is going to explode?!”

“I’ll explain that when DJ gets here so that I don’t have to repeat myself,” I said.

A countdown on the viewport kept track of how long we had before *Qriosity*’s self-destruct engaged, and the computer provided a helpful warning every five minutes.

Jenny glanced at Ty. "He apologized for shooting me and said he only did it because he thought I was working for Production. I've forgiven him, and you should too."

I snorted. "Yeah, okay."

"And we're not returning him to Production," Jenny added.

If Jenny wanted to get to know Ty, that was her business, but I didn't feel comfortable with him running around the ship without supervision. Forgiveness was easy; trust would take time, a resource we were low on.

DJ finally arrived, red-faced and buttoning his pants.

"Your shirt is on backward," Ty said. Jenny laughed and gave me a knowing smile, which I ignored.

DJ shoved past them both. "What's happening? Why are we self-destructing? Did Production do this?"

I leaned against the console and said, "Now that you're all here, I can explain."

"Explain what?" DJ asked. "Tell me what's happening."

Ty said, "I believe that's what he's attempting to do."

DJ glared at Ty. "Why are you here again?"

I cleared my throat to regain their attention. "Production controls *Qriosity*. We know that. We can't shut down the fold drive; we can't access sensors or comms or navigation. We are, essentially, locked out of our own ship." I paused for dramatic effect. "Except that's not entirely true."

"Have you gotten into MediQwik's narcotics?" Jenny asked.

"Seriously, Noa," DJ said. "What's this about?"

I held my silence until—

"Warning! *Qriosity* will self-destruct in twenty-five minutes. Warning!"

"There were a few times while I was stuck in the loop that it was simpler to end the day early and begin again. I discovered that I could initiate *Qriosity*'s self-destruct, and blowing up the ship was a quick and convenient way to hit the reset button. Once, I did it just because Jenny finally beat my high score on the pinball machine at Any Way You Slice It, the pizza shop in Bell's Cove—"

"You dick!" Jenny shouted. "Do you know how many hours I've wasted in front of that machine?"

Ty nudged her arm. "Maybe this isn't the best time?"

I mouthed *Sorry* to Jenny before continuing. "The first time I used the self-destruct, I did it to see what would happen. DJ attempted to stop me, but initiating the self-destruct requires inputting a sixteen-digit alphanumeric code. And that same code must be entered in order to cancel the self-destruct. Without the code, DJ was helpless, and so, I think, was Production."

DJ was biting his thumbnail. "How'd you come to that conclusion?"

"Easily," I said. "We know that you were in contact with Production during the loop. If you couldn't shut off the self-destruct, you would have asked Production to do it for you. But they didn't, and I think that means that they couldn't."

"Maybe they chose not to," DJ said.

"Possibly." I had to admit that there was a slim chance DJ was correct. "But I think it's more likely that Production simply overlooked the self-destruct system."

Jenny threw up her hands. "Because only a lunatic would blow themselves up!"

Ty motioned at Jenny with his head. "I'm with her."

"Noa?" DJ said.

"If this is the only choice Production has left us, then I would rather end this program on my own terms than wait for Production to strip away parts of who I am." I looked at each of them in turn. "Maybe they only remove three days from our memories this time, but how many will they remove the next? If we don't take a stand now, we never will."

Cautiously, DJ took my hand like I was going to explode instead of *Qriosity*. "I know you think this is the way—"

I touched my temple. "I've got memories of a family that I miss, but they're not real. You're real. You and Jenny are my family."

"What about me?" Ty asked.

"You're the weird dude who shot Jenny."

Jenny nodded. "Every family needs one of those."

DJ laced his fingers tightly through mine. "I understand what you're doing, but we can find another way. Production can't keep us apart."

I kissed his knuckles. "You'll find me or I'll find you or we'll find each other. Our love is epic and all that. I get it, and I believe it. But what happens then? Production pulls us apart again. Over and over. The endless cycle of finding you and losing you is tragic and romantic, but I'm over it. I'm making my stand here on *Qriosity*."

Jenny looked like she was going to argue but then seemed to change her mind. After a moment, she shrugged, reached into her pocket, and pulled out a Nutreesh bar. "Fine, let's blow up the ship or whatever."

Ty raised his hand. "I'm still vigorously opposed to exploding."

"Hush, sweetie," Jenny said. "Your job is to look pretty; you don't get a vote."

"Noa—" DJ said, but before he could raise his objection, photons swarmed from the vents and took shape in front of the viewport.

"Hi! I'm your host, Jenny Perez, whom you probably remember from earlier when I explained that your situation is hopeless and your only option is submission. It seems you've activated the Explodovat SD-23X self-destruct appliance. When you need your ship obliterated, trust Explodovat. Explodovat is a fully owned subsidiary of Gleeson Foods."

A few seconds passed where no one spoke. Finally, Jenny nudged me in the back. "Noa?"

I cleared my throat and steeled my spine. I did my damnedest to prevent the terror I felt from reaching my eyes, I turned my full attention to Jenny Perez, and I said, "We're rejecting your offer."

"Are we absolutely certain?" Ty asked. "I'm not sure we were quite finished discussing it."

DJ squeezed my hand and smiled at me with those dimples. "Yeah," he said. "We're sure."

I wanted to kiss him so badly. It was difficult to think about anything else, but I had to stay focused. "We will not submit to having our memories rewritten, and we will not hand over Ty."

"Thank God," he whispered.

"In addition to rejecting your offer, we have some demands of our own."

"We do?" DJ said.

"Sure, why not?" I shrugged and continued. "You will release control of *Qriosity*, you will shut down all surveillance equipment aboard the ship, and you will set us free and never bother us again."

"I'd also like to never see her again," Jenny added. "I want to be the only Jenny on this ship."

"Fair enough," I said.

Jenny Perez's face remained serene throughout my speech, as if I was simply listing the ingredients for brownies rather than attempting to blackmail her. Finally, when the palpable silence was nearly unbearable, Jenny Perez said, "No."

"No?"

"No," she repeated.

"Just like that?" I said. "You're willing to let the stars of your highest-rated program blow themselves up and end the show without a fight? Without even attempting to negotiate?"

Jenny Perez folded her arms across her chest. "Is this a negotiation, then?"

"It can be," I said.

"Production will not accede to your demands."

I hadn't thought they would. "Okay," I said. "But maybe we can reach a compromise that will make everyone happy."

"There's no arguing with Production," Ty said. "This is fairly pointless."

DJ stepped forward. "Let us come aboard your ship and talk to you face-to-face. Maybe we can hammer out a solution that doesn't involve anyone blowing up."

Seconds passed, and I held my breath. Jenny Perez's eyes were blank, like she wasn't there. A moment later, she blinked and said, "Agreed. We will dock with *Qriosity* in one hour." The photons dispersed, and Jenny Perez was gone.

Ty spoke first. "You can't honestly believe they're going to negotiate with you in good faith. If you board their ship, you might as well submit to rewrites."

"We still have the self-destruct." I turned to Jenny. "Jenny, you and Ty will stay here. We'll reset the timer on the self-destruct and I'll give you the code—"

Jenny rubbed her hands together. "Finally, some real power."

"Keep it armed, and if Production tries anything, blow up the ship."

DJ's eyes widened like a puzzle piece had finally clicked into place. "Production will be docked with us, so their ship will explode along with *Qriosity*."

I looked toward the ceiling, even though I didn't actually know where the cameras were located. "Did you hear that? If we die, you die."

"It's a good plan," DJ said.

I sighed. "It's really not, but it's all we've got."

TWO

PRODUCTION'S SHIP LOOKED LIKE A SUPPOSITORY. IT had no windows, no doors or seams that I could see as it approached. I couldn't even locate thrusters. It was bland and boring and white, and it arrived exactly sixty minutes after the end of our conversation, just like Jenny Perez said it would.

DJ and I stood on our side of the airlock, waiting for Production's ship to finish docking.

"Hey," DJ said. "About what happened earlier—"

"I'm sorry," I said. "But I thought if I woke you up, you'd try to talk me out of it."

"I meant before that."

"Oh." Heat rose into my cheeks, and a smile touched my lips.

"We didn't get to talk about it," DJ said, "and I want to make sure you're okay."

A laugh escaped. "Better than okay."

DJ beamed. "Really?"

I reached my arms around his waist and pulled him against me. "That's why I'm doing this. For you. For us."

"We can still find another way."

My lips lingered on DJ's lips as I kissed him slowly. "What's the point of being in love if you can't remember falling in love?" I kissed his nose and his cheek and his chin. "I don't want to forget falling in love with you. Not again."

The umbilical bridge from Production's ship connected to *Qriosity* and created an airtight seal. The lights above the door switched from red to green, and the door opened.

"Come on." I took DJ's hand and pulled him along. I wished I could feel as confident as I was pretending I was. My heart was beating spastically and I felt clumsy, like I was going to trip and fall and smash my face into the floor. DJ was all that kept me from embarrassing myself in front of our captors.

"Whoa," DJ said as we entered their ship.

Like the outside, the inside was glossy and white. There were no corners and no seams. It was like the entire ship had been carved from a single block of plastic. "I bet this place is a pain in the ass to keep clean of fingerprints."

"Do you think they have fingers?" DJ asked.

I hadn't exactly considered who or what we would be meeting. Production, sure, but what was Production? Were they living people? Sentient robots? Aliens? Ty believed Production was an algorithm, and DJ thought they were an artificial intelligence, and either of those was plausible, but the truth was that we didn't know.

"What now?" As soon as the question left my mouth, a green arrow appeared on the floor.

"I guess we go that way," DJ said.

I squeezed DJ's hand so tightly that his knuckles cracked, causing him to flinch. I was scared. Terrified, really. We didn't know what to expect, and my mind churned out a million possibilities. A hundred Jenny Perez clones could be waiting to take us into custody. Production might capture us, saw off the tops of our skulls, and replace our brains with tiny robots. We might learn that everything we'd experienced had been a simulation, and that our real bodies were in a vat of goo in an enormous, dark storage room. We were absolutely out of our depth. DJ was the only reason I could bear the fear. The only reason I could keep moving forward.

The arrows led us to an egg-shaped room that was devoid of decoration except for a bench and a chair, both located in the center. The furniture looked like it was made of the same material as the ship. Like it had simply flowed up and out of the floor.

"Should we sit?" DJ asked.

"Might as well." We chose the bench, and I was surprised to find that it wasn't as unyielding as it appeared. The surface contoured to my butt and back like memory foam.

"How come Production gets this," I asked, "and we're stuck with that sagging, busted piece-of-crap couch in the rec room?"

"Because anything more stylish would not have matched *Qriosity*'s scrappy, patchwork aesthetic."

The answer originated from behind me, and I turned around so quickly that I nearly pulled a muscle in my neck. "You," I said.

"Me!" Jenny Perez walked casually around the bench and took a seat in the chair across from us. She was smiling, wearing a pastel green suit, and she looked solid. Her edges didn't shimmer. I was pretty sure she wasn't a hologram. "Hi! I'm your negotiator, Jenny Perez."

"Are you real?" DJ asked.

Jenny Perez laughed. The delicate sound filled the stark room and then cut off sharply. "No."

"Then what are you?" I asked. Learning more about Jenny Perez might not have been the reason we'd willingly boarded Production's ship, but I was genuinely interested. She'd told me a great deal about her life as a child actress when I'd been struggling to come to terms with being trapped on the ship. I'd even felt some sympathy for her, but she had probably lied about her past the way she'd lied about everything else.

Jenny Perez crossed one leg over the other and leaned back in the chair. "This shell is a temporary self-contained environment for my personality matrix to inhabit during our negotiations. Production thought you would respond better to me this way."

"Personality matrix?" DJ asked. "Are you Production? Are you in charge?"

Jenny Perez laughed again, but there was a jagged edge to it this time. "Heavens, no. Jenny Perez is a fully licensed personality matrix owned by Kharis Talent Organization and leased to Production. KTO is a fully owned subsidiary of Gleeson Foods."

I was even more confused than before. "If you're not in charge, then why the hell are we talking to you?"

"Tsk, tsk, Noa." Jenny Perez sighed. "I am authorized to speak for and negotiate on behalf of Production. Any agreements I reach with you are binding."

I threw a questioning look at DJ, and he shrugged. I didn't believe for a second that we could trust Production, but I didn't see that we had a choice. We were on Production's ship, our Jenny was safe on *Qriosity* with her finger on the button that would blow us all to atoms, and Jenny Perez had gone through the trouble of stuffing herself into a body. It would be a waste of time to give up now.

"Where do we begin?" I asked.

"That depends on you," Jenny Perez replied. "This was, after all, your idea."

"Fine." I leaned forward. "The first thing I want to know is who Production is and what we're involved in. You said we consented, but I don't remember consenting to anything."

Jenny Perez waved her hand, and a sphere a little larger than a basketball appeared in the air between us. Its surface was divided into hundreds of squares, each of which displayed what appeared to be a program, though the facets were too small to make out much detail.

"Production is an arm of Programming. Programming decides what is broadcast, and Production decides how. The rest is, unfortunately, covered by a confidentiality agreement, therefore I'm not at liberty to divulge any further information regarding the organization. I am also barred, by the terms of your contracts, which you are both currently in breach of, from revealing who you were under any circumstances until the completion of your contracts."

I started to speak, but Jenny Perez added, "And, no, I cannot tell you when your contracts are due to be completed."

"That's convenient," DJ said. "If you're going to erase our memories, why not tell us anyway?"

"Because, as Ty has exposed, the rewrite procedure isn't always one hundred percent effective." Jenny Perez smiled graciously. "Now, we would greatly appreciate it if you would disarm the Explodovat SD-23X self-destruct appliance and submit to rewrites."

"Why?" I asked. "What do we get out of it?"

"Nothing."

DJ frowned at Jenny Perez. "This isn't how a negotiation works. It's about compromise. We get something and then you get something." His voice was even and calm. He had the patience of a kindergarten teacher, whereas I wanted to tear Jenny Perez's head off. The only thing preventing me from leaping off the bench was that she was as much a victim as we were. Whoever Jenny Perez had once been, this simulacrum wasn't her.

"You have nothing we want," she said.

"We have us," DJ countered. "If you agree to let me, Noa, and Jenny remain together, we might consider surrendering."

"DJ!" I yelled. "No!"

Jenny Perez was already shaking her head, though. "Until the conclusion of *Now Kiss!*, we can't separate you boys, but Jenny's character is scheduled to die in a horrible accident in the next episode, and she will be replaced."

I couldn't believe what I was hearing, and then it got worse.

"Furthermore," Jenny Perez said, "after audiences grow weary of you, and your program is inevitably canceled, you will never be permitted to perform in the same program or co-locate in the same transition school again."

"That's not fair," DJ said. "You're not even attempting to negotiate. Why did you let us come here if you weren't planning to make an effort?"

As DJ and Jenny Perez continued to argue, their voices became little more than buzz. It didn't matter what they were saying because they weren't negotiating a contract, they were negotiating my life.

I don't remember standing, but I found myself looming over Jenny Perez, and DJ was tugging my hand, trying to get me to sit down again.

"Who the hell do you think you are?" I yelled.

"Jenny Perez. Obviously."

I went off, ignoring her. "Production or Programming or whatever else. What gives you the right to exploit us? To exploit our stories and profit from them as if they were your own?"

Jenny opened her mouth to answer, and I was sure it would be an absolutely thrilling reply, but I was done with her, and I shut her down with a single withering look.

"My story belongs to me." I shook my hand, still joined with DJ's. "Our story belongs to *us*. We are the only people who get to tell our story. Not you, not Programming or Production. Us. We decide, not you." I was yelling. Tears were running down my cheeks. The entirety of the anger and frustration I'd been holding on to since that first day burst out of me. But when I was done, and I'd run out of things to say, I let DJ pull me back down onto the bench.

Jenny Perez waited a beat before beginning a slow clap. "Very pretty speech, but you wouldn't have a story if it wasn't for Programming. They put you together. They gave you the backdrop for your romance to blossom. Without Programming and Production, you would have never met."

DJ said, "I don't believe that. Something keeps drawing us together. Something stronger than you. Maybe it's fate or maybe we knew each other from before."

Jenny Perez brushed our words aside. "Irrelevant. Your story belongs to us."

"Then this is where our story ends," I said.

"Wait," DJ said. "You told us we had the highest ratings of any program—"

"Other than *Murder Your Darlings*, of course."

"But still," DJ said. "Our ratings are good."

Jenny Perez nodded. "Especially after last night in the shuttle."

It took me a moment to realize what she meant, and when I did, I felt like my soul had left my body. Like I was floating in the air, looking down upon myself.

"You didn't," DJ said.

"Oh, but we did."

They'd seen everything DJ and I had done. I wasn't ashamed

of it, but that had been for us alone. It had been special. "How?" I asked. "We used Ty's EMP device to eliminate your surveillance equipment."

Jenny Perez beamed. "Cleaning bots make wonderful spies."

"So the whole universe saw me and Noa together?" DJ asked. He was trembling with rage.

"Only the beginning," she said. "*Now Kiss!* is still a family show, so we tastefully faded to black at the appropriate moment. It was all very sweet."

"I hate you," I whispered. "I hate you, and I am going to destroy you."

DJ squeezed my hand, and I thought he was going to tell Jenny Perez where she could stick her ratings. Instead, he said, "What if Noa and I agree to allow you to continue recording us and our relationship?"

"Excuse me, what?" I looked at him in shock.

"Hear me out," DJ said, as much to me as to Jenny Perez. "We would stay on *Qriosity*, with Jenny and Ty, and Production could keep recording and broadcasting the show. In return, we would get control of the ship. We would be allowed to travel wherever we want, when we want, without interference from Production."

I couldn't believe what I was hearing. That DJ had suggested something so ridiculous. "Hell no," I said. "Even if I agreed to that, and I'm never going to, Production won't."

Jenny opened her mouth, paused, and then said, "Well, now. That's not actually a terrible proposal."

THREE

I GRABBED DJ'S ARM AND PULLED HIM OFF TO THE SIDE so that we could talk as privately as possible while Jenny Perez silently communicated with Production. I assumed Production could still hear us, but there wasn't much we could do about that.

Before I could get a word out, DJ said, "They're going to exploit us no matter what we do. This way, at least, we get to control how it happens."

"Would we be in a relationship?" I asked. "Or would it be a performance?"

"Noa—"

"I'm serious." I looked over my shoulder at where Jenny Perez was sitting. Her eyes had a blank, empty look that disturbed me immensely. "If our survival depends on ratings, how could we ever know if our actions were genuine? How could I know if you were kissing me because you wanted to kiss me or if it was because you thought it was what the audience wanted?"

DJ leaned his forehead against mine. "I don't care about the audience or about ratings. But this could be a way out for us. A way to hold on to who we are."

"But is this who we are?" I sighed in frustration because I understood where DJ was coming from, but I also felt like he wasn't listening to me. "We're not little paper dolls to be dressed up and posed. We're people, DJ. We weren't born into this universe so that strangers could watch us make out."

"Is it really so terrible that they want to?"

"It is if they don't see us as people first." I laced my fingers through DJ's. "The title of our show is *Now Kiss!*, right?"

"Yeah," DJ said warily.

"Because that's the only thing that's important to them. Not you, not me, not our lives. The things that are important to us are nothing more than the filler moments between the stuff that viewers really want to see—a couple of cute boys kissing."

It was one thing for DJ to say he didn't care about the audience, but the moment we sold ourselves to them, we would become beholden to their fickle whims. What happened if our relationship didn't evolve the way the audience wanted? What happened when DJ and I fought? What about when viewers grew bored with us?

I caught DJ's eye. I rubbed my thumb along his cheek. "We deserve more."

"Well said." Jenny Perez was wearing a deeply unsettling grin that sent a shiver through my bones. "Bravo, truly."

"Do you accept our proposal?" DJ asked as if everything I'd said had been for nothing.

Jenny Perez laughed. "No. Most definitely not. But we do have a counteroffer." She looked like a predator. She looked victorious.

"What?" I asked.

"Submit to rewrites and we won't have Jenny thrown out of the airlock."

I felt like I'd swallowed molten lead as Jenny Perez waved her hand through the air, projecting an image of Ops from *Qriosity* into the air. Jenny was sitting at her station, eating a Nutreesh bar, like all was right with the world.

"Have you finished?" Jenny Perez asked.

Behind Jenny, Ty nodded. He looked straight at us and said, "I'm terribly sorry about this, mates, but I'd prefer to live." He pressed a button on the console in front of him.

"Self-destruct has been canceled. Thank you for trusting the destruction of your ship to Explodovat. Explodovat is a fully owned subsidiary of Gleeson Foods."

Jenny stood and rounded on Ty. "You son of a bitch!"

Ty had the decency to look ashamed. The last thing DJ and I saw before Jenny Perez killed the image was Ty aiming his pistol at Jenny.

I lunged at Jenny Perez, but DJ grabbed me around the waist.

"That was hardly a challenge." Jenny Perez looked bored now. "You lost before you even set foot on this ship."

"What did you offer him?" DJ asked.

"A better life." Jenny Perez spread her hands as if to say, *What did you expect?* "He contacted us, after your clandestine meeting aboard the shuttle, and said he would help us if we rewrote him as the lead of his own program. We declined his offer, of course. We had no need for him, until you pulled your sneaky stunt with the self-destruct."

"How?" I asked. "DJ told me the encryption on the self-destruct was impossible to hack."

"We had no need to hack it," she said. "We simply provided Ty with *Qriosity*'s command override codes. That gave him back-door access to the self-destruct system, allowing him to shut it down. We would have done it ourselves, but it couldn't be handled remotely. It's a flaw in the system that we plan to rectify."

My shoulders slumped. I held DJ's hand limply in my own. "So that's it? It's over?"

"Not over," Jenny Perez said. "Noa North and DJ Storm have a bright future ahead of them. Production is even considering adding a third character to your relationship. Love triangles are back in vogue."

"So you're not gonna rewrite us?" DJ asked.

Jenny Perez rolled her eyes. "Oh, we're *definitely* going to rewrite you. Production wants to guarantee that you don't remember any of this and that you'll be more pliable in the future. Everyone hates repeats."

"At least we'll be together," DJ said.

"This isn't fair!"

"It's cute that you think life should be fair, Noa." Jenny Perez stood, her anger as swift as a summer storm. "Do you think it was fair that I sacrificed my childhood to people who saw me as little more than a resource to exploit? Do you think it was fair that I had to grow up under the perverted gaze of degenerate men who maintained a public countdown until my eighteenth birthday, as if that made their lust somehow less revolting? Do you think it was fair that I never truly knew whether my family loved me or whether they were simply sucking up to me to make sure I would maintain them in the lifestyle to which they'd grown accustomed?" Jenny Perez seemed to swell in size as she spoke, her voice filling the room.

"Life isn't fair, boys. We each have our part to play. This is yours; get used to it."

In a strange way, it was comforting to see Jenny Perez truly lose her temper, to see a side of her that wasn't polished and perfect. She might not have been real, but maybe she was human after all.

Jenny Perez looked like she was going to continue to lecture us, but instead she cocked her head to the side like she was listening to a voice we couldn't hear, and said, "What now?" She waved her hand, bringing up a picture of Ops. At first, it appeared that Jenny had tackled Ty and was attempting to wrestle the gun from him, but I quickly realized that's not quite what was happening.

Jenny's arms were wrapped around Ty, and she was kissing him. Though, if I'm being honest, it looked more like she was trying to suck the last breath from his lungs. In the background, *Qriosity*'s computer said, "Warning! *Qriosity* will self-destruct in five minutes. Warning!"

"Well," Jenny Perez said, "I did *not* see that coming."

It was my turn to grin. "I did say that we'd rather die than submit." With the hand that wasn't holding on to DJ, I held up Ty's EMP so that Jenny Perez could see it clearly. "Sorry about it." I pressed the button, and Jenny Perez collapsed to the floor.

NOW KISS!
EPISODE TEN, SCENE FOUR

INT. PRODUCTION SHIP *MUX* HALLWAY

NOA NORTH and **DJ STORM** flee from the meeting room after disabling **JENNY PEREZ** and ending the negotiations.

NOA

Killing Jenny Perez felt more satisfying than I'm comfortable admitting.

DJ

You know she's not actually dead, right?

NOA

Don't ruin the moment for me, DJ.

Noa and DJ stop running. Noa leans against the bulkhead, breathing heavily.

DJ

Which way?

NOA

Bleep if I know.

DJ

Are we doing the right thing?

NOA

What choice do we have? What choice have they left us?

DJ

I just want to make sure that *you're* sure. You know I'll follow you anywhere, Noa North. I'll even jump out of a ship for you.

NOA

How many times are you going to bring that up?

DJ

As many times as I can. I jumped out of a *bleep*ing ship!

Noa and DJ continue sprinting down the passageway, eventually arriving at the umbilical connecting Production ship *MUX* to *Qriosity*. DJ and Noa dash swiftly across.

INT. *Qriosity*—OPS—MOMENTS LATER

DJ and Noa run into Ops. **JENNY PRICE** and **TY DAVENPORT** are still locked in an embrace, exchanging oral bodily fluids. It is both visually and aurally displeasing. They separate when they realize they have an audience.

QRIOSITY COMPUTER

Warning! *Qriosity* will self-destruct in thirty seconds. Warning!

NOA

Thanks for not actually betraying us.

TY

Technically, I did betray you. However, Jenny changed my mind. She made a terribly convincing argument.

DJ

Gross.

JENNY

How is it gross when I do it, but it's totally cute when you and Noa slobber all over each other in the galley?

QRIOSITY COMPUTER

Warning! *Qriosity* will self-destruct in fifteen seconds. Warning!

NOA

I'm sorry it's ending like this, but—

JENNY

Don't say it.

NOA

At least—

DJ

Seriously, Noa. I'll break up with you if you say it.

NOA

We get to go out with a bang.

QRIOSITY COMPUTER

Warning! *Qriosity* will now self-destruct. Thank you for trusting the destruction of your ship to Explodovat. Explodovat is a fully owned subsidiary of Gleeson Foods.

EXT. SPACE

Production ship *MUX* detaches from *Qriosity*, and quickly flies as far from the other ship as its thrusters can propel it.

Qriosity explodes.

FADE OUT.

EPILOGUE

I WOKE UP ON A SPACESHIP. AND I WAS DEAD.

It wasn't the first time.

DJ slung his arm around my shoulders and leaned his head against mine. I slid my arm around his waist. We stood in Ops on board a ship called *Qriosity* and watched the stars. There was nothing on the viewport. No planets, no space school, no Production.

"Did it work?" Jenny asked. "Because I'm sick of wondering if I'm being watched by a bunch of pervs."

"Production is a computer program," Ty said. A violet hickey the size of golf ball peeked out from under his collar.

Jenny glared at him. "I don't care. Computers can still be pigs."

DJ coughed to remind them that they weren't alone. He turned his attention to Ty. "Well? *Did* it work?"

Ty nodded. "I did as we discussed on the shuttle. I betrayed you, suggested to Production that I could assist them with disabling the self-destruct but that I would need the command override codes to do so, and then used those codes to gain control of *Qriosity*."

"What about their surveillance equipment?" I asked.

"The program I wrote should have disabled the systems they were using to monitor us at the exact moment the fold drive engaged." DJ shrugged. "To Production, it should've looked like we blew up."

There were so many unknowns. So many things that needed to happen for our plan to work and that could have gone wrong. "But do you think Production believes we're dead?" I asked.

"I certainly believed you were going to kill us," Ty said. "And I was privy to the scheme from the beginning."

I had brought up the self-destruct while we were freezing our butts off on the shuttle. It was, it seemed, one system Production didn't control, and one we could exploit to our advantage. I suggested using it as leverage, but it was Jenny who came up with the idea to use it as means to take control of *Qriosity* and fake our deaths. Ty and DJ helped fill in the details.

Honestly, I was surprised it had worked.

"So we have full control over navigation?" I asked. "Communications? We won't be skipping randomly through space?"

DJ was leaning over a console, tapping the screen. "It does seem that way. We can go where we want."

"What about the other stuff?" I asked, glancing at Ty.

"I downloaded that information from Production's ship myself," Ty said. "Not only do we have a functional map of this section of space, but we also know the location of every transition school Production operates."

Jenny pulled out a Nutreesh bar. "So, what? We're going to zip around space, attacking space schools, and freeing the students?"

"Have you got a better idea?" Retrieving the locations of the schools had been done at my request. We had escaped, and that was great, but I wasn't comfortable taking our success and running away with it. If we didn't hold the door open for others to escape, we weren't really any better than Production. Only, I didn't plan on just holding the door. I was going to blow the damn door off the hinges.

"We could go home?" DJ said. "We know Earth's location now. We could fire up the fold drive and be there in ten minutes."

I looked around at the three of them and then shook my head. Even if we reached Earth, and even if the people I had memories of were still alive, they wouldn't know who I was. No one could tell me who I was but me. My name was Noa North. I was in love with DJ Storm. My best friend was Jenny Price. I still wasn't sure about Ty, but I had plenty of time to figure it out.

"I'm already home."

"Barf," Jenny said.

"We're going to ensure that Production can't do to anyone else what it did to us," I said. "Then I want to find Programming and take them down too. We're not going to stop until we've dismantled the entire system."

Jenny cleared her throat. "Cool. Can we wait until after lunch, though? I'm starving."

DJ laughed. "You just finished eating a Nutreesh bar."

Ty took Jenny's hand and led her toward the door. "Personally, I would like to finish the conversation we were having before we were interrupted."

"It's called kissing, Ty. We were kissing." Jenny shoved him into the passageway.

I stood in front of the viewport and watched the stars. There was more out there than I had ever imagined, and I was going to get to explore it with someone I loved. With someone who loved me. This was not the life I had expected, it wasn't the one I'd wanted, but it was the one I had, and I was okay with that.

DJ hugged me from behind. "Do you think we're really free?" he asked. "Do you think this is the end?"

"I think we're free," I said. "But this definitely isn't the end. Our story is just beginning, and this time we're going to tell it our way."

It turned out that Jenny was right. We always have a choice. I chose DJ. I chose to live. I chose to fight.

But that's a story for next season.

ACKNOWLEDGMENTS

When I started this book, I was calling it *Gays in Space*, and all I had was this nebulous idea that it would be about—surprise!—gays in space. Getting from that initial idea to this finished book was a journey of a million steps, and I couldn't have done it alone.

My agent, Katie Shea Boutillier, has been Noa and DJ's champion since day one, just as she's been mine.

Everyone at Donald Maass Literary is a rock star, and none of this would be possible without them.

Liesa Abrams, my tireless editor, kept me going in the right direction even when I felt a bit lost.

The entire team at Simon & Schuster and Simon Pulse and Simon & Schuster Books for Young Readers are simply incredible. I wrote the words, but they made sure the words made sense; they gave this book a beautiful cover, designed the layout, packaged it, promoted it, got it into bookstores so you could read it. There are so many people who work their butts off to make a book happen, and I'm grateful to all of you every day.

Julian Winters, who was the first person aside from my agent I told about this wild idea, for encouraging me every time we spoke. His excitement for this book kept me going during the times when I thought I'd never finish writing it.

My friends and family continue to be an unending source of material for future books. Keep being weird; I love you all.

The librarians and teachers and booksellers are out there working their butts off to put books into the hands of readers. None of us would be here without them. You are my favorite people. Thank you.

Thank you to all the gays in space out there who make me proud to be part of the community. We are legion, and we are fabulous.

Finally, thank you, readers, for giving me a little home in your heart.

ABOUT THE AUTHOR

SHAUN DAVID HUTCHINSON is the author of numerous books for young adults, including *The Past and Other Things That Should Stay Buried*, *The Apocalypse of Elena Mendoza*, *At the Edge of the Universe*, and *We Are the Ants*. He also edited the anthologies *Violent Ends* and *Feral Youth* and wrote the memoir *Brave Face*, which chronicles his struggles with depression and coming out during his teenage years. He lives in Seattle, where he enjoys drinking coffee, baking, and eating cake. Visit him at ShaunDavidHutchinson.com or on Twitter @shauniedarko.